Wendy Perriam

was born in 1940 and educated at a convent boarding-school and St Anne's College, Oxford. After a stint in advertising and a succession of more offbeat jobs, ranging from the bizarre to the banal, she now writes full time.

Her novels, which include *Born of Woman, The Stillness The Dancing, Sin City, Devils, for a Change, Fifty-Minute Hour* and *Bird Inside*, have been acclaimed for their exuberant style, their provocative mix of the sacred and the profane, and their extraordinary power to disturb, amuse and shock.

She is currently working on her eleventh novel and some new short stories.

D1054915

By the same author

CUCKOO
AFTER PURPLE
BORN OF WOMAN
THE STILLNESS THE DANCING
SIN CITY
DEVILS, FOR A CHANGE
FIFTY-MINUTE HOUR
BIRD INSIDE
MICHAEL, MICHAEL

WENDY PERRIAM

Absinthe for Elevenses

Flamingo
An Imprint of HarperCollins*Publishers*

Flamingo
An Imprint of HarperCollins*Publishers*
77–85 Fulham Palace Road,
Hammersmith, London W6 8JB

Published by Flamingo 1993
9 8 7 6 5 4 3 2 1

This revised edition previously published by Paladin 1991

First published in Great Britain by
Michael Joseph Ltd 1980

Copyright © Wendy Perriam 1980, 1991

The Author asserts the moral right to
be identified as the author of this work

Photograph of Wendy Perriam by Jane Bown

ISBN 0 586 09129 7

Set in Baskerville

Printed in Great Britain by
HarperCollinsManufacturing Glasgow

All rights reserved. No part of this publication may be
reproduced, stored in a retrieval system, or transmitted,
in any form or by any means, electronic, mechanical,
photocopying, recording or otherwise, without the prior
permission of the publishers.

This book is sold subject to the condition that it shall not,
by way of trade or otherwise, be lent, re-sold, hired out or
otherwise circulated without the publisher's prior consent
in any form of binding or cover other than that in which it
is published and without a similar condition including this
condition being imposed on the subsequent purchaser.

For Gloria Ferris,
most generous of friends

Yea, Lord, a little bliss,
Brief bitter bliss, one hath for a great sin;
Nathless thou knowest how sweet a thing it is.

Swinburne *Laus Veneris*

1

Ian hated Harrods. Especially the lingerie department. He skulked at the entrance to the pink frilled boudoir, glaring at flimsy nighties and flaunting bras. He wished there were a few more men around. The only male for miles was in tow to a megalithic matron with a felt flower-pot on her head. Ian tiptoed in behind them, trying to look as if he belonged. All three landed up in Corsets.

Ian trailed away and hid himself among the housecoats. The department was hushed and hallowed like a mausoleum, with silken shrouds draped over defunct dummies – armless, eyeless effigies, arrayed in their burial clothes. Even without eyes, the dummies stared at him. He slunk between two rails of lacy gowns, feeling almost claustrophobic in the stifling hothouse air, which seemed made of pink foam rubber. Gilded plaster cherubs closed in on him around the walls, dangling scarlet suspender belts only inches from his nose. Feather boas serpented towards him, whalebone corsets poked him in the ribs. Salesgirls were smirking at him, customers whispering. He was an intruder in their sanctuary, a man in a dirty raincoat, defiling a female shrine.

He glanced furtively in the mirror. His raincoat wasn't dirty – Ginny saw to that. None the less, he slipped it off. You couldn't be too careful, not in Lingerie. The mirror frowned back at him: shabby jacket, shapeless pullover, fawn face wearing a permanent apology, fair-to-middling teeth, unambitious nose. Ordinary. He narrowed his eyes and sucked in his cheekbones, trying to look like Byron at Missolonghi. It didn't work. Byron had flashing black eyes and tumbling curls. He supposed he was lucky to have any hair at all. Half his contemporaries were beginning to read the toupee ads, or resorting to colour-restorers. His was still thick (and mouse). He was reasonably tall and his waist was just perceptible, if he breathed in. And for Christ's sake, even Byron had a club-foot.

'Can I help you, sir?'

He saw himself jump in the mirror and pretended he'd merely been straightening his tie. He wished she were one of the prettier ones.

'Yes, er . . . thank you. I want a nightdress for my wife.' Why couldn't Ginny settle for something sensible, like a pressure cooker, or a garden fork?

'What sort of thing did you have in mind, sir?'

Ian dragged his mind back from garden tools. He and the salesgirl were nose-high in nightwear. Froth, feathers, flounces, frills, whirled before his eyes as she rotated the display rack. She gestured to a prawn-pink peignoir hiding its shame in marabou, and an overgrown T-shirt with 'Night Student' blazoned across the front in bold black letters. Ian flashbacked into breakfast. Marabou in the marmalade wouldn't be hygienic. And he was too tired at night to teach her anything.

'Something, perhaps, a bit more . . . ordinary?' That word again. And it wasn't really fair. Ginny wasn't ordinary. But you didn't grill bacon in pink plumage. And did his wife wear pink? He couldn't quite remember. Fifteen years married and he didn't even know her favourite colour.

The salesgirl led him over to another rack – the Ordinary Department, he assumed. The nighties there looked limp and sanctimonious. He recoiled before a khaki cassock and an ashen winding-sheet.

'What colour do you want?'

The girl had dropped the 'sir'. She'd be tapping her foot next, or sighing heavily. Salesgirls terrified him. He clutched at the nearest garment on the rail. 'I'll take this one,' he barked, trying to sound haughty and decisive. It was baby-blue brushed nylon, with high neck and long sleeves. Ginny felt the cold.

He followed the girl over to the pay-desk, where she disappeared in a cloud of tissue paper. Suddenly, the tissue billowed and surged, as six-foot of wolfskin coat stormed the counter, and a good two dozen pairs of scarlet panties cascaded on to Ginny's chastened nightdress.

'Just take these for me, would you, angel? I've got a taxi waiting.' The intruder's smile was sugar-coated dynamite.

'I'm already serving this gentleman,' the salesgirl stammered, sticking in the sugar. It didn't sound convincing.

Ian looked up indignantly, trying to extricate himself and his nightie from a halo of cigar smoke. The face above the wolfskin hammered at his memory, somersaulted into consciousness, and fell neatly into place. 'Caldos!' he cried. 'Caldos de Roche. It must be twenty years.'

De Roche smiled a vague, jolly smile.

'You don't recognise me, do you? Ian Barnes. Fellow student at St John's.'

'*Ian*, old chap. Wonderful! Capital! Would have known you anywhere. Don't look a day older. Trust me to find an Oxford man in the knicker department.' He seized Ian's arm and gave it the pump-handle treatment. His laugh boomeranged across the counter. 'And what little wickedness have I caught you in?' De Roche scooped up his crimson booty and thrust it at the salesgirl's bosom. The blue nightie lay revealed in all its quiet decorum. Ordinary.

'Blue for babies, old chap, scarlet for redheads, black for blondes.' De Roche obviously didn't bother with brunettes. 'What's she like then, Ian?'

'She's my wife,' admitted Ian, feeling half-ashamed.

De Roche let out a guffaw. 'I'm not swallowing that one! I remember you at Oxford – no woman was safe within a hundred yards.' He secreted his account card into the salesgirl's palm, closed her hand over it, and sealed it with a kiss.

Ian counted on his fingers – he'd had exactly two and a half girlfriends in the entire three years, and one of those had been a hand-me-down. De Roche must be confusing him with Emir (Randy) Sharif, who'd had tattooed testicles and a harem. It was quite a nice confusion. He switched on his Don Juan swagger. 'She's blonde,' he conceded. It was almost true.

'Congratulations!' De Roche had kidnapped the salesgirl's other hand, and was deciding on a ransom. 'Though, confidentially, I reckon you should start a new mistress just after Christmas, and discard her the week before.' He dropped the hand. 'Saves a hell of a lot of shopping. Or you can standardise the whole business and buy them all the same thing' – he prodded his pile of panties – 'at least it stops them scratching each other's eyes out.'

Ian struggled back into his raincoat. 'I thought you had a taxi waiting.'

'Good God no! I only tell them that to get them off their arses. Besides, I can't allow an old college chum to maltreat a blonde!' He hauled Ian over to a mock seraglio labelled 'Naughty Nighties' and sorted swiftly through the rack. 'That's the one!' He grabbed a sin-thin scanty in black-eyed lace – more holes to it than substance – slit to the thigh and totally transparent, a skittish pair of micro-pants sneaking underneath.

Ian backed away. 'Look, I really don't think . . .' It was freezing in the mornings. The thermostat had broken and their boiler threw tantrums. Ginny boiled eggs in her bedsocks.

'Buy her that and she's your slave.' De Roche held the nightie up against him, black lace trailing beneath his five o'clock shadow. 'No woman in her senses could resist it!' He pirouetted and one wing of the nightie floated across Ian's face. He gazed up at de Roche through a haze of black transparency, began to feel excited. They could always buy an oil stove.

De Roche strode back to the salesgirl with the nightie looped around his neck. Several shoppers stared. He was a big bulky man with too much of everything. His voice brayed and boomed, his eyebrows embraced each other, his stubble seemed to rebel against the razor, his smile was a rainbow. His wild wolf coat shouted King of the Beasts. He was Lucifer in church.

Ian thought back to the quiet quad of St John's and saw a younger, slimmer de Roche, in a scarlet-lined opera cloak, exchanging witty rejoinders on Wittgenstein with the notorious Dean, or downing his eleventh pint after victory in Eights Week. Strange they should have rowed together. It was really all they ever had in common.

'Cash or account, sir?' The salesgirl had retrieved the 'sir'. Ian sprang out of the College Eight and took the bill.

'Cash,' he said, unfolding it, then clutching at the counter for support. It was in three figures. De Roche was heavily involved with a second salesgirl, a red-haired Scot with freckles. With any luck, he couldn't hear. Ian leant across the counter and whispered:

'So sorry, but I think I'll take the blue after all. My wife feels the cold.'

De Roche abandoned the freckles. 'Chicken!' he shouted. Both salesgirls giggled nervously. He rallied their support. 'Look, girls, I put it to you. This is your ardent Lothario, bearing gifts. Which would it be – blue geriatrics or black extravaganza?'

The blue looked suddenly senile, didn't stand a chance. Both girls were mesmerised by the black, especially as modelled by de Roche. He had draped the pants across his chest like the briefest of bras and was ogling the redhead with them. She leaned across to stroke the lace.

'I'd do anything for a bloke who bought me that!'

Ian fumbled for his cheque book. Harrods' staff had obviously deteriorated. He wrote the cheque as slowly as possible, filling in the amount last of all. There was just a chance that de Roche would leave.

'Why don't we have a drink together? Catch up on those twenty years. And you can tell me all about your *femme fatale*.' De Roche flung a rough wolf paw across Ian's shoulders and capsized them.

'The pubs are shut.' Ian wrote 'and ninety-nine pence' and passed the cheque across as if it were a nasty smell.

'There's the Dress Circle just round the corner,' said the red-head, helpfully. 'You can get tea and things there.'

Ian rammed his biro back into his pocket. Harrods must be scraping the barrel for their staff – ill-bred opinionated eavesdroppers, interrupting private conversations. No wonder England was going to the dogs. British Leyland bankrupt and divorce among the royals. He made a swipe at the bag. It was surprisingly light for what it had cost – as light as his bank balance.

De Roche was gesticulating with his gift-wrapped scarlet pants. His cigar blazed a pungent trail in front of him. He elbowed a middle-aged matron out of his way and swept towards the Dress Circle. The queue was so long, it trailed into the adjoining coat department.

'Look, Caldos, I really can't wait. I've got to . . .'

'Itching to tear that nightie off your tame Aphrodite, is that it?' De Roche's laugh was like a pneumatic drill. He marched to the front of the queue and whispered to the steward, who let them through. There was a second queue at the self-service counter inside. De Roche waved a bank note at a waitress, pushed Ian ahead of him and bagged the last pair of free seats. The waitress returned with frothy cappuccino, and two generous slices of what de Roche described (in a perfect German accent) as Schwarzwälderkirschtorte, a cholesterol-loaded chocolate cake, sagging under an avalanche of cherries and whipped cream. Ian would have preferred lemon tea and a plain digestive biscuit. Everybody else was queuing. De Roche demolished his cake in three bites and wiped cream from his chin.

'Well, old boy, spill the beans. How are you making your millions these days?'

'I'm with Imperial Biscuits. Personnel.' Ian wished he could say Sales Director, or Production Manager, or member of the board. He thought enviously of Messrs Holsworth and Perry up on the executive floor, with their fitted carpets and their antiqued walnut desks (with secretaries to match), and potted palms from Rentapalm, and Bahamas-blend coffee in a Spode cup and saucer, instead of paper cups from a dyslexic machine. His own desk was metal, and the floor was Marley tiles, and he had only a scant third of a breastless secretary with bad teeth. And no armchair. Armchairs were of paramount importance in Imperial Biscuits. One armchair was the gateway to heaven; two armchairs was coming close to God.

Ian stared glumly at his cake. It oozed heart attacks and strokes. The factory doctor said you couldn't be too careful, not at his age. He pushed the plate away. 'How about you?'

'Are you enquiring about my health, or whether I want that second piece of Torte?'

'No, I was wondering about your work. Did you stick to medicine or were you lured back to the business world?'

'You speak as if the two were incompatible.' De Roche made a foray into Ian's cake. 'I may be one of London's leading psychoanalysts, but I still run a few little side-shows, dabble on the Stock Exchange, you know the sort of thing.'

'Christ!' Ian choked into his cup.

'What's wrong? Don't you approve of speculation? Or do you want your cake back?'

'Yes, er . . . no. It's not that. It's the psycho bit.'

'The perfect profession, my dear chap,' de Roche enthused through a moustachio of whipped cream. 'Your patients rarely die and equally rarely ever recover. A wrong diagnosis is most unlikely to be fatal. And if there's any complaint, you can always attribute it to their own latent hostility and so have a perfect excuse for continuing treatment – for years and years, if necessary.'

Ian stared, gulped down his coffee, fighting with the white meringue of froth.

'I did consider surgery.' De Roche picked up his knife and made a careful incision through the remainder of the Torte. 'Hogging the headlines by transplanting a pig's heart into some smashed-up swine of a motor-cyclist. But there's too much competition – all that hanging about waiting for dead men's shoes, and having to be civil to the anaesthetists.' He stuck a finger in the jam which was oozing out of his dismembered cake. 'Besides, I hate blood.'

Ian thought back to Oxford. De Roche had been just the same then. All that farce and farrago to make sure no one ever guessed he had a heart. But Ian had seen his heart. He remembered the business with his room-mate – de Roche had saved his life, more or less. And, two months later, flogged all the way to Wales and worked for nothing in the Merthyr Tydfil pit disaster, though claiming he had gone there simply for the scenery and the chance of mountaineering. He wondered if the de Roche heart had survived. The appetite most certainly had. De Roche had finished both pieces of cake and was now assaulting the sugar dish.

'There's not the same status, of course. The surgeons are the princes of our profession. Psychiatry is just the chambermaid. That's rather apt, come to think of it.' His laugh hit the ceiling. 'But I was lucky. I was taken up by a Professor Sigmund Schrot. He'd been analysed by Freud himself – even took his name. That counts. He was almost senile by the time I met him, obsessed with constipation. He was working on a project with constipated catatonics, curing them by dream analysis. In the end, they shat in their sleep and all the nursing staff gave notice.'

Ian glanced nervously behind him. He had trouble with his own bowels, for heaven's sake, but you didn't broadcast it to the whole of Harrods.

'There was nothing closer to the Prof's heart than the anus.' De Roche continued at the same volume. 'And I played along with it. Why not? It made a change from the interminable phallus. I was even co-author with him on a slim little volume entitled *Anal Character Traits of the Capitalist Instinct* – a collector's item now, in fact. The whole thing paid off handsomely. The Professor advanced me within the Institute, loaded me with patients, and I've never looked back.' De Roche lit another of his fat Partagas. The No Smoking sign applied only to lesser mortals. 'I've two healthy private practices – one in Harley Street and one at my home in Chelsea. Titled heads, actresses, you know the sort of thing. I mustn't mention names, Ian, but you'd drool at some of them. I've even got a royal. Of course there's been madness in the royal family ever since poor George III, but they try to hush it up, distract themselves with horse-racing and corgis. More coffee, Ian old chap?'

'Caldos, I really must be . . .'

De Roche blinded the waitress with his smile. 'Two more coffees, *Liebchen*. And perhaps another piece of that delicious little Torte.'

It was dark when they left Harrods. De Roche ushered Ian out of the back entrance, through the menswear department. The doorman looked pained.

'Terribly sorry, Len. I've been a naughty boy, haven't I? I know I said five minutes, but I couldn't tear myself away from this whiz-kid. Top brass in the biscuit world, Len, and one of my very old chums.'

'Pleased to meet you, sir.'

Ian wondered whether you shook hands with doormen. But Len didn't have a hand. He had been entrusted with the panties, and was helping de Roche disentangle himself from the wolfskin. Years of chocolate cake had made their mark. There were the beginnings of a paunch and the oarsman's chest had run to fat. But the exquisite dove-grey suit did its best to conceal such imperfections, and was so obviously distinguished it distracted both the attention and the eye. Ian glanced down at his own off-white nylon shirt, then back at de Roche's silk one in a subtle shade of aubergine which exactly matched his tie.

'Where's the car?' de Roche asked, pushing back an unruly strand of hair.

'She's right outside, sir. I managed to move her along.'

Ian looked up expectantly. Would she be a blonde? No, she was red; her long limbs sprawled voluptuously, her elegant extravagant bonnet curving out in front, surmounted by the prancing bull which swanked and shouted Lamborghini. It was the Espada, this year's model. He'd only ever seen one in a magazine. He stroked the bonnet reverently, admired the tinted windows, the twin exhausts streaking from the back. Len ignored him, too busy with the wolfskin and its owner, settling both in comfortably, removing non-existent specks from the gleaming polished windscreen. Another bank note changed hands.

'Happy Christmas, sir.' Len touched what would have been his forelock, before he lost his hair.

'See you on the sixteenth,' de Roche shouted to Ian through the window. 'And thanks for the invitation. I can hardly wait to see your country villa!'

All three and a half bedrooms of it, Ian thought glumly, as the scarlet vamp sprang forward. He plodded round the side of Harrods to the Brompton Road. His own sludge-green Ford Escort was half a mile away. The store loomed up, a great ship strung with golden lights; Union Jacks shivering on the rooftops, rough-handled by the sharp December wind. Tinsel Christmas trees shimmered in every window, festooned with scarlet feathers and silver plumes. There was a sudden volley of music and a lady in a bonnet shoved a collecting-tin into his ribs. The Salvation Army band was out in force.

'God rest ye merry, gentlemen.' As a boy, he'd always got the comma wrong. He wondered whether he'd rather be rested, or merry. He rarely felt either these days. He turned away and struggled through the crowd of shoppers across the busy road. Strains of the music followed him. He could hear the words growing gradually fainter and fainter as he trudged towards the park: 'Ti – i – dings of co – omfort and joy.' He turned a corner and even the last note of joy had disappeared.

2

The traffic was impossible. The whole world seemed to have converged on Kensington. Angry drivers shouted wild obscenities, impatient horns repeated them. Ian inched forward and then braked sharply. The lights were red again. De Roche would have jumped them, or tossed Santa Claus a fiver to tow him behind his sleigh. They changed, at last, and he scorched away at ninety. He was driving the Lamborghini, feeling it respond to his lightest touch, as it sprang like a cheetah down the Fulham Road. He pressed the remote-control button and the window noiselessly rolled down. He flicked a switch and the London Philharmonic poured into the back seat with a quadraphonic fanfare of brass. Beethoven's 'Eroica' crescendoed to an ugly volley on the horn. He had almost hit the bumper of the car in front. The driver stuck his head out of the window and swore in at least five languages. 'Fucking weekend drivers,' he concluded.

Ian tried to dispose of the Lamborghini, or at least get rid of de Roche. But somehow he persisted, his cigar smoke coiling round the car, his fur coat flaunting, his Harley Street practice flying like a triumphant flag. His own flag was only a plastic pennant, drooping at half-mast. The semi-detached in Hinchley Wood with its eighth of an acre of begonias; his unexceptional office with its cardboard coffee and its khaki walls; the endless stream of problem personnel – women who had lost their sugar-coating and men who had lost their hair and their libidos, dragging their fraught Mondays and their fraying Fridays and their snuffling nose-running progeny along with them. There was so little he could do for them. He listened interminably to the scraps and scrapings of their lives, and longed to be the omnipotent God they thought he was. But Imperial Biscuits confined its gods to the executive floor, and he was only a threadbare Saint Peter, keeping this one on, and flinging that one out, and only sorry there wasn't more of heaven to go round.

He jabbed his car into second gear and turned off the bypass. The traffic was thinning now, as he cruised along the A307 and turned right at the lights, and right again into his own tree-lined avenue. Miss Hodgkins was watching, as usual, through her immaculate net curtains, spying on his movements, probably noting he was late. His house looked somehow smaller than he'd remembered it; the front garden bare and brown, a mulch of rotting autumn leaves littering the path. He fumbled for his key, couldn't find it, knocked instead. Ginny skittered to the door in rubber gloves and a rush.

'Ian, where on earth have you been? I've been worried sick about you.'

Ian winced. He only forfeited his hard-day-at-the-office kiss if things were pretty bad.

'It was my orphans day today and you promised to be back. Diana's got flu, remember, so I was running it on my own. I told you so at breakfast.'

'Oh hell,' said Ian. 'I'm sorry.'

Ginny always prattled over the eggs and bacon, but half the time he was worrying about his bowels, or the bank-rate, or continuing a dream where he'd been Casanova fused with Don Juan. He hadn't heard a thing about orphans. She had the little monsters over once a month for a bun fight and a binge. It was always a riot, but mostly in the best sense.

'It was absolute disaster! Jamie tried to stuff the cats down the lavatory, and Spencer and Bill had a bust-up. And all the rest joined in and flung biscuits at each other.' She started to laugh. 'It does sound rather funny, but . . .'

The laugh changed key, hovered on the edge of a sob. Ian stepped gingerly over a headless teddy bear and hugged her. 'I'm sorry, love, I really am. It was Harrods' late-night shopping and the traffic was murder.' He walked into the living-room, dodging a lake of pink blancmange. Half a jam sandwich was embedded in his favourite chair, and broken crockery trailed across the carpet. 'Good God, Ginny, it's like Armageddon in here! Where's Dad, for heaven's sake? I always thought Dad was your Lady Bountiful on these occasions.'

'Oh he is. He was. I don't know what I'd have done without him. He calmed them all down and did his Wild West act and doled out Liquorice Allsorts. They all adore him. But Bill hurt his wrist in the shindy and screamed the house down. George took him up to the hospital. I don't think it's much, but you know your father!'

Ian grinned. He did. He joined Ginny on the carpet and surveyed the carnage. Ginny dropped the dishcloth and leapt to her feet.

'The girls! I've forgotten clean about them. They need collecting from the swimming baths – rang up half an hour ago, but I hadn't got the car.' She slipped out of her apron and dashed towards the front door.

Ian flung her the car keys. 'I'll carry on with the carpet,' he called. He commandeered a half-chewed doughnut and the wreckage of a dinky car and dropped them in the waste bin. He could have done without the orphans. Caldos bloody de Roche and Bruiser Bill on the same afternoon was just a shade too much.

The carpet was drying, the girls were in bed, and George had returned from the hospital. He'd done an encore with his saga of the casualty department and had finally padded upstairs with a flush of triumph and one of the cats. Ian and Ginny were sipping their late-night Ovaltine. Ian laid his hand on Ginny's thigh and tried to picture her in the black lace exotica. He couldn't. She was wearing her faded camel dressing gown with a darn on the sleeve, and blue winceyette pyjamas, her long fairish hair tied back in a rubber band.

'Imagine, Ginny, it must be almost twenty years since I last laid eyes on him. He didn't even recognise me. But I'd know Caldos anywhere, even though he's run to fat.' All right, she wasn't quite the bombshell de Roche had assumed, but she was luscious underneath. Went in and out in all the right places. And her skin was so soft, it was like the very bottom of a horse's muzzle – that tender, almost trembling bit, which felt like warm velvet.

'It's a funny name,' she said, flicking the skin off her Ovaltine. 'Even for a psychiatrist. What is he, French or Spanish?'

'Oh, a bit of both – and lots more besides. I seem to remember he had a string of names in between, one from every country on the continent. Things like Leopold and Olaf. His mother was a Moravian countess, so he said. Not that we ever saw her. He always swore he was English, just because he was born on an English cruise ship – somewhere between Guadeloupe and Port of Spain, I think it was. First-class cabin, of course!'

Ginny broke off half her biscuit, gave it to the dog. 'I only wish you hadn't invited him here. This is hardly the setting for mixed-up Moravians who travel first class.'

'Sorry, darling. But he really invited himself. He said he was taking Gish to Sandown Park, so naturally I told him we were only a mile or two from the racecourse, though we'd never been in fifteen years. He was flabbergasted. Tried to talk us into going with them, but I draw the line at horses!'

'But if he's so rich and famous and everything, whatever can I give them for dinner? And the dining-room needs painting. And who on earth's Gish?'

'I think she must be his girlfriend. He doesn't seem to have a wife. He did admit he'd been engaged once, to a Russian prima donna, but he'd never actually laid eyes on her. She only sang in Moscow, so it was betrothal by letter. But then he claimed he lost her in the post.'

'I don't think I'm going to like a man who loses fiancées. He sounds jolly careless. And not much use as a psychiatrist.'

'He's not a psychiatrist. He's an analyst.'

'What's the difference?'

'Oh, couches and things. He did explain, but he kept making jokes, and I couldn't really tell what was serious and what was just a send-up. But you're right, you know. He seems more like an actor or a film producer. Even up at Oxford, we never knew why he'd settled for medicine. He'd already made his pile in business. But he had this thing about Hippocrates.'

'*Who?* Why do they all have such extraordinary names?'

'No, Hippocrates wasn't at Oxford. He . . .'

'Do you think he'd eat fish? I could do them trout, or something grand like that.'

'I should think he'd eat anything and everything. Judging by his tea! And he was always starving hungry at St John's, often wolfed two dinners. He'd make sure he sat next to this puny chap called Higgins, who had badly-fitting dentures and couldn't chew too well, and Caldos just reached over and took forkfuls of his steak and kidney pudding, or finished off his rhubarb tart and custard.'

'How perfectly obnoxious! I know I'm going to loathe him.'

Ian pushed Toby off his foot and replaced the lid on the biscuit tin. 'He's not as bad as he sounds, darling. I'm sure it's only a put-on. He likes to pretend he's a cross between Mephistopheles and the Aga Khan. But I suspect he's quite a softie underneath.'

'Well, I'd never dream of inviting the Aga Khan to dinner.'

Ian leant across and kissed her. 'Let's go to bed. I'm knackered.'

One way and another, it had been a bloody hard day.

3

'George, be a love and remove that rabbit from the sitting-room. I've got important people coming and he might wet the carpet.'

'Leave him be, lass. He's enjoying himself. If he makes a mess, I can always clear it up before they come.'

'But it'll smell, George. Like those awful advertisements where people wrinkle up their noses when they step into your house. Why can't he stay in his hutch like any normal rabbit?'

'It's sinful cooping up God's creatures.' George padded into the sitting-room and retrieved the rabbit. 'He *has* made a mess.'

'Hell!' said Ginny. 'I'm terribly behind as it is.' She redoubled her efforts with the egg whisk, spurting a shower of chocolate mousse across the salad, which was ready mixed and waiting for its dressing.

'Calm down, lass,' soothed George, settling himself on a kitchen stool with the rabbit on his lap, and offering it a chocolate-flavoured lettuce leaf.

'George, please don't smoke over my mousse. It's already gone funny. The egg whites wouldn't stiffen.'

George moved his pipe to the other hand and stuck a finger into the mixing bowl. 'Mm . . . Tastes all right to me. No one makes chocolate pud better than my Ginny. And if it's not good enough for your fancy friends, they can jolly well go without.'

'It's not a pudding, George.' Ginny sloshed a generous dollop of brandy into the mixture and stirred. 'And for goodness sake don't say "pud" in front of them. It's *petits pots au chocolat*.'

'Hey, Mum,' yelled Sarah, bursting in with Toby at her heels. 'Have you seen my roller-skates?'

'No, I haven't. And I can't think why you need them now, when it's pitch dark outside and you're meant to be doing your homework.'

'It's Saturday. You let me off on Saturdays. Anyway, it's William the Conqueror and he's a total wimp.' She tossed back her blonde pigtails, pulled crossly at the brace on her front teeth. 'Mum, can I lick the bowl out?'

'No.' Ginny tipped the mousse into five glass dishes and sprinkled each with nuts. 'I need every scrap I've got. It's all sort of shrunk in the saucepan. And please don't call me Mum. Especially not tonight. It's vulgar.'

'Mu-um!' It was Snookie now, naked except for her mother's high-heeled shoes. 'My nightie's all wet. It felled in the bath.'

Ginny groaned. 'Where's Daddy? I thought *he* was putting you to bed.'

Sarah grabbed a handful of nuts. 'He's trying to mend the stereo. It's all in pieces on the floor. He said "damn", twice, and then "bloody". I heard him. Mum, can Thumper sleep in *my* room?'

'Certainly not! George, could you get these girls to bed – *and* that blessed rabbit. Dr de Whatnot will be arriving any minute, and I haven't even changed.'

She took a last peep at the dining table, smiling her approval. She'd arranged button chrysanthemums with sprigs of fir, and ironed the best lace cloth. There were home-made *langues de chat* to go with the mousse, and the Beaujolais was swanking in a cut-glass decanter. She'd insisted on decanting it, to hide the Sainsbury's label. She wondered again about the *coq au vin*. A Dr de Roche was probably used to grouse and pheasant, not supermarket chicken, disguised with a foreign name. Or perhaps he was a vegetarian, or one of those weird vegans who wouldn't touch anything except vegetables and nuts. Psychiatrists were often cranks.

She went upstairs to dress, had changed her mind twenty times already about what she should put on. Her long-sleeved black was safe, but boring. Dared she wear the blue? It was an inch too tight, and glittery, and it might get splashed when she served the *coq au vin*. She settled for the black. It looked distinctly dowdy. She took it off again, struggled into the blue. Ian sauntered in, clad only in his underpants.

'Seen my cufflinks?'

'Ian, look at me a moment. Is this dress okay? It's awfully sort of daring.'

'Looks fine to me,' said Ian. He wasn't looking.

'Do you think this Gish person will be all dolled up?'

There was a roar outside, as George chased a streak of naked Snookie dripping from the bathroom. Ginny tugged at her stiff zip. 'Your father goes mad with those girls. They'll never settle down.'

'Oh come on, Ginny, they adore it. And they're his life now.'

'Yes, I know. It worries me. He's got nothing else to do. When they're at school, he just prowls around the house looking woebegone and then brings home half the wildlife of Surrey. Honestly, Ian, I draw the line at any more animals. I know he's a love, but how your mother put up with bats and boa-constrictors, I'll never understand.'

Ian smelt the sickly smell of lilies, watched his own surprising tears splashing on the wooden pew. He never cried. 'Dearly beloved, forasmuch as it has pleased Almighty God to take unto himself the soul of our dear sister here departed . . .' Almost exactly three years ago. 'Ashes to ashes, dust to dust.' Three thousand years ago. It was all the same with death. Dark earth piled beside the hole, cruel turf hacked out in squares. 'The days of man are but as grass.' The cold stinging air outside changing to the hot fug of the hall – chicken vol-au-vents sticking in his throat, as he chatted to old ladies in new hats. His frail, fond, five-foot-nothing mother, rotting in a hole, while the vicar quaffed cream cakes.

'Wake up, Ian! They'll catch you in your underpants if you don't hurry up and dress. And have you got the drinks out?'

'He took it very well, you know, Ginny. I mean, it was all so sudden and she was absolutely devoted to him. He . . .'

'Grrrrrrrrrrr! I'm a big black bear and I'm going to eat you all up!' George dashed past the door, disguised in a shaggy hearth-rug and Ginny's black fur hat, both the girls fleeing from his growl, bursting into their parents' room for sanctuary. Snookie flung her hot wet hands around her mother's lurex; Sarah stole an eye-pencil and gave herself black lips.

'Gosh, Mum, you do look posh! Is it the Queen that's coming?'

'Sarah, have you done your teeth?'

25

Sarah obliged with a toothpastey kiss. 'Yes, smell. Can I read in bed? It's too early to go to sleep.'

'Well, as long as you don't disturb us. They're very important people and they won't want a lot of . . .' Her voice was interrupted by the doorbell. She jumped, swung round to Ian. 'Oh lord! That's them. They're early. And I haven't done the rice. George, take that rug off – quickly! I need it in the sitting-room to cover up the rabbit stain.' She lunged towards the door, dodged back again for a quick glance in the mirror, frowning at her neat and boring features, her standard-issue mid-blue eyes, and her mess of wavy hair, which had once been blonde, like Sarah's, but was now more the colour of chaff, or clover honey. Ian said she was pretty, and her best friend, Kate, claimed to envy her complexion, complaining that it showed up her own blemishes, but it would be nice to look in a mirror and see someone completely different, for a change. One got tired of the same face.

She loped downstairs, holding in her stomach and forcing a four-star smile. They had no right to be early.

'We're collecting jumble for our Christmas fair,' said a minuscule boy-scout, who looked too small to carry any. Ginny switched off the smile and rushed into the kitchen. The *coq au vin* smelt good. She rummaged through the cupboards, found a broken toaster and a pair of owl bookends. Sarah was flirting with the scout, cavorting in her pink-frilled shortie nightie.

'I'll look out some more for you tomorrow,' Ginny promised, shutting the door on his salute. 'Now come on everybody. They'll be here any minute. Girls, go back to bed. Ian, come and do the ice.'

Ian was on his third drink. 'It really is a bloody cheek. Nearly two hours late and they haven't had the decency to phone. It's damn bad manners.'

'The rice is ruined,' Ginny moaned. 'I should never have cooked it in advance.'

'Perhaps they've had an accident,' George suggested brightly.

Ian switched to ITV. A gilt-edged female with a velvet voice abandoned her bridge party to prepare the Nescafé. '*I care* about the coffee I give my friends . . .'

Ginny leapt off the sofa. 'Coffee! I'd forgotten all about

it. The cups are probably dusty. We haven't used them in an age.'

'We'll be lucky if we ever reach the coffee stage at this rate,' Ian muttered, harpooning the lemon in his gin and swallowing it. He was starving.

Ginny fretted into the kitchen. The watercress was already wilting on the avocados, and the chicken looked shrivelled in its casserole. She climbed on to a chair and reached down the Royal Worcester coffee set, which they only used for very special visitors. Ian mooched out to replenish his lemon.

'I wish you'd never invited them in the first place,' Ginny called down from her chair. 'They've obviously thought better of it. Why should they bother to visit boring old us in the suburbs, when they're hobnobbing with famous actresses half the time and living on grouse?'

'Ginny, that's the fifth time you've mentioned grouse this evening. I'm sure the season's over, and even if it isn't, I wouldn't touch it anyway.'

'Well, it's so rude,' retorted Ginny. 'Was he always late at Oxford?'

Ian tried to think back. De Roche loomed up like a colossus: dark, loud, bitter, bombastic, clever; dressed in drag at the College Ball and singing a spoof version of the *Liebestod*; speaking at the Union amidst the howling counterpoint of fury and applause; winning a bet that he couldn't eat fifty toasted crumpets at a sitting; driving down a No-Entry street with a busty blonde sitting on the bonnet. Even to own a car in those days was something of a triumph, when most students had been grateful for a second-hand bike.

George joined them in the kitchen, hated being on his own. 'Why don't we start without them? It's not good for the stomach to keep grinding on itself. Mother always said eat little and often.'

'No, Dad, we can't do that. They may have been held up in traffic.'

'Traffic at ten o'clock at night!'

Ginny polished up the coffee cups, tried to find more teaspoons. 'Perhaps they had a big win at Sandown and they've just dropped everything and jetted off to France.'

'There's telephones in France.'

'Let's all have another drink,' Ian shrugged.

'Never drink on an empty stomach. That's what Bea always said.' George took an apple from the fruit dish.

'George, dear, don't do that. You've spoilt my arrangement. Look, I'll make you a sandwich, to tide you over until they come.'

'*If* they come.'

'I'll have another bash at the stereo,' said Ian. 'It'll give me something to do.' He took off his jacket and stomped back into the sitting-room. Ginny spread pickle on brown bread.

The stereo was in ruins and George on his second sandwich, when the driveway exploded in a hurricane of gravel. Ian rushed to the curtains. 'It's a different car,' he whispered.

The citron-yellow Porsche dived into the hydrangeas, backed hysterically on to the japonica and shivered to a halt. Something black, thin and feathered stepped gingerly out. There was a little shriek as it stumbled on the pebbles. 'It's like sodding Brighton beach!'

The emaciated blackbird slammed its door. The other door opened, and de Roche struggled out, with difficulty. Ian marched to the front door. Feathers, fur and cigarette smoke fell into his arms. Ginny stared, her smile now quite forgotten. Ian was disentangling himself from a tall angular female in black satin pantaloons and a sleeveless jacket fringed with black feathers, which shone and fluttered as she moved. Her hair was black, long and uncompromisingly straight; her nose also long and straight – a beak. Behind the huge dark glasses, her skin looked pale and fragile; the cheekbones high, the whole face tense and taut. Glittery jet earrings dangled in Ginny's face as Gish bestowed on her a bony kiss, preceded by a liberal exhalation of menthol-flavoured smoke.

'Darling!' she trumpeted. 'We're too too terribly late. We met these *divine* people and we promised to have just a teeny weeny drink. But I simply couldn't drag Tum-Tum away.'

'Who?' said Ian. He hoped to God they hadn't brought their poodle. Toby hated strange dogs.

Gish patted de Roche's stomach with a proprietary air and wreathed it in a halo of smoke. 'Tum-Tum,' she indicated, brandishing her king-size cigarette-holder with as much ceremony and pomp as if it were a mace.

Tum-Tum didn't seem to hear. He was booming into Ian's left ear; gave a sudden whoop of delight as he glimpsed a shimmer of blue Ginny through Gish's black feathers.

'*Quelle enchanteresse!* Ian, old boy, she's gorgeous! Don't know how you biscuit chaps do it. So you're the dazzling Mrs Barnes? *Le ciel redevient azur!*' His lips kissed her hand, brushed their exultant way to the delicate inside of her astonished elbow, lingered there a moment, before moving slowly upwards.

Ginny felt the rasp of a rough chin, contradicted by the soft caress of cashmere pressed against her chest. Her nose swooned in 'Eau Sauvage'. She drew back to look at him, eyes stopping at his shoes. They were exquisitely hand-made in charcoal-coloured lizard skin, double stitched along the sides. Ian bought his shoes at Freeman Hardy & Willis. Her husband suddenly seemed shabbier and smaller, and she could tell he was still fraught. He ushered Gish into the sitting-room, kicking bits of broken stereo under the sofa. George was chuckling over Ronnie Corbett and had pickle on his chin. He shambled to his feet, still clutching a cat.

'You're late,' he said. 'Pleased to meet you.'

Gish backed away with a quiver of her feathers, whinnying with fear. 'I'm sorry, but I simply can't abide cats. Nothing personal. It's a sort of phobia. I'm being treated for it, actually.'

George tucked Mishka under one arm and went to prise Thompson off the window-sill. All three looked deeply hurt. Ian was pouring drinks.

'No, really darling, I never *look* at whisky. Give me just a drop of Punt e Mes.'

Ian froze. He'd heard of Punt e Mes, even seen it in advertisements, or in smart Italian restaurants, but he'd never ever tasted it, let alone bought it for his humble English sideboard. He clonked a few bottles together to make his search sound more convincing. 'Would you believe it, Gish? Not a drop left! We must have finished it last Sunday. Terribly sorry, how about a sherry?'

Gish was generous with her shrieks. 'Suicide!' she screamed. 'Absolute suicide with my stomach. Look, for goodness sake don't go to any trouble, I'll just have a Perrier water with a thimbleful of Pernod.'

Ginny groaned silently. Why couldn't Ian admit that he only had cheap sherry and cut-price Sainsbury's whisky, and maybe they could retrieve the last charred relics of her *coq au vin*, before it was cremated in the oven? De Roche had settled for an uncomplicated double Scotch. She almost loved him for it. She sat beside him on the sofa, wondering how soon she could drag them in to dinner. It was nearly George's bedtime. Gish sulked into her tomato juice, while de Roche surveyed the sitting-room as if he were an estate agent. She knew he'd seen the large crack in the fireplace, and the coffee stain on the battered rocking chair. She only hoped he couldn't smell rabbit.

'What amazing prints,' he said.

Ginny hesitated. She wasn't quite sure what 'amazing' signified. Ian barged in.

'Yes, charming aren't they? Sarah got them on a school outing to the V & A. Thirty pence each, believe it or not. They're the old bridges of London. I framed them myself.'

'Gish collects Craigie Aitchison, don't you, darling?'

'Who?' said Ian.

Ginny tried to catch his eye, stop him with a frown. They mustn't reveal their yawning cultural ignorance before they'd even started dinner. 'I'll just go and check the oven,' she said brightly. It was a good excuse to look for George, who had not bothered to return. She found him comforting Mishka with titbits from her casserole.

'George! What *are* you doing? There's almost nothing left of that chicken as it is. You'd better go and tell Ian we'll have our dinner now, before the cats do.'

George fed Mishka a last morsel of choice breast, then chugged into the sitting-room. 'Ladies and gentlemen, dinner is served. And about time too.'

Ian forced a laugh to cover his embarrassment. 'My father,' he said, tersely, since George had not been introduced.

Gish looked suspicious, as if he might still be secreting a cat or two beneath his green home-knitted pullover. Ian took her arm, and seated her at the table, as far away from George as he could manage. De Roche was placed on Ginny's right. She was fussing over the avocados.

'I only hope they're ripe. The greengrocer did assure me, but you can never really tell when you buy them . . .'

Gish smiled dazzlingly. 'I never touch them anyway. Sorry, darling, but my stomach draws the line at avocados.'

'How about a grapefruit?' Ian suggested. Ginny tried to kick him under the table, but encountered de Roche's knee instead. De Roche let it linger.

'Oh no, wicked bloody things. They absolutely *ooze* acid.'

Ginny relaxed – there weren't any grapefruit anyway. De Roche was shovelling in his own avocado with impassioned concentration, then reached across and kidnapped Gish's plate. 'They're quite superlative, Virginia. You can tell your greengrocer I shall toddle down to visit him myself.' He scraped the green skin naked, then flung himself on Gish's pear.

'My name's not really Virginia,' she explained.

'It suits you, *mon ange*. Blonde, beautiful and chaste Virginia.'

Ginny giggled nervously. Gish lit a cigarette and yawned through it.

'You shouldn't smoke, you know,' said George. 'If you've got a dicey tummy.'

Ian turned on his father. 'You old hypocrite, Dad. You know you smoke yourself.'

'Only a pipe,' countered George. 'And I eat everything I'm given.'

Ginny kicked her chair back. 'I'll get the next course,' she flurried, as a peace offering.

The *coq au vin* still smelt delicious as she removed the lid, though the sauce was dry and brown around the edges. 'I'm terribly sorry. I think I've ruined it. I'm afraid the chicken's gone all sort of mushy.'

'Oh, chicken,' pouted Gish, spitting out the word as if it were synonymous with arsenic.

'Don't keep apologising, lass. Meals will spoil if they're kept, and I can't see it's your fault.'

Ginny quelled George with a look; ladled out rice and a large chicken leg for Gish. There was another little shriek.

'Oh no, no, darling, stop! Just a teeny weeny bit of breast for me. And no rice at all. I'm allergic to the starch. Give that one to Tum-Tum.'

Tum-Tum pounced on the plate and swamped it with salad, then turned to George, speaking through a mouthful of tomato. 'And what's your role in life, Mr Barnes?'

'He's retired,' said Ian. 'Only six months ago. His firm was taken over. You miss it, don't you, Dad?'

'Forty-two years with Mainstay Mutual General. And now, nothing. It's a shock, my lad. You always hear about retirement, but it's worse than what they say. I'm lucky, of course. I've got Ian and Ginny here, and the children, and my animals. But it's not the same. A man needs his job to give him self-respect. I'm fit and capable and I've got years of work in me yet. But you reach a certain birthday and suddenly you're shaking hands with old Philpott and all you're left with is a reproduction carriage clock. It's a dreadful business, dreadful.'

Ian filled his glass, to comfort him; noticed Gish toying with half a piece of cucumber, trying to remove it from the tide of winey sauce. 'Ginny, look, poor Gish has eaten nothing. She's probably not allowed rich sauces. Remember Colin and his ulcer? It was steamed fish and semolina all the time. Can't you get her something lighter?'

'How about an egg?' Ginny tried to sound benign. She'd hardly had a mouthful herself, what with replenishing Caldos and restraining George. Ian was obviously bemused by Gish's feathers, which were now shuddering and rippling as their owner bent her body into agonised contortions.

'Oh, I wouldn't dream of bothering you. It's just that sauces really are murder for my stomach. And please don't fry the egg. Just poach it for three minutes, and make sure you don't add vinegar. Or salt.'

Ginny trailed into the kitchen. The cats were mewing piteously outside the back door. She let them in – Gish would have to lump it. If they'd come much later, they'd have been in time for family breakfast, and Gish would have had her egg, not just with salt (and bacon), but also with Sarah's sniggers and Snookie's obscene garglings as she sucked up milk through a straw. She chose the smallest egg, cracked it into the poacher. The yolk broke and ran into the white. She tipped the whole mess into Toby's dish and began again, wearily. She could hear de Roche booming from the dining-room. How odd to come to dinner in Spanish-style black trousers and a pale cream cashmere sweater. Though, actually, it suited him. He was overweight, of course, but she liked his powerful shoulders, his opera singer's chest. She tried to imagine him serenading in his bath, soaping his stomach and then each hefty thigh – the bass part from *The Merry Widow*.

Suddenly he was there beside her, not singing but confiding. 'Virginia, my darling, you mustn't mind Gish. She's the nicest kind of nervous wreck.' He had brought his wine-glass with him, held it to her lips. He was so close now, she could see the faint shadow on his chin, and a few stray pinpricks of dark hair which had outwitted the razor. She sipped the wine, confused. It tasted strange and dangerous, seemed to surge straight to her head. She tried to step away, return to poaching eggs.

'Would she like it on toast?'

He pulled her back towards him, kissed her on the neck. 'You're a beautiful creature,' he murmured, his breath warm against her breasts. She almost dropped the poacher.

'We'd better go back,' she stammered. But that dangerous wine was still smiling on her lips.

Before the cheese and biscuits, George excused himself. If they didn't mind, he'd go on to bed – he was an early riser, force of habit.

'I'll come and do your Ovaltine,' Ginny said, relieved to see him go. He would keep praising her in front of Gish and telling anecdotes about the children. Gish had not the slightest interest in what Snookie said to Father Christmas, or how Sarah made the porridge out of Polyfilla. But Caldos seemed to like him. They'd had a long involved discussion about how to tell the sex of newts, and whether gerbils were superior to guinea pigs.

Ian confided in de Roche, once George and Ginny had both safely left the room. 'He's quite a headache, my old man. Fit as a fiddle, but nothing much to do. Ginny adores him, but he's getting on her nerves. He spoils the kids something rotten, and his room's full of hedgehogs he's rescued from the A3. He can't bear anything to suffer.'

'Wonderful old chap,' de Roche enthused, reaching for the cheese-knife. 'And with that splendid silver hair, I should think the old ladies succumb like flies.'

'Oh, they do,' Ian assured him. 'And not just the old ones either. He's such a softie, everyone starts pouring out their hearts to him. He's wasted really, just pottering round the place. And there I am in Personnel, and can't even find a job for my own father. It's his age that's against him. After sixty, you may as well be dead, as far as work's concerned.'

Gish was nibbling on a small dry biscuit, recoiling from the Brie. 'It must be quite a bore for you, having him underfoot all day.'

'Well, it isn't always easy,' Ian admitted frankly. 'He's a grand old man, but we're never on our own. Ginny wouldn't say so, but I know she feels the same.'

Ginny returned with coffee on a tray. Gish declined, though her shrieks were getting softer now. 'It's the caffeine, darling. Wreaks havoc on the heart. You must have read that article about it – Professor Blum and his thirty-six white mice. He fed them on crushed coffee beans for eighteen months and every one dropped dead.'

'But mice only live for eighteen months in any case.' Ginny was pouring coffee for the rest. She knew all about white mice. George kept them in his bedroom along with the sick hedgehogs.

'For God's sake, Gish,' snapped Caldos. 'They weren't white mice, they were albino rats. And you're not either.' He unwrapped his seventh chocolate mint and diluted it with a generous swig of port. He seemed to loom larger and larger as he downed everything in sight. He had finished Gish's mousse, demolished half the biscuits, made serious inroads into the cheese, and had even started on the rind.

'Why don't we take our glasses into the other room?' Ginny said, valiantly. Gish was clearly sulking and a change of scene might help the heavy atmosphere. She glanced up at the clock. It was nearly half past one – five short hours till their alarm-call in the morning. Sarah was competing in a Sunday swimming gala, and they had to be up with the lark.

She felt more like a dormouse than a lark, as the clock ticked on inexorably and she fought to keep her eyes open, tried to play the hostess still, respond with interest to de Roche's flood of words. Ian had lost the battle and was actually half-dozing, Toby snoring shamelessly. She wondered if they'd take a hint, bobbed up from her chair. 'I'll just put the cats out for their last prowl.'

Mishka and Thompson were still banned from the sitting-room, in deference to Gish, who was examining her fingernails, fiddling with her bracelets, finally unwrapped her long lean body from the sofa. 'Tum-Tum, darling, I think these early birds may want to go to bed.'

Caldos leapt up from his chair like a catapult, seemed completely inexhaustible. 'Memorable evening! Unsurpassable feast! If this is how they live in Hinchley Wood, we must move down here immediately. Virginia, darling, you're quite the most splendid cook and hostess. You must give me the recipe for that indescribably delicious chocolate mousse.'

The 'Eau Sauvage' was weaker now. He smelled warm and male and smoky, as he took her in his arms. The embrace went on and on, until at last Ian interrupted it by offering de Roche his coat, pushing it against his chest as a substitute for Ginny. De Roche scrambled into the wolfskin, and then clasped Ian instead, almost extinguishing him in a fierce and furry hug.

'Ian, old man, wonderful place you've got here. Absolutely splendid evening!' He drew back a little, to let Ian fight for breath. 'Now, look here, about your father – I've just had a wheeze. There's a caretaker-receptionist job going at my house in Harley Street. Free accommodation. Adorable basement flat. Decent little wage. They're looking for a married couple, actually, but I'm a great chum of old Crankshaw, and if I drop a word in the right ear, there's your dad fixed up.'

'A caretaker?' Ian looked hurt. 'Look, Caldos, he may not be executive material, but they thought very well of him at . . .'

'Nonsense, Ian! These jobs are like gold-dust. Fellows fighting for them, though most don't stand a chance. They'll only take the cream – highest references, personal recommendation, you know the sort of thing. Look at the responsibility they hold! All the keys to everything, and a dozen or more consultants to look after. Topnotch doctors, all of us – professors, OBEs, the latest brains in transplant surgery – not to mention famous patients swanning in and out. Your father would adore it. And it would help us out of a spot. We need a replacement as soon as we can get one.'

Gish was looking bored, pulling at his sleeve. 'Come on, Tum-Tum. It's freezing in this draughty hallway.'

'Well, if she will turn up half-naked except for a few feathers, what can she expect?' Ginny griped, when the door was safely shut and they could hear the Porsche roaring down the road.

'What an extraordinary woman,' Ian yawned, swilling down a last half-inch of port.

'Frankly, I can't see what he sees in her.' Ginny counted Gish's cigarette ends – seventeen – brushed a scurf of ash from chair and carpet.

'Did you notice, though, he hardly spoke a word to her. He seemed much more taken with you.'

Ginny smiled a secret smile. 'I hate fat men,' she shrugged, strolling into the kitchen for a tray. 'Come on, cats. You're reprieved.'

Mishka jumped up into her arms – large, exotic, handsome, purring, warm. She laid her cheek against his soft black fur. 'Mishka de Roche,' she whispered.

4

'She likes the free fresh
Wind in her hair,
Life without care.
That's why the lady is a tramp . . .'

Ginny was singing, out-droning the hoover as she vacuumed the sitting-room, her spirits far less buoyant than the song. 'Damn!' she said, as the phone shrilled from the hall, cutting off the 'free fresh wind', which she'd repeated four times over, since she couldn't remember any other verses.

She snatched up the receiver. She'd had three phone-calls already – one from George's contact at the RSPCA, one from the electricity board about installing a new meter, and the longest and most trying from Mrs Erskine-Taylor, who had problems with her husband, car and womb.

'Virginia darling, wonderful to hear you! Caldos here. How are you?' His voice was like a great fur hug.

'I'm fine,' she said. Suddenly she was.

'I wanted to thank you for a simply splendid evening. It was *thrilling* to meet you.'

She tried to find some words to match his own. He dynamited everything. Even the dull drizzly morning had exploded into fireworks. 'How's Gish?' she asked, after what seemed an endless pause.

'Oh Gish.' He made it sound like the name of a lavatory cleaner. 'Let's talk about *you*, shall we, Virginia? Tell me about yourself. We didn't really have much chance to talk on Saturday.'

It seemed a little odd, recounting one's life history at ten o'clock on a Monday morning, though Caldos wasn't listening.

'Have you and Ian discussed that caretaker's job?'

'Well, we weren't quite sure whether you meant it seriously. And George has never done a job like that before. He's not even lived alone. He moved in with us the very day Ian's mother died. He's very sociable.'

'Virginia, *mon ange*, he'll be completely in his element. Comings and goings all the time. Piccadilly Circus! I'm there every day myself and can keep an eagle eye on him. He can even bring his cats.'

'Oh, they allow pets, do they?'

'Rattlesnakes, if he fancies them. And he can conjure a little garden at the back. Tell the truth, Virginia, *chérie*, it'll be doing me a favour. The previous couple left very unexpectedly and we're frantic for a replacement. It's the agents who actually employ them, but they're so slow and cautious, it may be weeks before they fill the gap. And what with Christmas just around the corner . . . If I tell old Crankshaw what a find your father is, I can get things moving right away. He'll only need one interview and he's in.'

'Ian's not sure,' Ginny said, uncertainly, disappointed that the focus of attention had moved so speedily from her to George. 'He doesn't want his father to feel we're getting rid of him. Look, I'm sorry, Caldos, but I can't discuss it any more. George has just walked in.'

'Fantastic! Let me have a word with him. I know he'll love the job.'

Ginny tried to eavesdrop. The conversation lasted quite some time, though George seemed more concerned with his hedgehogs and his cats than with his duties as a caretaker, or his own wages and conditions. At last, he put the phone down.

'You might have let me say goodbye,' wailed Ginny. Dismal Monday had returned, all the fancy fireworks fizzled out.

'Dr de Roche is going to ring you back. He wants us to go up and see the place.'

'George, you don't know what you're taking on. It's a totally new way of life. And you'd be living on your own in a snooty part of London. I'd be worried sick about you.'

'The Doctor says I'm the only man he'd trust. It's a responsible job, you know. Most applicants don't stand a chance. They've turned down scores already.' The phone interrupted him – a de Roche ring, loud and lordly.

'Right, Virginia, have you got the arrangements straight? You'll bring George up this morning, I'll show him round the place, and if he's happy with it, he can go straight on to the agent for his interview.'

'This morning! But I haven't made the beds . . .'

'I've given George the address. Come to Oxford Circus tube, and just walk up Harley Street. Ring the bell with my name on, and make it by twelve sharp, please.'

Ginny sank into a chair. She was wearing frayed blue jeans and one of Ian's old shirts. She'd have to change, look smart. She'd planned to make a fish pie for the children, hadn't bought the fish yet. Supposing they came home from school and found the house still empty, and nothing for their tea? She'd better ring her mother. And shouldn't Ian be told? She tried to dial his number, found herself speaking to a Brixton betting shop, slammed down the receiver. Absurd to get in such a state, misdialling numbers, pacing round the room. All she had to do was make two simple phone-calls, leave the house-keys for her mother, then catch a train to London. George had already gone to change. She peered in through his door. It was six months since she'd seen him in a suit, and he was utterly transformed, a solid city man again, respectable and suave. She'd become so used to seeing him shambling about in cardigans and carpet slippers, she'd forgotten how distinctive he could look. His silver hair relieved the sober navy of the suit; the tie was safe, but elegant, the shirt high-principled.

'You do look smart,' she told him, felt a sudden pang. The budgerigar was clamouring in its cage, and there was a mess of straw on the carpet from his latest convalescent mouse. He was so different from her own cold-hearted father, who hated pets – and children.

'Come on Ginny, lass, we'd better catch the fifty-two.'

Ginny smiled to see him back in harness, schedules and train times marching through his head. Perhaps it would be good for him, this new opportunity, rescue him from hoovering and hedge-hogs. She nipped to her own room, started searching through her wardrobe, which seemed to offer little save shabby skirts and boring baggy T-shirts. Her only decent suit, the one she wore for weddings, christenings, Prize Days, hung stiff and chaste beneath its plastic cover. It made her look a little like a social worker, but it was the most stylish and expensive thing she had. She added a small hat, and the social worker turned into a JP, so she jettisoned the hat and clipped on large pearl earrings. Now she was Lady Bountiful. Lady B. tried to phone her husband.

'I'm sorry, but Mr Barnes is in a meeting . . .'

All right, all right, she'd try again from London. Surely he wouldn't mind his father simply looking round the place? He could still refuse the job.

She slung Kit-e-Kat into two saucers, scribbled a note for her mother and the girls, and slammed the front door behind her. George was already in the car, lolling against the seat with his eyes closed. George Barnes in Insurance had been a somebody, Grandpa Barnes in Hinchley Wood was a pathetic end-of-bin. But G.E. Barnes, Esquire, of Harley Street, was a man with a future.

They emerged from the fug of the underground into the sharp slap of December. A clotted leaden sky scowled down on the hordes of Christmas shoppers. George pressed his nose against lighted shop windows, admiring cotton-wool snow and cardboard reindeer.

Ginny squeezed his hand. 'You'd keep a herd of reindeer in your bedroom, if we'd let you.' She knew how George loved Christmas, still hung his stocking up at the age of sixty-two. She took his arm and they turned off Oxford Street and crossed the road into Cavendish Square. The statue of Cavendish-Bentinck looked stiff and grey with cold, its proud head splashed with bird-droppings, pigeons perched on both its hands. They left the crowds behind them as they strode up Harley Street, the houses sternly elegant, the window-boxes brave with glossy evergreens. How strange that Ian's own father might be living here. Such a stand-offish faceless street – no washing lines, nor corner shops, no cats, nor Christmas trees, no children, no front gardens.

They reached de Roche's number far too soon. Ginny paused, hung back, glanced across at George, who looked tense himself and sombre, in his best black overcoat. He'd bought it for the funeral and barely worn it since. She remembered him standing tall and terrible, tears sheeting down his face amidst the mocking scent of flowers. He'd picked every bloom in his garden, stripped

40

it bare and showered them on the grave. Ginny longed to hug him, say a word about that loss, which must still feel sharp and crushing, but the coat was like a barrier between them.

'Want to turn back?' she asked him, with a sudden hope he would.

'Whatever for?'

The door was solid mahogany, and flanked by a whole pride of large brass plates, Dr C.E.S. de Roche boasting at the top. She touched the R a second, heard his voice, ardent, in the kitchen; his warm and winey breath exhaling on her cheek as he bent passionately towards her. 'You're a beautiful creature.'

'Name?' barked an enamelled receptionist, with hair out of one bottle and talons from another.

'Barnes,' said Ginny lamely, and tried to explain about the job.

'I'm sorry, but Dr de Roche has been called away.' She didn't sound at all sorry. 'He said nothing about you, anyway, so I don't think I should let you in the waiting-room. You'd better go in there.'

She gestured to a slightly superior cupboard, with a table, two small chairs, and a tattered square of carpet. The receptionist closed the door on them, shutting out the Persian rugs and hot-house roses in the hall. Ginny felt infectious.

'I thought he said the dot of twelve,' grunted George from the depths of his pipe. It was quarter past already.

'He must have had an emergency,' Ginny said despondently, hearing sirens in her head, as foaming writhing patients were bundled on to stretchers, or flung themselves off bridges into the cold and heartless Thames. She wished they hadn't rushed so much. She didn't look her best, could have spent far longer putting on her make-up, or even stopping for a sandwich. 'Are you hungry, George?' she asked.

'Starving! We should have grabbed an ice at Waterloo. They do those really posh ones with sauce and nuts and whatnot.'

Ginny rummaged in her handbag, found a scrap of paper and jotted down a shopping-list. 'Ice-cream, ice-cream sauce . . .' She continued with detergent, frozen peas, sardines. At least it helped to pass the time. George was reading *Punch*, chuckling at the jokes. She found some magazines herself, thumbed through all the recipes, and then read three short stories, all with happy

41

endings. Would they ever see de Roche, reach their own finale? The clock was striking one now. She turned to the knitting feature in a dog-eared *Woman's Realm*. George would need more pullovers in a draughty basement flat. 'Oxford blue or Cambridge, George?' she asked, already working out the wool.

'Oxford, any day!' roared a disembodied voice. The magazine ricocheted out of her lap as the door burst open and de Roche flung himself upon her, and included George, the table, chairs, carpet, floor and ceiling in one universal hug. Exclamations and cigar ash showered all over them, as the cupboard burgeoned into a castle flying all its flags.

'Virginia! *Ma colombe, ma douce aubépine*. Adore the earrings! And that divine shade of chartreuse really sets off your eyes. Terribly sorry to keep you, George. Little change of plan. Crankshaw wants to see you straight away. My motor's panting right outside. Drop you at the door.'

'But he hasn't seen the flat,' Ginny objected. 'And he doesn't know a thing about the job yet. Ian doesn't even know we're here.'

De Roche ignored her. 'Pure formality, George, old chap. Absolutely nothing to it. You're not committed to a thing. Just see Crankshaw for the hell of it, and you can refuse it there and then. He's seen hundreds, literally. Wouldn't touch any of them, anyway. He's insisting on a really top man.'

De Roche grabbed each by an arm and swept them through the front door. His scarlet Espada was double-parked outside, the engine running still. Ginny sank into sand-coloured suede, gazing through the windscreen at half a mile of shiny swanking bonnet. George's mouth was open. 'Wow! What a smasher!' he enthused.

Ginny winced. Why couldn't he pretend he was boringly familiar with cars like this? He'd be asking what it cost next. The car slid into the road like liquid silk. Caldos was wearing a silvery-coloured suit, tight across the thighs, so that the fabric strained and rippled as he changed gear. The shirt was the colour of an oyster shell, its silky sheen contrasting with his large dark head, his chunky hirsute hands. Coarse hairs sprouted on his thumbs, tangled down his wrists, disappeared beneath the dazzling shirt-sleeves. He sat powerful in the driving seat, like a wild beast dressed by Savile Row, an animal warmth exuding from him, which both frightened and excited her. His voice was loud and vehement as he explained the job to George, described the likely pattern of the interview, yet she was aware that he was watching her, as well; somehow wooing her, including her, despite the fact he was still addressing George.

'Crankshaw will adore an ex-Insurance man. You can't get sounder than that! Mainstay Mutual will be music in his ears . . .' He pulled up outside a narrow building, wedged between a bank and an embassy. 'You stay here, Virginia, and amuse the car. I'll just steer your father-in-law in Crankshaw's direction. Back in two ticks. We can have a drink together while we wait for him.'

Ginny fumbled with the door. 'Look, Caldos, I think I ought to come with George. He's . . .'

'He's a grown man, Virginia.' It was the first time she had heard him sharp. 'Who's been in business all his life, and hardly needs a nursemaid now.'

Ginny flushed, though she could see that George was flattered. He seemed to have come to life again, ever since he'd donned that city suit; standing taller, straighter, with a new look in his eye. She subsided on the seat, enjoying the caress of the luxurious suede upholstery; waved goodbye to George. She shouldn't hold him back. He needed this new chance. They'd all taken him for granted; giving him potatoes to peel and punctures to mend, and forgetting he'd once had status and a decent salary. It was easy to forget. George had never really made the grade, unlike her own long-distance jet-propelled father, who hurtled to and fro across the world, and dismissed the universe as small and second-rate.

She heard a door slam, watched Caldos leap the flight of steps in one athletic bound, then frisk back to the car.

'First-rate chap, your father-in-law. Crankshaw's over the moon with him! I left them knee-deep in mutual adoration.'

'Caldos, I simply must ring Ian.'

'Relax, *carissima*, I've just phoned your husband myself – got him at the office and fixed up everything. He's taking care of George's references. He even spoke to Crankshaw.'

'And did he mind me being here?'

'Mind you being in the tender care of his oldest college chum? Virginia, be reasonable.'

Ginny tried not to notice where his hand was straying, and what

43

exactly it was doing to her thigh. 'It sounds so funny when you call me Virginia. My name's really Jennifer, but no one calls me anything but Ginny.'

'An abomination!' Caldos kissed her delicately between the eyes. 'You're far too delectable to be abbreviated. Now, how about a little lunch?'

She paused, flustered by the kiss, still breathing in his smell – cologne and nicotine, overlaying the barest hint of beast. 'But . . . But what about George?'

'Oh, he'll be an age yet. Crankshaw's taken quite a fancy to him and they're bound to have a drink together. Then he'll have to see another chap as well. Just a formality. But it all takes time.'

'Well, thank you . . .' It sounded awfully lame. She wished she had Gish's husky voice and wicked repartee.

They shot off like a rocket, weaving through the traffic, hooting at all laggards, then scorching round a corner and stopping very suddenly outside a haughty-looking restaurant with tall twin bay trees standing guard outside. A liveried doorman emerged from behind the right-hand tree and did obeisance to the car.

'Good morning, Dr de Roche, sir. Not so bright this morning, is it, sir?'

'It's a magnificent morning!' Caldos insisted, ignoring the grey rain-clouds and the fact it was already afternoon. The doorman slunk abashed behind his tree.

De Roche bounded towards the door, pushed it open, and was swallowed up in a sea of smiling faces and waving hands.

5

'*Che onore, Dottore!*'
    '*Benvenuto, signore!*'
    '*Che piacere rivederla, Dottore!*'

Three Latin lackeys prostrated themselves before de Roche. The head waiter was pumping him by the hand and flicking his fingers at the minions to prepare the best table. Various VIP acquaintances leapt up from their chairs and started braying salutations at him. Even the chef popped his head round the kitchen door and waved a floury hand.

'May I take the lady's coat?'

Ginny was trying to hide behind a pillar, but the smallest of the minions had already sniffed her out and was sneering at her Marks & Spencer's mac. It joined the minks and cashmeres in the cloakroom, like a scholarship-boy at Eton. The head waiter whirled her across the restaurant and sat her beside a vase of hothouse roses. She stared down at the daunting array of fearsome knives and forks, tried to disappear into the décor, as de Roche's rumbustious friends thronged around his chair. De Roche was talking loudest, jabbing out words like a machine which punched holes. He seemed to win his point. Cigar smoke cleared and his worshippers drifted back to their tables. An oily waiter pounced.

'Dr de Roche, sir, the *trota affumicata* is superb today. Or perhaps the *lumache*?'

'No, Giuseppe, I'm going to be a splendid Italian peasant and stuff myself with your sublime pasta. Give me a large dish of spaghetti – the one with the clams.' He broke his roll in two, larded it with butter and stuffed the larger half in his mouth.

'And the lady?'

'Oh, Virginia. How about a little *zuppa di tartaruga*, darling? Or the *gamberetti all'uccelletto*?'

Ginny fiddled with her knife. The only Italian words she knew were pizza and piazza. The dishes he'd just mentioned sounded almost dangerous, like Italian motorbikes. She was very fond of whitebait, but wasn't sure whether you were meant to eat the heads or not, and didn't want to look uncouth, or unused to ritzy restaurants. Perhaps melon would be safer, but very unadventurous. She'd have to choose most carefully, since any shrewd psychiatrist could judge her by the foods she liked, checking every mouthful, like a gastronomic Rorschach test. Melon for dull and watery sort of people, and snails for insecure types who longed to sneak back to the womb. There were hazards lurking everywhere. Her eyes scanned the endless menu, finding neither inspiration nor translations.

'Right, that's settled then. *Gamberetti* for the lady.'

Ginny squirmed with embarrassment as Giuseppe bowed in her direction.

'And to follow, sir?'

De Roche shut the menu with a bang. It was as large and heavy as a bible. 'Oh, the venison for both of us, no question. It's absolutely superb here, Virginia. It would be downright sinful to miss it.'

Ginny hated venison. She'd only had it once, and once was enough. But she didn't want to sin. So she suppressed heretical thoughts of rump steak and Dover sole and tried to look agog. De Roche was already deep in vegetables, Giuseppe reeling off a litany of what sounded like Italian cardinals: '*Zucchini, spinaci, cavolfiori, piselli* . . .'

De Roche closed his eyes. He seemed as absorbed as if he were about to choose the next pope. '*Quanta roba! Siamo golosi, vada a prenderci un assaggino di tutto.* Oh and a little béchamel on the cauliflower, Giuseppe. Right, that's it. *Va bene così.*'

Giuseppe bowed again, more deeply, and bore away the holy book. Another waiter returned with two aperitifs.

'Piero says they're on the house and a very merry Christmas to you, Doctor.'

Ginny tried a sip, spluttered as the liquid scorched her tongue.

Caldos raised his glass to a short swarthy man juggling bottles at the bar. 'I see you haven't lost your skills, Piero.' He took a long draught, then touched his glass to hers.

'I want to drink to a profoundly beautiful woman.' He had suddenly given her his full attention, and for the first time she looked into his eyes – dark fathomless eyes, with large black pupils and lashes as long as a calf's. They were forested by wild and overweening brows, which jutted forward, met across his nose. The hair on his head was more restrained, the dark mane sternly coiffed, a few grey threads gleaming at the sides. The lips were full and generous, the forehead broad, the hands strong, with fleshy fingers. He seemed to be breaking out everywhere: his stomach pushing past his belt, his neck fighting with his collar, the dark shadow on his chin threatening to erupt again, despite his morning shave. The quiet-toned silvery suit seemed unable to subdue him; his chair too small to hold his weight and bulk. She was beginning to feel fragile in comparison – pale and small and weak, and lost for words.

'Don't say that,' she blushed, at last. 'No one's ever called me beautiful before.'

'You have a beautiful potential. Don't you realise, Virginia, you're the sort of gentle modest woman every man dreams of? Fair and truly feminine, submissive, unassuming . . .'

Ginny wished he wouldn't talk so loudly. The man at the next table was eyeing them between noisy mouthfuls of his steaming minestrone. Yet de Roche's words excited her. She only hoped he wasn't mocking – it was so difficult to tell. She changed the subject, to be safe. 'What exactly do you do, Caldos? I know you're a psychiatrist, but . . .' He'd hardly touched on the subject when he'd come to dinner at their house. He seemed to wave his work away, as if it were a mystery or a joke.

'I'm an analyst by training and a scapegoat by necessity. I tell people beautiful lies that life is complicated, but good. I turn ugly ducklings into swans, and swans into birds of prey, so they can tear me to pieces with their talons. I throw tightropes across the void, and my cloak across puddles. I make a lot of money.'

'But don't you work in a hospital?' Ginny's experience of doctors was trifling, but she was enjoying the new serial on BBC1 – all those white coats and throbbing emergencies. Caldos would look dazzling in a white coat.

He banged down his empty aperitif glass on the table. 'Hospitals!' The table shook. 'What are they but a cross between a prison and a morgue? Comatose abattoirs which stamp out genius along with the germs, mummify their patients and massacre all ideas and initiative.' He snatched a third bread roll and began to tear it into shreds. 'And for the privilege of ministering to two million moribund morons, they pay you enough to keep your canary in birdseed. One modest night at the Mirabelle, *gioia mia*, would take a full week's earnings on our stone-hearted NHS.' He moulded a pellet from the innards of his roll, as if he were preparing bullets for a siege. 'What is more, Virginia, I have the distinction of quarrelling with half the hospitals in London. It's not only their patients they put in straitjackets, you know. Now I go my own way. I'm a pioneer, a prophet. I'm also rather partial to the Mirabelle!'

'But don't you enjoy your work?' Ginny wished she didn't sound so boring. Her conversation was like cold lumpy porridge, served with neither cream nor sugar. She had never really noticed it with Ian.

'Enjoy!' De Roche's voice went up another twenty decibels. 'Does one normally enjoy panic and compulsion, hysteria and pain?' He ground the bread pellet into the ashtray and left it gasping. 'How can you break and reshape and scoop up the pieces and not get cut in the process? How can you not bleed?'

The spaghetti arrived just in time to staunch his wounds. Ian was right – he sounded more like a barn-stormer than a doctor. Several other diners were staring at him, and he was clearly enjoying this new audience.

'But then I never talk about my work,' he said, and smiled, turning his attention to the acre of pasta which Giuseppe had placed reverently in front of him. Ginny wondered if he'd been serious about the pain and horror of his job. He had a strange mocking way of talking, which seemed to undercut everything he said, leave it glittering and ambiguous, as if he were sending himself up.

'*Gamberetti all'uccelletto!*' A second waiter was standing to attention, a huge silver platter poised at shoulder-height. He sounded as if he were announcing a famous prima donna. Ginny felt she should curtsey, or applaud. She shrank humbly away while he whisked the platter from heaven to table, and she peered into the supercilious faces of twelve deceased pink prawns. She was almost disappointed, had expected something more exotic, from the long Italian name. The prawns still had their shells on and were swimming in a lake of liquid garlic. *Lady's Journal* advised you never to eat garlic unless your partner did as well. Now Caldos would be recoiling from her all afternoon. And whatever did you do about the heads? They were almost worse than whitebait. There was probably a perfect way to peel a prawn. There were always rules for things, like filleting a fish – never turn it on its back. Or was that artificial respiration? She'd learnt so many things, but then they all got jumbled up together.

Nervously, she picked up her first prawn and pulled at its long whiskers. A waiter was hovering near their table and she could almost see him smirk. The prawn yielded up its small soft corpse and she gulped it down in gratitude.

Caldos was shovelling in spaghetti at an impressive speed and with total concentration, sucking in stray strands and abandoning himself wholly to the aroma of the sauce. He wound a forkful into a cocoon and poised it above the tablecloth. 'Try this, *tesoro*. It's sheer ambrosia!'

He eased the fork between her lips. She opened them and swallowed. The ambrosia was hot and fishy, and fought with the flavour of the prawns. She always told the children not to eat things from each other's plates; was relieved that they weren't watching. Spaghetti was dangling down her chin and there was butter on her nose.

She plodded through the prawns, trying to avoid garlic and antennae, and not to talk with her mouth full, none of which was easy. As soon as she had swallowed a morsel, Caldos would pop another prawn between her lips, or top her up with a sticky spoonful of his sauce, and then ask her opinion on Bramante or bel canto. She had never heard of either, so she just munched on politely, and tried to make discerning little grunts through mouthfuls of spaghetti. He didn't seem to mind. He had opinions and pasta enough for both of them.

Francesco approached with a bottle of Haut-Batailley 1964.

Caldos sat up straighter. 'I can see you're not a serious drinker, Virginia. This is one of France's noblest clarets, a classic, you realise. I visited the château last October, when I was whizzing through Bordeaux. Monsieur Borie showed me round himself – an amazing little man – almost as distinguished as his grapes.' He clasped his hands around his wine glass, closed his eyes ecstatically, and sniffed the bouquet. 'Do you know about wine?'

Ginny considered. What was one meant to know about it? Ian always swore by Sainsbury's. 'We don't drink a lot at home – usually stick to water, except when we have guests. Ian has to be very careful about his weight and his cholesterol and things.'

Caldos laughed derisively. 'Poor old Ian! He was just the same at Oxford. Cold showers and decaffeinated coffee. He always blamed the rowing, but I managed to pull my weight without all those tedious privations.' He drained his glass, which was immediately refilled. Waiters were hovering six deep. 'Were you also up at Oxford, Virginia?'

'Good gracious no! I went to a convent and learned embroidery and deportment. They didn't believe in girls being clever. Only good.'

'A real little convent lady! I might have guessed. Were you a Roman Catholic?'

'My mother was, and my father most definitely wasn't. I sided with my mother, and the nuns all backed me up. We used to pray for him together.' She giggled. The wine was running circles in her head and her limbs felt free and floaty, as if they didn't quite belong to her.

'And are you still a Catholic?'

'No, I gave it up. It was always rather difficult. My mother used to cry if I didn't go to church, and my father jeered if I did. Then I met Ian and he was vaguely C of E, and it all sort of lapsed and petered out. I still feel guilty, though.'

'My line of business makes half its money from lapsed Catholics.' De Roche cut into his venison, spurting sauce all down his shirt front. Two waiters rushed to succour him, but he waved them imperiously away, and they joined his audience at a discreet two paces. 'Sometimes I think it's a sort of remunerative divine contract. The priests get their clutches on you lot young enough, lard you with worthlessness and guilt, and then hand you over sick and screaming to the analyst. That way, they do their job, we pay our bills, and God has a damn good laugh.'

'I'd never dream of going to an analyst,' Ginny retorted, the Haut-Batailley imbuing her with courage. 'I used to love being a Catholic – all the services and incense, and that sense of being superior to the Protestants – you know, *we* were the true Church, and they were just the upstarts. I miss it, yes, and I do feel guilty, but that's because my mother minds. I'm certainly not at screaming point. And Ian would hate me to be practising. We'd have sixteen kids by now!' She was talking far too much, disobeying rules. You shouldn't run down Protestants, or hint at risqué subjects such as birth control. But France's noblest claret was removing the shackles from her tongue, slipping like bright peacock feathers down her liberated throat. Even the venison tasted tolerable.

'Where did you meet him, your low-cholesterol, decaffeinated Ian?'

Ginny put her fork down, beginning to feel disloyal. 'He was a management trainee at EMI. I was a receptionist there, and he asked me to the firm's dance.'

'So, love blossomed over the slow foxtrot. You're wasted, you know, Virginia.'

Ginny gasped. Wasn't Ian his friend, for heaven's sake?

'No, I don't mean Ian.' Caldos discarded Ian as if he were a scrap of gristle. 'I mean your whole situation. There's more to you than embroidery or the St Bernard's Waltz, don't you realise? You're a fairy princess in a tower, and you need someone to climb up your golden tresses and rescue you.'

The venison really did taste better. She swallowed a mouthful with a little shudder of delight.

'And I'd like to be that someone.'

She had never heard his voice so soft. Even the waiters shrank away. She felt a rainbow swinging through her stomach, a roller-coaster roistering in her head. Somewhere, miles below on the table, her hand was squeezed in a strong seductive grip. It must be somebody else's hand. Ginny Barnes's hands did the washing and the ironing, bathed grazed knees, made fish pies and beds, fed cats, brushed dogs, demolished dust and cobwebs, but never presumed to hold a crystal wine-glass at hoovering-time on Monday, or touch it to a famous psychoanalyst's, as he gazed deep into

51

her eyes. They were toasting each other, drinking up each other, and Monsieur Borie's little château in Bordeaux was covered in bunting and ringing all its bells.

'To my fairy princess.' Caldos leaned forward, so that his hair was almost touching hers. She could see herself reflected in the dark pupils of his eyes, two tiny rag-dolls, trapped in the black treacle of his gaze. She remembered the garlic and kept her mouth discreetly closed; felt he was sucking out the juices of her soul.

'The strawberries, sir.' Francesco's voice was reverential. 'Exceptionally good, sir. Flown in today, from California.'

The rag-dolls capsized and drowned. She had lost his attention to a dish of soft fruit. Francesco selected the largest berry, anointed it with sugar, placed it on a small silver platter and proffered it to de Roche, a precious sacrifice. 'The Doctor would like to try?'

Caldos cut the strawberry with a silver fruit-knife and placed a morsel on his tongue. He rolled it round his palate. There was a moment of suspense. Francesco was watching breathlessly, a suitor awaiting judgement.

'Yes, strawberries for both of us. They're absolutely Elysian.' Francesco mopped his brow. 'Soak them in a little Calvados, will you. I don't care for Kirsch.'

Caldos crushed each berry lingeringly against his tongue and swallowed it with slow worshipping indulgence. A waiter whisked his plate away and returned with coffee cups. Ginny was still eating. There was an intense debate about the brandy. Piero confided that he had an exceptional vintage cognac, and brought it up, dusty, from the cellar.

'Only for my very special customers,' he purred.

Ginny declined. She wasn't that special, and anyway, the strawberries had reminded her of George. He grew them in their garden, cosseting them with compost and devotion. 'Won't George be wondering where we are?'

'Virginia, relax! I refuse to rush a brandy that's had the sense to do nothing but sit around and improve itself for fifty-odd years. Besides, I asked Crankshaw to take George back to Harley Street and show him the flat. He'll be busy for a while yet.'

'Oh, I hoped I could see it too. And Ian doesn't . . .'

'Caldos, wonderful to see you!' A creepy man with cigar-coloured hair and tinted glasses threw himself across the coffee cups. 'Sir John is here, you know. Just spotted you this instant and insisted that you join us at our table.'

Caldos paid extravagant farewells to Ginny, seized his brandy glass, and sprinted to the far end of the restaurant. Ginny span out her last strawberry as long as possible, finished up the dregs of her cold coffee. She would have liked another cup, but the waiters were ignoring her. Five of them were clustered round Sir John, flinging curaçao on to flaming crêpes Suzette. Caldos was the centre of attention, pounding on the table with a soup spoon to emphasise his point and drawing diagrams on the starchy linen cloth.

Most of the other customers had left. Giuseppe had put the Closed sign on the door and was re-laying the tables for dinner. Ginny scraped the sugar from her empty coffee cup. The children would be almost home from school. She hoped her mother would remember Sarah's medicine and ban Mishka from the new armchair. Caldos was right – she *was* a prisoner. Her mind kept returning to her tower. But it was a safe and cosy tower, and no one spoke in riddles or Italian.

'*Signora, la colazione andava bene?*'

It was Francesco, looking grim. She couldn't understand a word he said. He was probably ordering her to leave immediately. Everyone else had gone, except her and Caldos and Sir John. She only wished she could go. Monday was her busiest day and she hadn't done the washing yet, but Caldos looked entrenched. She eyed the dish of bon-bons – dark chocolate mints oozing cream, each nestling in a green and silver ruff. The girls would really love them. She glanced around the restaurant, to see who might be watching. The two men were totally absorbed, and most of the waiters preparing to go home. She moved the dish in closer, plopped a dozen mints on to her lap. She'd secrete them into her handbag as soon as Francesco walked away.

'Virginia! Desperately sorry to abandon you, my angel.' Caldos was suddenly in front of her, brandishing his napkin and a glass. 'I've just confounded the brilliant Sir John. Resounding victory for Socrates de Roche! Except now we're late for George. We'd better leave immediately.'

Ginny scrambled to her feet. A dozen chocolate mints cascaded from her lap on to the floor. In the hush of the almost empty restaurant, they sounded like Niagara. Ginny flushed to her ears and crawled under the table, more to hide her confusion than to retrieve them. A herd of waiters stampeded to the scene and joined her on their hands and knees.

'Virginia, my dear. Why didn't you *tell* me you were still hungry? We could have had some Stilton.'

'They . . . they're for Sarah and Snookie. I thought . . .' Two of the creams had squashed against her skirt, one sticking to her shoe.

'Don't tell me those wretched cats of yours eat chocolate mints?' Caldos chortled, as he drained his glass. 'Giuseppe, the usual arrangement with the bill. And here's a little something for Christmas. Share it out between you.' He made no attempt to conceal the twenty-pound note.

Giuseppe simpered, grovelled. 'A very merry Christmas to you, Doctor.'

At least it would stop them sneering at her, Ginny thought, struggling into her mac, her face still scarlet and her fingers smarmed with chocolate.

'And to you, *signora.*'   •

Ginny shut her eyes. The train was crowded, and she was wedged between a lumpy-hipped Amazon loaded down with parcels and a man with a self-opinionated pipe. George sat opposite, with the *Evening Standard* open on his knee, though she was aware he wasn't reading it; couldn't read herself. So much had happened, she felt a hundred years had passed, yet it was still only Monday afternoon, and she was going home to steam fish, mash potatoes, wash dirty shirts and socks.

Caldos seemed to fill the train, hovering like a huge dark shadow, breathing through her pores. He was crowned with a laurel wreath of hot spaghetti; his tongue a slice of rich rare venison, his eyes dark chocolate mints. She dragged her thoughts back to George – solid sensible George, who sat staidly and serenely, fingers clasped, feet neatly side by side. He was keen on the job, no doubt about it – said they needed one another. But it was such a humble job. She didn't like the thought of telling friends and neighbours that her father-in-law was working as a caretaker. They might even suspect she'd pushed him into it. She had complained, yes, but only about trivia, like his comparing wars each morning with the milkman, and always having birdseed in his shoes.

She wished she'd seen the flat. Not exactly a palace, George had told her, which probably meant a slum, but Caldos had promised he could arrange some renovations. Caldos. It still seemed strange to say his name – a wild unaccountable name, the letters brimming over with claret and champagne. It flung through her head like a peal of bells – Caldos, Caldos, Caldos. George returned her smile, though she hadn't even known that she was smiling. He'd be lonely, of course. You could drop down dead in London and people simply stepped over your warm corpse. No, that wasn't likely, not with eleven doctors in the house. Eleven brass plates on the door. Dr C.E.S. de Roche. C for Caldos, S for special, E for exceedingly ecstatic.

She was still alarmed about the break-in. Two days after the previous caretaker had left, there'd been a serious burglary – so Crankshaw had reported – and half of de Roche's stuff had disappeared. Strange how Caldos hadn't even mentioned it. But that's why they were so keen to fill the post; wanted someone in by Christmas, to prevent any further vandalism. Ian wouldn't stand for that – George always spent his Christmas with the family.

Should they let him go at all? He'd have no one to look after him in Harley Street, no one to trim his hair or cook his favourite puddings. But Caldos had warned her of the psychiatric consequences if she tried to hold him back – delayed reaction to bereavement, danger of infantile dependency. It sounded most disturbing. He'd even cautioned her that George might suddenly break out, if she tied him to her apron strings, become violent or aggressive. She glanced across at George – he looked sane and calm enough, puffing on his pipe and gazing into happy space.

'What's for supper, love?' he mouthed. 'I'm starving! No one seems to stop for lunch in Harley Street.'

'Oh George,' she said. 'I'm sorry! I'd no idea you hadn't eaten.'

Venison and strawberries joined with Haut-Batailley in a red-carpeted rebuke. She tried to look concerned, but the silly smile kept sneaking back. It was hard to concentrate on George's empty stomach, when hers was full and overflowing with château-bottled Caldos.

6

'For Christ's sake, Gish, I've told you not to pay these social calls on me in Harley Street. I'm a doctor, not a duchess.'

Gish decanted eleven Fortnum & Mason bags from her aching arms to de Roche's leather couch, then ensconced herself in the softest of the armchairs. 'Well, if you will ignore me for a fortnight, and then ruin our only Saturday together by dragging me down to the bloody backwoods to dine with some semi-detached school-chum . . .'

Caldos took refuge in a Partagas, concealing himself in an impressive cloud of smoke. 'I thought it was a rather splendid evening.'

'Oh yes, I could see you were bemused by that unspeakable blue lurex. Though why the Persil Mum of the Month should rig herself up to look like a cut-price Christmas cracker defeats me. I can just imagine her the rest of the week, scrubbing out dog kennels in her traffic warden shoes, and crocheting toilet-seat covers in her Marks and bloody Spencer Crimplene twinset.'

Caldos tipped his chair back and stretched his legs up on the desk. 'Superb firm, M & S – Mecca for foreign tourists. If Virginia buys their twinsets, then she's helping our balance of payments, and we should all be on our knees to her.'

'Balls! She's so naturally boring, she makes Patience Strong look like a sex symbol.'

Caldos adjusted the cushions a shade more comfortably behind his head. 'Do I detect the faintest snarl of the little green-eyed monster?'

'Don't insult me, Tum-Tum. I could hardly be jealous of some twopence-off hausfrau, stuck in her home-spun kibbutz, and surrounded by monstrous wild animals and impertinent hand-knitted fathers-in-law. Oh, I know you *adore* them like that – dumb and demure and domesticated and hanging on to your every word . . .'

'Well, it does make a change, sweetest.'

' . . . and pale and passive and placid, and doing disgusting things with babies, and slaving over hot stoves . . .'

Caldos was drawing dyspeptic Donald Ducks on his leather-bound blotter. 'Yes, she *is* a rather clever little cook. I'm surprised you noticed, when you didn't eat a thing.'

'Christ, Caldos, I spent the entire night trying to get her shitty sauces out of my system.'

'You spent the entire night, treasure, snoring blissfully beside me on your water-bed.' Caldos sprang to his feet, scattering cushions like birdseed. 'And considering you can't even boil an egg without the concerted assistance of Mrs Beeton, Larousse, and the Southern Region timetable . . . But, I'm afraid, *mon petit chou*, your time is up.'

'Don't you dare treat me like one of your patients. I'll stay as long as I like.' Gish kicked off her shoes, curled her bony toes beneath her bottom, and closed her jolt-green eyes.

'I wouldn't touch you as a patient, angel. But my solicitor's arriving in exactly half a minute.'

'Oh, Philip bloody Mossman. I loathe the man.' Gish lit a cigarette and settled back for the night.

Caldos marched over to the couch, scooped up all the Fortnum's bags, heaved the window open, and dropped them on to the paving stones outside. He listened contentedly as Gish's shrieks died away down the corridor; watched her erupt through the front door and tangle with the wheels of an elderly Rolls-Royce drawing up outside, then shrugged and closed the window.

'Philip!' Gish yelped, banging imperiously on the windscreen. 'I must have a word with you! I'm absolutely frazzled.'

The small frail man in the driving seat looked dwarfed by the dimensions of his car. He wound the window down and stuck out an undistinguished head of thinning greyish hair. 'Nothing doing, I'm afraid. I've got an immediate appointment with His Highness.'

'Oh no you haven't! He's otherwise engaged. You'll have to wait, so you may as well wait with me. He's got a patient with him.'

'What, at this hour?'

'Philip, let me in *immediately*.'

Philip groaned and opened the door her side, dodging the blast of mingled Sobranie and Chanel.

'That beastly Tum-Tum's two-timing me, I'm almost sure he is. You're closest to him, Phil, and I insist that you find out.'

'For heaven's sake, Gish, I've enough to do discussing exchange control and trust deeds, without exploring de Roche's high-octane love life.'

'God alone knows what you both get up to – always closeted together, hatching your nefarious little schemes. You're the two most legalistic crooks I've ever met. Look at Tum-Tum! His car isn't paid for, he hides from his tailor, even his house is owned by some devious property company, which I suspect he controls under another name.'

'Total fantasy, my love. De Roche is just a brilliant doctor who happens to be fascinated by the world of high finance. All right, he throws his cash around, but he also works damn bloody hard. Look at him now, slaving away at this ungodly hour!'

'What, sitting on his arse, while some gold-plated loony yammers on about her potty-training. And then charging double what any self-respecting shrink would dare. It makes me laugh.' She snarled instead, snatched one of Philip's Gauloises. Mossman hid the packet.

'You're wrong, Gish. Analysts simply can't make that sort of money – not in England, anyway. They're very limited in how many patients they can take on in the first place. And it's exhausting unrewarding labour half the time.'

Gish expelled a gust of smoke into Philip's left ear. 'I've never seen Tum-Tum exhausted in his life. He told me once that analysts never listen to a word their patients say. They sit behind them on the couch, not because Freud told them to, but so they can finish off the crossword without anybody noticing, or pick their noses, or sort through all their mail. One of his female colleagues always knits. Tum-Tum said she reckons a Fair Isle sweater every patient-year.'

Mossman grinned. 'Nonsense, Gish! Caldos just adores people to believe that he's a brute. But there's a heart underneath, I'll guarantee it. You couldn't be an analyst without one. He also happens to get his patients better – which is extremely rare in his profession. He breaks every rule in the book, tramples on the collected works of Freud, but . . .' Mossman shrugged, 'it works. He's one of the world's originals. Didn't you see those articles he wrote in the *IJP*? Bloody genius! He's working on a scheme for treating patients in an entirely different way. The Establishment is up in arms about it – which is all the more reason to suspect he's on to something.'

'Okay, I know you think he's brilliant, we *all* think he's brilliant . . .'

'But?'

'But nothing. He's just wonderful. A crook, a bastard, a lecher, and a swine.'

Philip yawned. 'Isn't that what all women say when they've been given the boot?'

'Philip, I'd like you to understand, I have not, repeat not, been given the boot.'

Philip opened the car door and eased himself out. 'Well what's all this about two-timing, then? I thought you wanted me to sound him out on some devastating rival.'

Gish clutched at the hem of his coat and dragged him back beside her. 'Devastating! You must be joking. She's just some pusillanimous suburban little sycophant. But he's already lured her up to London. I happened to cast my beady little eye on them, lolling like lovebirds in his car. The cheek of it! He's going abroad on Thursday, and he told me he simply didn't have a single moment spare. Next thing I know, he'll have taken her with him. Well, if he wants to squander his après-ski on some Pride-of-Surrey Sunday School teacher . . .' Gish stabbed out her Gauloise viciously against the dashboard. 'The trouble is, Philip, he likes that type – ankle-deep in Wonder-mash and being so thoroughly, boringly *nice* all the time.'

Philip tried to edge himself towards the door again. 'If he likes them nice, Gish darling, how in God's name did you ever last the course?'

Gish flounced out of the car and slammed the door in Philip's face. He scrambled out the other side. 'You could always take lessons,' he suggested. 'Perhaps that pusillanimous suburban little sycophant could teach you.'

7

George removed the mothballs from the pockets of his best city suits. He was a working man again! Crankshaw was impressed with his references and wanted him to start immediately. They'd come to an arrangement over Christmas – he'd spend Christmas Day with the family, then Ian would drive him up on Boxing Day. He already had the keys and his instructions.

It was a peculiar Christmas Eve. Snookie kept bursting into tears and clinging on to George's left leg, as if that way, she could anchor him at home. George made lists, and packed and re-packed his suitcases, in between the cold ham and the first mince pies. Ginny stowed vol-au-vents in Tupperware cartons marked 'George' and printed labels saying 'heat slowly at 150°C', or 'store in fridge'. Sarah made a travelling-case for the guinea pig, and painted 'Henry' on his bowl in plum-coloured nail varnish.

In the afternoon, George took the girls to the shops. He'd run out of toothpaste, and Sarah wanted tracing-paper. Ginny wilted on to a kitchen stool. Christmas was hectic enough, without all this upheaval. She'd still got the turkey to stuff and the stockings to fill. Ian wasn't home, and would probably be late, what with drinks at the office and hold-ups on the roads.

'Blast!' she said, as she flopped down from the stool again. The doorbell was squalling and Toby skidding down the hall, with his death-to-intruders bark.

'Fierce little beggar you've got there!' winced the tall man in green uniform. 'Happy Christmas, ma'am!' He thrust a ten-ton confection of cellophane and scarlet ribbon into her astonished arms, scrabbled Toby's ears, and stomped back to his van.

Ginny peered into the faces of twelve exotic roses, lolling on a cushion of green fern, looped and latticed with arabesques of ribbon, their thorny stalks caressed by a scarlet satin love-knot.

She tore off bows and cellophane, seized a small white envelope, tucked between the blooms. Inside was a card with the proud insignia of a Mayfair florist, and sprawled across it: 'To my Princess in the Tower.'

She collapsed on the hall seat. The roses had affected her like cognac. Their deep blush-red had seeped into her skin, their thorns were prickling up and down her spine, their cloying scent had squeezed inside her head and made it spin and reel. Toby pounced on a piece of errant cellophane and killed it. Ginny crash-landed back to earth. The girls would come bursting in at any moment, could well have been around and seen the florist's van. Caldos was a madman, taking risks like that – a magnificent, irrepressible, unbelievably romantic madman.

She rushed upstairs with the flowers. Where could she hide a dozen tall-stemmed roses? She bunged the wrappings in the waste bin and the ribbon in a drawer – it would do for Sarah's plaits. The flowers looked slightly less conspicuous without their under-pinnings, but their lush throats still accused her. Couldn't her mother have sent them, as an extra Christmas gift? No, Mother was coming tomorrow, and would be astonished if they all began to thank her. Besides, she hated forced flowers – always said the poor things didn't stand a chance.

Ginny fished out all the cellophane again. If she put it back, she could re-address them to Ian. An unknown admirer had sent him a bouquet. Ian's hairy old tweed jacket nudged her in the ribs – leather patches on the elbows, bulges in the pockets; the way he talked at parties about weed-killer and work-appraisal systems. No, nobody would send Ian red roses. She could say they arrived with no enclosure. But Ian was so damned honest, he'd be round the road knocking on doors, or ringing up the Post Office. Anyway, she hated telling lies. She picked up the bouquet and trailed miserably downstairs. The sharp wind rebuked her, as she walked out to the dustbin, dug among the empty tins and tea-leaves to make a smelly grave. Her mother was right, the poor things didn't stand a chance. She couldn't do it to them – or to him. A true princess wouldn't asphyxiate red roses. She dragged them out again. The cold air had revived her common sense. It was suddenly quite simple.

She arranged the roses in a vase and found a plain white

postcard. 'To dearest George,' she wrote. 'To wish you a wonderful new start. From all of us.'

As she climbed the stairs again, to George's room, the front door cannoned open and the two girls raced each other in.

'Grandpa bought us jelly babies!' shouted Sarah. 'And three iced buns.'

'And he says we can all make toffee apples!' Snookie stampeded up the stairs.

Ginny was standing on the landing, smiling like a seraph. 'And we've got something for Grandpa,' she confided. She didn't even notice that they'd brought mud in on the carpet.

They were late to bed that night. Ginny was in the kitchen making brandy butter. Ian was wrapping a bear.

'I'm whacked,' he said. 'Ready for some shut-eye.'

Ginny licked the fork. 'You go on up. It's funny, but I don't feel tired any more. It must be the excitement.' Or the roses.

'You're worse than the children,' he mumbled, giving her the fag-end of a kiss. The office had been hell.

He grunted when his wife climbed in, at least fifty minutes later. She curled her cold toes around his feet. 'Ian,' she whispered.

'Mm . . . ?'

'Let's make love.'

He made a noise between a yawn and a groan. 'I'm dead beat, Ginny. Can't we leave it till the morning?'

'What, Christmas morning, with the girls up at the crack of dawn and half a dozen teddy-bears in bed with us!'

Ian turned over, struggling between lethargy and guilt. 'I don't think I can make it, darling. There's just nothing there.'

It did feel rather wizened, though Ginny tried to coax it into life. She was never normally so blatant, preferred to leave the first moves to her husband. But red roses were burning in her blood, and the wicked little card from the Mayfair florist had unfurled across the ceiling like a banner. She edged her body close to Ian's, rubbed it up against him. He loosened the cord of his pyjamas, but didn't take them off. Ginny climbed on top of him, threw her head back, pistoned up and down – a mistress and a courtesan, lying on a bed of scented petals, pleasuring her score of ardent lovers.

'Useless bloody thing!' griped Ian. 'I can't get it up.'

The useless bloody thing certainly seemed inept. It kept flopping out, skulking away, and bending in the middle. Ian sat up and swore. 'I'm sorry, love, I really am. Look, wait a minute . . .' He pushed her off and tried a little artificial respiration, Ginny joining in, but their three concerted hands couldn't raise a flicker. It was still a little soft pink prawn, sneaking back between the sleepy comfort of his thighs, a deceased *gamberetto*.

'It's no good, Ginny. The spirit is willing, but the wretched flesh is limp.' He tried to laugh, but the laugh spread-eagled into a yawn. He gave his wife an apologetic nuzzle and turned back to the wall. Sixty seconds later, his breathing had deepened to a snuffling wheezy growl.

Ginny slumped back on the pillows, fighting off her twenty rampant lovers. 'Go away!' she begged them. 'My husband needs his beauty sleep.' But her body was still fizzing like champagne, and she longed for some admirer to uncork her, so she could explode up to the roof-tops and let all the bubbles out. She tried to count sheep – dumb white foolish creatures, lumbering across the walls. Thirty-six, thirty-seven . . . The white wool began to darken, the lumber quickened to a caper, the bleating crescendoed to a boom, and suddenly, a furry four-legged Caldos hung upside-down from the ceiling, ogling her with his brown sheep's eyes.

She crept out of bed and into the cold bathroom, locked the door and pulled her nightie up. She spread the fluffy bath-mat on the floor, and sprawled wantonly across it, leaning against the shoulder of the bath. She began to rub herself, imagining his dark hands prowling up and down her body. She turned her own small finger into his thrusting throbbing thing, as large and hard as a bottle of Haut-Batailley. It tore her inside out. She bit her lips, to stop herself from moaning – didn't want her father-in-law to come looking for a wounded cat. Her legs were braced against the bathroom wall, her thighs spread wide, every muscle taut. Caldos was ramming into her, sucking at her nipples as if they were hot pasta-shells, sauced with garlic butter; crushing hothouse strawberries on her tongue; ejaculating cognac-flavoured cream. As she came, her head tipped back and hit the edge of the bath, and she cried out in a last blazing stab of pain.

She closed her eyes, clasped the furry bath-mat to her chest, trying to caress it into Caldos. But slowly, unbearably, Caldos sneaked away, and she was left, cold, cramped, and ridiculous, kneeling on a strip of damp green lino, with a lump on the back of her head. She shivered. Masturbation was a sin – that's what the nuns had taught her at her convent boarding school. Those blatant women's magazines might take a different view, but they believed in abortion on demand, and divorce, and TV dinners, and more or less insisted on universal masturbation, as a cure for loneliness, bad marriages, acne and neurosis; or championed the Feminists, who preferred masturbating to men. She'd tried to be persuaded by their arguments, but every time she touched herself, it still felt gross and shameful – well, not when she was doing it: that was quite ecstatic – but afterwards, when she was out of breath and slimy, and her fingers smelt of sin.

She soaped herself savagely with Wright's Coal Tar, trying to remove the traces. Worst of all was bringing Caldos into it; betraying Ian with one of his own friends; indulging in obscene and sordid fantasies with a man she hardly knew. That was sinful, too. Even if you didn't do a thing, the desire was enough to damn you. An adulteress through desire, was what the nuns would call her. They'd urge her to pray to Saint Thérèse of Lisieux, who had never had so much as one fleeting sexual fantasy in her whole irreproachable life. She lathered on more soap. Saint Thérèse of Lisieux had never met de Roche. She'd lived in a strict convent, and it was easier in convents – people didn't seduce you over venison and brandy, or weaken your defences with red roses. The roses! They were almost worse. Deceiving guileless George, and hiding Caldos' card in her underwear drawer, cradled between the cups of her best bra. Deceitful and disgusting, and doubly so on Christmas Eve. Christmas was a sacred time, when decent women thought only of their families, and didn't fornicate on bathroom floors with phantom psychoanalysts.

She rubbed viciously between her legs, rebuking them with the rough slap of the towel. Sleep seemed even more impossible. She could hear Toby snoring in his basket and Snookie's heavy breathing through the open bedroom door. Caldos wouldn't be asleep. He was winter-sporting in Kitzbühel, celebrating Christmas with hot spiced rum and sugar plums, dancing the *Schuhplattler* across the midnight snow, drinking his fill of brandy-steeped hosannas. She crept downstairs, still restless.

She'd left the kitchen clean and tidy, door shut against the cats, the breakfast dishes laid, and dangling over them, the chaste silver angel the two girls had made from milk-bottle tops and foil. The turkey crouched like the great white rump of a pagan goddess, the centre of the feast. She'd be tired tomorrow from the endless Christmas round – cooking and clearing up and carols and charades, and making soup from turkey bones, and trifles, salads, sauces. She prodded the turkey's bottom. It looked too plump and proud to end up as a carcass in a cooking-pot, a mess of bones and gizzards. Perhaps she'd light the oven now, give it a long slow roasting. Only a few short hours to Christmas Day – that sugar-coated day which seemed looped with tinsel ribbon, contained a special magic which never let you down. No one could be sad or bad or wretched or remorseful – not on Christmas Day – only kind and fun and jolly, like Santa Claus himself. The magic hadn't dawned yet. The night was cold and bleak still, the dark panes etched with frost, the stealthy clock tick-ticking.

Two A.M. As a child, she'd be coming home from Midnight Mass, the church a blaze of candles, the taste of God between her lips. So simple, then. Christ in the stable with the ox and ass, and God in her stomach, and her mother's black-gloved hand in hers, and her sneering magnificent father fast asleep in his chilly separate room.

She smelt nicotine and Brylcreem as the priest approached, the faintest whiff of altar wine exhaling in her face, as he bent towards her, placed the fragile wafer on her tongue. '*Corpus Domini*,' he whispered, and she bowed her head in worship, the Host dissolving slowly down her throat. She couldn't taste God this time, but only ripe red strawberries, and the frantic scent of roses was choking the whole church, stifling all the pious smells of candle-wax and incense.

Tears were seeping through the chinks in her clasped hands, trickling down the pale corpse of the turkey. Bones in the stock-pot, flowers in the dustbin, God in shreds and tatters. 'Caldos,' she murmured. 'Caldos. *Corpus Domini*.' She crumpled up two disintegrating Kleenex, tried frantically to pray, tried to bring that child back, that devout and trusting child who'd found a safer Father. 'Father,' she implored Him. 'Help me now.'

But neither God nor Caldos answered. Neither was at home.

8

Kitzbühel was desolated, London triumphant – de Roche had returned. Ginny abandoned the ski-ing reports in the *Daily Telegraph*, stopped agonising over avalanches in Austria, and began to fret about George instead. It seemed suddenly imperative to check on his health and his larder. She had been up twice already, and painted half the flat, but with Caldos away, those visits hardly counted. This one would be different. She bought a bold new lipstick, called Rocket-Launcher Red, and squirted 'Je Reviens' behind her ears.

George was doing fine. He was already on Christian-name terms with all the secretaries, and was fast fitting faces to the brass plates on the door. The agent had hired a well-upholstered woman with capacious cardigans and Crimplene hair, who came in every weekday to help him with the doorbell and the phone. He'd discovered five different pubs in as many minutes' walk, and had made a makeshift (miniature) garden in an abandoned china sink. He'd even adopted a kitten, an orphan and a stray. Caldos had persuaded him to leave his other animals at home, but he couldn't last a week without a cat.

Ginny found the kitten holding court in a converted cubbyhole. It sprang up on the table and sauntered self-importantly between the eight white telephones, each labelled with the name of one or more consultants. Three were shrilling at once. George seemed as imperious as his cat, gestured to her grandly, and manoeuvred all three phones in an impressive sleight-of-hand. 'No, I'm afraid he's not here at the moment, Lady Bamford, but if you'd like to . . .' 'Hello, Miss Alexander. Certainly I'll change the time. Just let me get the book . . .' 'No, Signora Baresi, I . . .'

Ginny waited respectfully until all the phones were quiet, then dropped her bags and packages and hugged him. It was still something of a shock to see him in that formal suit, that dapper new silk tie. A faint whiff of aftershave, which he'd never worn in his life before, always labelled 'sissy', had taken over from straw and garden twine.

His day was almost finished. He switched the phones through to his flat, and locked the waiting-room, then led her to the basement down a flight of carpeted stairs. She preferred that way to the steep stone steps outside, which plunged down from the street, and smelt of damp and urine. She always felt uneasy when she ventured down those steps; trapped by prison-railings, dodging coal-holes, squeezing past the dustbins – another world entirely from the brass and mahogany luxuriance of the patients' territory.

She unpacked home-made jam, home-made curtains, a veal and chicken pie, a pink hot-water bottle, and a slab of Christmas cake. George plumed and prattled and spooned extravagant amounts of tea into his cracked brown teapot. He left it to brew, while Ginny stood on a chair with a mouthful of pins and tried to judge the curtain hems.

'They're dipping slightly this end, love. Don't they look grand, though? I love the crimson poppies.'

Ginny stooped down, re-adjusted half the pins. 'How's that?'

'Absolutely tophole!'

Ginny lost her footing and the pin-box. The voice was far too loud to be George, who had swept towards the door.

'Good evening, Dr de Roche, sir. I trust you had a pleasant trip. My word, the suntan suits you!'

She wobbled on her perch, horribly aware of a six-inch gap of naked flesh between her shirt and jeans. She hardly dared look round, but the voice was coming closer, lapping against her legs.

'Virginia, you look quite magnificent! Venus ascending Mount Olympus. No, don't get down – I love my girls on pedestals!'

Caldos swept through the flat like a sirocco. She could feel his breath burning in her cheeks as she stepped down from the chair, returned to earth literally as well as metaphorically.

'George, can you find another cup?'

Thank heavens they matched and George hadn't plonked the milk bottle on the table, or exposed the broken biscuits. Even so, Caldos looked incongruous in these small and shabby quarters.

He was wearing a suit the colour of crushed damsons, and an oatmeal shirt with a slight weave to its texture and expensive fiddly buttons. The pale collar and cuffs set off his golden suntan, which had suddenly made her and George look wan. He sat down at the rickety table with as much enthusiasm as if he had arrived at the Lord Mayor's feast. He paid homage to the chicken pie, and munched his way through two generous portions. He raved about the Christmas cake; praised the strawberry jam, digging out the strawberries with the wrong end of a fork. He applauded the newly painted kitchen, eulogised the curtains. George plied him with tea and extra almond icing, while she explained the problems of pinch-pleating and false hems. At last, he licked his fingers and lolled back in the groaning kitchen chair.

'Well, George old man, how does it feel to be indispensable? The whole of Harley Street is humming with your praises, so I hear. I bumped into Dr Harrington an hour or so ago, and he said the house has never run so smoothly. He even said you'd started learning Arabic.'

'Only just the odd word, sir. I find it helps to put the Middle Eastern patients at their ease.'

'Ah yes, our little friends, the Arabs. They more or less keep Harley Street in business. Though not in my specialty, alas. I don't think Freud ever made it to Dubai.'

'More tea?' asked Ginny, hoping it was hot still.

He passed his cup across, allowed his hand to linger, brush against her own. 'And you, Virginia, are a born home-maker! You've turned the place into a palace. I simply didn't realise you were an interior decorator, as well as a *chef pâtissier*.'

George beamed proudly at his new saffron walls. 'That she is, Doctor. You should see my bathroom. It's more luxurious than a lounge.'

Ginny wished he wouldn't mention bathrooms. It wasn't in good taste. But Caldos didn't seem to have noticed, was leaping around the flat, praising shelves, curtains, colour schemes, even the old and tatty carpets.

'The Barnes family obviously *oozes* talent,' he concluded, straightening a dingy picture of a stag at bay. 'Well, I suppose I'd better toddle back to Chelsea. Lady Carruthers will be banging down my door. Can I offer you a lift, Virginia? It's pelting down with rain.'

She glanced nervously at George. 'I had intended to finish off the curtains . . .'

'You leave them, love. There's no rush. I don't like the thought of you traipsing round those dreadful undergrounds. Someone was mugged in Tufnell Park only yesterday. Would you be so good, Doctor, as to take her all the way to Waterloo?'

'Delighted, George. I'll see her on the train myself.'

Ginny fetched her coat and handbag from the bedroom. She should never have eaten that second piece of cake. Her stomach was objecting, her whole body strangely fluttery.

'First-rate chap, your father-in-law,' Caldos observed, as they cruised down Wigmore Street, rain thwacking at the windscreen.

'Mm,' said Ginny, racking her brains for something more profound to toss into the velvet dark between them.

They had reached Hyde Park Corner before she thought of it, and by then she was distracted. Caldos was whizzing round the roundabout and turning into Knightsbridge. Her geography had always been C minus, but even so, she was aware that Waterloo and Harrods weren't exactly side by side. She dropped the dazzling remark she had spent the last ten minutes polishing, and murmured timidly, 'We're – er – going the wrong way.'

Caldos clapped a bronzed hand to his forehead. 'Stupid of me, Virginia! Do you know, I was so deep in thought, I didn't even notice. I go this way so often, I do it in my sleep. It's a little tricky turning round with all this traffic, and now we've gone so far, it's hardly worth it. Tell you what, why don't I take you all the way to Hinchley Wood? We're on the right road, and it'll save you getting drenched.'

'But it's miles, Caldos.' His name still sounded frightfully daring. 'I'll only make you late.'

'Late for what, angel?'

'Well . . . Lady Carruthers. I thought you said . . .'

'Who? Oh, Lady C. Yes, of course. Well, why don't you drop in at Chelsea for a little glass of something and meet her ladyship? Or, even better, stay for a spot of supper with us both. I've got a whole smoked salmon twiddling its fat fins in the fridge.'

'But we've only just had tea, and . . .'

'Nonsense! It's the very *ne plus ultra* in salmon – sent all the way from Scotland, packed in ice. And a Corton-Charlemagne '73. No one in his senses could decline.'

She gazed down at her shabby jeans, her scuffed old winter boots – not quite the right apparel for dining with a titled head. 'I'm worried about the girls,' she frowned. 'Ian's late home tonight, so I'll have to pick them up from Kate's – my friend's.'

'No problem! You can telephone from my place and ask your chum to keep the little loves a trifle longer.'

'But Ian . . .'

'Late, you said. Poor fellow! My heart bleeds . . . It's all grind with these biscuit chaps. But there's no point in your returning to an empty house.'

'But, he might not . . .'

'Look, Virginia, I need your help. I'll be totally frank about it. I want to pick your brains. I've got this nonsense of a house in Chelsea – a little bijou slum, which is crying out for some tender loving care – a face-lift, an *outré* colour scheme, you know the sort of thing. You're a natural when it comes to colour. I realised that at George's. It's rare, you know, especially in a woman. I'd be overjoyed if you could spare me just a moment and cast your expert eye upon the shambles.'

Ginny clutched the arm-rest for support. Interior design was simply not her forte. She only messed about with Woolworths' Easy-On emulsion because Ian refused to pay a proper painter. All she'd reckoned on was a chance hello at Harley Street, not this extended venture into home-making. Snookie ought to have an early night and Sarah hadn't . . .

'I can't thank you enough, Virginia. What my house really lacks is the woman's touch, you see – that feminine *je ne sais quoi* which can transform the basest living-space to home.'

They were already skimming down the King's Road, past bistros and boutiques; must be only minutes from his bijou Chelsea slum. How could she refuse to help, or stop for just a moment? It would seem churlish and ungrateful after all he'd done for George. But she knew she lacked that vital woman's touch. If only she'd been to Art School, or taken a course in . . .

'Well, Virginia, *chérie*, tell me the story of your life.' Caldos lit a fat cigar from the built-in lighter on the dashboard and waved it graciously in her direction. 'No, let me guess! You were born in a ruined castle on the Rhine.'

'Well, not *exactly*.' It was a bungalow in Basingstoke, but she wasn't going to tell him that; started at the age of three, when they'd moved to genteel Cobham. She'd only got as far as her First Communion, at seven, when he suddenly turned right, into a street of shuttered houses which seemed to recoil from the flotsam of the life around them; pulled up at number ten, a tall four-storeyed mansion with beetling black-iron balconies and a door like a portcullis.

He selected a brass key from the massive bunch he carried, unlocked the door and stepped across the threshold. Ginny followed, jumping at the shrill and sudden salvo from the burglar alarm, which Caldos disengaged. He pressed another hidden switch and all the lights flashed on – concealed and cunning spotlights which haloed precious objects, whilst leaving background corners dramatically obscured. She gazed around the room, marvelling at the contrast between soft shadows and fierce glare. Everything was black – paintwork, ceiling, sumptuous thick-pile carpet, stately leather chairs – black on black on black. The gleaming midnight walls were crowded with enormous canvases, each one individually lit. Random daubs of colour shrieked against each other, or struggled to escape their frames; twisted, convoluted bronzes writhed in pools of light. Ginny spelled out letters on plinths and pedestals: 'Celebration of a Hole', 'Hiroshima', 'Parabola 3'. A huge carved figure with three bulging eyes, one arm and no neck, glared down at her from its redwood pedestal. A quartz crystal clock measured the millionth fraction of a second on the alabaster mantelpiece. It was a most unusual slum.

Caldos threw her coat across the chess table, submerging two ivory bishops and a queen. She dived into a shadow, to obliterate her jeans. So this was his princely pigsty, his five-star shambles, which she was to insult with her suburban dabblings and her Woolworths colour schemes. She could no more help him renovate this dream-house than a schoolboy's sums could succour Einstein's genius.

He vanished for a moment, returned with a tall bottle and two fluted Victorian glasses. The wine was very cold and very dry, sent shivers down her spine. She kept glancing round her nervously, wondering when Lady Carruthers might arrive, and whether her ladyship would be annoyed to find another woman there, especially one so patently inferior as far as rank and breeding were concerned. Though a threesome would be preferable in one sense, might help the conversation, which was languishing at present. Caldos seemed much quieter than his usual buoyant self, and there was no food as yet to engross him or inspire him. He disappeared again, and she listened for the hopeful sounds of clinking knives and plates. At least a whole smoked salmon would serve as a distraction. Instead, she heard the faint flick of a switch, and a triumphant burst of music exploded through the room; the disembodied voices of some magnificent church choir pleading for eternal rest. '*Requiem aeternam, aeternam*.' Cellos and basses surged above the choir in a sobbing crescendo, as the voices begged for light – '*luceat, luceat*' – hushed, repeated, rapturous; voices crying in the darkness.

Ginny dared not move. She was back in her convent school, back with the deportment, and the spotted dick for dinner, and the solemn Mass for the dead. She suddenly remembered a summer trip to Rome – a stifling-hot school pilgrimage, when they'd all had their missals blessed by the Pope and their bottoms pinched by his faithful, and she'd heard a Requiem Mass weeping through the gloom of Santa Maria Maggiore. But not this Requiem. She'd never heard this fervent Mass before.

The choir was singing the *Kyrie*: Lord have mercy, Christ have mercy. '*Eleison, eleison*.' A bassoon tore through the voices, while the cellos keened beneath them. Ginny felt she should be on her knees. She glanced across at Caldos. His face was half in light and half in shadow; eyes closed, hands clasped, head thrown back against the chair. She dared not speak, disturb his concentration.

Altos and tenors began to chase each other through the Offertory, the orchestra joined in, and there was a gradual swell and surge of sound. Ginny recalled the words in English, still familiar from school: 'Deliver them from the mouth of the lion, nor permit the dark lake to engulf them, nor darkness to overcome them.' And now the baritone blazed in, his bare proud voice standing alone before God, begging that they should pass from death to life.

In the tiny pause which followed the Amen, Caldos floated to his feet and moved towards her on the sofa. His eyes were still half-closed, as if he were walking in his sleep. He sat beside her, silent and engrossed, still listening to the music. The mood had changed with the *Sanctus*, and for the first time, the violins meandered into the score, and the harp anointed it with quicksilver.

Slowly, solemnly, Caldos removed his arm from the back of the sofa and placed it round her shoulders. '*Sanctus, sanctus, sanctus,*' the sopranos were insisting. His face moved closer, so that she was wandering through the dark forest of stubble on his upper lip, and trailing her fingers in the black pools of his eyes. There was a sudden shout from the brass – '*Hosanna!*' – and she felt his mouth crush against hers. She tried to pull away, but his mouth was a hosanna, exulting, eloquent. He used his tongue to capture her, inveigling it between her lips, prising them apart, exploring crannies of her mouth she hardly knew were there. The treble solo capered above the choir, blithe and innocent, and her mouth began to move and grow, surging with the violins into harmony with his, until she was all opening softening moistening moaning mouth. '*Qui tollis peccata mundi,*' implored the tenors. But there were no sins any more, only the cadenza of his tongue against her mouth, and his skilled hands bowing and plucking her body, and the dark yelp of the bassoon.

Suddenly, from miles away, she heard the chastened baritone begging God to deliver him from eternal death; the sopranos fleeing from the wrath to come. An avenging trumpet cut through the room with a whip-lash *Dies Irae*, threatening and discordant. She dragged her mouth away from Caldos, almost bit and shook him off, as she shrank into her own corner of the couch. She was surprised to see her shirt unbuttoned. Her face was wet and stinging, her mouth misshapen, mauled.

Caldos reached out urgently towards her. 'No,' she whispered. 'Please no, Caldos.' '*Libera me, libera me*' – the choir supported her, pleading to escape, and the iron voice of the baritone cried out along with her: 'Deliver me, Oh Lord, deliver me.'

Caldos seized her by the wrists, slammed his mouth against her neck, grazing with his teeth. It was a breathless pain, punishment for her blasphemy – sacrilege even – to smooch throughout a Requiem Mass. She no longer recognised her own mouth. It had betrayed her, taken over, behaved wildly, irresponsibly. She tried to force him off again, almost fighting with him now, but heard his voice reproaching her, gentle and seductive, as his mood changed with the music – trumpets banished, harps beguiling; the *In Paradisum* plaintively entreating. She was aware that she was weakening, ravished by the violins, bewitched by his bravura words; finally jerked up from the sofa and stood trembling by the door.

The organ rolled behind his voice – a very different voice now – agitated, vehement, angry like the brass. He was telling her she needed him, that to deny sexuality was to deny God, whereas to celebrate the body was to outwit pain and death; that love and death and pain were all inseparable; that fidelity was outmoded and chastity neurosis; and that she, Ginny Barnes, was a boring predictable suburban little prude.

The silence was deafening. The room, which had roared and threshed with sound, had now shuddered to a halt. Ginny stood, half-paralysed herself, listening to the faint swish-swish of the still-revolving spool. De Roche's face was closed and hard, his brows drawn down like shutters. He turned his back, strode into the kitchen. She followed nervously, blinking against the fluorescent glare, the stark white walls and worktops. She had been wrenched from the snug darkness of the womb into the cold white stare of the delivery-room. A forceps delivery. A still-birth.

Caldos didn't bother with plates. He slapped smoked salmon on to pumpernickel, slung the slices on a tray. She could taste his scorn like lemon, the wine cold against her bruised and smarting mouth. They ate standing up, leaning against the futuristic table in moulded white glass.

'Even Fauré is against you,' muttered Caldos, with the icy dregs of a smile. 'Do you know what he said?'

'No,' said Ginny, trying to dislodge an obstinate crust of pumpernickel from the ruins of her throat. She'd never even heard of him, and there was still no sign of Lady Carruthers.

Caldos crammed his mouth with salmon and spoke through it. '*L'art a toutes les raisons d'être voluptueux.*'

9

George cleared the tea table and drew the new flowered curtains. A spiteful rain was lashing at the windows and he hated to see the bare panes wet and buffeted. Thank heavens Ginny was not out in the downpour. Decent of the Doctor to have offered her a lift to Waterloo. He was such a busy man, it was a wonder he could be bothered with all the social niceties. Funny fellow, really – downright eccentric, but brilliant none the less. Everybody said so. You heard the nasty rumours too, but that was jealousy, no doubt. His secretary treated him like Jesus, and the patients simply wouldn't keep away. Some of them came five times every week, and then they phoned between-times. Miss Hammond, for example, insisting that she ring at the crack of dawn tomorrow, when she'd already phoned three separate times today; sobbed for ten whole minutes with the other phones all hollering, and a whole tribe of Arabs picnicking in the waiting-room. The poor kid was just a schoolgirl, barely seventeen. Bea would have hated it. All that suffering, and hardly out of socks.

George turned on the television, but kept the sound right down. A mean-eyed man with a Colt 45 strode into the saloon and put a bullet through the barmaid. He switched her silent screams off, unlaced his shoes, rubbed his aching feet. It was damned hard work looking after eleven doctors, eight insistent telephones and umpteen fretful patients. Perhaps he'd go to bed. He'd tidied up the waiting-room, locked all the other doors, and jotted down his schedule for the morning. The kitten was lying dozing on the eiderdown, as if he, too, was knackered by his day. George picked him up, took him to the kitchen to prepare their Ovaltine; whipped round from the gas-stove as the doorbell rang upstairs. The agent had advised him to ignore it after hours – half the time it was only tramps or troublemakers. But it always made him nervous.

He poured hot milk in his cup, jumping as it rang again, louder, longer, and sounding almost ominous. He hurried up the inside stairs and along to the front door. The bell was squalling now, as if the caller had his finger on the bell-push and refused to take it off. He drew the bolts back cautiously. 'Who's there?' he growled, trying to ape the mean-eyed gunman. You had to be really careful after dark.

He heard muffled sobbing, a broken jagged voice: 'I want to die. I just want to die.'

George unlocked the door, and a small frail girl, wearing a fur coat over a nightdress, swayed unsteadily towards him. The fur was sleek and streaming with rain, like a seal, and her hair dripped in streaks across her forehead, mixing with her tears. She threw herself down dramatically on the marble flagstones of the porch.

'I can't bear any more. I want to die. Please let me die.'

'Miss Hammond!' George exclaimed, trying to coax her from the floor and half-carrying her inside. He had never seen her so disturbed, but did his best to keep his own voice calm and kindly. 'You come down to the kitchen, lass, and I'll make you a cup of tea.'

'I don't want tea. I want to die. Where's Dr de Roche? I must see Dr de Roche.'

George steered her along the passage, and downstairs to his flat. The house felt cold, unwelcoming; the clock ticking almost angrily, as if annoyed at being bothered after hours. 'I'm afraid the Doctor's not here in the evenings. But I do know where to phone him, so if you'd like to . . .'

'No!' she shouted, clutching at his arm. 'Please don't go away. Don't leave me.'

'I'm not leaving you, lass. The phone's only in the passage.'

'I don't want you to phone him. He'll only be annoyed. He told me to wait till tomorrow. It's so long till tomorrow. I just want to die.'

George sat her down on the sofa and removed her dripping coat. The nightie flapped against her bare legs. He was surprised that such a sparrow of a girl should contain so much grief. It seemed to well out of her, like a tap without a washer. He settled her back

77

against the cushions and tucked a rug around her legs. She was all eyes and bones, like some abandoned fledgeling, peering at a hostile world. He must alert de Roche – this was an emergency.

'Look, Miss Hammond, I think you need that cup of tea. It'll help to warm you up.' He could do with one himself, and it would give him an excuse to slip out to the phone, without her noticing. The agent had warned him about hysterical patients, told him not to get involved. But how could he avoid it, when she was clinging to his sleeve?

'I know you don't want me here. You're going to send me away. I won't go away. I'm going to die.'

That terrible refrain each time. He found it most distressing – all that talk of dying, when she'd only just started on her life. 'It's all right now, Miss Hammond. I shan't send you away. You can stay here for a while. But why don't you tell me what's the matter?'

She shook her head and shrugged. 'Nothing much to tell.'

George said nothing either, simply picked up his pipe and filled it, as if all his attention were concentrated on half a gram of St Bruno. He struck a match, a tiny explosion in the hushed brown room. Miss Hammond jumped, and he saw her frightened eyes, watching him in the sudden snap of light, eyes too big for her small-boned fragile face, her short and spiky hair. He put his arm around her shoulders and sat beside her, puffing quietly on his pipe.

Suddenly she began to talk, words pouring out of her, instead of tears. She was no longer looking at him, seemed to be speaking to her hands, which lay inert and pallid on the rug. 'I lie awake at night and pray to God. I don't believe in God, but I just say "let me die". I've thought about doing it. I've got all the pills and stuff. I wouldn't cut my wrists. I hate blood. Pills are tidier. But I'm scared, scared of waking up in another world even worse than this one. Or being alone for ever. At least when I'm alive, I've got Dr de Roche. I can talk to him about it. I can't tell anybody else. You're not allowed to want to die. It upsets people, makes them really angry. They say, "You're young, you've got everything to live for. You're rich. You could do anything you want." But I don't want to do anything, or spend my rotten money. I'd like to be rubbed out, like that white

78

stuff typists use, covered over like a misprint.' She laughed, a grotesque laugh, which sounded like a cry.

'I had a friend once. Deirdre. Her father used to call her "sweetheart". He never said "Deirdre", always "sweetheart", like a lover. I loathed her guts. So I invented this person of my own, who was just like Deirdre's father – tall and thin, with freckles on his hands, loads and loads of freckles, blotched all across the backs. He was always there, available – not like my own father, who pissed off when I was three. So when I starting seeing Dr de Roche, I pretended he was him; used to close my eyes and hear him saying "sweetheart", or imagine him holding both my hands in his great big freckled ones.'

George laid his pipe down, moved his leg a fraction. 'And did the Doctor ever say it?'

'Oh no. No, no, of course not. I never told him, anyway. He's very kind, but there's a sort of barrier between us, a great wodge of something getting in the way. It's as if he's talking from a long way off, like the wrong end of a telescope. And I'd never dare to touch him. It's like he's wearing armour. But you mustn't think he doesn't care. He does – I know he does. But he's got all these other patients. Deirdre was an only child, didn't have to share her father. And, anyway, I don't have that much time with him – only . . .'

Tears fell on her hands. She hardly seemed to notice them. George edged a little closer, rummaged in his pocket for his handkerchief, wiped her nose and eyes, as if she were a child, then began to smooth her hair. That had always worked with Sarah when she'd been overwrought or tearful – a gently rhythmic stroking – the sort of thing the cats liked, which soothed them, calmed them down. She was lying very awkwardly, her whole body tense and wary, as if at any moment she might yelp and spring away. He continued stroking, and, at last, the girl relaxed, closed her eyes, slumped against his shoulder. He tried to keep as still and quiet as possible, to merge into the room like a piece of solid furniture, though his arm was getting stiff and he had cramp in his left foot. He could hear the rain droning down outside, the muffled roar of passing cars, a few lonely footsteps startling the dark street.

There was a sudden mew and flurry as the kitten capered from the kitchen and jumped up on the sofa. Miss Hammond shrank away, but the kitten frisked across her leg, sniffing at the tartan rug, searching out the softest spot.

'What's its name?' she asked, reaching out to touch him with one cautious finger.

'Harley. Because he lives in Harley Street.'

She tried the name, repeated it. The kitten purred and shook his ears.

'It's more than time for his milk. I wonder if you'd be kind enough to hold him for me, while I go and get it ready?'

George slipped into the kitchen, poured milk into a saucepan, then sneaked out to the phone. De Roche's Chelsea number was engaged. He filled a saucer with warm milk, tipped the rest into a mug and took it to the sitting-room. 'Do you like Ovaltine?' he asked.

Miss Hammond made a face, pushed the cup away. Harley was lying right across her chest. George left the cup beside her, tried the phone again. Still engaged. He dialled the operator, to explain the situation.

'The receiver has been taken off,' the operator informed him, once she'd tried the number herself. 'It may be unintentional, of course, but I can hear background music. It sounds a bit like a church. I could put the howler on, if it's important.'

George pondered. Maybe de Roche had gone to bed and wouldn't relish being woken up. But would he sleep to music? And why church music – unless he was comparing records with a music-minded analyst or priest. He was such a busy man, perhaps it was wrong to bother him, in any case. There were emergency numbers pinned up on the board, or he could always ring the hospital, or Dr Stewart-Davies, though Miss Hammond wouldn't care for strangers.

He crept back to look at her. She had both hands round the kitten, which was still curled across her chest, but the hands were limp, relaxed, and she was breathing very deeply. George sank into a chair. Better let the poor kid sleep, though Mrs Massey wouldn't like it – a young girl in her nightie, spending all night with the caretaker. It wouldn't do his reputation any good at all. He trailed out to the passage, tried de Roche again. Still busy. He dithered for a moment, then dialled the hospital. If he sent her home, she might do something desperate; if he let her stay, he was breaking all the rules.

'Hello. Middlesex. Can I help you?'

George tried to find his voice, sound forceful and assertive.

'Middlesex Hospital. Hello caller. Are you there?'

'Yes – er – no. I'm sorry. I must have got a wrong number.' He returned to the sitting-room, glancing at his hands – gnarled old hands, with blue veins standing out, roughened from all weathers and his gardening. There were no freckles on the backs, only a scratch from Harley's claws, but they'd simply have to do. He sat down on the sofa, just beside her feet, paused a moment as she whimpered in her sleep, then reached out both his hands. He closed his fingers over hers, moving very gently for fear that he might wake her, then trying to get comfortable himself. The night might be a long one, and he mustn't let her down.

'Sweetheart,' he said softly.

10

Their local record shop didn't stock the Fauré *Requiem*.

'You'd better go to HMV in Oxford Street,' the wild-haired youth suggested, once she'd spelled it for him.

'Thanks,' said Ginny, drifting to the pop section and picking out a record for Sarah instead. These last two weeks, she'd been snapping at the girls so much, the least she could offer them in recompense was an ear-splitting LP by a group of acned punks. As for HMV in Oxford Street, forget it! She refused to go traipsing up to London in search of sentimental memories, just because some self-opinionated over-sexed Chelsea doctor was too ill-mannered to phone. Thirteen and three-quarter days precisely. She marched out of the shop, and into the small café two doors down; found herself a niche.

'Yeah?' The waitress had a faint moustache and a transatlantic twang.

'A black coffee, please – a strong one.'

He was a busy man, for heaven's sake. Wasn't George always telling her how long and hard he worked? He probably couldn't find the time to phone, with demented patients pestering him all day, not to mention Gish. Crazy to imagine she could compete with all those feathers. He was bound to have a score of Gishes, all sharp and sexy and devastating, who wore Gucci jeans and had absinthe for elevenses, instead of ginger nuts. Why on earth should he bother with dreary Ginny Barnes – a boring predictable suburban little prude? She flung a third lump of sugar in her coffee cup, jabbed it with her spoon. She was a piece of living Tupperware, overflowing with Brillo pads and baked beans, Washing Whiter and Baking Lighter and Killing Germs Other Cleaners Couldn't Reach, dashing from the sink and stove to the Women's Guild bazaar, then back to chores and children. 'The sort of gentle modest woman every man dreams of, fair and truly feminine . . .'

Those were his own words. But that was before the Requiem, before he'd changed his mind about her, and, anyway, he probably hadn't meant it. Or perhaps he had it off by heart and said it to them all. Could they *all* be fair, submissive, modest, unassuming; all be Princesses in Towers? Princess. She spun the word out – a happy-ever-after word. Perhaps she'd hurt his pride. It was a funny thing, male pride – made men rush around the place sleeping with sixteen-year-olds, or choosing dolly birds as secretaries, to give them instant glamour; or always having to win at games – golf or darts or football, then downing ten pints afterwards, to prove what sports they were.

All except for Ian. His secretary was menopausal, and he didn't like Lolitas; played no games at all save Scrabble with the girls. And he never propped up bars; rationed himself to one cut-price Cyprus sherry in the safety of their sitting-room, before his low-cholesterol dinner. She should be grateful really. He was marvellous at making rabbit hutches, and could prune trees and poach eggs, and even find his way around Sarah's hazardous New Maths. It was wicked to want more. Kate's Alan went to Special Saunas, the ones with kinky massage, and forgot his own son's birthday. And Emma Bamford's husband had been discovered in Le Touquet with his blonde receptionist.

She pushed her cup away. Caldos was out of the question. If she saw him any more, it would be opening the door to danger and depravity and all those things which *Lady's Journal* warned against. 'Dear Patience Soul, I am a happily married woman with a lovely home and children, yet I'm shouting at my husband, kicking cats and . . .' 'Dear Patience Soul, It is thirteen days, fifteen and a half hours, since I last saw Dr Wonderful. I am neglecting my chores and writing "C de R" in the dust on the dining-room table.' 'Dear Patience Soul, I am a boring predictable suburban little prude.'

Was fidelity outmoded, as he'd claimed? *Lady's Journal* didn't seem to think so, but Kate and Alan did. And if chastity caused neurosis, then perhaps that's what was wrong with her. She had sex, of course, with Ian, but it was chaste and timid sex. Ian just didn't have a mouth like that, or hands like that, or . . . She ran her tongue round the inside of her lips. She could still taste sugar; still hear '*Sanctus, sanctus*' thrilling in her head. She beckoned to the waitress. 'Another coffee, please. With cream. And a piece of strawberry cheesecake.'

It was inexcusable, wasting time like this, with the girls' tea still only a frozen package in her shopping bag. She seemed to have returned to adolescence, or perhaps she was more seriously disturbed, even turning into one of Caldos' patients. Maybe she should talk to him about it, or at least try to reassure him if she'd hurt his feelings, or appeared petty and unfair. And she could explain her deep belief in old-fashioned things like loyalty and love, her commitment to the children, and then he'd give her one last kiss, just a brief and unexceptional kiss, and that would be the end of it.

Except for George, of course. She'd have to visit George, and George was living only one floor down. Well, if she ran into Caldos in Harley Street, she'd simply have to smile and say wasn't it amazing how the snow had held off, and yes, the traffic was much worse these days, and no, she didn't think nurses' pay was . . .

She checked her watch, grabbed the bill in panic, and rushed back to the car, praying Kate would be delayed herself, and not be sitting fuming outside the Barneses' semi. She zoomed round the corner on two wheels, heart sinking as she saw the battered Volkswagen; Kate slumped in the driving seat reading *Cosmopolitan*.

Ginny wound the window down. 'Terribly sorry, Kate, I was . . . held up in Safeway's.'

'D'you reckon you've got an identity crisis?' Kate shouted from the depths of page fifteen.

'What?' Ginny turned the engine off.

'Twenty per cent of women are suffering from it, apparently. Do you have rashes, headaches, nausea, irritability, irregular periods, or cold sores?'

Ginny wished Kate wouldn't talk so loudly. Their next-door neighbour was always listening in, then relayed the choicest titbits to Mrs Edgeworth opposite. Snookie clambered out of the car. 'I've got a cold sore and I'm starving,' she complained, scuffing her school shoe along the gutter.

'Don't *do* that!' Ginny griped.

Sarah banged out the other side, slammed the door behind her. 'I'm sure Mummy's got one of those crisis things. She's always shouting at us.'

'Nonsense, Sarah! Your mother's so bloody saintly, she makes us all sick. My horrid brats don't get home-made éclairs and their socks darned.'

'Who wants their socks darned, anyway? Debbie's mother just throws them away when they've got holes in, so she gets new ones all the time. And Mummy hasn't made éclairs for ages. All we've had is rotten tinned spaghetti.'

'I love tinned spaghetti,' Kate's son, Steve, protested from the floor of the car, where he was crouching in imitation of James Bond.

'Why don't you all come in for tea and I'll damn well make you some éclairs?' Ginny scrabbled for her key, scooped up all her shopping.

'That's called guilt, love. It's one of the symptoms.'

Kate was large and not quite plain, her full mouth and grey-blue eyes redeeming straight and mousy hair, which hung ragged and uneven. She didn't believe in hairdressers, just snipped bits off in front, when fringes were in fashion, or hacked hunks off the back, if it took too long to dry. She seemed permanently at 'take-off'; never still, but leaping, laughing, darting, often doing several things at once. Her son was small and shy, as if deliberately reacting to his mother's bulk and vigour.

She breezed in through the door, almost tripping on a cat. 'Good God, Ginny! No wonder you've got an identity crisis. It's like Pets' Corner in here.'

'I haven't got an identity crisis. I'm just a bit on edge.'

'What's the matter?'

'Nothing. Hell, I'm right out of cocoa. Farewell éclairs!'

'Glad to know you're human. Jane used to say you're the only woman she knows who's never run out of anything in fifteen years of marriage. All those shopping-lists and freezer-logs. It's unfair on the rest of us.'

'Oh, don't be stupid, Kate.' No, she mustn't snap. A fortnight wasn't really all that long. Perhaps he'd gone away again – wine-tasting in St Emilion, or a medical conference in Mexico, glamorous interpreters whispering in his ear. 'I'll have to make flapjacks, I suppose. I know I've got some treacle.'

'Didn't know your taste in music went this low.' Kate had a habit of unpacking other people's bags.

'Oh, that Yellow Skunk thing. It's Sarah's.'

Kate pounced. 'There you are, you see, what other martyr mum would actually encourage their kids to listen to that racket? Alan sold our stereo the very day Steve learned to put it on.'

The children had already gone upstairs to change. Sarah trailed down in grey school knickers and a violent-orange T-shirt with 'Shout louder' on the front.

'Someone's nicked my jeans. Skunk YELLOW! Mum, you angel! I *do* like tinned spaghetti.'

'It's real spaghetti, if you don't mind. And flapjacks.'

Sarah wasn't listening, had dashed back to her bedroom. The thump-thump-thump of drums resounded from upstairs, thundered round the landing, followed by a whine from the guitar, then a wailing cockney voice began to murder both the language and the lyric.

'Shall I make the tea?' asked Kate, wincing at the noise.

'Thanks,' said Ginny, counting on her fingers. If he'd gone to Mexico, he'd be away at least a fortnight. Another fourteen days of rushing to the phone and almost murdering any caller because it wasn't Caldos; or trailing into Safeway's and buying best smoked salmon instead of pilchards in tomato sauce. She measured out the oats. If he wasn't in Acapulco, he'd be in Chelsea – always was on Wednesday afternoons; saw the ones who didn't come to Harley Street. And Wednesday afternoon was her day for the orphans. The house should be resounding with them, the kitchen table groaning with sandwiches and cakes. She stirred the saucepan glumly. All those lies she'd told to the Children's Home, just because she couldn't face another bun fight. If only he'd phone her, she'd invite all the starving millions round for tea, make flapjacks for the entire Third World, if necessary. But without his call, she was just an orphan herself.

'Kate?' she ventured.

'Yes, love? It amazes me the way you won't succumb to tea-bags. All that grot down the sink.'

'Ian likes a proper cup of tea.'

86

'Ian doesn't happen to be here, ducks. And there's nothing wrong with tea-bags. I . . .'

'KATE!'

'What?'

'I wondered if you'd make a phone-call for me.'

'Have you lost your voice, or something? Or is it Sarah's piano teacher again? I categorically refuse to phone her any more. She practically spat at me the last time – *and* in Serbo-Croat. Do your own dirty work. If Sarah keeps on losing "Great Studies for Tiny Hands", then . . .'

'It's not a piano teacher. It's a doctor.'

'What, Dr Nichols? I thought his wife was one of your best friends.'

'She is. But it's not him I want. It's a specialist.'

'What's wrong, Ginny? Forgotten to take your Pill? Or have you found a little lump and you're too embarrassed to have Nichols touch you up?'

Ginny showered oats into the saucepan. She did have a lump, but it was somewhere in her throat. Kate looked up.

'Okay, love. Give me the number. I can see it's serious. What do I say to this eminent consultant? You're on the edge of a nervous breakdown, or you've run out of cocoa?'

Ginny tried to look busy with the treacle. 'Just ask who's speaking, and if it's not Dr Caldos de Roche, find out if he's there.'

'Dr de *What*? Look, if you're that desperate, darling, I know a very sound chap in Wimpole Street.'

'259 1875.' Ginny was surprised how well she knew the number. 'And don't you dare say anything stupid.'

'Has it ever been known?' Kate ambled into the hall and picked up the phone. 'God, what a racket! I can't compete with those screaming bloody Skunks.'

Ginny ran upstairs to turn the record down. Sarah was still in her grey school knickers, mooning about the room in time to the music, her eyes half-closed and a look of total ecstasy on her eager spotty face. Snookie and Steve were lying on the floor on their stomachs, sharing Desperate Dan and a bag of Liquorice Allsorts. She could hear Kate's voice booming from the hall, turned the music up again – couldn't bear to eavesdrop.

'Gosh, Mum, I do believe you're getting to be a fan! Here, want to dance?' Sarah pulled her mother into the centre of the room and started dipping her elbows down to her knees and jerking back her head. 'That's what they do on Top of the Pops. Oh listen, it's Coffin Icecream! Isn't it fantastic?'

'It's 'orrible,' said Snookie.

'Ssh!' said Steve, as he removed a piece of liquorice from his mouth, peered at it, and put it back.

Ginny dipped her elbows, jerked her head. It was absurd to be teeny-bopping round her daughter's bedroom at four o'clock in the afternoon, with a cockney vocalist wailing at a hundred decibels and her heart broken into pieces.

'You're not half bad at dancing, Mum. You ought to come to one of our discos.'

'Not half bad!' Ginny launched into one of her English language lessons, then shrugged and let it go. Skunk Yellow didn't care about grammar. 'Don't call me Mum, darling.'

'Mama, Mother, Mater, Mummy. MUM!' Sarah whirled her mother round the room, collapsed giggling on the bed. Ginny hugged her suddenly. She didn't want Caldos intruding here. If this was her tower, it was a shining solid tower, safe from the horrors and heartbreaks outside. Her children were well-mannered and well-fed, their teeth anointed with fluoride, their eyes tested, their hair trimmed. They'd had their vaccinations and their vitamins, their piano lessons and their extra milk. Sarah was netball captain and Snookie top in art. Ian still had his own hair and his ECG was normal. The freezer was stacked with food, the garden . . .

'For Christ's sake, Ginny, for a girl at death's door, you don't seem overkeen to hear from your doctor.' Kate had cantered up the stairs and was standing, panting, on the landing. 'I've been screaming at you for the last half hour.'

'What's wrong with you, Mummy? Are you going to die?'

'Kate's just joking, dear. Now clear up all this mess and get your jeans on.' Ginny lured Kate into her bedroom and slumped down on a chair. She did feel almost dead. 'Well?' she asked expectantly.

'He's just left and she doesn't know what time he's coming back.'

'*Who* doesn't?'

'I dunno. Some bird that answered. She was bloody rude, actually.'

She. De Roche didn't have a secretary at Chelsea. 'What do you mean, rude? What did she say?'

'She didn't say anything. She just sounded stand-offish, as if she couldn't be bothered to speak to a worm like me.'

'But she did say he'd been there? He hasn't gone away?'

'For God's sake, Ginny, who is this guy? If I didn't know you were Chastity personified, I'd begin to get suspicious. At least you could tell me what it's all about, in exchange for the phone-call.'

'The flapjacks! Oh no . . .' Ginny sniffed the air, stampeded downstairs, too late; scraped the black sticky mess into the waste-bin.

'It *will* be tinned spaghetti at this rate,' Kate muttered, choking in the smoke. 'Or dog-biscuits. Look, I'll rustle up the nosh. You sit down and put your feet up. You look all in.'

Kate banged about in the larder and returned with two tins. Ginny sipped her tea. The unknown girl in Chelsea began to fill the kitchen – dark, voluptuous, sultry, face distorted with desire, mouth open to her toes – probably more than one girl. A second *femme fatale* with auburn curls and cruel scarlet talons mocked her from the tumbled pillows. Suddenly, the room was full of girls – jeering greedy females, gasping out 'Hosanna!' as they cavorted on the bed, their naked shadows taunting on the wild black reeling walls.

'Dinner is served!' Kate announced, plonking down a saucepan of congealed spaghetti rings in the centre of the table.

'I'll just get the children.' Ginny loped upstairs to shoo them down. 'Start without me, will you. I've got to phone Daddy.' She sneaked into the bedroom – there was a phone extension there – picked up the receiver, put it down again. She mustn't act impulsively, ought to have her tea first. But if she didn't phone Harley Street before half past five or six, there'd be no one there but George. She dialled the first digit – paused again, uncertain. She should be with the children, discussing their school day, easing any problems with their homework. And how about Kate? Supposing she got suspicious and said something to Ian? Nonsense. Kate opposed all husbands on principle. And if she didn't make this vital fateful phone-call, she'd have another of those wretched nights, creeping about at three o'clock in the morning, with Caldos' ghost snapping at her heels. She dialled, dithered, carried on; heard the number ringing – hollow, vacant, mocking. Ringing, ringing . . .

'Hello, this is Mrs Ginny Barnes.' Should she say Virginia? 'I want to leave a message for Dr de Roche. Yes, I realise he's at Chelsea.' (Though Kate had said he'd left.) 'No, I haven't tried him there.' (Didn't want to speak to some obscenely naked female warming up the bed for his return.) 'Could you kindly leave a note for him – say I'm coming up tomorrow to see my father-in-law. There's a small problem with the flat. Yes, I know it's nothing to do with Dr de Roche. Yes, I have already tried the agent . . . All right, I understand, but could you simply tell him I'll be there tomorrow afternoon. Thursday. And I'll probably stay on late.'

Damn those snooty secretaries, playing God and fending people off. That plummy-voiced Miss Petulant was probably mad about de Roche herself, didn't want to share him. Well, she'd simply have to learn to be more generous. On Thursdays he worked late, and she was determined to grab ten minutes of his time. She mooched downstairs, found Kate spooning up spaghetti from the saucepan. 'Look, Kate, I hate to ask you. I know it's my turn tomorrow, but . . .'

'Going to see your doctor friend about your little lump?'

'*We're* not allowed to eat out of the saucepan,' Snookie observed, with an admiring look at Kate.

'Snookie, don't be rude. No, Kate, not a lump, late-night shopping – I've simply got to get this garden fork from Selfridges.'

'There's a garden shop in Hinchley Wood,' Sarah offered helpfully.

'I want *you* to pick me up,' wailed Snookie. 'My teacher's got to see you about the school bazaar and I promised you'd be there.'

'Oh, don't be such a baby,' Ginny barked. 'And turn that racket off.' She seized Sarah's transistor and switched off Banshee Brown in mid-caterwaul.

'Try a Valium sandwich for your tea.' Kate snatched up her son, and her handbag. 'Come on, Steve, we're going.'

'I'm sorry, Kate, I really am. I just don't know what's wrong with me.' (Lies, all lies.) 'But please help me out tomorrow. It's vitally important.' She pressed three chocolate biscuits into Steve's grubby hand – an ally might be useful. 'I'll do double next week, I promise faithfully. Just keep the girls at your house, could you, and I'll get Ian to pick them up.'

'Okay okay. But don't saddle me with that paragon of a husband, I beseech you. The little stinkers can stay the night, as long as they don't expect home-made meringues for breakfast. Give my love to Selfridges. Goodbye.'

''Bye,' called Ginny, laughing with relief. Kate was an angel. It would have to be LPs all round, at this rate. One way and another, Caldos de amazing Roche was going to cost her quite a lot.

11

How George did go on! Ginny had almost forgotten the sheer length and lavish detail of his sagas. He'd been talking to her now for a solid four hours, and they'd moved from Mrs Massey's gynaecological history (an epic in its own right), through Dr Bartley's stand on corruption in the Special Branch, and on to the vicissitudes of the kitten's bowels. He was lonely, she supposed, and still not used to evenings on his own. He'd been pathetically pleased to see her, cut her a whole truckload of cheese-and-pickle sandwiches, and told her admiringly she looked more like Sarah's sister than her mother. She sneaked a glance in the sideboard mirror. She did look rather good, had made an effort this time, determined not to be caught out again in shabby jeans and boots. She'd chosen a tight-fitting dress in what she hoped was a subtle shade of beige, found almost matching shoes, coaxed her hair into reluctant curls, and burrowed around in Sarah's bedroom drawers for blusher, shiner, lipstick, shadow, gloss. Perhaps she'd overdone it. She craned her neck again, to check on her reflection, frowning at the emphatic crimson lips. Yes, she did look a little like Miss United Kingdom, runner-up. She scrubbed her lips with a tissue, checked her watch – tenth time. Surely all his patients would have gone by now. Unless they stayed the night.

'George,' she mumbled.

'What, love?'

'Does Dr de . . . ? No, it doesn't matter. Nothing.' She mustn't bring his name up any more. George would get suspicious. She'd already slipped it in at least half a dozen times. Was de Roche extremely busy? Did he take his secretary to lunch? Did he live alone?

There was still hope. George kept popping upstairs between Mrs Massey's fibroids and the kitten's diarrhoea, which meant

92

some of the consultants must be still around. She closed her eyes, her lashes stiff and sticky from all the gunge she'd larded on them. Please God, let him be one of them, let him still be there.

The eye-shadow was wrong. She'd have to swab it off in any case, before she got home. She didn't normally wear eye-shadow to Selfridges, and no one would believe she'd been dashing round the sales with Dawn Purple eyes. She'd give him exactly eight more minutes, and not a second more. 'Please God,' she begged again, hardly daring to glance down at her watch.

George was explaining the system of appointments, and how busy each consultant was. 'Do you realise, Ginny, you have to wait six or seven weeks to get a first appointment with Dr Colwyn-Jones, and even longer for Dr Harrington. And that's private, would you believe. You're better off National Health.'

'Really?' Ginny murmured. He must have got her message. Unless that supercilious secretary had forgotten it on purpose. At least he could have phoned. She pulled crossly at a Shirley Temple curl – all that agony with the Carmen Rollers wasted on George. Though George looked pleased enough, had just zipped down from upstairs again, waving his bunch of keys.

'That's the last of them, Ginny. Now I'm all locked up, so we can settle down with a nice glass of sherry. I'm so glad you've got the girls looked after. I hate it when you have to rush away.'

'Well, I can't be too long, George. You know what Ian's like on his own. Excuse me just a moment, will you? I'll just pop to the bathroom.'

She glared at herself in the bathroom mirror. She looked like the supporting role in a bad B movie. She scrubbed at her rouged cheeks with a piece of toilet paper; picked up George's comb, dipped it in water and tore it savagely through her hair. The curls subsided. He'd be lolling about in Chelsea with a redhead on his knee – a stunning natural with a forty-inch bust, who didn't need two and a half hours to make herself look like a second-rate barmaid. A multi-orgasmic nymphomaniac with perfect pitch. A Nubian slave-girl who spoke faultless Italian and knew about wines. Or at least a normal un-boring non-prudish female, who didn't scuttle back to suburbia as soon as she was kissed.

The phone was ringing in the passage. Another frantic patient, or a doctor who'd forgotten his appointment-book. It was pointless coming to visit George in any case. He was so damn busy, they never had a moment's peace.

'It's for you, love. The operator. Says she's got a call for a Mrs Barnes.'

Oh, God, she thought, grabbing the receiver. Sarah must have cut an artery, or Ian was being scraped off the A307. 'Hello,' she said uncertainly, as she watched a fleet of ambulances shrilling to the scene, police cars skidding on two wheels as they panted in pursuit. 'Oh, *hello*! Yes, fine. Well, yes, I am, but . . . No, I really think I ought to . . . Yes, I know, but . . .' There were a lot more 'buts' before she put the phone down. George was hovering anxiously.

'What's the matter, Ginny dear? You've gone quite pale, you know. Is everything all right?'

'Yes. No. It's nothing really. It's just that . . . er . . . It's Toby. Yes, Ian's having trouble with Toby.'

'But why the operator?'

'The . . . um . . . phone's out of order. Look, George, I'm really sorry, but I'd better go straight back. Toby's sicked his dinner up and . . .'

'Poor little lad! You want to rest his stomach. Just fluids for a day or two. It always does the trick.' George parcelled up the remaining cheese-and-pickle sandwiches and stowed them in her handbag. She needed feeding up. 'You don't look too good yourself, love. You've lost all that colour in your cheeks. I only hope I haven't tired you out with all my chatter.'

Ginny turned away. She was a wicked wicked woman to worry him and lie to him, and it would serve her right if she had a fatal accident on her way to shameful Chelsea. Yet she had never felt so happy in her life. The stars were shining when she stepped outside, and the air smelt cold and special, and a waiting taxi was throbbing at the door, just as he'd assured her, the handsome driver a twin to Robert Redford.

Park Lane melted into Hyde Park Corner. She admired her face in the dark pane of the window, cascaded perfume down her neck. Brompton Road was full of angels. She could feel her own wings growing, almost lifting off. King's Road slowed her down, the first wave of apprehension churning through her stomach. The taxi stopped and she scrabbled in her purse.

'Don't worry about that, miss. The Doctor's taken care of it.'

She shivered on the doorstep. She could still go home – underground from Sloane Square, change at Charing Cross. The door suddenly burst open. She glimpsed embroidered golden dragons, elaborate black silk toggles. Caldos looked resplendent in a Chinese smoking-jacket, the silk smooth against her cheek as he pressed her to his chest. She tried to pull away, convey her new resolve, explain her firm decision not to see him any more. He didn't listen and she couldn't speak. His tongue had fused with hers, and was smouldering inside her mouth, forcing her to sin – unforgivable sin, glorious, astounding.

Her coat had somehow been removed, and she heard the zip on her tight dress sighing with relief as it succumbed. Beneath the silky jacket his chest was bare and hot, the dark hair like a second skin, furring his whole body. That hair was almost shocking in its animal profusion, tangling on his shoulders, creeping down his back; dark sworls on his stomach, pushing past his belt, disappearing beneath the tight black trousers. She had to touch it, stroke it, experience that sense of softness/roughness mixed. Her hand stopped at the belt, but he was tugging at the buckle, removing his last clothes, then commandeering hers. Her skin looked starkly white against his tanned and hirsute body; paler still against the black pile of the carpet. He had forced her down beside him, his greedy mouth grazing both her nipples, lapping down her thighs, flicking wildly back to her ears, her eyelids, lips. Her own mouth was opening wider than it ever had before, opening to her breasts, opening to her legs, and then between her legs, making strange high noises through his kisses.

Suddenly, he rolled away, eased up to his feet, vanished for a moment to a corner of the room. She felt instantly bereaved – widowed and abandoned; her body crying out for him, her back arched up, both thighs spreading wide. She could see his brawny naked legs returning now towards her, the great right-angle still standing stiff between them – obscene, magnificent.

He held a glass against her lips, and some strong and fiery liquid baptised her tongue in a new erotic sacrament. She could already hear the music, slow and sacred music, swelling through the room.

She was drinking down great draughts of it – an intoxicating mixture of trumpets, strings and timpani – half-choking on the rising head of woodwind. Oh no, she prayed, not another Requiem, her legs beginning to close against the threat of sacrilege.

'The *Missa Solemnis*,' Caldos murmured, offering her the glass again, and tonguing up a drop of amber liquor as it oozed between her breasts. 'The most passionate religious music ever written by a mortal man.'

She tried vainly to object, as the ecstatic choir cried '*Kyrie!*'; the tenor voice repeating it, spinning out the syllables; then the soprano taking over, reverent yet impassioned.

'My incredible Virginia, this is holy, don't you see? I can only make love to church music because only that is worthy and sublime enough. Sex isn't something sordid, some hole-and-corner grope, but a taste of life eternal, a sacred ritual, a vital part of . . .'

She heard no more, because he was explaining with his mouth again, a mouth no longer on her lips, but clamped between her legs; the *Kyrie* resounding still, as he explored her with his tongue; the dark voices of the baritones expressing her own heady sense of shock. And suddenly, explosively, his mouth was back on hers, and she could taste her own wet strangeness on his lips.

He entered her to a rushing avalanche of strings, her sudden gasp of pain swamped by strident voices; relentless cries of '*Gloria!*' exploding through her body as he slammed and pounded into her. She was assailed by shrieking woodwind, torn by stabbing brass; too small for him, too grudging, as he thrust again, again. His rough chin chafed against her face; her mouth felt crushed, invaded; her back and shoulders ground into the floor.

He reprieved her for a moment, releasing her, consoling; lips lingering and sensuous, as he kissed her throat and fingers; brushed soft and teasing lashes against her own closed lids. She let herself relax, the music tamed and tranquil now, a reprieve itself, as deep-throated velvet cellos throbbed beneath the horns.

She stroked a finger down his face, outlining his brows, running subtly, softly, round the inside of his lips. She heard his mew of pleasure, echoed by the tenor, his ardent anguished voice suddenly ringing out beyond them both: '*O, misere, O, misere!*' But Caldos had no mercy, turned her on her front and entered her again;

96

percussion dashing her to pieces, brass and drum inside her. She sank into the pain now, accepting it, submitting; swept along impetuously as the shattering squall of music broke about her body; exultant trumpets blazing through the room. She was part of the whole rhythm, a fanfare in the orchestra, a high voice in the fugue; in thrall to him, and worshipping, as she insisted with the choir that he only was most holy, he only most high. '*Quoniam tu solus sanctus.*'

She could hear him crying out as well, both their voices foundering in the majestic sheet of sound; then the sudden frantic flurry towards the last 'Amen, amen'. But it was not amen, not final; he still frenzied, thrusting; she panting from the unrelenting build-up; willing, begging him to come – come as she was coming, wild and loud and wonderful – amen, amen, amen. He didn't come, seemed tireless and insatiable, threshing even harder now, until an electric whoop of glory from all four soloists seemed to galvanise, release him, and with the last triumphant '*Gloria!*' he plunged shuddering against her, shouting out so violently he submerged the whole great Mass, then slumped inert across her back, sweating, out of breath.

'*Credo!*' thrilled the choir. '*Credo, credo, credo.*' I believe. Ginny ran a hand slowly down his body, felt its strength, its damp but scorching heat. She did believe, believed in her new God; she his humble acolyte repeating '*Credo, credo*' with the overawed contraltos, the enthralled and fervent baritones. And she hardly knew whether it was Beethoven she was worshipping, or Almighty God on High, or his detumescent penis dribbling sperm.

12

His bathroom was also black. The bottles of scent and aftershave were black; his towels and flannel black. Even the soap was black. The taps were gold, gold swans.

She lay in his royal playground of a bath, glancing at her scarlet-painted toenails. She had varnished them that morning, to match his Lamborghini. That alone was proof of her depravity. Would she paint her nails for Ian, or buy new lacy underwear? Ian! She dared not think of him – struggling with his supper, mending broken chair-legs, wondering where in heaven's name she was. She must come down to earth immediately, return to guilt and shopping-lists, children and lamb-chops. She stretched out in the water, breathing in the scent of pines, the haze of fragrant steam, wallowing a moment more in wicked blissful indolence.

Her eyes opened to a flash of scarlet silk. Caldos had crept in on her, carrying a tray, and dressed in a kimono the red of sin and roses. He seemed to have as many leisure out-fits as he had positions on the carpet. He sank down on the goatskin bathmat, a bottle of wine between his thighs, a dozen small glass dishes marshalled at his feet. His hand sneaked across her breasts, disappeared beneath the pine-green water, and did sinful things between her legs. The other hand crammed her mouth with caviare. He was feeding her in the bath, selecting morsels from the tray: a prawn, a brandied quince, a sliver of smoked salmon, secreting them between her lips. She was feasting at both his hands, purring as he stroked and foraged her. He opened the wine, filled two large tumblers, and poured the rest into the bath. The bubbles pricked and fizzed.

'The next best thing to asses' milk, my pale Cleopatra.' He took a mouthful from his glass, and dribbled the wine from his mouth into hers – lips warm, wine cool and tingling. A drop or two trickled down her breasts.

'I want to re-christen you, my water nymph, find a glorious new name for you. You're not a Virginia any more. And I won't have you a Ginny.'

She lay back in the bath. How did he make everything so holy? 'Unless you be born again with water and the Holy Ghost . . .' But to be re-christened with bath-oil and Corton-Charlemagne in a state of mortal sin . . .

He was munching on a chicken breast, gazing up at the black ceiling as if the Holy Ghost were already crouching there. 'Estrella!'

Ginny jumped. 'I beg your pardon?' Did he have another woman hidden in his bathroom?

'*Alfonso and Estrella*. It's Schubert's first opera and the one he liked best. I'll be the brave and banished King Alfonso, and you're the bewitching and beauteous Estrella.'

Opera. Ginny took a large gulp from her glass. Didn't they usually end up dying of consumption? 'Who . . . was she?'

Caldos swallowed five olives in quick succession. 'A fair princess who needed rescuing.'

'And does it have a happy ending?' Ginny's thoughts had turned to Madam Butterfly, deceived, deserted, and dying by her own sword. Or Carmen bleeding in the bull ring, stabbed by her jealous lover – the only operas she'd ever seen, and both on television.

Caldos demolished half a dozen prawns and wiped his mouth on Ginny's shoulder. 'Ecstatic! Alfonso marries Estrella and is restored to his throne. The only problem is, the other chap – Adolfo – has by far the best music and he's very definitely the villain of the piece. Tell you what . . .'

'What?' Ginny hoped he wouldn't launch into the whole story of the opera. She always found them hopelessly confusing, and she had quite enough problems with her husband at the moment, without breaking her heart about Adolfo. 'Look Caldos, I really must get home. Ian will . . .'

Caldos swooped her right hand from the water, slid it inside the folds of his kimono, and positioned it between his thighs. Even at rest, he was large.

'We'll call *him* Adolfo. He's a real prima donna, and most definitely a villain.' Adolfo began to plume and swell, in response to his new name.

Ginny removed her hand reluctantly. 'I'm sorry, but I'm already frightfully late, and . . .'

'No, you're singing the wrong words, *mein Liebchen*. That's not in the libretto. According to the plot, you're wholly, inescapably, in Adolfo's fiendish power.' Caldos abducted both her hands this time, and assigned them to Adolfo, who stood stiffly to attention. 'Why don't I take you to the opera? Not that one – they hardly ever do it, except at Scunthorpe University Church Hall, or the Wigan Triple Festival of Arts. But something glorious else.'

Ginny flexed her toes in the warm and foamy water; couldn't really concentrate on Schubert in Scunthorpe, when Ian was doing his nut in Hinchley Wood.

'What's your taste in opera, *mon ange*? Verdi or Monteverdi? Or do you agree with our doughty Bernard Levin that Wagner is God and Bayreuth very heaven?'

She stared down at the soap-dish in search of inspiration, Adolfo twitching in her hand, Ian tweaking at her conscience. 'I cried in *Madam Butterfly*,' she offered.

Caldos winced. 'Puccini's pop, beloved – sheer saccharine and schmaltz. I can see I'll have to educate you.'

Ginny/Estrella stepped frowning from the bath. Conversation with Caldos was full of hidden traps. In Hinchley Wood, Puccini spelt highbrow, so why was Caldos consigning him to the Jimmy Young Show?

Opera seemed forgotten as he thrust his mouth against her dripping thatch. 'Real blonde pubic hair is exceptionally rare, *meine Süsse* – sign of a true princess, like the pea under the mattress.'

'Caldos, darling . . .' Maybe a darling would dislodge him, though it felt extremely daring. 'I simply must go home.'

Caldos groaned dramatically, held his forehead in his hands. 'Since my punctilious princess is determined to return to her dilapidated tower, and to repugn her unabashed Adolfo, nothing remains but abject surrender and a call for her coach-and-four.'

Ginny swathed her giggle in a huge black fluffy towel, dabbed gingerly between her legs, which still felt sore, inflamed. She could hear Caldos phoning for a mini-cab, his voice urgent and peremptory, as if he were buying shares on the Stock Exchange. They kissed again, whilst waiting for the cab; she dressed, he naked still, *Gloria* and *Credo* resounding in her ears. She stepped outside, a million stars dazzling the dark sky. He closed the door, and stars capsized; clarinets and trumpets stifled by the panting of the cab.

The journey home seemed endless. Every light was red, Ian's worried face reproaching her from every house and hoarding. She spelt out all the shop-names in straggling Putney High Street – Dorothy Perkins, W.H. Smith, Adultery. ADULTERY. They had blazoned it in scarlet letters all along her route – one of those strange spiky words which belonged in bad films and the Bible, or in other people's messy muddled lives. It had never had a place in her own snug cosy world – Ovaltine at bedtime with her husband warm beside her; ice-cream cornets in the park on Sunday afternoons. It was a treacherous and tainted word, leaking sperm and lies, polluting every mile of road from Chelsea to her home.

'Could you stop at the end of the road, please?' she asked the kindly driver. Their next-door neighbour wouldn't want adulteresses pulling up outside.

'No, please don't help me out.' She winced at his 'Goodbye!' carolled loudly after her; wished he could reverse without so much noise and flurry. Miss Clifford lived at number three, often talked to Ian. Thank goodness it was dark.

She crept on down the street, trying out excuses, inventing alibis. Ian fell on her as she slipped in through the door.

'Ginny! Oh, thank God! I've been worried sick about you. Wherever have you been?'

'I . . . er . . . met this girl I haven't seen in years. She used to be head girl at school.'

'But couldn't you have phoned, for heaven's sake? I've been absolutely frantic wondering where you were.'

Ginny tried again. 'The shops were murder. I didn't feel too good.' That was true, at least. Her face was crumpling up, her voice splintering and skidding.

'Ginny, darling, please don't cry. What's wrong? What's the matter?'

'I . . . I meant to go to Selfridges to buy your garden fork. I

101

didn't forget, honestly I didn't. I know which one you want – one with an ash-wood handle and . . . I did mean to go. I did.'

'It's all right, darling, don't worry about the fork. What's a stupid garden fork, so long as you're all right? What happened, though, to hold you up? Why on earth are you so late?'

She couldn't get the words out, couldn't lie to him. She pressed her face against his hairy jacket, smelt the faint whiff of lead pencils, a trace of last week's bonfire. She clasped both arms around his chest, longed to merge with him in one simple, safe and everlasting hug; buy him the most expensive garden fork in all of London. 'Oh Ian,' she sobbed. 'Oh Ian.'

'Darling, please don't cry. I hate it when you cry. Nothing matters, so long as you're all right.'

'Look, all that really happened was . . .' She broke off, scoured her face. There were only lies, and he was far too good for lies. 'Ian,' she murmured finally.

'Mm?' He was holding her against him, head bent towards her own. He felt smaller, after Caldos, as if he'd shrunk in just one night.

'I love you,' she insisted. It was almost not a lie.

13

Ginny wedged the car between a battered Mini and a Cortina Estate. All the cars looked domesticated, women's cars, piled with cardboard boxes of Shredded Wheat and toilet rolls, or fitted with baby-seats; cars with Snoopy transfers on the mudguard, or 'Fight Abortion' stickers on the back – another world entirely from his wild-beast Lamborghini. She took his letter out again, smiling to herself. She knew it off by heart now, except for the Italian bits. (If only they'd taught Italian at her half-baked convent school, instead of the Latin Mass and the Immaculate Conception.) The Italian seemed to be in verse and looked completely baffling. His writing leapt and bounded right across the page, large loops on the upstrokes, t's crossed with a flourish, drawings in the margin, and a separate (English) poem in the shape of a tall tower. She sat there grinning stupidly, the rich soft-centred phrases melting through her mind again. That letter had transformed her day. She'd left the dirty dishes, and sauntered out with Toby, floating through the streets, singing snatches of old love songs. 'Don't throw bouquets at me,' she'd warbled to a florist. 'P – ee – eople will s – aaa – y we're in l – oooo – ve.'

She'd broken off uncertainly in the middle of 'Unforgettable', suddenly remembering her lover's taste in music – though it wasn't exactly easy to croon the *Credo* from a Beethoven Mass at nine o'clock on a drizzly Monday morning. She'd got as far as '*Jesum Christum*', then ditched Jesus and returned to Nat King Cole. She'd hardly even noticed it was raining. When, at last, she'd got back home and saw Toby's muddy paw-prints embroidering the floor, she'd just shrugged and sipped a sherry, read the intoxicating letter three times through again.

It was a unique amazing letter, which gave off so much charge she couldn't settle to a thing. She'd tried to peel potatoes, but she'd

103

put the peel in the saucepan and the potatoes down the sink. And princesses didn't peel potatoes anyway.

Principessa. That was one of the Italian words, the only one she understood. She tucked the letter in her pocket and walked towards the library.

'Could you tell me where I'd find an Italian dictionary?' She bestowed a radiant smile on the small shrivelled lady, scowling behind the desk. Everyone looked adorable today.

She sat at a desk with the dictionary and spread the letter out again. P, pri-, *principessa*. Yes, she was right. Princess. The stupid smile returned. Now for the next one, *spina*. She turned to the s's. *Spina* – a thorn. She didn't like the sound of that, but perhaps it was only a thorn on a red red rose of love. She searched for something which looked rose-y, soon discovered it. *Rosa*, a rose. Well, that was simple enough. Perhaps she could do a crash course in Italian. Italian for lovers. Sing along with Nat King Cole in a gondola.

She'd need to know Italian, anyway. She was embarking on an extensive study course in Italian Renaissance Art, with the old school chum she hadn't met in Selfridges. Her tutor would be Caldos. He'd dreamed it up as a fool-proof alibi. She was to tell her family she was up to her ears in da Vinci, instead of in de Roche. It was partly true, at least. Her course would include anatomy and extensive study of the nude.

She opened the dictionary again. After an hour, her confidence was waning. She had an indigestible jumble of words, but they didn't seem to add up to anything. Princesses, roses, thorns, hearts – yes, they were all delightful. But what about a vulture, a plumb-line, villein as in feudalism, to nick or pilfer (*colloq., ungrammatical*), or a confraternity of voluminaries (which looked foreign, even in English). Some of the words weren't even in the dictionary. And being poetry, they all seemed the wrong way round. What the hell was a *ghiandaia*? Or a *scodinzolio*? There was nothing for it, she'd have to ask Giulietta. She was the only girl she knew who spoke Italian.

She began to copy out the verses. It was a slow and tedious business, struggling with a language she didn't understand. She stopped in the middle of *ghiandaia*. Supposing it were porno-graphic? Or searingly personal? Dare she entrust Caldos' poetry to some vague acquaintance who might disapprove – or gossip?

She tore the paper into shreds. A gangling student at the next desk glared at her. She smiled her best Italian smile. All was not yet lost. She could reply to the rest of the letter and just ignore the Italian, or simply make a casual joke about *principessas* with *spinas* in their feet.

Reply. Oh God! She'd totally forgotten that he'd be expecting a reply. Fine to slop about all morning, smirking over five-star love letters, but another thing entirely to try to answer them. The student glared again as she slammed the book shut, slumped back in her chair. She hated writing letters. Even bread-and-butter letters took her a whole morning. Dear Dr de Roche, Thank you for the lovely . . . It was just what I . . . I hope you had a . . .

Impossible! She had to be deep and dazzling, take the skin off the page with the cut and thrust of her irrepressible pen, scatter quotations like grass seed, dash off witty little verses in assorted shapes, drown herself in golden metaphor. She spread out a sheet of clean paper, sharpened her pencil, and began: 'Dear Caldos . . .' Well, it was a start. But wait a minute – wasn't she meant to call him Alfonso? She crossed out the Caldos, then the dear, and began again. 'Beloved Alfonso.' Absurd! Perhaps she should just start – daringly – in mid-sentence: 'Sitting bemused by my Italian dictionary . . .' No, that wouldn't do, he'd take it for granted she was multi-lingual. 'Dear and most esteemed Sir, Soliciting a continuance of past favours and thanking you in anticipation of a favourable reply . . .' Secretarial School was a piece of cake compared to this. She slunk out of her chair and crept past the student, back to the enquiry desk. The librarian look more shrivelled, distinctly less appealing. 'Yes?' she growled.

'I wondered if you had any books of letters – other people's letters?'

'What kind of thing did you have in mind? Political correspondence? Gladstone, Disraeli? Lloyd George?'

'Oh no, nobody too famous. Sort of lesser-known letters.'

'Well, if they weren't well-known, we wouldn't keep their letters.' The neat grey bun quivered with contempt, as it returned to sorting tickets.

Ginny tried again. 'What I really meant was . . . er . . . personal, private sort of letters.'

105

'You mean *love* letters?'

Ginny flushed. She made it sound obscene. 'Well, yes. Elizabeth Barrett Browning, that sort of thing. My daughter's doing a project on . . . um . . . "Sickness in Art".'

'I thought you said you didn't want anyone famous.'

'No. Well, not exactly Elizabeth Barrett Browning in person. But someone like her.'

'There's no one like her.'

A second, jolly-looking woman barged into the conversation. 'I know the sort of thing the lady means, Maud. She'll find a lot in the biography section.'

Ginny could have kissed her. They went together to the far end of the library, and the jolly lady made lots of loud jolly comments about inflation and pollution and the torture in South Africa. Ginny tried to keep her mind on love.

She staggered back to her seat with eight tomes, opened one at random – someone called John Donne. 'I make a count that the writing of letters is a kind of ecstasy.' Lucky guy – she'd stick with him. Pencil poised, she read on. 'Everything refreshes and I wither, and I grow older and not better, my strength diminishes and my load growes . . . I have over-fraught myself with Vice.' Ginny groaned. J. Donne's ecstasy was even shorter-lived than hers, and the last thing she wanted to think about was vice, especially with a capital V.

She snapped the book shut, tried another one – Wordsworth at Brighton: 'I am doomed to be an idler through my whole life. I have read nothing this age, nor indeed did I ever.' Good God! If Wordsworth was an idler, she was a drone. All those daffodils and rainbows, and endless improving dialogues with celandines and leech-gatherers. They'd done it all at school. (The nuns had permitted Wordsworth because of the 'trailing clouds of glory' bit, but had played down Dorothy.)

She dipped into the book again. 'Owing to a set of painful and uneasy sensations, which I have, more or less at all times, about my chest, from a disease which chiefly affects my nerves and digestive organs and which makes my aversion from writing little less than madness' – she knew exactly what he meant – 'I deferred writing to you. During the last three years, I have never had a pen in my hand for five minutes, before my whole frame becomes one bundle of uneasiness; a perspiration starts out all over me, and my chest is oppressed . . .'

She warmed to Wordsworth. Obviously the leech-gatherers had taken their toll, but Caldos was a doctor, and if she copied all that stuff about her chest and digestive organs, he'd take her pulse and whisk her off to hospital before she could say 'Dove Cottage'. Anyway, Wordsworth was so wretchedly famous, Caldos probably knew his letters backwards, or had translated them into Japanese. Nobody ordinary seemed to have written letters, not the sort she wanted.

She stared out of the window. A blotting-paper sky and a bank-rupt tree stared back at her – no inspiration there. She turned back to her desk again, and Coleridge: 'The withered Passions weave a holy spell.'

Now that was good! Not a letter, but a line of real live poetry, which would fit wonderfully well with solemn Masses and pas-sionate seductions. She hoped it sounded nonchalant – the sort of thing she reeled off on the spur of the moment, while sorting out the washing. She toiled on through the poem, searching for a second little gem. She'd keep it brief – brief but brilliant. Another hour dragged by. She had written and re-written just five lines. They sounded rather jerky, as if they didn't really jell – which wasn't surprising, when she'd cobbled them together from five quite different books. She wove a little padding round them, swopped the second sentence with the third, then signed her name. G. She turned the G into an E, kept forgetting who she was. Did Estrella have two l's? She checked his letter to find out, reading it right through again. Sadly, half its magic had somehow seeped away.

She stumped back to the car, neck aching, fingers cramped. The kitchen was still littered with the breakfast things, and the smell of bacon hung in the air, a greasy reprimand. She pushed the porridge dishes to one side, cleared a space and read through her masterpiece one last time. Funny, now it sounded almost *too* pat – simply wasn't conversational enough. Perhaps she'd make a few mistakes on purpose. She found a clean sheet of paper and laboriously rewrote it, taking care with the mistakes. She added a small blot, as if she had dashed it off in two minutes, between her harpsichord practice and lunch at the Ritz, then tore up the old draft and took it out to the dustbin, which was becoming quite a feature in her life. She poked the fragments under a grease-bespattered *Surrey Comet*, then drowned the lot in cold congealing porridge.

Back indoors, the letter seemed to scream at her. She must get rid of it immediately. Once it was posted, she could banish Caldos from her kitchen, and continue with the chores. She felt completely drained, as if she'd copied out in longhand all twenty-nine volumes of the *Encyclopaedia Britannica*. She trekked along the road to the post-box at the corner.

'Dreadful day,' called Miss Hodgkins from next door.

'Yes,' said Ginny, feelingly. 'Appalling!'

The pillar-box sneered at her. Instead of 'No. 3', it said 'Whore!' Maybe she shouldn't have written back so soon. It looked eager and childish, as if she weren't used to getting letters. She placed her hand in the opening of the box, but still held on to the letter. Perhaps she shouldn't have written back at all. A woman lumbered over, with an overweight spaniel at her heels. 'Good afternoon,' she trilled.

Ginny jumped, and the envelope dropped in. The yawning mouth of the post-box was hissing insults at her, telling her how lewd she was, how wicked and adulterous, wasting all day writing love letters, instead of making shepherd's pie.

'Not so bright today, is it?' The woman lingered, smiling, while her spaniel did his business in the gutter.

'No, the rain doesn't look like lifting. Good boy! What's his name?'

'Rover.'

Not very original. Caldos was right – they'd had all their joy and juices drained out of them in Hinchley Wood, like human shepherd's pie. Eking out their lives with left-over bits and pieces, instead of insisting on expensive prime red steak. Caldos was like tournedos – robust and full-blooded.

She crossed back to her house and the dingy patch of garden – dry sticks of hydrangeas, empty barren flowerbeds. The porridge plates were difficult to wash. Porridge! The only copy of her precious letter was coffined in cold porridge. Supposing Caldos quizzed her on the poetry, or continued the quotations? She'd forgotten already how that bit of Wordsworth went. And if he replied to her letter (God forbid!), she'd have to write again. It would be shameful to repeat herself, or use the same adjectives, or muddle Coleridge up with J. Donne. She should have kept a record, filed all her jottings for reference, so he couldn't catch her out. She dashed back to the dustbin, scooped up all the tattered shreds, plonked the whole damp glutinous mess in the centre of the table and tried to sort it out. The ink had run and the paper was disintegrating. 'Holy spell,' she deciphered with some trouble. Drat! There was nothing holy about this fatuous lark. It was stupid, sordid, self-indulgent, and totally absurd – and clearly all his fault. Did he have to be so clever, spouting all those foreign languages and knowing Shakespeare off by heart? He'd probably dashed off his own letter in three minutes flat, while fondling Gish with the other hand. She pictured him at breakfast, eating his egg in iambic pentameters, translating his toast into Gaelic, filling in his tax-returns in Linear B. He probably succoured his patients in Sanskrit, and tore up the *Shorter Oxford Dictionary* to wipe his bottom in the lavatory.

The back door slammed. 'Good God, Ginny! Have you only just got up? Is that your coat, or your dressing gown?' Kate swanned into the kitchen, three children in her wake, cast a triumphant eye over the congealing mound of paper porridge mulched across the table. 'You're becoming one of us at last, love. It won't be long until the tea-bags! By the way, Snookie's in a tizz about her homework.'

'Oh Mummy, help! It's English tonight and we've got to write a letter, a letter to a friend. Miss Smithers says it has to be original and not just boring things like "I hope you are well".'

Ginny shrieked, flung off her rubber gloves. 'Bugger the tea-bags, Kate! Let's have a sherry.'

Kate raised her eyebrows. 'That doctor of yours has obviously worked wonders. Bring on the Amontillado!'

'Dear Debbie,' laboured Snookie, from the other side of the table. She put her pencil down and groaned. 'Mummy, what *next*?'

14

George coaxed Harley into the cat-basket, then clamped the lid down firmly. The kitten spat and clawed, mewing frantically, the doorbell suddenly cutting through its cries.

'There should be a law against doorbells at weekends,' he murmured to himself, as he picked up cat and basket, grabbed his coat, then trudged upstairs and unbolted the front door.

Miss Hammond was standing stiffly on the step, dressed in jeans and leather jacket, which looked rough and almost brutish against her slender frame. 'Hi,' she muttered, shoulders hunched, eyes wary and dark-ringed.

George did his best to smile. He'd seen her in the waiting-room almost every day, but she'd been embarrassed and withdrawn, sitting in the corner and hardly even glancing at him, as if she'd regretted all she'd told him on that wet despairing night. Then, once de Roche had seen her, she'd sidle out immediately, hail the nearest taxi.

'I'm afraid Dr de Roche isn't here on Saturdays.'

'I know.'

George hesitated. He shouldn't really ask her in. De Roche would strongly disapprove and, anyway, what about the vet? Harley seemed to read his thoughts, let out a piteous howl. Miss Hammond jolted back.

'Don't worry – it's only the kitten. I'm afraid he's not too well. I was just on my way to the vet.'

Miss Hammond said nothing, stared down at the ground, traced a nervous pattern with her gym-shoe on the step.

'I'd love to ask you in, lass, but the vet's quite some way away, and I really must get off. It's probably only a touch of conjunctivitis, but best to get it looked at, just in case. He's off his food, as well, you see.' George glanced at her stick-wrists, emerging thin

110

and bony from the sleeves of her black jacket. She didn't look as if she'd been eating much herself.

She shrugged. 'It doesn't matter. Didn't think I'd find you in, in any case.' The voice was cool, offhand, but the feet were saying something else, writing desperate messages as she jabbed them on the step.

'Tell you what,' said George.

'What?' The jabbing stopped.

'Why don't you come with me to the vet's?'

Silence.

'I was actually wondering how I'd manage on the bus, with those bad-tempered conductors, and Harley in a fret. It would be quite a help to have another pair of hands. Could you take the basket?'

They waited fifteen minutes for the bus. George chatted about chrysanthemums and cat flu, and the problems of teaching budgies how to talk. His companion seemed immune – or deaf.

'Have you got a pet yourself, Miss Hammond?' Perhaps a few harmless casual questions might encourage her to open up.

She shook her head, pulling at a button on her coat. A lorry rattled past, two Kawasakis wove around the traffic, hooting at each other, a blonde youth riding pillion hurling insults at the throbbing bike in front. George was almost grateful for the racket. At least it helped distract him from the young girl's brooding silence.

'George,' she faltered suddenly. It was the first time she had used his name.

'Yes, what, lass?'

'Would you be allowed to call me Angela?'

George paused a moment, grinned. 'I don't think there's any rule against it – Angela.'

It suited her, the name. She was too sad and scared and skinny to be a convincing angel, but her oval face and wan blue eyes reminded him of the pictures in Bea's old faded prayer-book. The bus lumbered up, at last, a scarlet brontosaurus, belching its hot breath against their legs.

'Let's go on top. Oh please! I've never been on top of a bus. I usually take taxis.'

He kept forgetting she had money, especially dressed like that,

111

in jeans and yobbo jacket. But her accent was top-drawer, and he'd seen her in the waiting-room wearing really classy clothes, the sort of thing they featured in those glossy magazines which the patients always read. She probably divided her life between dress-designers' showrooms, the back of taxis, and Dr de Roche's couch.

'Oh, look, you can see the Post Office Tower! And there's a gigantic Irish wolfhound with a pudgy four-foot owner.'

The grimy lurching bus seemed to have changed her mood entirely. She was almost chatty by the time they reached the vet.

'I'd like to have been a vet myself,' she confided, sotto voce, as they found seats in the waiting-room, sharing the cramped space with two other cats, three dogs, a white mouse in a toffee-tin, and a very superior pink-eyed Angora rabbit.

'What *do* you do?' asked George, trying to distract Harley from a macho Dobermann.

'Nothing. I've never had to work.'

'Well, you could help out in an animal dispensary. They're always short of volunteers. You'd be very good at it.'

'No, I wouldn't.'

'Do you know how to hold a cat down? The vet might need some help.'

'Don't know anything.'

'Thank you,' said the vet, when he'd finished examining the kitten, and Angela had proved herself a creditable assistant. 'It's nothing serious – the eye will clear up on its own – but the cat's a bit off-colour. It looks to me as if he needs more fresh air and exercise. Have you got a garden?'

'No,' said George.

'Yes,' said Angela.

'Well, make sure he has plenty of space to run around. Cooping up a kitten never did him any good. And go easy on the food – nothing too rich. Okay, that's it.' The vet was clearing up, rinsing the thermometer, discarding his used gloves. 'But don't hesitate to ring me if you find he still seems poorly.'

George was silent on the bus back.

'Angela,' he said, at last.

'Mm?'

'Did you say you had a garden?'

'Yes.'

'What's it like?'

'Big. Too big. I live on the ground floor of this huge great Victorian mansion just off Holland Park, and I own the whole damn garden. I've always hated gardening. There's a man comes in to do it. But it's mostly shrubs and things.'

'Something for Harley to exercise his claws on?'

'What d'you mean?'

'It's not right to keep a kitten cooped up in a basement flat, with only three square foot of concrete for a garden.'

'But surely you don't . . . ?'

'Well, you heard what the vet said. It's doing him no good. With all my other cats, I had a decent garden with trees and grass and smells. It seems unfair on Harley to deprive him of those pleasures. In fact, I may have to consider finding him another home.'

'That's cruel – that's really cruel, George. I mean, giving up on him when you know he'd pine without you.'

'I'm never cruel, Angela – you can rest assured of that. The kitten will be fine if he goes to the right person.'

'There isn't a right person. He doesn't know anyone but you. You told me yourself you never let him near the patients.'

'He knows *you*.'

'Yes, but . . .'

'He seems to like you, Angela. He let you hold him at the vet's, without scratching you or anything.'

'But I've never had a pet, never in my life. Supposing he died?'

'Died? He's full of beans. And he needs someone to look after him, someone with a garden.'

Angela said nothing. She had the basket balanced on her knees, and was frowning down at it, one finger through the wickerwork, keeping contact with the cat. The bus was filling up, crawling through the traffic, a group of fractious children sparring at the back. Suddenly she cleared her throat, asked George almost fiercely, 'You mean, he'd be my own? You wouldn't take him back?'

'I've told you, I'm not cruel, lass. Now, we'd better make arrangements. He's got quite a lot of stuff, so you'll probably need another of your taxis, for his dishes and his basket and a tin or two of Kattomeat to tide you over the weekend. It's Sunday tomorrow, so you won't be able to buy him fish.'

'*Tomorrow?*'

'Yes, why not?'

'But . . .'

'Quick! We're going to miss our stop.'

Harley shook himself dramatically once they released him from his cage. George set to, collecting up the kitten's things, chugging from the kitchen to the sitting-room and back. He glanced across at Angela, who was standing by the mantelpiece, fiddling with a photo-frame. 'All right?' he asked, picking up a half-chewed rubber mouse.

She nodded. 'Will you come and visit him? Come and see the garden?'

George stowed three tins of cat-food in a plastic carrier. 'It's a wee bit awkward, Angela. I don't think Dr de Roche would quite approve. But I'll see you here, each weekday, when you come for your appointments, and you can tell me then how Harley's getting on.'

'But you won't see the garden.'

'No, I won't see the garden.' George looked up at Bea, who was watching from her frame, a younger Bea, laughing with her grand-daughters. 'But you could bring me a photograph – one of Harley on the grass, and I'll put it up there on my mantelshelf, with all the rest of my family.'

'Would you mind if I was in it, too?' Angela had taken down the photo and was peering at it closely, tracing the three faces with her finger.

''Course not. Angela and Harley relaxing in their garden. I'll give it pride of place, put it right bang in the centre.' He wrapped two enamel cat-dishes in a pale blue baby's blanket, and placed them in the carrier, on top. 'Right, I think that's everything. I've written out Harley's feeding schedule, and put his favourite rug in. I've ordered you a taxi, which should be here in just two ticks, and I'll see you on Monday morning in the waiting-room. That's not long now, is it?' George smiled and squeezed her arm. 'Don't forget to keep an eye on Harley. He'll need a day or two to find his feet. I wouldn't let him out on his own, not until he's settled down. Okay?'

George returned an indignant kitten to the basket, entrusted it to Angela, picked up the plastic carrier and led the way upstairs.

'Hey, George,' she said, stopping in the hall. 'We really ought to change his name. I mean, Harley won't be right when he doesn't live in Harley Street. Or d'you think he might object?'

'I'm sure he'd be delighted. Any particular name you had in mind?'

'Well, I suppose it's stupid really, but . . .' She broke off, chewed her nail.

'What's stupid?'

'Not the name. I really like the name. It's my favourite name, in fact. But . . .'

'But what?' asked George, reaching up to straighten a picture on the wall.

'Well, I wondered if you'd mind if I called the kitten something like . . . ?' She moved towards the door, turning back to look at him a moment. 'Like George?'

15

Ginny sat on a toilet in Waterloo Station and cried. It was agony to pee. There was a burning pain between her legs and the urine cut her like a knife. She bent right over, trying to inspect herself. Things didn't look too good. She must have caught some terrible disease – syphilis, most likely. She'd seen it on TV – Maupassant writhing on a pallet, blind and totally deranged, brute iron-jawed apothecaries struggling to restrain him. Al Capone had died of it, and countless other men been driven to insanity and suicide. It was even worse for women – left you sterile, as well as simply cretinous. Her daughters might be killed (or kidnapped) and she'd be unable to replace them, or give poor Ian a son. Every time she thought of Ian, she was swamped with guilt and shame, and now she'd probably infected him with some lethal spirochaete. He was already irritable, suspicious, and if he discovered her affair, her whole safe and cosy marriage would come crashing down around her ears.

How could she have treated him so shabbily? All those scanty salads she'd left him on the kitchen table, when she knew he hated beetroot, loathed eating on his own. And those scrawled deceitful notes, propped beside the salad cream, with the names of Renaissance artists casually inserted to prove how well her study course was going. And skipping Sarah's school bazaar, when she'd never missed a single function since her elder daughter's first lisped play at kindergarten. And promising both girls she'd . . .

She gasped with pain, as a thimbleful of urine seared and scalded out of her. How could she tell Caldos what was wrong? He might be really angry, put all the blame on her, insist that she had caught the thing from Ian. Thank God he wasn't expecting her tonight, but accompanying an old school chum to some way-out modern concert. She'd been glad to miss the music, and was even more relieved now. She must keep her distance from him – and she meant that literally. He might well harbour a whole plethora of germs, what with all that tangled body-hair, and the extraordinary things he did to her. It was Divine Retribution, the sort of thing they'd warned about at school. She'd thought it funny at the time – all that stress on purity, and having to wear chemises in the bath, and modelling one's life on the Blessed Virgin Mary's, which wasn't exactly easy, since most normal women couldn't have a child without a man. Perhaps the nuns were right, though. Men were dangerous and disgusting, just as Reverend Mother Mildred always claimed. She'd have gladly entered a convent at this moment, so she'd never have to see a man again. Sex simply wasn't worth the dire results – pain and shame, sterility and madness.

No, she must keep calm. VD was as common as the common cold – or so Kate had once informed her. Other girls wouldn't waste their time cowering in a cramped and smelly lavatory. She'd only gone there in the first place to find the address of what they called a Special Clinic, so she'd better stop snivelling and hurry up and find one.

She mopped her eyes, looked up from the floor-tiles. The notice was facing her, tacked up on the inside of the door. 'Venereal diseases are DANGEROUS.' Yes, she was well aware of that, but where to go for help? Albert Dock was the first name on the list, sounded unnervingly like prison. St Thomas's was the nearest, but two of her old school friends worked there as nursing sisters, and it might leak back to Reverend Mother Mildred. University College Hospital – that was the one! – a dignified and scholarly name, and straight up the Northern Line with no changes on the tube. She dabbed gingerly between her legs with a shiny piece of toilet paper, which felt like glass, or sandpaper, and had 'Government Property' printed on each sheet. They could keep it! They probably made it uncomfortable on purpose, as a punishment for anti-social syphilitics.

She sprang up from the seat. Hadn't her mother always told her not to sit on toilet-seats, and here she was, the sort of feckless Jezebel she'd been warned against since childhood – a toilet-seat-infecter, depositing her germs all over London's lavatories, fouling innocent schoolgirls, or even pious nuns. Supposing

Mother Mildred was caught short at Waterloo? She rummaged in her bag for the bottle of 'My Sin' she'd bought in a post-Christmas sale, the name horribly appropriate; poured the precious perfume on her hankie, then used it like a cleaning-rag to douse the toilet-seat. She'd read in *Lady's Journal* that perfume killed most germs – though it seemed an awful waste. Even cut-price Lanvin cost a bomb. But she owed it to society, as an act of reparation. She tipped the last of the large bottle directly on the seat, then stumbled out, praying for forgiveness.

She continued praying on the tube, silently reciting the Litany of the Blessed Virgin Mary, as she was whisked along to Warren Street. Ark of the Covenant, Tower of Gold. She'd never understood those words as a child at boarding school. All the girls and Sisters had processed around the vegetable garden at five o'clock in the morning, chanting the whole Litany in Latin, blessing the swedes, and sprinkling holy water on the Brussels sprouts and cabbages. It must have worked, since the swedes turned up with depressing munificence every other dinner-time. But even as a schoolgirl she'd been worldly; her thoughts on chocolate shortbread or what she'd get for Christmas, instead of on the Virgin.

Ora pro nobis. Ora pro nobis. Only now did she begin to understand the need for such devotion. Pray to Blessed Mary long and hard enough, and she'd keep you out of mischief, out of Special Clinics. It was too late now – she hadn't prayed in years, and Our Lady was clearly taking her revenge. Refuge of Sinners, Virgin Most Prudent, forget the swedes and succour a sinner. She tried her best to concentrate, pray with true sincerity, but impure thoughts kept creeping in like weeds. Would the clinic ask for names? That notice had said SECRECY, in bold black capitals, but none the less she'd better be prepared. She could call herself Estrella, except no one would believe it, and Estrellas would go private anyway. Smith and Jones were far too obvious. She glanced around the carriage, scanning the advertisements, in hope of inspiration. BROOK STREET BUREAU GOT BIG BY BOTHERING. Brook? Yes, that was safe and sensible enough. Susan Brook. There'd been a girl at school called Susan, who'd joined the Carmelites. She'd be Mrs Susan Brook.

'Name?'

'Brook.' Ginny blushed.

'Name of your GP?'

Oh God, she'd never thought of that one. The nurse was tapping her pen.

'Don't you *have* a doctor, dear?'

She and Ian knew their GP socially, his bubbly wife one of her good friends. And Chris himself had only ever treated her for hay fever and flu, minor ailments which were socially acceptable. But the Brook bit would confuse them, and perhaps she'd spell his name wrong.

'How many years have you been married?'

It sounded a long time. Though an enjoyable long time – at least it had been up till Christmas. Guilt swooped down again. Ian had been a pretty decent husband, all those fifteen years – maybe not the last word in excitement, but steady and reliable and good at mending things.

'Wait over there, please.'

She waited, feeling like the damned in hell as she glanced around the small and stuffy basement. The Special Clinic was housed in a grim annexe, traffic roaring by it on the busy road above. She had slunk past the main entrance of the hospital, with its impressive marble pillars and graceful pediment, and had trudged down steep stone steps, along a dank and dismal passage, to this ignominious cellar with its grudging light and gurgling water-pipes.

Well, she supposed they'd done their best with it. There were posters on the walls, and goldfish in a tank, and they'd painted the cracked ceiling a sickly shade of pink to try to counteract the gloom. She riffled through the leaflets on the table – rape, abortion, alcohol and drugs. There seemed no end to the horrors of being human. If only she hadn't strayed beyond the Elysian Fields of Hinchley Wood into the reeking hell of Chelsea. She crossed her legs, jigged up and down, desperate for a pee again. But peeing was forbidden until she'd seen the doctor. There were notices on all four walls, so no one would forget: 'DO NOT PASS WATER UNTIL INSTRUCTED BY THE NURSE'. The very word 'water' made things worse, so she kept her eyes averted from the fish-tank, tried to think of deserts – the Sahara, the Mojave. The last few nights had been equally uncomfortable: leaping out of bed every half an hour, or less, sprinting to the loo and passing lava; Ian worrying, solicitous, which only fuelled her guilt.

She crossed her legs, continued jigging – the longest jig she'd endured in all her life. There appeared to be one lone doctor for a score of syphilitics. She found a woman's magazine, tried to distract herself by reading. 'How Your Little Gestures Give You Away. *Naked Ape*-man Morris reveals how we betray our secret thoughts.' She leafed on through the article. Apparently, they could tell if you were lying by the way you tapped your foot or touched your face. She'd been lying to Ian for weeks, and would have to lie to Caldos now – couldn't tell him where she'd been, couldn't sleep with him. She'd have to pretend she'd got weeping boils, or scrofula – something quite disgusting to turn him off entirely. He wouldn't accept a headache or the curse. Lies, and still more lies. And even if she maintained a wary silence, according to the article any shrewd observer was bound to find her out. 'Non-verbal leakage', it was called. She shuddered at the words. There was enough leakage in her pants.

'Mrs Brook.'

That must be the lady in the see-through plastic mac. How amazingly relaxed the others all appeared – even downright bored. One of them was chewing gum and had a badge on her right breast saying '*Je ne regrette rien*'.

'Mrs *Brook*!'

Oh, God! Oh, yes! I'm coming! Susan Ginny Estrella Guilty Brook.

The doctor was dark and swarthy, not Indian exactly, but something like Armenian, or Turkish. He unfolded her pink form – which matched the ceiling – and began to ask her questions.

'I beg your pardon?' Ginny said, confounded, having failed to understand a single word. His accent was like porridge – thick and grey and lumpy – and he put most unusual stresses on the words. She did her best to lip-read.

'What? Oh yes, I see. Two days ago.' That was with de Roche.

'And with husband?'

She was blushing as she counted on her fingers. It seemed an age ago. Would the doctor think her decadent, consorting with her lover while cold-shouldering her spouse? Whatever he thought, she had failed to catch the gist of it. 'I'm sorry, I didn't quite . . .'

Weren't there courses he could take – Elementary English or Bedside Chat, Grade One?

'Is he regular boyfriend, or casual?'

Heavens! What a choice. Dr C. E. S. de Roche could hardly be described as anybody's boyfriend, and 'regular' was the last word she'd apply to him. But then wasn't 'casual' every bit as wrong?

'Any other partners?'

Ginny shook her head. Surely two was quite enough, or was the doctor simply out for kicks? The questions grew still worse. Anal? Oral? And something completely unintelligible, until he sketched it for her. Her cheeks were deepest crimson as she mumbled 'Yes' to all of them.

At last, he had completed her pink form – though she wondered in what language – and after another tedious wait, she was ushered into the examination-room, told to strip below the waist and lie down on the couch. No chance of a brief shut-eye. Her legs were thrust apart, her feet jacked up above her head, and rammed into iron stirrups which looked like instruments of torture; her private parts shamefully exposed, and only inches from the doctor's dusky face. An ice-cold teaspoon was shoved up her vagina, followed by a spatula, as if the nurse and doctor were two eccentric chefs who'd decided to make a cake inside her. The next utensil felt so large, she screamed.

'Good girl,' clucked the nurse, with a little smile of sympathy. Ginny turned her head away. She wasn't good at all, but thoroughly depraved. 'CONTAMINATED MATERIAL' read the label on the box beside her. Yes, that was more appropriate. She should also wear a label branding her 'contaminated', or ring a bell like lepers did, warning all she met to keep their distance.

The afternoon dragged on – blood and urine, temperature and pulse, more pink forms, pink ceilings. Thank the Lord that Caldos wasn't waiting for her, with two glossy concert programmes and a carnation in his buttonhole. Did *he* have symptoms, too? Perhaps he'd invented the concert purely as an alibi, and was skulking in the male department just two doors along, a Punjabi-speaking Indian squinting at his penis?

No. Men like Caldos didn't catch diseases, only passed them on to frailer mortals. And he'd never stand for all this inefficiency. She was still hanging around for her preliminary results, back now in the waiting-room, squeezed between two fatties on a bench. The whole interminable process seemed to have slowed to a near-halt, yet more and more patients were still flocking through the door. Half of London must be riddled with VD. She glanced up at the posters on the walls. 'Come to Beautiful Norway', they enticed. Fjords and snow-cowled fir trees, and underneath, a row of dead grey fishes, grilling on a spit. Bright flames leaping up – the flames of hell – sheep and goats again. The just among the fir trees and the damned amidst the flames.

Once more, she tried to pray, fumbling for the half-forgotten words of the *Salve Regina*. 'To you do we cry, poor banished children of Eve. To you do we send up our sighs, mourning and weeping in this vale of tears . . .' They'd lisped it from the age of five, when tears were confined to cut knees or confiscated sweets. Those wretched nuns were right again – it *was* a vale of tears.

'Holy Mary, let me not have it. I know I've neglected you, but please let me be clear . . .'

'Mrs Brook?'

The doctor was almost dropping with exhaustion. He opened her file. 'Monilia,' he murmured, in a wilting voice which matched his sagging back.

If only he spoke English. She gestured her bewilderment.

'Thrush,' he said, scrawling on his pad. 'Monilia is Latin word.'

She stifled her annoyance. Why in heaven's name speak Latin when this was the UK? He'd alarmed her without cause. Thrush was nothing, really – unpleasant, but not threatening. And if you judged by all the readers' letters in women's magazines, half the female population had caught it at some time – even nuns and virgins.

He shook his pen, which appeared to have gone on strike in protest at its work-load. 'And also trouble with your waterworks.'

She could have told *him* that. She knew about cystitis, had returned with it from her honeymoon, like a painful souvenir. But was that all she had? What about VD – the dread and drastic kind? His accent was so thick, she might have missed it. Had he said syphilis *en passant*? Or maybe in Armenian? She tried to question him.

'These tests very quick.' (What did he mean, for God's sake?

She'd been waiting now for two hours, twenty minutes.) 'Culture needs grow. We give it time, okay? One week, no sex, no boyfriend. You come back here. We tell.'

A week! She could have wept. Seven endless days of worry and suspense. He was writing out a chit for pills and pessaries, about to hand it over, about to say goodbye. Surely he knew more, was probably hiding something, didn't dare to tell her, or was simply plain sadistic, enjoyed his little tortures. 'Doctor, please, I beg you, tell me what you . . . I mean, could it be . . . ? Have I got . . . ?' Her own command of the language seemed to be deserting her.

He looked up wearily. 'Is possible you have gonorrhoea. We do not find in microscope. But in culture maybe. One week you wait. No boyfriend. No sex one week, okay?'

She never wanted sex again, not in her whole life, let alone a week. She made another appointment, aghast at all the hours and hours which had to tick away before she'd know the verdict. Gonorrhoea. What a disgusting word it was, made her feel defiled; germs swarming in her knickers, polluting her whole body. She glanced up at the poster as she waited for her pills. The flames looked fiercer now. She could almost feel their scorching tongues licking against her gonorrhoeal loins.

'There we are then, Mrs Brook,' the Irish nurse said cheerily, as she passed across the package. 'It's snowing, so Nurse Johnson said. Don't catch cold now, will you?'

Ginny shook her head, turned wretchedly away. There was very little danger of catching cold in hell.

16

'I still can't quite decide,' said Caldos, bounding from the entrance of the Queen Elizabeth Hall, 'whether an aleatory fugue isn't a contradiction in terms.'

'For God's sake, Tum-Tum, *wait*.' Gish draped herself decoratively around a concrete pillar. 'That putrid concert has left me totally paraplegic. Why you have to drag me to hear farmyard noises interspersed with wailings of the damned . . .'

'Simply, my sweet, because you insisted on seeing me again, complaining bitterly of de Roche withdrawal symptoms. And since my role in life is to succour those who suffer . . .' He leapt up the stone steps towards Waterloo Bridge, three at a time. 'As for the concert . . .' Gish shuddered, on the bottom step. '*Fantastico!* That last piece was bare-faced revolution, a march to the scaffold for civilisation, a sock in the jaw for our cultural complacency. I used to know the chap at Oxford. We played Meade Lux Lewis together on the Dean's piano. He's a new messiah, Gish, and all we do is crucify him.'

'Christ Almighty! It's me that's been crucified. My ears are still bleeding from the shock. He's jolly lucky to have you to applaud. Almost no one else did. Mind you, Tum-Tum, I sometimes suspect you do all that bravo-ing bit merely to make an exhibition of yourself.'

'That's exactly the sort of remark, my precious, which persuaded me to give you up.'

'Just for the record,' panted Gish, still teetering up the first few steps, 'I gave *you* up.'

Caldos sprang on to the bridge and hurled a little Wordsworth to the stars:

> 'Earth has not anything to show more fair,
> Dull would he be of soul who could pass by
> A sight so touching in its . . .

Wrong bridge! Wrong time of day!' He kissed his hands to a dilapidated barge. 'None the less, the scansion is admirable.'

'Tum-Tum, where are we *going*?'

'I can't answer for you, my darling. I'm going to Cherokee's.'

'Shit! Not that dump. They're the rudest set of waiters I've ever encountered. And all as queer as coots.'

Caldos was humming an unhummable phrase from the concert. 'That's most unfair to coots! They're paragons of heterosexual devotion. The males even build nests like the females. Though, come to think of it, that *is* rather camp.' He changed the humming to a coot noise. 'Besides, Gish, all my best friends are queers, or Jews, or Gay Lib Jewish analysts. Except dear Philip. I've arranged to meet him there.

> Dear God! the very houses seem asleep,
> And all that mighty heart is lying still!'

'Tum-Tum, do stop showing off. I loathe poetry after nine o'clock at night. And as for Philip, I can't think of a more lethal combination than Cherokee's un-*haute cuisine* and that noxious little creep.' She tripped on a loose paving-stone and swore impressively. 'Trust you to have a solicitor who's ninety per cent a con-man.'

Caldos was now playing an imaginary trombone, one fist clenched hard against his lips, and the other hand sliding back and forth towards the pavement. 'It makes the other ten per cent such marvellous value, darling. Phil's bound to be late anyway, so you can have me all to yourself, at least as far as the clam chowder.'

He *was* late. Caldos compensated by hoovering half a dozen Beautiful People into his entourage. Gish glared at a blonde Amazon with triple-decker eyelashes. Caldos was doing battle with an oversized chicken carcass and an undersized psychiatrist.

'Balls, Joshua! Analysts today are blinkered and constipated. You can tell that by our journals – chewing the same regurgitated cud and refusing to look beyond the cowshed at adjoining fields. We should be out, wolfing down new shoots in those lush new meadows – epistemology, ethology, anthropology, sociobiology . . .'

Joshua choked on a piece of tomato. 'We'd all get mental indigestion. One of our problems as doctors is pressure of time. We're

125

weighed down by our work-load, as it is. We can't be philosophers as well as practitioners.'

'But we bloody well can be. We must be.' Caldos jabbed his baked potato, spattering the butter. 'The way we work, we haven't even time to think. And if we don't think, we die. Look at our profession! It's already fossilised, rigid, terrified of new ideas . . .'

Joshua was dabbing butter off his shirt-front. 'I already work eleven hours a day.'

'Then you're a fool. We're all fools. Half our patients don't need the extensive, expensive, concentrated, introverted treatment we insist on. They're lonely, bored, cocktail-belt neurotics, suffering from absentee husbands and nothing to do. They want somewhere to go and someone to listen. I do listen, very carefully, but I'm a rather expensive ear, and largely irrelevant, as far as they're concerned. They don't want to get better – or they daren't. They've become so used to their symptoms and their sessions, they'd be lost without them. They come for analysis, when all they really want is sympathy. We could dole out their sympathy in quite a different fashion, jazz the whole thing up a little.'

Joshua pushed his plate away. He had hardly touched his Seafood Special. 'What on earth do you mean, Caldos? We're not some sort of circus.'

Caldos kidnapped the seafood and divided his attention between the scallops and his chicken. 'Ah, but maybe we should be. Bread and circuses are basic human needs. Even the mental hospitals have clubs and sprees and social junketings. A lot of my patients have nothing in their life. So they put me at the centre of it. Why me? An occupational therapist would do as well, or even a masseur. We want to get them out, about. I'm wasting twelve years of specialised training on a gaggle of Knightsbridge neurotics, half of whom would be better off with a lover, or a coffee morning. I'd rather reserve my skills for those who can make real use of them.'

'And abandon the Depressives Anonymous to drown in their pool of tears, I suppose?' Joshua watched disapprovingly as Caldos made inroads into his crab.

'Not at all. Just have the imagination to prise them off the couch into some more productive form of self-absorption.'

126

'More *profitable*, don't you mean?' Mossman interjected. He had crept up on the conversation from behind a pillar.

'Philip!' Caldos leapt up from his chair, which clattered to the floor. Three waiters picked it up. 'Philippo, wonderful to see you! Though you look fearfully pale and wan. Overdoing it again, I suppose, with your twenty-one-hour days. How's the new motor?' Caldos disentangled himself from rimless spectacles and sober dark-striped tie, turned back to the others. 'Phil's just bought himself a Corniche Convertible.'

Gish looked up with interest, began a lightning reappraisal of the 'noxious little creep'.

'Philip, come and join us. Gish you already know – all too well, I fear. But may I introduce Clarissa, who spends half her time cavorting on the cover of *Vogue*. Sun-suits in Siberia, wasn't it last week, darling?'

The triple-decker eyelashes set up a slight breeze in Philip's direction, then re-turned their attention to the under-age actor at the next table.

'And this is Dr Joshua Levine – brilliant little footnote to the late Sigmund F. And Jerry, fiendish Jerry, who put the J. in J. Walter Thompson. Meet Mr Philip Mossman, one of my dearest chums, and dare I say it, my solicitor.'

Mossman smiled and nodded. There wasn't time for more, since Caldos was stampeding on. 'Overjoyed to see you, Philip! You illustrate the very point I've been trying to lead on to. Here's a man who takes sixty per cent of the profits and does ten per cent of the work.'

Mossman opened his mouth to object.

'No, hold on, Philip. It's a flexible system and one I really envy you. Without your clerks, or legal executives, or whatever you call them, you couldn't handle half your existing clients. As it is, you pile them all in, and then turn them over to the minions. Everybody's happy, your practice flourishes, and you toddle about in your new Corniche.'

Philip abducted a waiter and ordered himself a Tequila Sunrise. 'Let up about the car, can't you? The sodding thing's already developed a wheeze.'

'Rotten luck! You should drive something with staying power. A Lamborghini, for instance.'

'What, and pay a hundred pounds for a piddling set of sparking plugs! No thanks.'

Gish glanced irritably at her watch. Car-talk always bored her, and the advertising wimp had been pontificating endlessly about USPs and loss-leaders. She flinched as Caldos returned to the attack.

'Yes, Philip, psychoanalysis could use a system like yours. You take the overall responsibility, and your staff do the dogsbodying. Wonderful! If I had your clerks, I could triple my work-load, and yet reduce the pressure. As it is, I'm turning away wealthy patients I could really be of use to.'

Philip drained his Tequila and ordered a replacement. 'Come off it, Caldos, a human being isn't as simple as a lease.'

'Judging by the mess you made of mine, there's nothing simple about a lease. But that's not the point. Look, Philip, it's the human beings I care about. I'm working on something which might well be a godsend for them. Someone's got to reorganise the system. We cling to theory and jargon at the expense of patients' welfare, half the time. And the way we work, we can only see a handful anyway. My scheme will change all that.'

Joshua was trying desperately to object, through a mouthful of whipped cream. Gish had pushed her plate away and was watching with distaste while her rival wolfed the cherries from a gigantic banana split. Females called Clarissa were invariably tedious. 'Ghastly dump, isn't it?' she said.

'What, Cherokee's? I adore it! You meet such *delicious* people.' Clarissa chomped her final cherry, then made a little boat out of her paper serviette, and launched it with a gale from her long lashes, steering it in the direction of the actor. Gish turned back to Joshua, but he was crossing swords with Caldos, or at least brandishing his knife.

'Psychoanalysis . . .' he began, dogmatically.

Caldos jumped straight in: '. . . has become an élitist over-elaborate system, a defensive profession clinging to its rituals. Just look at us! We limit our horizons and our membership, and if anyone disagrees with us, let alone attacks us, we accuse them of irrational hostility, or react so vitriolically we display all the classic pathological defences of repression, projection and denial, which we're always struggling to treat in our own patients. Holy

Christ! I want to split the whole thing open, let in some light and air, work with bright new therapists, energetic people who haven't lost their wits and their ideals in our twelve-year morass of irrelevant medical training.'

'And what about charlatans and quacks?' Joshua retorted, flinging down his knife. 'Untrained gurus rushing in, pulling people apart and being totally unable to put them back together. Damned irresponsible!'

'Even quacks have something to teach us, Joshua. We can't afford to be so bloody intellectual all the time. Psychoanalysis has never been a science, however hard our dear Freud tried to make it one. We need something to graft on to it – something experimental and instinctive – the folk thing, the body thing. That's absolutely crucial, isn't it Clarissa?' Caldos leaned over and kissed the southernmost point of Clarissa's plunging cleavage.

Gish glowered down at her own concave chest. 'I'm sorry, Tum-Tum, but I can feel one of my bad migraines coming on.'

'Purely psychosomatic, darling. You need our brilliant Dr Joshua Levine. On second thoughts, let's all go on to Annabel's.'

'Hold on a second, Caldos, I haven't even eaten yet.' Philip prised the last plump prawn from de Roche's fork, gulped it down himself.

'Grab Gish's. I was just about to start on it myself. It's virgin territory. She's only flirted with a lettuce leaf and one sliver of tomato.' He fished about in Gish's unscathed salad, dug out half an artichoke and waved it under Philip's nose.

'Eat up, Mossman, you need all the strength you've got. I want your advice on this little scheme I'm hatching – my first foray away from the couch.'

Philip disposed of the artichoke, drowned it with Tequila. 'More damned theory, I suppose. You analysts forget we don't all live by psyche alone.'

'But that's exactly my point, dear Philip. I agree with you entirely. And I want to use my patients to prove it.'

'And what do you want to use *me* for?'

'To make me a nice fat profit, of course! What else?'

17

Ginny knelt in the very last pew of Westminster Cathedral, and gazed up at the dark immensity of the nave. Common daylight had been banned from this sacred place of glinting gold and shimmering mosaics; the highest, widest nave of any cathedral in England. God felt very far away, but after fifteen godless years, was it any wonder that He preferred to keep His distance? Yet these last few days, she'd been praying more intently than ever in her life. Only one more day to go before her next crucial visit to the clinic. Her symptoms had abated, but that might be a fluke. She'd looked up gonorrhoea in a medical encyclopaedia – sterility, arthritis, blindness, peritonitis – there seemed no end to its horrible effects. She wondered if Caldos had all the ghastly symptoms they described – pussy yellowish discharge seeping from his penis. No, she mustn't think of Caldos, not in church. He was an Occasion of Sin – to use a term the nuns loved – and she was going to give him up.

An old man in carpet slippers joined her in the pew and rummaged in a paper bag. She stole a sidelong glance at him, recoiling from the smell of sweat. He was unwrapping sardine sandwiches from a piece of greaseproof paper. What an unholy lot we are, she thought, guzzling and lusting even in God's presence. She must remove herself at once from such profanity. She crept out of the pew and walked along the aisle, past the gleaming gold of the side chapels, across the south transept to the splendour of the Lady Chapel. The rich mosaic ceiling was spiked with angels' wings, the walls swirling and rippling with dazzling ornament. Confessions were in progress, just behind her. She could hear the priest's soft murmur, the stealthy noise of feet as they shuffled to and fro between the pews and the confessional box. It would be her turn any moment. Was it sheer neurosis to be returning to

130

confession after a gap of fifteen years? They'd changed it all, in any case, so she wouldn't know the rules. And how could they forgive her, when she wasn't even a Catholic any more? No. Once a Catholic, always a Catholic. It was something ineradicable, like the colour of your eyes. You couldn't cast it off, despite all those thorny problems which Ian had always balked at: the Immaculate Conception, the Virgin Birth, the Infallibility of the Pope. And how about the Pill? She couldn't go back to those passion-killing diaphragms, which larded you with jelly and smelt like babies' plastic pants. Durex were still worse. Ian went limp at the very thought of condoms, and Caldos would simply hoot. But why bring Caldos into it, when she'd decided to renounce him? This was her new start, a return to God, and to conformity and purity, and she'd no right to be thinking about penises in church.

Renunciation was the very stuff and heart-blood of religion. If you wanted a favour, then you had to pay for it. It was like a sort of bargaining with God – one she'd learnt at school. Their hockey team, for instance, would give up sweets on Saturday, in return for thrashing Woodford High six-nil. You do this, Lord, and I'll do that. She hoped the Lord was listening now. You forget about the gonorrhoea, and I'll forget about de Roche.

She moved right up to the altar, as if there were more chance of being heard there. Getting rid of Caldos would be like cutting down a tree. His roots had already gone so deep, she'd only dislodge him with a mighty crash, a terrible upheaval. He was like some lofty elm, magnificent, imposing, yet diseased inside and rotten; and his tangled branches had overshadowed all the smaller, frailer saplings in her life. She'd been living like a bird at the top of his tall tree; a wild free life, but unstable and precarious, and basically quite wrong for her. She was really just a wren – a small drab bird which nested low and crept along the ground – a jenny wren, as her mother used to call her. She rummaged in her bag for her battered childhood missal, which she'd found abandoned in a drawer. 'To Jenny Wren, with loving prayers from Mummy.'

Her mother would be thrilled to see her now. She'd been praying for a decade for her only daughter's return to Mother Church. And her father would be furious – sneer at Papist prejudice or Irish superstition, as he sneered at Venice and Tchaikovsky and modern youth and English cheese and women novelists. He'd probably take to Caldos – they could sneer in harmony – and both would clearly be appalled at the sight of Ginny Barnes, kneeling in her black lace mantilla, with a missal in her hands, as if both Freud and Darwin had lived in vain. She'd tried to read up Darwin in one of Sarah's school books, and had once dipped into Freud, but found it all thoroughly confusing. The more she searched for Truth, the more it seemed like Father Christmas – something longed-for and worthwhile, but which failed to quite convince you after the age of six or seven. Ian still believed, and he'd been to Oxford and got to grips with Einstein, but then the Anglican religion was simpler altogether – just garden fêtes, and christenings, and smiles and hats on Sunday. The so-called Church of England was a quiet pat on the head, while the rigid Roman Catholics ripped the skin off your whole life. You could renounce the Catholic God, but it would never be reciprocal. He'd keep striking, stabbing back, and your wounds would be so serious, they'd pierce right through to the bone.

She leafed through her old missal, turning to the prayers before confession. 'Oh God, wicked as I am, it is only due to thy great mercy that I have not fallen into still more serious sin and have not been called to judgement and damnation.'

She closed her eyes a moment, to try to blank the words out. If she died in mortal sin, she would be cast into the infernal fire. There'd been a painting of hell-fire in her dormitory at school – evil gloating demons sticking pitchforks in the damned; the gaping jaws of hell engulfing naked wretches in a choking pall of flame. One of the officiating devils had looked distinctly like de Roche – dark, sardonic, hairy, and superior.

Away Satan! Why did her prayers begin with God, but always end with Caldos? She turned sternly back to the Examination of Conscience, the print hazing before her eyes. 'Have I been immodest or impure in thought, word, or deed, with myself or with others? Have I sinned against the law of God in my married life?'

Holy Mother, she was guilty of it all! Masturbation, contraception, shameless fornication. She couldn't give them up. If she threw away the Pill, she'd have ten more children, bankrupt Ian, and land up in the workhouse. 'Immodest deeds with oneself' was a Catholic euphemism, and would most certainly include her new triple-speed vibrator, which Caldos had presented to her on condition he could watch her making use of it. She slammed her missal shut. This was shameless sacrilege – bringing triple-speed vibrators into Westminster Cathedral, even to the very threshold of the sacraments. She crossed herself hastily, slunk back along the aisle. She'd never change her life, so why delude herself? She slipped out through the doors, blinking as harsh daylight dispelled the sacred gloom.

A pallid winter sun was shining in the square, three young girls sitting on a bench, eating sugared doughnuts. Ginny watched a spurt of jam oozing down a chin, suddenly felt ravenous herself. There was a McDonald's right in front of her; posters in the window portraying two-foot-high Big Macs, a trail of greasy chips dropped and squashed outside. She dodged the chips, walked up to the counter.

'Two chocolate milk shakes and a piece of apple pie.' Wicked to be hungry at this time of spiritual crisis, and surely further proof of her depravity. The whole place looked so jolly – the serving girls in cheerful orange pantaloons and matching stripey hats; tumpty-tumpty music whooping through the room; prankish clowns with scarlet-bobble noses beaming from the walls. Yet everything was plastic and disposable – paper cups, polystyrene cartons, cardboard food, fake froth. She felt pulled between two realms – this breezy world of thirty-two flavours and triple-whip indulgence, and the stern spirituality and soaring beauty of the Church. And Caldos seemed compounded of them both – fleshy and celestial, delicious and degenerate, a flaming seraph and a voracious beast; a scoop of Double Chocolate Ripple on top of a church spire.

She drained her first milk shake, started on the pie, which was hot and sweet and filling, though bore no resemblance whatsoever to home-made apple pie. She plunged her straw into the second chocolate shake, slurped it greedily. She resented Caldos trying to keep her slim. He was overweight himself, stuffed everything in sight, and then he had the cheek to ration her. He liked his women sylph-like.

Did she really want to cling to him, when he bullied and dictated? After all, there was more to life than wild black thrusting

133

sex. And if she didn't give him up, she'd infect poor innocent Ian, who'd develop stricture, scarring, sterility, and endocarditis. (The medical encyclopaedia had threatened all of them.) The priest would understand. They were known to be progressive at Westminster Cathedral, which was why she'd chosen to go there in the first place. She'd noticed the difference as soon as she'd walked in – all those racy pamphlets on 'Why God?' and 'Can We Trust the New Testament?', which would have given Reverend Mother Mildred an instant heart attack. The Church was freer altogether, no longer carped about mixed marriages, or insisted that you fasted during Lent. Some easy-going priests even turned a blind eye to the Pill, left it to the conscience of the individual woman, so perhaps she needn't mention it at all. She wiped froth from her lips, scooped up a last fragment of her pie, and ventured out again.

The tall tower of the Cathedral stretched its finger up to God, the cross right at the top glinting in the sunlight. She craned her neck to look at it, wishing she could bridge the gap between hamburgers and heaven; then pushed the heavy door, and was swallowed up in gloom and heady grandeur. All her senses seemed enthralled – the smells of flowers and candle-wax, the rumble of an organ, her eyes beguiled by gleaming bronze, rippled swirling marble. She glanced around her, dazzled, admiring the majestic domes which flung their dark dramatic curves against the floor of paradise; the gold and scarlet gash of the gigantic crucifix. The man with the sardine sandwiches was still sitting on the bench, picking his teeth with a clasp-knife; discarded crusts beside him, and two empty Guinness cans.

She crept along the aisle once more, spelling out the names of all the side-chapels – St Gregory, St Patrick, St Andrew and St Paul. The Communion of Saints. Even without Caldos, she would never be alone. The whole host of heaven would be there to keep her company. She stopped to light a candle in front of the alabaster statue of Our Lady of Westminster, which stood close to the confessional. The candle was for luck. She watched it flame and flicker, then took in a deep breath, and walked into the pew reserved for penitents.

The pew was empty now, confessions almost at an end, though one last woman was kneeling in the box, her scuffed brown shoes sticking out beneath the purple curtain. The other side was free. Ginny tried to ignore the pounding of her heart as she stole across and slipped into that side. Behind the heavy curtain, it felt dark and hushed and secret, like the womb. She was captive now, committed, couldn't run away. She could hear the woman speaking, an indistinct and murmured drone, which made her still more nervous. Suddenly, the priest drew back the wooden slide on her side of the box. She glimpsed his face, his profile, pale in the dim light, a flash of priestly purple, the glint of spectacles. She dared not look at him, but gazed instead into the recesses of the box, her eyes cast down more in fear than piety.

'Bless me, Father, for I have sinned.' The words came automatically, though her voice was hoarse and faltering, had petered out already.

'Yes?' the priest said, prompting her. He didn't say 'Yes, my child', as they had done in the old days. She'd feel small and safe and wholesome if he'd only say 'my child'.

'Father,' she began, then broke off once again. Perhaps you didn't call them Father in these progressive days, but Mike or Dad or something. 'It's . . . er . . . fifteen years since . . . I mean, I haven't been to the sacraments for' – she swallowed – 'fifteen years.'

She waited for his gasp, his instant reprimand, but he didn't react at all. Perhaps he hadn't heard, was maybe even deaf. She shuddered at the thought. Impossible to shout, boom out all her mortal sins for any passing worshipper to hear. She started with the venial sins, raised her voice a fraction. 'Father, since that time I have neglected my religious duties, used bad language, told lies . . .' The old familiar phrases. But there were no lulling and familiar words for adultery or VD. Her voice kept croaking to a halt.

'Yes?' he said, encouragingly. His own voice was kind, unfazed, but she'd hardly told him anything as yet. 'I . . . er . . .' However did she phrase it? 'Sexual intercourse' was far too formal, like a heading in a text-book, and 'fornication' sounded quite depraved. Her stomach churned and gurgled. Those two milk shakes had been a grave mistake. 'I . . . I have sinned against the sixth and ninth commandments.'

She stopped in mid-confession. She had distinctly heard a

135

chuckle from the priest. No. She must have been mistaken. No priest would laugh when administering the sacraments. Priests were holy men, anointed, set apart, guardians of morality, representing God Himself on earth. She reeled back in consternation as she heard a second guffaw through the grille. No doubt about it this time. God's sacred representative was laughing.

18

Ginny tramped along the Embankment, towards Waterloo Bridge and her train to Hinchley Wood. The Thames looked soiled and sluggish. The words of absolution had washed no contagion from her soul; sounded strange in English anyway. There had always been more magic in the Latin. She didn't feel absolved. The priest had been so liberal and light-hearted. Fancy him even laughing in confession, teasing her about the terms she'd used. He'd told her she was twenty years behind the times, that things were different now; that religion was a joyous liberation, not hell and wrath and rules. True, he said, extra-marital sex was still a sin, but not as heinous as those hidebound nuns had claimed. God would understand. Hadn't Christ Himself consorted with Mary Magdalen, mixed with publicans, adulterers?

And then he'd changed from priest to pop psychologist, raked up all her childhood, blamed her traumas on her father and the nuns. She'd recoiled at all that soggy spineless sympathy, that bending over backwards to be mod and merciful. It had totally unnerved her. She hadn't even told him about the Pill, let alone the gonorrhoea. He'd been rattling on about how God welcomed sinners, and she couldn't get a word in. It was probably a false confession, totally invalid. She'd kept things back, important wicked things. Her soul was spotted still, like the mottled bark of the plane trees planted all along the river, graceless blemished trees.

She stopped a moment to touch their roughened bark, still hearing the priest's words, still unable to believe that he had shrugged off flagrant Caldos in such a cool and casual manner; just told her to forget him. *Forget* him! Did he really think that possible? Yet every time she'd dragged her lover in again, the priest had capped his name with Christ's; told her half a dozen times that

Christ had died for sinners. He'd seemed strangely keen to give her absolution. Perhaps he had an aching back, or was dying for a pee, or maybe there was treacle tart for lunch. Or could he be a renegade, about to be defrocked? God Himself never bent the rules, was always strict and castigating. She knew the sorts of things God said; had read them in the Bible: 'Depart from me ye wicked, into everlasting fire'; not 'No wonder you're in the soup, my dear. Convents have a lot to answer for.' And was it fair to blame the nuns, who'd done their simple best? All this progressive lily-livered Christianity was only a snare and a delusion, like those pupil-powered schools where the children did no serious work, but messed about with finger-paints, then landed up in Borstal.

She should never have gone to the Cathedral in the first place – wallowing in all that pomp and gold, and expecting God to be gift-wrapped, and come with froth on top; should have been more humble, chosen a small modest church where the stern priest knew the difference between psychology and sin. She rubbed her eye, removed a piece of grit from it. The wind was blowing off the river, disturbing grime and sand, fretting the brown water into ripples. She glanced across at Hungerford Bridge, cutting brash and scarlet between dark wavelets and drab cloud. Normally, she liked this view, liked the wrought-iron dolphins sculpted round the lamp-posts, the red-beaked terns preening on the parapet, but today it seemed ugly and depressing. She sat down on a metal bench, supported by a sphinx's head, and suddenly the river disappeared. All she could see now was the stained façade of the dreary soulless Shell building, and a stretch of muddy slime.

She pulled out the New Testament she had bought at the Cathedral shop, and started leafing through it to find Corinthians I. The priest had instructed her to read it as her penance. That was odd, as well. The usual penance in the old days had been three Our Fathers or three Hail Marys – something short and simple, and invariably in threes. She'd hardly even heard of Corinthians; had some trouble finding it in this cheap edition with its tiny blurry print. 'If I speak in the tongues of men and of angels, but have not love, I am only a resounding gong or a clanging cymbal . . .'

But of course she knew it, everybody knew it – except this was a modern version, and in her day, they'd called it charity, not love. The words were hugely different. 'Charity' was formal and official, a safe and sanctioned term – knitting socks for soldiers, or spooning soup into starving refugees. But 'love' was an abandoned word – open and unnerving, impassioned, indefinable. Love included lust and passion, nakedness, elation. Love invited lunacy, threatened loss, despair.

She forced her attention back again. 'Love is patient, love is kind . . . It always protects, always trusts, always hopes, always perseveres.' That was Ian's sort of love, and a vitally important kind. She *did* love Ian – well, almost – and both her lovely daughters, and her sweet safe cosy life in Hinchley Wood. But she also loved Caldos, and there was nothing kind or quiet or patient in that desperate dangerous love. 'Love does not envy, it does not boast, it is not proud. It is not rude, it is not self-seeking, it is not easily angered, it keeps no records of wrongs.' But Caldos was proud and rude and arrogant, angry and vindictive. And she loved him with a wild, rude, boastful, furious love. And even after the Cathedral and Corinthians, she could still feel his tongue pushing into every hole she had.

She eased up from the bench, leant against the cold stone of the parapet. There was very little river traffic. Most of the craft were stationary: tawdry pleasure-boats waiting for the summer, or dirty barges tethered like old dogs. She opened the New Testament again, propped it on the ledge, rebuking herself for misreading the text. It was nothing to do with human love, let alone with lust. She was dethroning God and setting Him up in Chelsea, defiling Holy Writ. Her confession didn't count. She hadn't said her penance and she'd left out half her sins. Her mind was still on holes instead of holiness. If she were truly forgiven, then heaven should be rejoicing at the fact, as it said in St Luke's Gospel (the bit about Lost Sheep and Prodigal Sons), but everything was flat and grey and dour. The sky pressed low against the sullen river, grey weeping into brown, and small droplets oozed like tears down the dolphins' metal snouts.

She closed the book, scrambled for her gloves. She knew what she must do – take the train to Norbiton, instead of Hinchley Wood, and make a second confession at St Ursula's – a small and simple church with a fearsome Irish priest, who preached hell-fire and damnation; spewing out words like 'lust' and 'lechery' as if they were burning holes in his mouth. She hadn't been there for a decade, but her Catholic friend Theresa kept her up with it, faithfully reporting his latest spitfire sermon. If Father Patrick Maloney could forgive her, then God Himself would.

She checked her watch, broke into a run. If she really put a spurt on, she'd catch the thirty-four, make that vital detour to St Ursula's, and still be back in time to meet the children.

Ginny unlatched the battered door of drab St Ursula's, stepped into a plain and bare interior: stark white walls, harsh and glaring light. No beguiling gloom here, or soul-ensnaring glamour, but a strict no-nonsense building which didn't tangle God with art and artifice. The church was cold and empty, smelt of piety and damp. The few flowers on the altar looked unloved, their faded petals falling on the bare unpolished wood. Tacked up in the porch was a gilt-framed certificate proclaiming 'The Association of Total Abstinence'. It seemed symbolical, the furthest cry from Caldos and his total self-indulgence. Again, she tried to boot him out of church, as she lingered for a moment in the porch, inspecting the small rack of religious books and pamphlets: 'Thy Will Be Done', 'Rites and Rules for Life's Long Journey'.

Here were the sense and solidity she craved. She picked up a small book on sexual ethics and opened it at random: 'unbridled exaltation of sex', 'dissolute carnal union', 'unrestrained licentiousness'. These were the phrases she remembered, even Reverend Mother Mildred's favourite word, concupiscence. She found a lengthy section on masturbation – a word too blatant and disgusting for the nuns even to pronounce. As an innocent young girl, she'd thought it was some unfortunate disease, something like mastoid, or mastitis. Only in her twenties had she actually indulged in it. 'Masturbation is an intrinsically and seriously disordered act,' the pamphlet thundered out.

On and on it went. There was scarcely a sin she hadn't committed. Fornication, adultery – she never quite remembered which was which, but she was bound to have indulged in both – impure thoughts, corruption of morals, dissolute companions, gluttony, intemperance. They all seemed different ways of saying Caldos.

She slotted several coins into the box set in the wall. She'd better take the booklet home, as a shield and a remembrance. There was a row of other money-boxes, each labelled with a tag: 'For the

Homeless', 'For the Holy Souls in Purgatory'. She opened her purse again, removed her last remaining five-pound note, folded it in four, and stuck it firmly into the box marked 'Sinners'.

She paced slowly round the church, wondering if she should try to find the presbytery – and Father Patrick Maloney – or instead return on Saturday, when confessions were officially heard, according to the notice in the porch. But she might be dead by Saturday – dead and swiftly damned – run over by a lorry and sent straight into the arms of smirking Satan. The words of the catechism were chiming in her head: 'Our natural inclinations are prone to evil from our very childhood, and if not corrected by self-denial, they will certainly carry us to hell.' She stampeded down the aisle, back towards the porch. She'd had enough of hell, must find the priest and beg him to absolve her, in case she met her death on the way home.

'Who's there?' a peevish voice called, which stopped her in her tracks.

She swung round to see a shock of ginger hair, flaming from a florid face, which was peering at her sternly from a small connecting door which led into the sacristy. The jowled and fleshy neck was constrained by a tight dog-collar; the massive shoulders lost in a black cassock, now billowing towards her.

'What do you want?' the cassock growled.

'I'm sorry, Father, but I've made a false confession and I wish to put it right.'

The priest perked up immediately, as if his favourite pastime was condemning the iniquitous. 'It's not the proper time for confessions. If you abuse the sacraments, then you can't expect overworked and busy priests to rally round and bail you out.' He vanished for a moment, reappeared with a purple stole around his neck, obviously unable to resist a mortal sinner. He entered the confessional box, beckoned Ginny in. She cowered the other side, voice skulking in her shoes. The light was much less merciful than it had been in the Cathedral, and she could see the priest's grim narrowed eyes threatening through the grille. She began her saga tremulously.

'And how many times did you indulge in these forbidden acts?'

She paused. She and Caldos had never thought to count. Perhaps all erring Catholics should keep a secret record, like a freezer log. Three beef and mushroom casseroles, stewed 31 March; three hot devilled Caldoses, screwed 25 January. Though counting would be tricky. Did you tot each separate orgasm, or only count the sessions? And if you indulged in two consecutive bouts, one after the other, did you chalk up one, or two? Whichever way she counted, the numbers in her head were mounting up alarmingly, so she divided them by three. Even so, she knew she'd shocked the priest, who was breathing very heavily, as if trying to control himself.

'And did you have intercourse in ways forbidden by the Church?'

'Yes, Father.'

'Did any shameful acts take place?'

'Yes, Father.'

The priest paused in his interrogation, to lash her into self-disgust, his voice a flailing scourge. 'Spiritual neglect of your children . . . total disregard for your marriage vows . . . a web of lies and deception . . . sinful and self-indulgent contraception.'

Yes, she had admitted being on the Pill, but still not dared to broach the gonorrhoea. As she'd realised in the Cathedral, the vocabulary was perilous. If she said just brief 'VD', it might sound like some religious abbreviation. After all, the Jesuits signed themselves SJ, and Mary was often called the BVM. It could even be a new religious order – the Valiant Divines, or the Victorious Devotees. It would be terribly embarrassing if the priest failed to understand. He looked far too old and angry ever to have heard of Venus, yet venereal disease, spelt out, sounded blatant, almost blasphemous. She wasn't even certain that she had it, but safer to confess it, just in case. She'd know the worst tomorrow, but couldn't bear to face this church again after another gruelling session in the clinic, spoons and forks thrust up her private parts.

'Father, I . . . I think I may have contracted a sexual infection.' Contracted was a clever word. It sounded legal and somehow less deliberate. None the less, she still felt hopelessly debauched as she glimpsed his stern face through the grille, wrinkled up as if to guard against contagion. No joy in heaven yet, alas, but at least this was a real confession. No pastoral psychiatry, no namby-pamby lenience. Sexual infections were obviously rare in Norbiton, and he'd been saving up his spleen to deal with this one;

his disgusted voice lambasting her again, branding her vile body with a G – G for guilt and gonorrhoea, godlessness and greed.

'And for your penance, you will say the Stations of the Cross, and you will reflect on how your lewdness and iniquities have torn your Saviour's flesh and pierced His side, and how it was YOU' – Ginny jumped as he raised his voice dramatically – 'who nailed Him to the cross, YOU who crucified Him.'

She bowed her head, listened to the words of absolution. Once he'd finished, he began again in Latin, and her heart leapt up in joy and recognition as she heard the vital phrase she remembered from her childhood: '*Ego te absolvo.*' The priest might abominate her person, but the Latin was so ancient and inviolable, it made her feel infallibly forgiven, which no down-to-earth vernacular could ever do as well. She was sure God spoke in Latin when At Home.

'Amen,' she said, with feeling. The priest crossed himself and shot out of the confessional, as if he feared contamination; stomping back across the church and slamming the connecting door. She emerged herself, more shakily, checked her watch, then started on her penance, which seemed even more important than being home in time to make the children's tea. She thumbed swiftly through her missal to find the Stations of the Cross – prayers and readings from the Psalms were given for each station. 'Lord, thy hand presses me hard . . . my wounds stink and are corrupt, because of my foolishness. I am troubled, I am bowed down greatly; I go mourning all the day long. For my loins are filled with a loathsome disease, and there is no soundness in my flesh.'

How horribly appropriate it was, as if it had been written for herself alone. She looked up at the painting of Christ on the cross, blood dripping in gross gobbets from His anguished thorn-crowned head; His body racked, contorted – a slender body, palely white and hairless. She closed her eyes and forced herself to pray, as the image of another body – hulking, dark, and hirsute – stretched, equally contorted, on a black-pile Chelsea carpet.

'Oh, no!' she cried in torment. She'd had three separate absolutions in the space of one short day, the last of them in sacred solemn Latin, yet had still not banished Caldos from her heart.

19

De Roche was reclining on his own expensive leather couch in his stylish room at Harley Street. 'Come in,' he called to George.

'Oh, I do beg your pardon, Doctor . . .'

'Not at all, George, not at all. It's good for me to get the couch-eye view, for once, besides the fact it's really rather comfortable. I keep an electric blanket switched on in the winter, underneath this rug. Clever little ruse, I feel. There's nothing like a spot of heat for boosting one's reputation.'

'Dr de Roche, sir, I wondered . . .'

'What you need to understand, George, is that many of my patients have extremely complex feelings about the couch. One particular female (a titled head she was, in fact) refused categorically to lie on it for almost eighteen months, and when, at last, she succumbed, she wept uncontrollably for the entire fifty minutes, and confessed that she had dreaded yet desired to be seduced.' De Roche leant up on one elbow, glancing with approval at his new Italian kid-skin shoes. 'I always think it's rather droll that the couch is seen as vital, almost a symbol of our profession, yet one of the main reasons why dear Sigmund favoured it is because he hated being stared at by his patients – especially the disturbed ones, and especially all day long. He preferred to remove himself entirely from their range of vision, by sitting just behind them while they were lying down. That's always struck me as just a trifle paranoid – to be so patently uneasy about eye-contact – or maybe any other kind of contact. You probably won't believe this, George, but my own analyst confided to me, donkey's years ago, that Freud would never touch a female patient, and was actually quite terrified of sex – which is probably why he wrote about it so much. But then I suppose the arch-exponent of theories about neuroses ought to be allowed to have a few neuroses himself.'

George cleared his throat politely. 'Dr de Roche, I . . .'

'Mind you, the fact the analyst's out of sight has often been abused, of course. I mean, all those jokes about doctors grabbing forty winks while their patients ramble on, do have a grain of truth in them. One of my own colleagues actually defended it – said he always fell quite deeply asleep with one particular patient, who'd been coming four times every week for a good eight years or more. Apparently, she nodded off, as well, and they both slumbered very peacefully through a good half of the session. My colleague always claimed that this shared intimacy of "sleeping together" was highly therapeutic for his patient, recreated the mutual trust between an infant and its parent – you know, that vital mother/baby bond, which had been lacking in her earliest months of life. But a damned expensive sleep, I fear, since he was charging more than anyone else in Harley Street. Have a date.' Caldos gestured to a wooden crate weighing down his Queen Anne rosewood table. 'Fresh Israeli dates, George, sent direct from Tel Aviv this very morning. Present from a grateful patient – an insomniac, this time.' Caldos stuffed a handful into his mouth and spoke, with difficulty. 'Is this a social visit, George, or has the boiler blown up?'

'It's Miss Hammond, sir.'

Caldos spat out six small stones in swift succession, replaced them with six more dates. 'Miss Hammond's blown up? Surely not.'

'No, Doctor, it's . . .'

'You're fond of Miss Hammond, aren't you, George?'

'Well, yes, I must admit I . . .'

'Leave her alone, George, strictly alone. She's a difficult patient with a deep-seated desire to destroy herself. She's fixated all her infantile dependency needs upon me, sees me as a father. If you get involved as well, it will only confuse her, and may do positive harm. You've gone too far already.'

'I only thought . . . I mean, surely it won't hurt to have just a friendly chat with her, or the odd cup of tea together? After all, she's just a kid, and . . .'

'She's older than she acts, George. You shouldn't take her entirely at face value. Her case is much more complex than it seems. Look, old chap, you've proved absolutely first-rate in the job. Everybody's thrilled with you. You're marvellous with the patients, fantastic in emergencies, but don't get involved with Miss Hammond. Right? You don't know what you're up against. More dates?'

George shook his head and went on shaking it. He didn't like the way de Roche was turning Angela into some delinquent nut-case. The Doctor might be brilliant, but he was deluding himself if he thought he could act the father. That was his own role, and without blowing his own trumpet, he had to admit he'd played it pretty well. That night she'd spent downstairs in his flat had been something of a triumph. She'd slept through the whole night without a murmur, even managed a boiled egg for breakfast. He'd cut her toast into soldiers for her, the way he'd always done for Snookie, and dug out his best teapot, the one shaped like a cottage with roses running round the spout; told her how he'd had it thirty-seven years. He hadn't mentioned Bea. She'd had enough of death.

'I don't see how the occasional visit could do her any harm, Doctor. I could go to her place, maybe, just the odd weekend – show her someone cares.'

De Roche spat a date stone into an alabaster vase. '*I* care, professionally, George, and Miss Hammond is aware of that. I consider the subject closed. I'm doing everything I can for her at present, and I don't want any interference. You're untrained, inexperienced, and you don't even see the problems.'

George glanced up at the wall, where a portrait of the Doctor hung in a gilt frame; the crude and messy paint daubed on just at random, and bearing almost no resemblance to a human face at all. The skin was jaundice-yellow, the eyebrows wild black splodges, and the Doctor appeared to be suffering from a dislocated neck. It had probably been painted by some schizophrenic patient, who had delusions of grandeur but no shred of skill in art. Snookie had done better at her nursery school.

'Ah, you're admiring the Auerbach. Amazing likeness, isn't it? He only paints intimates, you know – family and rather special friends. Though, come to think of it, you'd make a good subject for Auerbach yourself. You've got a very splendid head, George, do you realise?'

George peered into the mirror which hung above the couch.

He'd never really thought about his head. He was lucky to have kept his hair, of course, and it had obliged him by turning a distinctive shade of silver. He sucked his cheekbones in, tried to see his artistic possibilities. But he could only see Miss Hammond, lonely and abandoned.

Caldos dislodged a piece of date skin from a tooth. 'I've no wish to circumscribe you, George. If you've got social-work ambitions, I can certainly make use of them. I'm aware you have potential, a natural gift for handling people, a genuine compassion, and all those things have commercial possibilities. Just give me time, and I'll make Mr Barnes a name worth reckoning with.'

He lazed up from the couch, sauntered to the bookcase and removed *Who's Who in the Arab World*, a weighty tome, bound in scarlet leather. George edged away a little, always found de Roche's books intimidating. Half the titles were double Dutch and the other half obscene. And it was bad enough working out who was who in Harley Street or Hinchley Wood, let alone Dubai.

Caldos shifted two more volumes, cursing to himself. 'I could have sworn I hid my bourbons underneath the Arabs. I've got an absolute passion for McVitie's bourbon biscuits, George. Aha – got 'em! The little buggers were lurking behind *Identity and Madness*.' Caldos lined up six biscuits in front of him, like dominoes, and tossed the rest to George. 'Look, old chap,' he confided, after a brief McVitie interval. 'I plan to expand my line of work, open it up, take on more patients, treat them in a different way. I'm bored with disembodied psyches – I want to treat people as integrated individuals, with bodies, souls, intellects, and appetites. I'll move them to a social setting, set up a Creative Living Centre, perhaps a sort of club for holistic health and happiness.'

George's mouth dropped open. Caldos plugged his own mouth with a bourbon. 'I'll need assistants, George, and they won't all be analysts, or even psychotherapists. Oh yes, we'll offer every therapy in the book, and a lot more out of it, but man cannot live by Freud alone. There'll also be masseurs, musicians, buskers, beauticians, dance and drama teachers, top French chefs and German philosophers, Indian gurus, herbalists, gymnasts – anyone who can make man whole and holy. Holiness and hedonism will be at last united.'

George glanced at the bookcase, where *Jane's Fighting Ships* and

147

Debrett's Peerage rubbed shoulders with P.G. Wodehouse. He never quite knew when de Roche was being serious. He was like his books, a mixture of the absurd and the sublime.

Caldos was building a castle out of biscuits. 'Solicitors have their legal executives, so surely I'm entitled to my therapeutic executives – and therapeutic in the wildest, widest sense of that as yet puny underdeveloped little word. You, George, would make a most creditable therapeutic executive on the horticultural side, bringing patients peace through plants. Ian tells me you're a whiz with the begonias. And begonias are far less hazardous than Miss Hammond.' He added a tower to his castle, which ignominiously collapsed. 'But if you want to help patients, the possibilities are endless – nature-study classes, still-life painting sessions, group creative gardening, back-to-the-soil regression schemes, dynamic flower arrangement, botany, biology, zoology . . . You could even help them overcome their snake and spider phobias. "How I learned to love Mr Barnes's boa-constrictors!" No, seriously, George, patients are people first, and people need more in their lives than fifty minutes on the couch, and a few high-powered monosyllables from an aloof and distant analyst.'

'You don't get many snakes in West One,' George ventured, gazing out at grey pavements and grim railings. 'And we haven't got a garden.'

'But my dear chap, we'll certainly be moving. This scheme requires luxurious new premises, somewhere extensive and exclusive. A promotion, George, a smart new address, a step up in the world. You've proved yourself already in this job. You're everybody's blue-eyed boy. Why waste all that potential? You've dealt with people in Insurance all your life. Why stop now? You need stretching, George, developing. Look, old chap, I've simply got to toddle. We'll talk about it later and I'll fill you in on spider phobias. We'll start on your metamorphosis right away.' He twirled his coat around his shoulders like a bull-fighter, waved at George and billowed through the door.

George strutted grandly back to his apartment, already a budding Horticultural Therapeutic Executive. It took a man like de Roche to recognise his gifts. The good Doctor had believed in him right from the start, rescued him from premature retirement, from cribbage and carpet slippers and bingo in the church hall. Ginny was a grand girl, no doubt about it, but she couldn't understand there was more to life than making rabbit hutches out of orange-boxes, or popping down to Safeway's for half a pound of lard.

He was smiling as he dialled Hinchley Wood. 'Ginny?' he boomed, appraising his artistic head in the mirror in the hall.

'Mummy's out,' said Sarah. 'She's always out now.'

'Ssh!' warned Ian, grabbing the receiver. 'Hello Dad. How's things?'

'Grand! In actual fact, I'm going to be . . .'

'Ginny did intend to phone you, but she's at an evening-class. She's studying Renaissance Art with some old school-chum she bumped into at Selfridges. Somewhere in Chelsea, I think she said. She's up to her neck in it.'

'Do her good! She ought to get out more. She hasn't been up here for an age, and last time I saw her, she was looking very peaky. She'd put all that muck on her face – you know, rouge and stuff. But I wasn't born yesterday. She was as white as a sheet underneath. Is she eating enough?'

Ian thought back to their last meal, and remembered he'd cooked it himself. His cooking was improving. 'No,' he grumbled. 'She should have gone to cookery classes. She's out of her depth with all that Renaissance stuff.'

'Nonsense, son. We all need stretching. I may be embarking on a spot of scholarship myself – horticulture, botany, boa-constrictors – even a little psychiatry perhaps. Ian, for heaven's sake, stop *laughing*.'

20

Ginny gambolled up the stone steps from the clinic, humming a happy catchy tune, which had only four brief words to it: 'I haven't got it.' She repeated them again, again, declaring to the sky, the road, the traffic, and the whole of Greater London that she hadn't hadn't hadn't hadn't got it. She skipped around the corner, crossed the road to the tube. 'I haven't got it,' she confided to the ticket machine, almost hugging the West Indian standing at the barrier. She glided down the escalator, trilling the same glorious refrain to a brooding Julie Christie on a poster. '"No gonorrhoea present." I saw the words myself, written on my form.' It was all right to use that shameful term – the train had just roared in and drowned her voice. She found an empty seat, glanced up at the advertisements.

'I haven't got it,' she informed the lady from the Brook Street Bureau.

'Bad luck! You should have tried us first. We Got Big By Bothering.'

She grinned, didn't care if no one understood how utterly ecstatic she was feeling – saved, safe, healthy, clean, reprieved. 'Haven't got it,' sang the train, as it swaggered along the rails. 'Haven't haven't got it,' crooned the escalator, depositing her at Waterloo main station. Her train was in already. She climbed into a carriage and introduced herself: new-model Ginny Barnes, loving mother, faithful wife, totally devoted to family and home, speeding back there even now to darn socks, dust shelves, make spice cake and profiteroles. (She'd already bought the cocoa and the cinnamon.)

They sped past Clapham Junction and she waved to a factory chimney belching smoke; beamed at dirty terraced houses with flower-gardens of shirts and pants fluttering from their washing-lines. The high-rise flats had never looked so elegant, their stained grafittied concrete shining in the wan but valiant sun. They passed a sprawling cemetery, and even the graves seemed cosy and convivial, crowded companionably together and shaded by solicitous trees.

'I haven't got it,' she hollered through the window to a large white marble angel, weeping on a tombstone, then got a pad and pencil out and made a shopping-list. She'd buy best rump steak for supper, and coley for the cats, chocolates for the children, a good red wine for Ian. And real leaf tea (again), and decent Kenya coffee, and half a dozen dusters, and . . .

She collapsed in a heap of parcels in the hall, surveyed the house in horror. She'd certainly neglected things. The silver needed cleaning, and there were cobwebs on the curtains. Why didn't she spring-clean? It wasn't really spring yet, but it felt like it inside. She could turn out all the cupboards, defrost the fridge, wash the sheets and blankets. She'd start on the fridge, then the ice could be melting while she stripped the beds upstairs. She was shocked to see its contents – hardly remembered buying all that junk-food: congealing cardboard curries, half-eaten Instant Whip. She flung them in the waste-bin, grimacing at a half-full can of some evil-looking liquid, labelled 'Country Vegetable Soup', which had clearly never seen the country in its life. She scoured the shelves with Cleen-O-Pine, to remove not just the germs, but her own laziness and negligence. It would be back to normal now – decent home-made meals, with not a chemical in sight, a freezer packed with goodies, a larder full of love.

She rested for a moment, glancing round the kitchen – both the cats purring by the cooker, the battered biscuit tin with its portrait of the Queen, Snookie's drawing of a dragon pinned to the larder door, legs lopsided and grease spots on its scales. 'FEERCE DRAGON' said the caption underneath – though it looked less fierce than friendly. Caldos would scoff because the china wasn't Spode, and the saucepans came from Woolworths, and Toby's only trace of pedigree was a vaguely spaniel look around the ears. But how could she explain that this shabby mongrel kitchen was both beautiful and precious? Sarah was growing cress on a pair of Aertex knickers, and Snookie had made a rabbit out of empty toilet rolls, and Ian had put the shelves up, and George had fixed the blinds, and she was queen of it all.

She blew a kiss to the dragon and zipped upstairs to start clearing out the wardrobes. She'd begin with darling Ian's. She'd hurt him most and owed him most, though thank God he'd never discovered her affair. She'd try to make it up to him by strengthening her marriage, as the first priest had advised, showering him with gratitude and love, never looking at another man again.

She took out all his clothes – baggy corduroy trousers, worn and shabby suits, hanging forlornly on their hangers, like Ian without his stuffing. They even smelt of Ian, a faint elusive smell of bonfire and wet dog. Her lover's scent was more potent altogether – 'Eau Sauvage' and strong cigars – and he would have a hundred suits in some vast majestic wardrobe, not Ian's pathetic three, and somehow they'd hang solid – puffed-out and three-dimensional, not flat and limp like these. Oh, if only she could rid herself of that terrible tenacious man, who seemed to have no qualms at all about intruding in their bedroom, even crouching in her husband's private wardrobe. She turfed him out, along with two left insoles and a broken wooden hanger, then started on the drawers.

'Haven't got it, haven't got it,' she was still humming to herself, Jack Jones harmonising as he sang a different number on the bedroom radio. The bottom drawer was jammed, Ian's thick-knit cricket sweater bundled in on top, which appeared to be preventing it from opening. Strange, she thought, as she tried to work it free – Ian hadn't played cricket since the summer. At last, the drawer jerked open, and she released the crumpled jersey, heard the faintest rustle underneath her hands. Hidden right inside its folds was a dark green Harrods bag. That was stranger still. Ian ventured into Harrods only once a year, to buy her Christmas present. He loathed the shop, feared its ritzy prices, and this Christmas he'd cried off, given her a Marks & Spencer's nightdress, a pink one with long sleeves. She'd been disappointed, actually, liked the Harrods label, even if no one saw it but the cats.

She opened the bag, unfolded swathes of tissue, stared in shock at two wicked wisps of black seductive lace – the top transparent, and slit almost to the waist; the shameless pants so scanty they'd have barely covered a thimble. She jabbed her finger roughly through the crotch, remembering a letter she'd read in Kate's last *Cosmo* – a frantic Mrs B. of Borehamwood, who'd found her husband dressing up in bras and frilly nighties. Could her own husband be the same, have secret sexual problems, want to be a girl? No, the truth was much more terrible – Ian must *have* a girl – some sultry piece who drove him wild with her exotic sexy lingerie.

She sank down on the carpet, utterly incredulous – patient, plodding Ian with his leather patches and his limp and drooping penis. But perhaps his penis only drooped because he'd worn it out with some brazen nymphomaniac, and his exhaustion every night was nothing to do with pay structures or pension-protection schemes, as he tried glibly to convince her; but simply a result of stolen hours in another woman's bed. She checked the black lace top. Despite its skimpiness, the bust-size was a large one. The Other Woman probably had huge breasts – a Page-Three girl, or a latter-day Jane Russell. No wonder Ian was stricken.

Yet it still seemed so unlikely. Ian preferred gardening to girls, and was home most nights by six. Though perhaps he was playing truant from his work, enjoying a 'siesta' after lunch, risking their whole livelihood by absconding from the job. He must be up to something. Why else would he hide lingerie inside his cricket sweater? Their usual hiding-place for presents was a suitcase in the loft, which they'd been using now for years. She rummaged in the Harrods bag, still baffled, found the bill crumpled at the bottom, gasped as she unfolded it. No one in his senses would spend that sort of money on a nightdress, least of all Ian. He must be totally besotted with the girl, must have lost his reason. What a swine he was, allowing her to suffer so much torment over her own modest infidelity, while he went in for the big time with three-figure Harrods call-girls; urging her to buy the cheapest Cheddar and to economise on coal, so he could lavish all his salary on an overgrown scrubber with pretensions. She screwed up the nightie into a furious little ball, hurled it at the wardrobe door. Why waste her time sprucing up his clothes, so some tainted little trollop could take them off again?

She stumbled to the phone, tears sheeting down her face. 'Kate, I . . .'

'What on earth's the matter, Ginny? Have you hurt yourself?'

'No, it's Ian. He . . .' She couldn't speak, couldn't find the words for Ian's betrayal.

'Well, what? Has he had an accident, or . . . ? I'm sorry, I can't hear you, love. Look, I'm coming round, okay? Give me just two ticks.'

They sat in the damp kitchen, soggy peas and sausages defrosting all around them, water drip-drip-dripping from the fridge on to the floor. There were constant cracking noises from the ice-box, then sudden startling thuds as lumps of ice cascaded to the floor. Ginny's tears were diluting her pint-sized mug of coffee-laced-with-brandy, which Kate had just concocted.

Kate swigged her brandy neat. 'You're such an innocent. Alan's been sleeping around for bloody years. I'm afraid it's simply the nature of the beast. I must admit I'm a bit surprised at Ian, but it only goes to show how men are all the same. Better to accept it, grit your teeth and look the other way.'

'But Kate, I'm *not* an innocent, you don't understand.'

Kate drained her brandy glass, reached out for a biscuit. 'You're innocence incarnate, duckie. You've never looked at another guy in fifteen spotless years. You read *Lady's Journal* instead of *Cosmopolitan*. You fill Ian up with Ovaltine and home-made treacle sponge, then wonder why he sweats off all that excess energy on private little work-outs in the sack. You should be harder on him, Ginny – ease off the flapjacks and start on the flirting – with someone else, I mean.'

'But that's exactly what I have done.' She dared not look at Kate, stared intently at the label on a bag of thawing corn.

'*What?*'

'I've been having an affair since Christmas,' she confessed.

'Ginny, you utterly amaze me!' Kate was on her feet now, her voice strident and appalled. 'There I am, rambling on each week about my latest little fling, and you never say a single word, let me think you're living like a nun. Yet all the time you're rutting away as wildly as the rest of us. You might at least have told me, trusted me, for God's sake.'

'You know I trust you, Kate. It's just that . . .'

'What?'

'Well, you always take these things so sort of . . . casually. To you it's all a game, but to me it's real and terrible. I feel everything's collapsing round my ears. I don't know what to do. I'm in love with both of them.'

Kate poured another tot of brandy for them both. 'Get one thing straight, my girl – it's nothing to do with love. You'll only get hurt if you bring feelings into it. It's just a matter of urges – modern marriage, if you like. He has his black lace floozie and you have your . . . Hey, who the hell *is* this mysterious man?'

Ginny dodged the question. 'I can't live like that, Kate. It's so cold-blooded and clinical. I feel guilty all the time, and I'm having ghastly nightmares, waking up at three A.M. and screaming. And I can't decide whether to tell Ian or not. Perhaps it would be kinder to come clean.'

'Absolutely not! That's sheer emotional indulgence. It's far more mature to say nothing and do everything. Oh, make him his meringues if you really feel you must, but enjoy your bit on the side. Guilt's outmoded these days, belongs to an old morality which has lost its point and . . .'

Ginny interrupted. 'That's what Caldos says.'

'Who?'

'Caldos de Roche. My mysterious man, as you put it.'

'Oh, good God! I'm beginning to see the light. Well, I suppose it's better than some dread disease. If you really want to know, I was getting quite concerned – thought you'd found a lump.'

'It's worse than any lump.' Ginny mopped her eyes with the black lace extravaganza, which she'd brought down to show to Kate. 'And another little problem – what do I do with *this*?'

'Nick it! And wear it in bed to turn on what's-his-name. Or take it back to Harrods and demand your money back – tell them Great-Aunt Ethel didn't think it suitable, then splurge all the lovely cash on chocolate creams. Serve him right!'

Ginny didn't laugh, had no wish to join her mocking friend in a cosy web of secret infidelities, to dump love and trust in the waste-bin, along with the Instant Whip. She felt horribly alone, cut off from everyone – from cunning calculating Ian, who hid his lust (and lingerie), pretended to be faithful; from casual Kate, who made sex sound like a stud, and even from Caldos, who scorned her suburban stronghold, and wanted her bigger, brighter, bolder, than she was. But maybe she'd maligned him. Perhaps she *was* unappreciated, as Caldos always claimed – cooking and cleaning for a sly deceitful husband, who kept complaining about the mortgage rate, while pouring money down the drain of some ungrateful little tart. And then blaming her lover for horrible diseases which she might well have caught from Ian. She hadn't slept with Caldos for a fortnight, had almost turned her back on him and torn him from her life, for the sake of a bare-faced hypocrite who didn't know the meaning of fidelity or trust.

'Look Kate, I can't face Ian, or even the children. I feel absolutely torn to shreds.'

Kate proffered the brandy bottle. 'Okay, I'll fetch the kids. It's my turn anyway, and they can stay the night at my place. Why not just flake out, put yourself to bed with a double one of these?'

'I couldn't sleep a wink. And Ian's home early tonight. What on earth am I going to say to him?'

'Nothing. I've told you, Ginny, absolutely nix. Put that nightie back for the moment, exactly as you found it. And then get the hell out.'

'Out where?'

'What about your doctor friend? Won't he welcome you with open arms?'

'I'm not too sure. He's always very busy and I've been sort of . . . unavailable.'

'Well, ring him up and tell him the red light's off and you're raring to go and randy as all hell.' Kate removed her brown suede boot from a rivulet of icy water. 'Honestly, my love, it's like Alice and the Pool of Tears in here, what with you sobbing one end and that beastly fridge flooding the whole floor. Whatever made you start it in the first place? Women don't normally defrost their fridges just because their husbands are having an affair. It would take more that that to make me tackle mine.' She found a kitchen-mop, stabbed the floor halfheartedly, the water rippling further out, trickling under furniture, trapping Ginny's feet. Kate lunged with the mop again, knocked a bag of frozen peas from the work-top to the floor; five whole pounds of garden peas showering, bouncing, rolling, sliding, skittering.

'Shit!' said Kate, letting out a guffaw. 'Well, I suppose it would make a good game for the kids – asking them all to guess how many peas in a sodding five-pound bag. I'd say approximately two million.' She extracted one survivor from the bottom of the bag. 'Two million and one,' she grinned.

Ginny hid her head in her hands. 'I just don't understand, Kate, how you can laugh at everything.'

'I don't have much alternative. No point sitting here discussing Life's Black Comedy in a swamp of peas and water. Quick! Go and fetch a broom. You sweep and I'll mop.'

Kate worked fast, peas and water capitulating. She flung sausages and vegetables back into the fridge, slammed the door, then tried to wrest Ginny from her broom. 'Come on, misery, I'm going to lend you my best red dress, slap a bit of gunge on your face, and pack you off to your medico for a spot of instant resuscitation. I suggest you ask him for the kiss of life.'

'We've missed some peas,' moaned Ginny. 'There's a whole load more underneath the table.'

'Sod the bloody peas! Ian can pick them up. He'll be all alone this evening, so he'll need something to amuse him.' Kate steered her friend with one hand, snatched the brandy bottle with the other, marched both to the door. 'And he doesn't deserve the Courvoisier. *I'*ll look after that!'

21

'Estrella, you look quite sensational! I simply wasn't aware your wardrobe boasted such attire.'

Kate had done a marvellous job – tacked in her own red vamp-dress a good three inches either side, so Ginny looked all curves; scooped up her hair on top, and sprayed it with her bottled Golden Glints; transformed her tear-stained face with blusher, shiner, gloss, and turned her into a most successful tart.

De Roche approved of tarts. 'Bright colours really suit you, my enchantress. I don't know why you always try to lose yourself in those dreary fawns and browns. And that dress is simply stunning – seems a shame to take it off.'

She was naked underneath it. Kate had insisted, and she'd felt too worn down to argue. Caldos kissed her nipples lingeringly, then pressed her naked body against his fully clothed one. Her breasts became soft cashmere, her thighs rough nubbly corduroy. Suddenly, he slapped her bottom, hard. She gasped and pulled away. He'd left an angry mark, branded right across her buttocks.

'You're a wicked faithless woman,' he said, smiling. 'Wicked and enchanting. You left me quite bereft for fifteen days, and I think you should be punished – very exquisitely punished.' He was still fully dressed, but she could feel the hard excitement of his body as he embraced her for a moment, then swept her through the door, and along the passage to the bedroom. She had never seen his bedroom, never made love anywhere but the carpet in the drawing-room. He laid her on the bed, an impressive bed with a luxurious black fur rug thrown casually across it, and an antique dark-oak headboard, carved with a cornucopia, disgorging fruits and flowers. Fur caressed her naked back, as she glanced around the room, which was large and dimly lit; a mural covering one whole wall, depicting strange and shadowy figures, half-human and half-beast. He seemed to own no normal bedroom furniture, such as chests of drawers, or wardrobes, only a bureau with more sculptures on, and a computerised chess-set laid out on a low mahogany table. Two saw-toothed ferns in copper pots threw spiky shadows on the sombre dark-toned ceiling. The room smelt male – a smell of musk, cigar smoke.

Caldos was standing by the bed, absolutely motionless, watching her, appraising her, following her gaze. Slowly, he approached her, turned her on her stomach, then arranged her as he wanted – face down, back humped up. Even now, he didn't take his clothes off, remained detached and somehow distant, only his voice seductive as he whispered '*Mia dolcissima*'. She closed her eyes, waited for his tongue to lick a magic stairway from the nape of her neck to the last bone of her spine. Instead, a stinging blow strafed across her buttocks. She struggled and cried out.

'*Dolce, tigretta mia.*'

Never before had she heard his voice so gentle, his soft bewitching kisses like a bandage on the blow. She let herself relax, accept the healing balsam of his lips, but the swingeing stroke burned into her flesh once more, the angry thwack of metal on bare skin. Again, he cancelled it with soft alluring words, distracting her by kissing every finger, his tongue gliding very gently up and down between the knuckles, then circling all the tips, suckling them like nipples. It was so sensuous, exquisite, she was almost off her guard again, spread-eagled on her stomach now, voluptuous fur tickling on her breasts. Then suddenly, abruptly, he was beating her and beating her, and she was scalded with sharp shocks of pain – pain which had a rhythm of its own. Her mind was being quenched inside her body, her body lashed into wild white-hot subservience. Every time she tried to speak, or surface, the dazzling pain caught up with her again, flung her into an unresisting frenzy. She had become the rhythm – responding to it, crying out in time with it, accepting it, surrendering, almost troubled when it stopped. The last blow was the fiercest, stinging through her body, leaving her on fire. She turned slowly round to look at him. His eyes were shut, his face closed off, that blank impassive countenance contrasting with the arousal of his body; a proud Adolfo pushing out his tight black corduroy trousers.

'Undress me,' he commanded. She struggled with his sweater, the stiff buckle of his belt, feeling clumsy and inept; tried to shrink away when he handed her the silver-backed hairbrush, embossed with fleurs-de-lis, which seemed too elegant, innocuous, to have made those ruthless marks across her buttocks.

'Punish me, my witch.' His voice was pleading, servile. She had never known her lover plead for anything, just seize it as his right. And he looked undignified and vulnerable, lying on the bed face-down, his bottom thrust towards her. Impossible to punish him. Not only did it feel quite wrong – and frightening – but she didn't have the strength. Her backbone was a sagging scarlet ribbon, her ribs just broken shells.

'Estrella!'

The voice was now imperious. She dared not disobey, brought the brush down, hard, across his back; heard him sigh with pleasure and relief. 'Harder,' he said tersely.

She shut her eyes, couldn't bear to see; kept beating with the brush's silver back, appalled to hear his frantic cries of pleasure, wild discordant cries, jarring through the room. She tried to find a rhythm, to alternate hard with soft, and fast with slow, as he had done himself; to move out of her head and stop caring how absurd she looked, how incompetent she felt. There was a skill in it – a skill she didn't have.

'Hold me,' Caldos whispered, and guided her free hand towards Adolfo, who began to move beneath her hand in the same counterpointed rhythm, as his body heaved and flinched beneath the blows. There was no music to help out, no ecstatic soaring choir or yearning woodwind; only his strident cries, his heavy rasping breathing. She longed for him to quieten, so she could rest, or run away; found it very difficult to co-ordinate her hands – one gentle, one relentless; abhorred the cruel red weals across his back. Then, suddenly, she realised he was coming, her left hand moving faster as Adolfo flailed against it like a wild and struggling bird trapped within her palm, determined to break free. She could barely hold the bird – he was too strong for her, too violent – making one last frenzied effort, then fluttering back and down, as if stunned, or even slaughtered, oozing hot wet sticky blood between her fingers.

She dropped the hairbrush like a stone, crept into the bathroom, scoured both hands, kept scrubbing them and scrubbing them, her body chilled and shaking. When, at last, he came for her, his hair was combed, his face composed, his dark and hulking nakedness concealed in a silk dressing gown; the smell of sweat and semen banished by the lemon tang of soap. He picked her up, as if she were a child, carried her along the passage, laid her very gently on the sofa in the drawing-room. His hands were now so careful she felt that she was made of wings; some fragile injured moth he only dared to handle with the lightest glancing touch. His lips whispered on her eyelids, murmured against the insides of her wrists. She felt her body sinking back, her bruised mind letting go, heard his voice like cream, or silk, feeding her, assuaging.

'*Dolcissima*,' he murmured, and suddenly the cruel remorseless rhythm was thrashing through the room again, and she was accepting it, surrendering, and she realised with a thrill of shame that never in her life again would she wholly block it out.

22

'How dare you stay out all night! How dare you, how dare you! Worrying me sick and making me look an absolute fool in front of that sluttish friend of yours.' Ian was pacing round the kitchen, fists clenched, face pale and tense, lunging out at Toby if he dared get in his way.

'Kate's not a slut,' said Ginny, still trembling by the door. 'You should be very grateful to her. I was called away urgently and no one else would take the children just like that.'

'They're round there far too often. I don't approve of it. She swears in front of them and stuffs them full of Lucozade and chips. And what the hell do you mean "you were called away"? It's not the story *I* heard.'

'Oh, really? So what did Kate tell *you*, then?'

'Some rubbish about your Renaissance evening-class, and the teacher being taken ill.'

'Well, that's exactly what I said. I had to go and help out.'

'I've never heard of evening-classes going on till dawn, and anyway the day's wrong. Perhaps it's slipped your mind, Ginny, but your classes are Tuesdays and Thursdays – or have been up to now. And why the hell should you help out? You're hardly qualified to teach the Renaissance, are you? I don't know what you're up to, but I don't like it at all. I've been awake the whole damned night, waiting for a phone-call. God Almighty! You didn't even leave a note, explaining where you were. And there was no supper I could find – just a fridgeful of defrosting peas, and more peas on the floor. I almost broke my bloody neck on them. And when I went upstairs to change, I found all my clothes scattered on the bed, drawers left open, the bedroom like a tip.'

Ginny slumped, exhausted, at the table. Never once, in fifteen years of marriage, had Ian raised his voice like that, displayed such outraged fury. Tears fell through her fingers on the bare scrubbed pine. Ian sank down beside her, reached out a weary hand. 'I'm sorry, Ginny, I didn't mean to shout. I've been in such a state about you, imagining you were dead, or . . . Look, darling, I just couldn't help wondering all those endless hours . . . I mean, where in God's name *were* you all damned night?'

Ginny shut her eyes. The glare of Caldos' red silk dressing gown was burning through her cheeks. 'I . . . I missed the last train. I had to stay the night with Eileen.'

'Who's Eileen?'

Black fur sticky with white sperm, bare body lashed and branded. 'Ian, you *know* who she is – the girl I go to classes with.'

'Well, *I*'ve never laid eyes on her. You're always raving on about her, but you never bring her home. Why not invite her back one night, so I can see what I've been missing? And you still haven't bothered to explain why you couldn't pick the phone up.'

'Eileen doesn't have a phone. I . . . I did ask Kate to . . . to tell you.' Black Chelsea walls closing in around her, eyes stinging like her body.

'Oh, hell, don't cry. I hate it when you cry. I didn't mean to make you so upset. I'm tired, that's all, completely bloody whacked. And concerned about the two of us. We're growing apart – can't you see that, Ginny? Okay, it's my fault partly. I'm so wrapped up in my work, it can't be too much fun for you, stuck home here all the time. It's only natural that you should want to get out more, make some sort of life for yourself. That's fine with me. I understand. But don't leave me out completely, will you, darling? Look' – he got up from his chair, put his arms around her – 'let's try to get back closer, do more things together, talk to each other more.'

She pulled away. His blue-striped towelling dressing gown felt rough against her breasts – yes, even through her clothes – breasts sore and chafed already. She and Caldos had made love again last night – love and hate, love and frantic pain. She glanced at the white V of chest above his open-necked pyjamas; a narrow hairless chest. Could she ever let Ian touch her after that blazing night with Caldos, and her shameful frightening pleasure in the pain? And what about his own affair? Had she got it wrong about

163

the nightdress? He appeared to care, to need her, seemed nothing like a husband who was betraying her himself. She fiddled with the buckle of her mac, longed to take it off in the hot and stuffy kitchen, yet how could she reveal herself in Kate's tarty low-necked dress? She could hardly think at all. Her mind was battered, bumbling; the beginnings of a headache hammering in her skull. She leant across, kissed the pale white V.

Ian took both her hands, squeezed them in his own. 'Let's forget about last night, darling – kiss and make up.'

Kiss. The word didn't sound the same on Ian's lips, nor feel anything the same. Even so, her lips hurt – had been over-used last night.

Ian unbuttoned his pyjama jacket, slipped her hand inside it. 'Hey, I've got a good idea. Let's ask your mother to have the girls this Saturday, and I'll take you up to London. I've got to go to Harrods to return something, but if you came too, we could really make a day of it – have lunch out in a pub, or a wander by the Serpentine.'

'Harrods?' Ginny's voice was dangerous.

'Yes, Harrods. What's the problem? I made a mistake with a Christmas present and I want to take it back. I could buy you a new dress or something while we're in the shop. Oh, I know it's rather extravagant, but why don't we splash out for once? You'd like that, wouldn't you?'

'I'd hate it and I *hate* Harrods.' The plates trembled on the dresser as the door crashed to behind her.

Ian shrugged and let her go. He couldn't understand his wife. She must have overstrained herself with too much studying. It was quite pathetic, really, all those books on heavy opera, when all she ever listened to was musicals, and struggling with Italian grammar, and French and German literature, when she'd never learnt a language in her life. Her convent hadn't been too hot on the academic side – Lourdes rather than Oxbridge. She was clearly trying to compensate, catch up in her thirties on what she'd missed at seventeen; or perhaps she felt inferior compared with her friend Eileen, who'd been head girl or something, and won a scholarship. He didn't warm to Eileen. She sounded bossy and self-satisfied, and was clearly irresponsible. He stretched and sighed, mooched over to the sink and filled the kettle. He'd make a cup of coffee and perhaps they'd both calm down.

'Coffee up, darling!'

Ginny slammed the door upstairs, as furious with Ian now as he had been with her. So his spoilt little minx of a mistress wanted something better, did she? A billion-dollar nightie simply wasn't good enough. Or perhaps it was a shade too tight across her D-cup breasts, and she'd ordered Ian to change it for a double E. The cheek of it! Expecting his wife to tag along, while he prowled around the lingerie department, with his fancy woman's cast-offs on display to everyone; chewing over her all too vital statistics with any smirking salesgirl who would listen. And then rewarding her with lunch – warm beer and a sandwich for boring Mrs Barnes, while Miss Voluptuous drowned herself in caviare and claret. And how about his promise of a dress? That was merely guilt, a blandishment to keep her sweet, stifle her suspicions, even buy her silence. It really was preposterous – almost too preposterous for Ian. Could he really change his basic personality? He'd never looked at another girl since the day of their engagement. Perhaps it was the start of the male menopause, a last wild fling before final impotence and hardening of the arteries and a bungalow in Eastbourne.

She couldn't go to Harrods anyway. Saturday was Transformation Day. A top-to-toe treatment, Caldos had called it – nothing sexual this time, but a whole day being pampered in a Bond Street beauty salon. Her lover wished to banish the last traces of drab Ginny, and summon forth the true Estrella, brilliant, blonde and beautiful. He'd told her she had beauty, but it was imprisoned in a tower and needed helping out. He put things so romantically, but she suspected what he really meant was that he'd rather not be spotted with a suburban little nobody whose fawn and boring clothes and face matched her fawn and boring mind. He'd prefer to have her gift-wrapped, so Bond Street would be paid to do the wrapping.

She couldn't really blame him. Saturday was special – the evening of the Gala, when they'd be sitting in the conductor's box, dressed up to the nines. Caldos knew conductors and composers like other people knew their hairdresser or butcher. They'd been invited to have dinner with the maestro afterwards, a really ritzy dinner, with several famous singers present; and Caldos had cajoled her to spend the whole weekend with him in Chelsea. A cold sausage in a pub and a tramp around the Serpentine simply couldn't compare.

The door opened very warily – Ian, with coffee in two Snoopy mugs, peering at her nervously, as if he feared she might explode again. She kept her voice as frosty as she could. 'I'm sorry, Ian, but I'm afraid Saturday's not on. I'll be away on a Renaissance weekend study course. They only let us know last night, and it's essential that I go. The subject's one we're doing at our classes – "The Influence of Masaccio on Filippino Lippi".' Caldos had suggested that, though she had a horrible suspicion she'd got their names the wrong way round, and that it was Filippino Lippi who'd influenced Masaccio.

'Who?' asked Ian, banging down his mug.

'Filippino Lippi,' she repeated, with a touch of condescension. 'He's absolutely crucial.'

'I've always managed well enough without him. And anyway, you've just told me that your teacher's lying delirious on her sick-bed, so how the hell's she meant to cope with this Philippino chappie?'

'Oh, *she* doesn't teach it. She's only an ordinary BA. There's a brilliant professor, coming all the way from Italy. That's why it's residential, so we get more chance to talk to him – stay up late, continue our discussions over meals – all that sort of thing.' Caldos had primed her well.

'Why this sudden scorn for ordinary BAs? You used to be impressed by mine. Nothing seems to please you any more.'

'Leave me alone, Ian, can't you? Do you have to begrudge me my measly bit of learning? You had all yours the easy way, and now you're trying to stop me enjoying even one weekend.'

Ian stared at all the photos on the dressing table – Snookie in a party frock, Sarah in a tutu, both girls as bashful bridesmaids, both girls in fancy dress. Ginny had made all those clothes, sometimes sewed until the early hours if she was making half the costumes for a play. There was truth in what she'd said – she hadn't had a lot of time for studying.

'Okay, you've got a point. I don't want to be unreasonable. Tell you what, if the course is not too far away, why don't I drive you there myself? We could take the children too, make it a real outing, find a bed-and-breakfast place and join you in the evenings.'

'No . . . er . . . children aren't allowed. And the . . . the evenings are all booked, Saturday especially. It's the climax of the course, you see. The Professor plans to show some slides of really rare unusual works, which no one's ever seen before, not outside Ravenna. Actually, I was hoping you might offer to take the children off my hands, so I can relax for once, and know they'll be okay – especially as you don't approve of Kate.' Ginny drained her coffee, wiped her mouth. That blatant black lace nightie made lying much less difficult. 'In fact, if you plan to go to Harrods, why not take them with you? They'd love to see the pet department, and you could buy them cakes or something in the Food Hall.' That would put him in a spot – trying to dispose of his girlfriend's lurid scanties with two eagle-eyed daughters in tow. Why shouldn't *he* feel guilty for a change?

'Okay,' said Ian, without conviction, peering gloomily into the bottom of his mug. The landing clock struck eight. 'Christ!' he yelped, springing to his feet. 'I've missed the 8.08.' He dragged off his pyjama top, started hunting for a shirt, discarded two with buttons missing, and scrambled into a third. He faltered up to Ginny, buttons still undone. 'I hate leaving you like this, darling, when we haven't settled anything, and I know you're still upset. Why don't we – you know – make it up, have a little cuddle?'

'What, now?'

'Mm.' He slipped off his pyjama bottoms, pressed himself against her.

'I thought you said you were late.'

'I am. But another fifteen minutes won't make that much difference. I can always tell Holsworth there was a breakdown on the line.'

Ginny backed away, clutched her mac around her. Headaches, periods, stomach pains – she'd used them all before. Ian seemed quite perverse, only showing interest at the most inconvenient times, when he was late and irritable, and she was sated, spent. But if she didn't try to humour him, she might lose her precious Saturday, and Filippino Caldos Lippi. Reluctantly, self-consciously, she unbelted her green mac.

'What on earth's that dress you're wearing, Ginny? I've never seen it before.'

'I . . . borrowed it from Kate. I spilt coffee on my skirt, just before I left.'

'I hate you wearing Kate's clothes. They make you look really cheap and vulgar. I told you we should go to Harrods, buy you something decent.'

'Oh, don't start that again, Ian.'

'Okay, but promise me you won't wear Kate's old cast-offs.'

'Cast-offs? I'll have you know this dress cost a packet. Kate bought it at a . . .'

'Ginny! Where's your bra, for God's sake? I suppose you've burnt it, have you, joined the Women's Lib brigade – pinched that from Kate, as well?'

Sarcasm was wasted. Ginny wasn't listening. She was clutching at the dress in desperation, before Ian could drag it off. She'd totally forgotten she was naked underneath. Even women's libbers didn't burn their pants, and how on earth could she explain those lurid weals criss-crossing her bottom?

'Hold on a minute, darling. I must pop to the loo. I'm desperate after all your lovely coffee.'

She locked the bathroom door, removed the dress, then twisted round, so she could check the angry marks. They hadn't faded much, still looked red and raised. Could she say she'd fallen, had some sort of accident; or pretend to faint, lose consciousness, so she wouldn't need to speak at all, but could be carried to her bed? She paced up and down the bathroom like a small caged nervous animal, praying for deliverance. Perhaps the postman would rat-tat with a parcel or a telegram. They'd won the pools and the photographers and pressmen were already panting on the step. Or the telephone would ring: Ian's boss had had a heart attack, so they needed Ian immediately to rush in and take the hot seat. Or a heavy-breather had phoned to proposition her, and she must grab her coat and contact the police. But phone and doorbell sulked in a conspiracy of silence – no sound at all, save a peevish husband calling from the bedroom.

'Get a move on, darling! If you don't buck up, the bloody thing will wilt.'

She willed the bloody thing to wilt, spent as long as possible peeing, washing, cleaning teeth (and basin). But he only called again, now sounding sharp and edgy. If they had another row, it might spoil her plans for Saturday, prevent her Transformation. She gritted her teeth, pulled on her dressing gown, and stumped back to the bedroom.

'Let's make love in the dark, Ian – pretend we're on our honeymoon and I'm a nervous little virgin bride again.'

'Oh, *yes*.' The wilting stopped. 'Remember how we were – a pair of total innocents! You refused to let me look at you, and I was such a greenhorn, we were fumbling in the dark for hours, before I even got it in. And in the morning, you got up at dawn and put all your clothes back on, in case they knocked with morning tea and found you in your birthday suit.'

Ginny tried to laugh. She had drawn the curtains as close as they would go, switched off all the lights. She nipped swiftly into bed, only relinquishing the dressing gown when she was safe beneath the covers.

'Let's play it all again.' Ian was cock-a-hoop. She hoped he'd come as quickly as he had done on their honeymoon, but without the hours of groping foreplay. At least it was an easy game. All she had to do was act tense, reluctant, passive – and no acting was required.

She hid her face in the pillow. 'Ian, I'm scared,' she stuttered, trying valiantly to recall her lines. The guest-house in the Isle of Wight seemed a hundred thousand years ago – cheap little G-plan bedroom with confetti on the sheets.

Ian was gurgling with delight, romping in 1960s Shanklin. 'Remember how we ate that wodge of wedding cake in the middle of the night – and dropped icing sugar everywhere?' He laughed and tweaked her nipples. 'I didn't tell you then, darling, but I was really in a state. Stan had given me this sex manual, and I'd been studying it for days, assumed all those weird way-out positions were essential first time off. Hey! Why don't we experiment, try a few right now? You won't believe this, Ginny, but I can still remember some of them. There was one called the Wheelbarrow, where the woman puts her arms on the floor and sticks her bottom up.'

'No,' said Ginny, shuddering. 'Let's stay on our honeymoon. It's . . . fun.'

'Oh, *please*.' Ian rolled her over, pawed her eagerly. 'Let's just try the Honey-pot. I've always wanted to have a bash at that one. I can see the illustration in my head, even after all these years. I've never liked to mention it before, darling. I didn't think you'd approve of playing games.'

Ginny called on Filippino Lippi for encouragement, though still fighting deep suspicions. Had her greenhorn husband been truly waiting fifteen years to try the Honey-pot, or had he learnt these specialities in just the last few months from some new and kinky mistress? He certainly looked expert – arranging her body with an undertaker's skill, and muttering instructions to himself.

'That's it. No, bend your right leg up a little, and let your head fall back, so it's almost touching the floor. Great! Relax a bit – you'll love it.'

She shut her eyes, winced as he jabbed in. Her head slipped back and hit the floor, but Ian clung on tenaciously. 'It's called the Honey-pot,' he panted between exertions. 'Because . . .' She grimaced as he ground her head into the carpet – a thin and scratchy carpet with no mercy. 'Because I put honey in your pot.'

She grabbed at the blankets, waited for the honey. It didn't come. The bedroom looked quite different upside-down. Her back was agony, and she could almost feel the floorboards pressing into her skull. Her husband seemed unstoppable. She tried to move her honey-pot against him, but it was more or less impossible with her body pinioned and her head right on the floor. He emerged still stiff, and gloating. If this was what he did with his new woman, then she must be a yogini with an India-rubber spine.

'Isn't this fantastic, darling? I don't think we've ever made love quite so well before. It's good for you, too, isn't it?'

'*Wonderful*.' Ginny grabbed the bed-legs, using them as leverage to return her to the horizontal. Although the room was still pitch dark, she made sure that she was lying on her back.

Ian mopped his sweaty stomach with the sheet. 'There's another one I've always longed to try. You do it with a cushion and a chair. I think it's called the Tiger-lily.'

Ginny remembered dancing-lessons from way back in her teens – an instruction-book with diagrams of feet, and little pointing arrows to show the line of dance. She had never really mastered the slow foxtrot. She could see her husband following his own book, trying to catch the rhythm, trying to learn the hold – slow, quick-quick, slow . . . He'd probably been mulling over that sex manual since the evening of the stag party. Never in her life had she known him so insatiable. The 8.20 and 8.31 had long since gone. He'd shrugged off the 8.50, ignored the 9.03. Imperial Biscuits had gone into liquidation. She was still bone dry.

'Happy, darling?' He was like a kid with a giant-sized ice-cream cornet. If only it would melt.

'Ecstatic,' she replied.

'Tell you what,' he puffed, pausing for a moment to regain his breath (and footing). 'I'll dig out that old sex manual and we can work through the whole ninety-six positions.'

'Great!' said Ginny, realising she would have to change her tactics. If she lay there like a ramrod, he'd still be erect by lunch-time, and she'd be creaking into position number ninety-five. She closed her eyes, and Ian's white body broadened, developed an instant jet-set tan; his palish, blueish eyes scorching into deepest wicked brown. She could feel her fingers grasping sworls of body-hair; her buttocks sore and smarting, yet submitting to his cruel benediction. She was moist, at last; her body heaving, firing into Ian's. She had mastered the slow foxtrot.

Caldos was whispering sweet obscenities between her throbbing breasts, his tongue so deep inside her mouth it had reached the silent bottom of her ocean. As she came, she longed to shout his name, and it was agony to murmur 'Ian', instead of roaring 'Caldos, Caldos, Caldos, Caldos, Caldos!'

23

Ginny gazed at the blonde bombshell in the mirror and wondered who she was. In the seven pampered hours since she'd left the porridge plates to soak, and stepped inside the pink and purple glamour of Babette's of Bond Street, Ginny Barnes had somehow got mislaid. The long and messy hair had fallen in swathes upon the purple carpet and been swept into a waste-bin. The natural face had disappeared beneath bottled glow and shine; the artless eyebrows plucked into an imperious arch. Her twenty standard-issue nails were now screaming scarlet talons; her body oiled, soothed, pummelled, cosseted.

A gaggle of pink-overalled minions had joined her at the mirror, all so sleek and svelte that even the humblest of them looked as if she'd been rented from Metro Goldwyn Mayer.

'It was absolute murder,' Jeremy informed them, collapsing on a sumptuous purple chair. 'Madame's hair has been utterly neglected, simply *chewed* off. I don't know how I coped.'

The minions swaddled him in suave pink admiration. The manager flounced over and added purple praise. Even the chubby gilt cherubs supporting the mirror looked singularly impressed.

Ginny went on staring. The hair was short, chic, curly, bouncy, blonde. Yes, blonde, real blonde, like Snookie or Marilyn Monroe – clever little curls, coaxed into an ingenious exuberance, fair as a new-hatched chick, shouting out to be admired; cruel crimson lips, jungle lashes, Polaris eyes. It was her, all her, not rented, borrowed, or just stuck on. She owned that new reflection in the mirror, she could even take it home. It was the new Caldos creation, inspired and financed by Dr incredible de Roche.

All day they'd been kowtowing to her, purely on the strength of him. She was 'Dr de Roche's booking' – a magic phrase in Bond Street, like being Saint Peter's mistress when you arrived at the

172

gates of heaven. You had to be rather special to have Jeremy at all. (He'd trained under Vidal and wouldn't speak to lesser mortals.) And on top of Jeremy, she'd had a smoked salmon lunch on a showy silver tray, with free champagne, compliments of Miss Babette herself ('And how's my wicked, wicked Doctor, then?'), and petits fours at teatime and a real bone-china cup.

They'd coaxed her hair into silver sausages and lulled her under the dryer, while assorted pink and purple minions had manicured her hands and toes, and hovered with *Vogue* and fresh-pressed orange juice. She was drunk on glossy magazines, had leafed through a score of emaciated model girls, all of whom looked bored as well as starving. She'd obviously have to practise looking bored. There were so many skills she didn't have, so many graces and accomplishments she lacked. Well, at least she'd made a start – had killed Miss Mouse stone-dead. The only problem was, they hadn't changed her soul. Underneath the icing, there were still lumpy tedious things like conscience and remorse. The mouse might be changed into a peacock, but every time she tried to spread her tail, there were little yelps of protest, anxious squeaks of guilt.

Why couldn't she sweep away her family, along with her anaemic hair and ineffectual eyebrows? She'd been streamlined and remodelled and swept into a different world, yet somehow Ian and the two girls were still so precious and insistent. The bitch in the mirror might abandon them, but the conscience in the chair could not. She tried to join her two separate halves together, as an obsequious pink seraph escorted her upstairs. The face felt strange, as if it didn't quite belong. She was almost surprised to see her shabby coat again and the Safeway's plastic bag. The seraph bowed her into a changing-room and laid them on a purple couch.

'Does madame require any assistance with her toilette?'

'Oh, no no, thank you, no.' She'd die with embarrassment if anyone should see her old and tatty shoes, and the hasty cobbled tacking-stitches in Kate's second-best dress. Even her bra looked a dingy shade of grey. She was just struggling with the hooks when she heard footsteps right outside, a soft tap-tap on the door. Had she missed a treatment? Surely not. She'd already had sauna, massage, facial, manicure and pedicure; four-power talks on her hairstyle, as if she were a fishing limit or a nuclear threat; club-cut, body-wave, bleaching; breakfast, lunch and tea.

'Delivery for madame!' The under-aged cherub lisping at the door looked as if he'd sprung from a Florentine fresco. He was carrying a large silver box, festooned with scarlet ribbon.

'There must be some mistake,' she faltered. But the cherub had flown off. 'Mrs Barnes' said the label on the box. She wasn't really sure whether Mrs Barnes was dead, but someone had to open her parcels.

She scrabbled at the ribbon, tore through a mass of rustling tissue paper, and shook out a flaunting streak of jet-black crêpe de Chine, a couture creation that might have tumbled out of *Vogue*. Reverently, she draped the gown against her – high chaste neck, contradicted by a devastating back, plunging bare almost to the waist; tight floor-length skirt, slit all along one thigh; full transparent sleeves, upgrading her arms to a new erotic zone; tiny fastidious buttons at the wrist. It was both decorous and debauched, trollop and nun.

She gasped at the label, which seemed almost unbelievable after a lifetime of M & S and Richard Shops. At the bottom of the box was something just as precious – a flamboyant scarlet card with the de Roche hieroglyphics leaping right across it. 'My Princess,' it said in a few languages she recognised and several more she didn't. She was smiling stupidly, her whole pampered body one sugar-coated smile, as she confined Kate's boring dress to the Safeway's plastic bag. Her body slid into the crêpe de Chine like a sword into its scabbard, straining a little at the curves, the way Caldos always liked. Now she was glad he had wolfed all her crêpes Suzette and reserved the second helpings for himself. She was as slender as the dress deserved. She fastened the fiddly little buttons at wrist and throat, hardly daring to look up. She closed her eyes, flung back her head, took a deep breath in and opened them.

Princess Estrella was standing in the mirror, her dress by Yves St Laurent, her hair by Jeremy, face courtesy of Miss Babette, total creation by C.E.S. de Roche. Ginny stared, astonished, at the stranger, the seductress. Her hair looked even blonder against the dress's sultry black. And what big eyes she had, what sensuous scarlet lips . . .

'All the better to damn you with, my dear!'

'Go away, God!' she implored Him in a whisper. She just couldn't get away from Him. Even when she'd hacked Him off with her hair, stripped Him off with her face-mask, He still managed to sneak back again, secreting His serpent-trail of guilt in the gilded case of a lipstick, or under the stitching of a sleeve. Princess Estrella didn't believe in God. She believed in Freud and Schubert and smoked salmon and Yves St Laurent and Château Lafite and Château de Roche – above all, in de Roche. Hadn't he created and redeemed her?

There was a tap at the door. It wasn't God, but Miss Babette. She was used to princesses, and only raised an eyebrow.

'*Magnifique*,' she drawled, fastening a last forgotten button at the neck. 'I think the good Doctor will agree, he and I have achieved a total transformation.'

24

Ginny swept into the foyer of the Coliseum, a bewitching blonde in a dress which plunged bare-back to the waist. The opera house was humming with excitement and celebrities. Hothouse flowers twined around plinths and pedestals, diamonds sparkled, cameras flashed. She floated towards the staircase, anxiously scanning the crowds. Princess Estrella wasn't quite complete without her Prince. He was standing with his back to her, holding court among his entourage, resplendent in a silk-lined opera cloak. She heard his laugh break like a stone hurled into a lake, surrounding him with ripples of applause and adulation.

'Bloody farces, these galas! Bleeding chunks of opera, Tito Gobbi called them – yes, Tito was a chum. An orgasm from one work, a death-throe from another, and a superfluity of spastic swans stampeding through Tchaikovsky. I'd wipe my arse on my ticket, if it wasn't for La Rosa.'

Ginny took advantage of the titter to insinuate herself inside the magic circle. Caldos flung out his arm, dropped to one knee and kissed her hand with the conviction of des Grieux and the showmanship of Don Giovanni. '*La mia principessa celeste dai capelli biondi!*'

His retinue were obviously impressed. Caldos introduced them: the owner of a Mayfair gallery in a puce velvet jacket and a face to match; the opera critic from the *Sunday Times* spitting at his rivals from the *Observer* and the *Telegraph*; the Romanian cultural attaché wearing medals; a pre-war actress wearing well; a dress-designer straining at his seams, and a sprinkling of eighteen-carat Arabs. Medals and turbans bowed in her direction; she was crushed against orchids and tickled by mink.

'Absolute riff-raff you get at these occasions,' Caldos confided to her later, in the quiet of the conductor's box. 'Anyone with an ounce of musical taste would keep a hundred miles away. The programme is geared for sub-normal socialites, gossip columnists, and the tone-deaf . . . DARLINGS!!! You look absolutely ravishing! Where *did* you get your tans?'

The conductor's wife had swooped into the box, two plain daughters skulking in her wake, hideous in jaundice-yellow dresses. She ducked away from Caldos' exuberant embrace.

'Really, Caldos, there won't be any suntan left, if you insist on mauling me like that. We've been trailing around Tahiti, actually, while Tubby crossed swords with the New York Philharmonic. Unspeakably tedious it was. The Pacific's much the same as any other ocean, when you're on intimate acquaintance with it – wet and blue and boring.'

The Tahiti tan was frowning as it shook Ginny's hand – it loathed glamorous blondes on principle. The daughters blushed and shuffled as Caldos compared them (at length) to Aphrodite and Athene. He was interrupted by the National Anthem, booming from the orchestra pit with an impressive roll of brass. The whole auditorium, orchestra included, had risen to its feet. Every eye but Caldos' was focused on the royal box. A plumply pink Queen Mother was gliding in, like a brocaded cushion on castors. The Gala had begun!

Ginny relished every moment. She'd never seen live opera, and no ballet save *Swan Lake*, an amateur production, thirteen years ago, in a grim provincial theatre with gangling toothy swans. And the two operas and one ballet she'd watched on television had seemed interminable; confused her with their sub-titles, or their incongruous commercial breaks. But excerpts were quite perfect, like extracting all the juice from a ripe orange, and discarding the pith and pips and rind. The performance opened with a fighting-fit Violetta, who spent a full fifteen minutes dying, and then revived to acknowledge the cheers. There were quite a lot of deaths. Romeo expired on top of Juliet, having murdered Paris first, to make the numbers up. Eurydice perished in the Elysian Fields, but was restored to life and Orpheus, even before the applause. A lean male dancer in lilac tights did obscene things with feathers, and half a *pas de deux* lost its fan. It was like drowning in the fizziest champagne.

Ginny turned to look at Caldos – he was lolling behind her in

177

the box, wedged between yellow daughters, and yawning. He had come only for La Rosa, and she was programmed last, before the interval. She hadn't sung in England for over seven years, and the moment she appeared, the audience went wild. She stood, a tiny figure, alone on the vast stage, haloed by a spotlight. Her pure reverberating voice seemed to pierce the dome of the building, and shoot like a meteor through the dark sky outside, lighting up all London. And all London was applauding; fans shouting, stamping, cheering; bravos and bouquets showering from the gallery. A crimson rose whizzed past Ginny's ear and landed on the ledge in front of her. She twisted round to offer it to Caldos, her private bouquet for his passionate performances. Tears were streaming down his cheeks. His hands clapped automatically, but his face was naked, undefended, as if he'd slunk away from this glittering auditorium and entered his own anguished world. She was shocked to see his mouth tremble, that mouth which scoffed and satirised and took the skin off other people's lives, and which knew its arrogant way round every niche and crevice of her body.

Applause was still roaring through the opera house. The conductor's wife was criticising La Rosa's slinky dress; La Rosa herself ankle-deep in flowers. Ginny could only gaze at Caldos – his mouth, his tears, his rapturous response to a voice which beggared him. Oh, God, she thought, still clutching her red rose, I'm recklessly, ridiculously, and irretrievably in love with him.

Caldos had been invited to join the royal party for a little light refreshment during the first interval. He scrubbed his eyes, reapplied his public mask, and began his court-jestering again, leaving Ginny in the tender care of Lady Zinnia Lamont, and a fat-faced film producer whose auburn hair-weave clashed with his red carnation. Various bin-end celebrities crowded in and out of the conductor's box, and the yellow daughters blushed still harder, and tried to cool themselves with Grand Marnier ice-cream. Other little delicacies were being proffered by a waitress, and a steward, dressed so nattily he looked like a grandee from *Don Carlos*, refilled all their glasses with champagne.

Ginny sipped and smiled. Smoked salmon and Veuve Clicquot twice in just one day! She was becoming quite a traitor to the humble fish finger. She was also beginning to realise, with a measure of astonishment, that she was one of the most stunning women there. People were actually turning round to stare at Mrs Barnes; distinguished men fighting to introduce themselves, asking her opinion on Janacek and Meyerbeer. She had no opinion on either, but it hardly seemed to matter. They were just as attentive when she talked about puff-pastry, or hard-pad in dachshunds. She was surrounded by a crowd of cordon-bleu dog enthusiasts when Caldos returned. He could hardly get near her for the crush. A ballet critic was pawing her bottom and a property speculator drinking from her glass.

The conductor's wife was carping still, insisting to a nervous Finnish flautist that her husband had rushed the semi-quavers in the Reznicek. They were both interrupted by a sudden high-pitched shriek, as a leap of silver cat-suit clawed itself across de Roche's shoulders, smearing kümmel-flavoured lipstick right down his frilled front. 'Tum-Tum!' trumpeted Gish. 'I'd no idea you'd be here. I thought *Parsifal* was more your line, not this pantomime. Introduce me!'

Caldos dabbed crossly at his frills. He introduced an archbishop and a counterfeit peer, then turned his back and kissed both hands to Ginny. But Gish was in pursuit, her gimlet eye boring into the Yves St Laurent. 'And the lady?' (She made it sound like a poisonous form of snake.) 'I don't *think* we've met . . .'

Ginny was aghast. How on earth could Gish not recognise her, when she'd actually been to dinner at their house, spent an entire (and endless) evening sulking on their sofa, or shrinking from their cats? She was suddenly aware of the sham she was, the dummy; just a painted mask, a wisp of crêpe de Chine. The false façade might crack at any moment, revealing her drab nakedness, the fawn and boring housewife underneath. If any of these people were to pop in to her home and catch her making pastry in her overall, they'd vow they'd never seen her in their life.

She held up her champagne glass, tried to use it as a mirror, her face mockingly distorted. Surely her features must be just the same, her voice, her shape, her character? Or had Caldos changed her totally, pepped her up and slimmed her down, taught her to put the r in 'orf' and to elongate her vowels? She had become his creature. Unconsciously, she was imitating him, learning his language, wearing his livery. She was a hybrid, a new model, with a new name, new morals, new opinions, and yet unable to cast off the old and the familiar, still pulled between Safeway's and Mount Olympus.

She drained her glass defiantly, refused to think of Safeway's – or of Gish. She was learning to be expensive and exclusive, and it took her total concentration. 'More champagne!' she demanded, with a new imperiousness she had learned from Lady Zinnia. Caldos handed her his own brimming glass, sipping from the other side. He pressed his cold winey lips against the inside of her wrist, kissed it lingeringly. If Gish could unravel her, then he could make her whole again.

Towards the end of the second interval, Caldos made his excuses to the conductor's wife. 'Terribly sorry, darling, but I promised to join Sir Alec in his box for the last act. Used to do a spot of business with him. Charming fellow. Auld Lang Syne sort of thing . . .'

He led Ginny past the crowds in the stalls bar, up a poky wooden staircase to the stage boxes, and through a little door marked A. They seemed to have walked almost on to the stage – high up, but looking straight down into the orchestra pit, and directly opposite the royal box, which was flower-festooned, but empty. The royal party were still in the retiring-room, taking refreshments with their second round of guests. Box A was also empty.

'But where's Sir Alec?' Ginny asked, titles tripping off her tongue.

'He's just left – lucky fellow! I saw him slip out with his wife five or ten minutes ago. Emergency session in the Foreign Office, I presume.'

'Then why . . . ?'

'First, because I'm suffering the advanced stages of Yellow Daughter Fever. One of those unspeakable brats picked her nose throughout the Jewel Song, and the other helped La Rosa out by humming the accompaniment in the key of F sharp minor. Secondly, because the acoustics are lousy down there. The conductor's wife may be tone-deaf, but I'm unfortunately not. Here, we're submerged by the strings, but at least we're not listening through a layer of butter muslin. And most importantly, because I intend to make love to you during *Madam Butterfly*.' He moved towards the front of the box and scanned the stalls below.

Ginny gasped. 'But Caldos, we simply can't! It's unthinkable. We're like a public exhibition up here. Everyone can see us – even the royal party. They'll be staring right across at us.'

'No, *moya milochka*, they always sleep through opera. And anyway, if we move to the back of the box and lie down, nobody will even know we're here. Anyone who's anyone assumes we're still in the conductor's box. And as for the assiduous wife, she won't take her beady little eye off hubby's baton. She's under the illusion *she's* principal conductor here.'

He took her hand and tried to lure her to the back of the box, kicking a gilded chair or two out of his way. He stretched out on the faded red carpet, as if he were reclining at a country picnic. Ginny stayed grimly put.

'I find your modesty quite entrancing, my beloved, but if you don't either sit down, or lie down, the royal bodyguard will have returned to their box, and be training their bayonets on you!'

Ginny peered down at the pit. The orchestra was back in place; a reverent and expectant hush warning her she had no time to waste. She crept nervously to the rear of the box, crouching down beside de Roche. He placed a hot and ardent hand on the bare square of her back, pulling her towards him. The house lights dimmed, and she felt his fingers inching down her thigh. There was a sudden sob from the orchestra, as wistful oboes rippled across melting clarinets, and two disembodied voices, a soprano and a tenor, poured like double cream into her ears. The actual words were indistinct, since she had her head pressed right against the carpet, and all she could see was Caldos' face in close-up, and the dark curve of the ceiling arching over them. They were in their own hazy horizontal world, where orchestra and singers were only incorporeal sounds, but the entwined impassioned voices of Butterfly and Pinkerton were like the music one would hear if one slipped inside the golden gate of heaven.

She raised her head a little, tried to make the words out; the soprano's voice now rising on its own – radiant, but tinged with apprehension:

> 'Rejected
> Rejected, yet happy . . .'

Caldos was already stiff. He removed no clothes, just unzipped his trousers, then pushed her dress right above her knees. He always forbade her to wear underwear, and in a dress as low and tight as hers, it would have been impossible. A draught from the door fanned across her pubic hair, and the carpet scratched and prickled her bare skin. She peered up at the ceiling, past the line of Caldos' chin, and saw a vast blue dome soaring up into a shadowy black cupola.

Somewhere, far below, Pinkerton was pleading with her:

> 'Till now you never told me
> never told me you loved me . . .'

Ginny resisted a little, as Butterfly repeated slowly, sadly:

> 'But if I were to tell you,
> I might die,
> I might die . . .'

Pinkerton consoled her, his voice molten like warm honey:

> 'Love does not kill you,
> Love is life . . .
> Its smile is a blessing from heaven.'

Ginny longed to believe him, to join in the exultant swoop of flutes, horns and clarinets, enfolding her in their unquestioning embrace. Caldos entered her, moving with a languorous stealth and slowness, lunging silently against her at half his usual speed. He did not speak, nor kiss her – seemed to be listening with at least one ear as a limpid solo violin turned torment into lullaby. Butterfly was imploring Pinkerton to love her like a child, to love her gently like a baby, and voice and orchestra and trembling strings were hushed into one whispering cradle-song.

Ginny was afraid still, Butterfly's own anguish tearing into her, with the wild discordant words:

> 'If a man catch a butterfly
> he pierces it with a pin
> and leaves it to die.'

But immediately, Pinkerton was comforting her, his smooth seductive voice outsoaring the cries of the woodwind, defeating the dissonant strings. And his words were somehow doubled by her lover – Caldos' slow deliberate movements like another sort of music, rhythmic, reassuring. Her own body had dissolved into the swell and fling of sound. She no longer cared whether people in the gallery could see her. The whole auditorium had become their private playground. Pinkerton was singing with a new restless fervour: 'Come, come be mine now'; singing for the two of them alone. 'Come, come!' he cried again, effusive and beseeching, though Caldos was still moving with an exquisite sensuous slowness, which matched the slow relentless music, easing the whole length of his body silently against her.

'I surrender,' clamoured Butterfly, a hundred miles below, and Ginny yearned to echo her, to cry out her surrender with the breathless harps, the enraptured violins.

'Come!' Pinkerton reiterated, insisting and entreating beneath Butterfly's rich voice; the whole orchestra exploding in a crescendo of desire. Caldos, too, had moved from *pianissimo* to *forte*, and was thrusting, swooping into her with the excitement of the score. She was struck, plucked, strummed, bowed, rung – swept by his baton into a tempestuous finale.

As he climaxed, the stage lights brightened and the whole ceiling was suffused with golden light. He had come much sooner than usual and she was still moving underneath him, but music and lights and throbbing harps climaxed for her instead. She lay back to acknowledge the applause. They were cheering not Butterfly and Pinkerton, but Estrella and Alfonso. Her Bond Street curls were crushed against the carpet, her left foot was entangled in a chair leg, Caldos' sperm drooling down her thigh, but she was floating high above the cupola, bowing amidst a barrage of bouquets. She was sandwiched between crimson carpet and golden ceiling, somewhere at the highest point of heaven, where she and Caldos had joined with all the gods and emperors sporting on the ornamented walls.

The applause was still thundering about them. Caldos used the cover of the noise to lift her to her feet. They sat together, hidden in the shadows, heads touching, fingers clasped. Ginny gazed out at the great arc of the auditorium, the hundred hundred heads,

183

dark blobs in the gloom, faint blurs of faceless faces – important stylish faces, but because she belonged to Caldos, she outshone them all. They were only robots, and she was a blazing seraph and a phoenix; more royal than the royals, sitting bored and obedient in their puny box; prouder than the ravening golden lions leaping into breathless space above the stage; higher than the sculpted eagles set above them, brushing their wings against the floor of heaven.

She turned her eyes back to the stage. The music still resounded, the acts still swaggered on, but she was aware only of her lover, could see him everywhere – in the bearded profile of Macbeth, in the grace of Romeo, in the electric grief of weeping Orpheus. He belonged in every century, straddled the whole globe. He was the hero of every opera, the frontispiece of every precious book, the face in every portrait, the final cadence in every symphony. Because his fingers were entwined in hers, the whole universe had become her prize and keepsake; the vast stage just a footstool at her feet.

The last chord swelled and faded, swallowed up in tempestuous applause; singers blowing kisses to the stalls, stately divas curtseying as they accepted huge bouquets, roars of approbation erupting above the blitz of clapping hands. Ginny lolled back graciously, acknowledging it all. The entire audience was on its feet, paying rapturous homage to the only star and idol of the evening – her own adored and unsurpassable de Roche.

25

'Recover all thy sigh-blown age
On double pleasures: leave thy cold dispute
Of what is fit, and not. Forsake thy cage,
Thy rope of sands . . .'

Caldos paused a moment in his loud dramatic reading, while he devoured the last fried mushroom. He had introduced Ginny to George Herbert over the cornflakes, and they had moved from 'The Church Porch' to 'The Pearl' in the time it had taken him to eat his four-course breakfast. (Ginny had been limited to orange juice and cereal.) Books and crumbs and bacon rinds littered the huge bed. George Herbert was propped against de Roche's naked chest; he leaning snugly back against four plump goose-down pillows, and Ginny curled beside the two of them in nothing but her skin. She had warmed to Herbert instantly. He seemed to share her own uncomfortable mixture of devotion, ecstasy and guilt. She still felt inordinately guilty about repeating all those sins she'd only just confessed, but her resolve to return to Ian and work on strengthening her marriage had been blown to bits by her husband's own deceit. She hoped that God might look on Herbert as a sort of compromise. He had all the right credentials, was priest as well as poet, and his sole poetic theme was devotion to religion – sin, repentance, prayer. He'd even translated a *Treatise on Temperance*, so Caldos had informed her, and had been enviably temperate in his own brief but worthy life.

She tried to make as little noise as possible crunching on her cornflakes (which she was eating dry, since the full-cream milk which Caldos drank contained three hundred and eighty calories a pint), while Caldos continued with the reading. Perhaps God would stretch a point, and regard it as a sort of Sunday service, with Caldos as the officiating priest. It *was* Sunday morning, after all, and Caldos read with genuine devotion.

> 'If thou do ill, the joy fades, not the pains,
> If well, the pain doth fade, the joy remains.'

The pain had already faded, and the angry red weals with it, and, yes, the joy remained – great four-course feasts of joy, golden like the egg-yolks, sizzling with the bacon. She had never known a night like that before, a night stretched in all directions, until it hit the stars and bumped against another constellation, then plunged reeling and triumphant into dawn. He had baptised her with white star-dust, confirmed her with dark fire; chastened and ·chastised her, and then redeemed and resurrected her; broken out of his own body and come roaring into hers. He was omega and alpha, saviour and seducer.

And he could even cook a gourmet breakfast, totally unaided; hadn't let her lift a finger, just told her to lie back and read Swinburne to him through the open door, while he leapt about marauding mushrooms and doing violent things to eggs. (He'd had a second kitchen installed opposite the bedroom – insisting life's two greatest pleasures should adjoin.)

She wasn't all that keen on Algernon Charles Swinburne, who was a pervert and an atheist, as well as alcoholic. Well, her lover was an atheist himself, but he hadn't been expelled from both Eton *and* Oxford, as A.C.S. had been. (Caldos called a lot of writers and artists by their initials – on intimate terms not just with the famous, but even with the dead.) He approved of A.C.S. because his father was an admiral and his grandfather an earl, and he was the patron saint of flagellation. She loathed that word, which reeked of dirty book-stalls, and lurid back-street Soho, and seemed to have no link whatsoever with the radiant death-in-ecstasy which her lover lambasted into her each time they made their raw and ravaged love. Yet A.C.S. *did* understand the feeling – there was no denying that; had captured the experience and put it into whiplash words in the most exhilarating way. She had read aloud in her best Veuve Clicquot voice, drawling a little, the way all Caldos' friends did, and making sure she put the h in whence:

'. . . whence, ripe to steam and stain,
Foams round the feet of pleasure
The blood-red mist of pain.'

'*Must*,' Caldos had corrected, darting from the cooker to the bed.
'What?' said Ginny.
'Must, not mist.'
'Must what?'
'The blood-red *must* of pain – though actually, I quite like
"mist". Estrella, you may well have the makings of an Ella
Wheeler Wilcox, besides having the most gloriously athletic cunt
in all Chelsea.'

She had lolled against the pillows, wallowing in the duvet of his
love. Ella Wheeler Wilcox was probably some outrageous profli-
gate, or Swinburne's satanic sister, but she'd been too content to
care. Ian had never mentioned her cunt, not once in fifteen years,
but Caldos had fed it morsels of smoked salmon, and christened
it with Dom Perignon, and now it was the preening queen of
Chelsea.

Caldos had continued with the Swinburne, reciting it by heart,
thundering out the lines with a little help from the fish-slice.

'The grief of cruel kisses . . .
The joy whose mouth makes moan . . .
The something, something, something – bugger!'

He had leapt away from the frying pan, as sizzling fat spurted
on his chest.

'Throbs through the heat of pleasure
The purpler blood of pain.'

Ginny had gazed fondly at his hot buttered chest. Strange to
cook breakfast in the altogether. Ian would never dream of it.
Well, her husband couldn't cook at all, but neither did he wander
around stark naked. As soon as they'd made love, he'd always
climb straight back into his thick blue-striped pyjamas, as if he
felt exposed and vulnerable without them. No. She mustn't think
of Ian. He and the two girls seemed a hundred thousand miles

187

away, tiny matchstick figures lost in a dark valley, while she'd climbed high high up, to the very summit of a dazzling snow-capped mountain. And she didn't even miss them – not a jot.

She had disposed of A.C.S., slammed him shut and hidden him under the pillow, as Caldos was now doing with G.H. It was time to give her full attention to Adolfo, who looked just a little droopy. Since she'd met Caldos, she'd begun to wish that penises could be continually erect, born stiff, as it were, sticking out rigid like a tusk. Unerect penises, even large ones like Adolfo, always had a hangdog look, and Ian's, in particular, seemed downright woebegone, coiling like a small damp snail between his thin white legs. Adolfo was in a different class entirely – a Martello tower to Ian's thawed fish finger. She still found it rather hard to breathe with the tower half down her throat, sometimes even gagged on it, but Caldos was instructing her, had become her tutor in all subjects – Fauré and fellatio, Birtwhistle and birch twigs. She often wondered how he found the time for all the things he did – Swinburne, Schubert, *soixante-neuf*, two exhausting private practices, frequent trips abroad from Biarritz to Bali Hai, rethinking his entire profession, and keeping up with the Lord Joneses. Even now, after a scant two hours of sleep, he was still firing on all cylinders.

They spent the entire day in bed, though not for the purposes of catching up on sleep. The pale March morning sun dwindled into lazy afternoon. It was cold and raw outside, with cruel red berries still bloodying the holly, but spring arrived in Chelsea just that afternoon. The sun sneaked into their bedroom on its way westwards and touched the forsythia with gold. Cherry-blossom confetti drifted through the bare brown garden, and the first jaunty daffodil trumpeted a fanfare to their love.

At four o'clock, Ginny poured tea. They were still in bed, but had stopped for light refreshments, having been interrupted by a long and awkward phone-call – one of Caldos' patients in a crisis.

'Caldos,' Ginny frowned, cascading milk and sugar into Caldos' cup, while leaving her tea strictly black.

'Mm?' Toast and peach preserve claimed most of his attention.

'Don't you get miserable with all those mental cases?'

'Estrella darling, you talk about them as if they're some sort

188

of incurable half-wits. Many of my patients are rich, lonely, middle-aged women, who use their analyst like a new baby, or a religion, or a love affair – something to build their life around.' He paused a moment to devour a chunk of peach. 'Some of them have been coming five days a week for a dozen years or more. And it's a bloody good investment. Just think what it gives them' – he larded extra butter on the last fat piece of toast – 'something to get up for, instead of brooding all day long in their nighties or their dressing gowns; somebody to talk to, when even their lap-dogs have stopped listening; a sense of self-importance that their psyches should merit so much devoted concentration; a subject of conversation with their friends – if they've still got any left – *and*,' he added, mopping jam off his chest-hair with a corner of the black silk sheet, 'a life-long supply of sexual fantasies. You've no idea how many women are screwing me, Estrella. In SW3 alone, I'm being seduced at least twenty times a night. And I don't charge them a penny more for the privilege. Fantasies are free.'

Ginny sipped her tea, wincing at the taste. She still didn't like Earl Grey, especially sugarless. 'It sounds very bleak to me – spending a whole lifetime lying on a couch. Wouldn't it be better for them to get a job, or something?'

'They don't want jobs, my sweet. They're looking for something to splurge their money on, not make even more. And who's to say tapping a typewriter all damned day is any more fulfilling than working on one's psyche? A large percentage of typists develop permanent postural defects. Lying on a couch straightens you out, literally at least.' He leaned down to kiss her nipple. 'You're right, though, *mon coquillage*, they do need something else. I'm working on it. I plan to prise them off the couch and spread some icing on their little lives.' He consoled the other nipple, until both were standing up. 'In fact, I'm even considering using *you* in my ingenious new scheme.'

'Me?'

'A blonde princess or two adds tone to any establishment.'

'Oh, Caldos, do be serious . . .'

'I'm absolutely serious. You're wasted, my sweet, in that semi-detached menagerie of yours. You're an intelligent perceptive woman, not a skivvy. You should be doing a socially important job, instead of cocooning yourself in all that cosy domesticity.'

'But I'm not trained or . . .'

He picked up the toasting fork and poised it delicately across her reddened buttocks. 'All you require, *mon p'tit chou de Bruxelles*, is a spot more regular tuition from a strict and well-qualified disciplinarian.'

She grabbed the fork, removed it. She knew he cared about his work, but he never let her see it. It was just the same when he told her that he loved her. Well, he hadn't really told her yet. He often almost said it, then shied away, started discussing Irish limericks, or Elizabethan lutists, or *soufflé d'épinards*. With a panting count-down, he would fling her soul among June moons, then just as she had orbited, he would make a cruel crash-landing on to Ezra Pound's use of hieroglyphics, or his preference for Stilton over Brie. But she was sure he almost loved her – well, nearly almost sure. He had nearly almost told her under the hundred-carat stars, and his frosty breath had drifted to the sky and set the almost-words shining like a new constellation. And he had kissed her in the cold quiet Chelsea garden, beneath Orion and the Great Bear, and wreathed winter jasmine in her hair and scattered words like diamonds.

'Oh Caldos,' she whispered, toppling her empty teacup into a hollow in the bed. 'I love you so dreadfully.'

He leapfrogged out of bed. 'Cherry cake or chocolate?'

In the cab home, she scrubbed at her nails with varnish-remover and arranged a headscarf on her hair. The bra was back in place, her buttocks soothed with camomile, and her limp green mac beginning to shed its creases. It had spent its dirty weekend in a Safeway's plastic bag. The Yves St Laurent had been left in Caldos' wardrobe. She'd tried to leave her heart there, but it wouldn't stay behind, and she'd found it quite impossible to get it back to normal, like her face. Lipstick rubbed off, but love was indelible. It soared up to the skies and scorched itself outstaring the new constellation; it plunged into the underworld and joined in the embraces of Orpheus and Eurydice; it outsung La Rosa and outshone the evening star. It was quite the plumpest peach in the preserve.

The driver set her down four doors away. She flurried up her own front path, fumbled for her key. A smell of burning wafted from the hall, as two pairs of legs came thundering down to greet her.

'Mummy's back, Mummy's back! Mummy Mummy Mummy! Daddy burnt the rice and Sarah's cut her thumb.'

Snookie jumped the last three stairs, and butted her blonde head against her mother's stomach, then reeled back in surprise. The headscarf had slipped off, and Ginny's streaked and sculpted hair shone like a Belisha beacon. Ian emerged from the kitchen with a dishcloth in his hand.

'How was the Renaissance, darling?' His smile wavered as it reached her head. 'Ginny, what in God's name have you done?'

Snookie burst into tears. 'You're not a mummy any more. You're all posh and horrid like a film star.'

Ginny tried to smile. Snookie sobbed. Sarah almost shouted. 'Gosh, Mummy, you look ghastly! Fancy going blonde at your age. I'd rather you went grey, like Debbie's mum. For goodness sake don't come to school like that. I'd die if Debbie saw you.'

'Don't be cheeky, Sarah. Your mother looks very ... er ...' Ian's wan voice died away, as he sought for a convincing word. Dear faithful, plodding, lying Ian, trying to forget he liked long, straight, natural hair; using the wet dishcloth to mop up Snookie's tears; a grease-stain on his jacket, one shoe splashed with paint. Could he really have a mistress, in those dreadful baggy corduroys, and when he was so obviously relieved in seeing her come home?

'Come on Snookie, darling, aren't you going to show Mummy that lovely cake you made her? It took her the whole afternoon,' he told Ginny with a wilting smile, planting an extremely wary kiss upon her cheek, as if frightened that her dazzling curls might take a swipe at him.

Snookie removed her hands from her face and dared another survey of the hair. 'It's horrible new hair,' she wailed. 'All stuck on like sausages.'

'Snookie made you a cake.' Ian was dogged, valiant. 'All on her own. Didn't you, darling?' Ginny almost wished he *was* unfaithful, then she needn't feel so guilty. But he looked fagged from chores and children, rather than swooning after love.

'Will it wash off?' asked Sarah hopefully. 'I suppose you could always wear a wig. Snookie's teacher does.'

191

'She *doesn't*!' shouted Snookie, jumping up and down.

'Does.'

'Doesn't.'

'Does.'

'Let's have supper,' Ian suggested, steering both the fractious children to the kitchen. Someone had been busy. The old pine table was camouflaged with the best white lacy cloth; in the centre a vase of sagging dandelions and one uncertain rose. The coloured plastic tumblers, stored away for picnics, had been found and dusted down (each boasting two tall straws); the paper napkins twisted into swans, and a quart of fizzy orangeade sparkled in a jug. Her largest saucepan bubbled on the hob, now blackened at the bottom. Ian dived across to stir it. 'It's risotto,' he announced.

'I helped,' said Sarah proudly. 'We looked through hundreds of your cook-books. But Daddy burnt the rice.'

'He didn't.'

'Did.'

Snookie turned her back on Sarah, took her mother's hand. 'Anyway, I made a cake – a real one. It's red. You can't see it until after the risotto. It's a s'prise.'

Ian dolloped brown-tinged rice on to the best rose-patterned plates, the ones they kept for special dinner parties. Ginny shook her napkin out, sipped tepid orangeade. She'd been away one short weekend, and they'd put out all the flags, welcomed her with rice and roses. It was shaming and unbearable and wonderful. Ian couldn't even cook, and there he was, attempting it, when all she'd left them was salad and corned beef. She forgave him his mistress, forgave him everything. It could have been just one brief fling, with the sort of forward little bitch who threw herself at men, or some young chit in the typing-pool who'd been hoping for promotion. She peered at the muddy hotchpotch on her plate, recognised the corned beef – small and shrivelled chunks of it, trapped in sticky gunge, along with wizened peas and bacon rinds – and love. She'd already eaten, actually, just an hour or two ago. Caldos had braised duck-breasts with double cream and brandy; whipped frothy zabaglione into two antique crystal wine-glasses.

'It's perfect,' she insisted. 'The nicest risotto I've ever, ever tasted.'

'I helped, I helped,' shrieked Sarah.

Snookie's face was crumpling up. 'It's horrible,' she sobbed. 'And your hair's horrible. Don't go away again.'

Ian put his knife and fork down, crouched beside his daughter. 'Hey, how about a piggy-back? Hold on tight and we'll go and get Mummy her surprise.'

Snookie clambered up. 'Shut your eyes,' she ordered, when they'd all three cantered back again, now whispering and giggling. Then, '*Open* them!' she yelled.

The cake sagged in the middle and was higher on the right side than the left. The icing was an alarming shade of red, though partially concealed by a rash of silver balls. 'WELCOME HOME MU . . .' was written in drunken script across the top.

'I didn't have quite enough room,' Snookie explained. 'I tried to finish the "Mummy" down the side, but the icing slided off. D'you mind? D'you like it?'

'I love it,' Ginny said. All the lumps in the lumpy grey risotto had marshalled in her throat. 'It's absolutely beautiful.'

'You've got to have the biggest piece, with the mostest silver balls.' Snookie was trying to cut it with the butter knife. 'The piece which says "MU".' She plonked herself on Ginny's lap and re-examined the hair. 'It's not completely horrible,' she said.

Ginny swallowed silver balls, soggy sponge and sickly scarlet icing. Ian was scouring out the rice saucepan, humming 'Over the Rainbow'. She squeezed a girl each side. Toby lolloped over and flopped down at their feet.

'It's so lovely to be back,' she said, trying to hug all three of them at once. 'I missed you – all of you. I missed you terribly.'

She had, she had.

26

Ian had haemorrhoids. He'd had them for at least three years, but they were not the sort of thing you talked about in Hinchley Wood. Coronaries or cancer were cocktail-party subjects, almost status-givers. But piles were relegated to the back pages of *Titbits* or the *TV Times*, along with pruritus, dentures and superfluous hair. No surgeon nor solicitor nor company director ever suffered their indignity, only hirsute failures with false teeth. 'Freedom of Movement in our Boneless Corset,' he read between clenched teeth. 'Say Goodbye to Denture Discomfort.' He resented being a back-page person, lumped together with bust-developers, incontinence pants, laxatives, and Dial-a-Date. He turned the page, came face to face with a pair of forty-four-inch D cups. 'Has Motherhood Wrecked your Bust?'

He must have a private word with Chris about these magazines. Other doctors had *Punch* or *Gardener's Weekly*, or at least the colour supplements. Waiting-rooms were bad enough in any case, full of lurid posters warning you of heart attacks, and inconsiderate people spreading lethal germs. Even the tradescantia looked sickly, had probably picked up something through its leaves. A delinquent baby out-bawled a rabid toddler, both their mothers joining in with entreaties, threats and smacks.

'Mr Barnes,' intoned the receptionist, her face and voice so gloomy they seemed more suited to a funeral parlour than a busy general surgery.

Ian got up gingerly – sitting was uncomfortable – limped into the doctor's room. Chris was an old friend. It was just a shade embarrassing discussing the defects of your rectum with someone you'd meet later over cocktails or roast beef. But the Imperial Biscuits doctor was a Nazi with bad breath.

'Sorry to bother you again, Chris. It's not just the piles – I've got these damned new pains. My whole stomach swells up like a football.' He climbed up on the couch. The ceiling glowered down at him, pale and pitiless. Chris's hands were cold.

'Does it hurt here?'

'Yes.'

'And there?'

'No . . . YES!!!'

'More here than there?'

Ian squinted up at Chris's left ear. Perhaps he was a front-page person, after all. Cancer of the bowel. He began to compose his epitaph – 'Not sleeping, but dead' – wondering how his wife would ever find the time to look in at his funeral. It was bound to clash with her classes, or a residential course. Maybe he should order the wreaths and things himself. Something really showy – lilies twined with laurel leaves.

'What?' he said, emerging from his coffin.

'I asked you – twice – do you still have the bleeding?'

'Oh yes, *pints*! Every morning, like those horror movies.' A buffet, or a sit-down meal? Wasn't it ham sandwiches for funerals? He'd go for something grander – a side of beef, or maybe goose.

'Right, put your clothes back on.'

Chris sounded most inordinately cheerful. Hardened, probably. A family man expiring in his prime would be nothing to a doctor.

'Nothing much to worry about, old man. I'm going to arrange a barium enema for you at St Mark's. That's the bum hospital in Islington. There may be a slight kink in the colon.'

Ian flushed. Why was everything about his body so damned undignified? It wouldn't look well on the forms – cause of decease: kinky colon. Atkins and Weller would snigger in the office. Unless he could find some impressive Latin name for it. Did they have colons in Latin? Entrails, certainly. They were always messing about with entrails in Roman times, to try to foretell the future. Well, as far as he was concerned, there didn't seem to be much future. He tried to concentrate on Chris's chubby face, which looked enviably healthy.

'On the other hand,' Chris pondered, 'it may be stress that's causing all the trouble. Are you worrying at all?'

Ian shook his head, contorting his expression into what he

hoped was courageous nonchalance. Hundreds of middle-aged men dropped down dead each day. Cancer was as common as the common cold. He had a good insurance – George had seen to that. And the way Ginny was behaving, she wouldn't even notice he was gone. He wondered if he could afford a marble plaque. Marble immortalised a man.

'Everything all right at home?'

'The girls are fine.' Orphans, very nearly. Snookie would look adorable in black.

'And Ginny?'

He couldn't see his wife in black, not since the Renaissance. It was always pulsing purple, or sock-it-to-me scarlet – though people would start talking if she wore scarlet to his funeral. 'She's out a lot,' he admitted. 'Bit of the Women's Lib bug, I suspect. It's been building up for months.'

'Oh, burning her bra now, is she?' Chris's laugh hit him like a shovelful of earth. 'Diana misses her, you know. And so does the Children's Home. We've been hoping she might lend a hand again.'

'Not a dog's chance at the moment, I'm afraid. She's trying to improve her mind. It was just the odd class to start with, but now she's out almost every evening. She's talking about going on to Higher Education, as if she wants to compete with me.' No, I'm afraid my wife didn't realise I was dead. She was otherwise engaged with Michelangelo.

Chris heaved his legs up on the desk, let out another guffaw. Doctors shouldn't laugh – it was cruel and condescending. He'd be offering him a jelly baby next, the way he did with Snookie.

'And how's old George these days?'

'We don't see much of him either,' Ian confessed. 'He's so damned busy now he's moved to Harley Street. To tell the truth, Chris, I don't much like the set-up there. He's working with a chum of mine – one of those trick cyclists, who's giving him ideas. Dad's even been swotting up psychiatry himself.'

'Wonderful!' said Chris. 'You used to complain he hadn't enough to do.' He swung his feet down, edged towards the door. Ian took the hint, got up; scowled at the receptionist as he plodded past the cancers and consumptives, and out into the rain again. He should never have mentioned George – it only made his mood worse. There was something really galling about his father's slick new manner, something crowing and superior which matched his new hand-tailored suit. Burton's off-the-peg had always been good enough for *him*. It wasn't easy, being outdressed by one's own father, especially when that father kept talking about libido and puffing Burma cheroots.

He crossed the road, weaving round the cars, turning up his collar against the persistent slamming rain. Perhaps he ought to buy some clothes himself – splash out for once and bypass boring Burton's. If he could only steel himself to take that bloody nightie back, he could ask if he could change it for something in the men's department, a classy city suit with a swanky Harrods label. He'd been trying to screw up courage for six months, but the thought of facing those supercilious salesgirls, or dreaming up some reason why the nightie wasn't suitable, always left him in a sweat. He hadn't even managed to spill the beans to Ginny. He'd kept meaning to regale her with the story, make a little joke of it, march her off to Harrods with him for moral support, but he'd never quite got round to it. She might not find it funny – especially in her present state – might even be annoyed with him for wasting so much money, when the roof needed repairing and they hadn't had a holiday for years – well, only tents and ground-sheets, and fry-ups on a primus stove.

Besides, he didn't like admitting he'd been bullied by de Roche. It had been pretty much the same at university, except at least he'd had the excuse of being younger then. In their very first term, Caldos had bludgeoned him into a double-date at Oxford's most expensive restaurant, and he'd been stuck with the ugly elder sister and three-quarters of the bill. He'd had to sell his bicycle and live on tea and lentils for the rest of the (long) term. The memory still rankled. No, he didn't want his wife to know what a chicken he was, compared with game-cock Caldos. He didn't really want to know himself. So he'd simply shoved the nightdress in a drawer, and done his best to stuff de Roche in the same baneful Harrods bag.

But the accursed man kept flouncing out again, entangled now with George, whom he was using as a glorified administrative assistant, entrusting him with new responsibilities, piling on more duties every day – though still paying him a pittance. The suits and the cigars were merely compensation, ostentatious perks tossed down to George's basement like handfuls of monkey-nuts. And he'd even lent him books – heavy learned tomes on highly unsuitable subjects (unmentionable, in some cases), as if trying to turn a simple old-age-pensioner into his psychiatric sidekick.

Ginny would be next. She'd probably get a First in Art or Anthropology, and become one of those plate-glass career women with her nose in the *Financial Times*, and a brass-bound leather briefcase with a combination lock. She'd already cut her hair, which was always the first (fatal) step. The Suffragettes had done the same, hacked their wavy tresses into ugly boyish bobs. He couldn't even touch her any more. Her hair was stiff with lacquer, her face all gunged with rouge. And she continually had headaches or the curse. How many other wives had heavy painful periods three weeks out of four, and raging migraine on the remaining seven days? And they lived on tins and TV dinners, and *beetroot*, for Christ's sake. Hadn't he told her twenty times how he couldn't stand the sight or smell of beetroot? And Snookie was having nightmares, and Sarah getting out-of-hand – latch-key kids, they were now, who'd grow up into hoodlums, or start snorting dope at pop festivals.

He dodged a muddy puddle, cursed the fact he'd forgotten his umbrella. Flaming bloody June. It had been raining almost every day for weeks. They hadn't even had a spring. The frost had pounced in April and killed all the apple blossom. There'd be no fruit this year, no autumn apple harvest. He'd be lucky if he lived to autumn anyway.

A boy on a skateboard rammed into his thigh. 'That's right,' he muttered. 'Hit a dying man. Bump into a cancer.'

She'd be sorry when he'd gone. He could see her tears sploshing on to the stylish marble plaque – except it would probably be chipboard, with the rates the way they were, and she'd be crying long-distance in the warm brown arms of that Philippino chap. He glared at a minuscule mongrel defecating hugely on the pavement. He couldn't even shit – outdone by a low-born lap-dog, outshone by all the family. George taking tea with R.D. Laing, and Ginny turning into a don or a director, and reminding everybody that he'd only got a Third. Well, he'd had to row, hadn't he? All that slogging on the Isis undermined the brain. You couldn't expect to be the toast of Henley and still do well in Finals. Except bloody Caldos had. De Roche had romped away with a First *and* a Blue.

'Damn de Roche,' he said out loud and kicked an empty Coke can into the gutter. 'Damn damn damn damn damn!'

Snookie snatched the letter. 'Daddy's got to drink castor oil,' she spluttered into her Sugar Puffs.

'That's what people take when they have babies,' Sarah announced grandly. 'Susie Doyle's eldest sister told me.'

'Damn Susie Doyle,' said Ian, spreading Flora thinly on Ryvita. (He didn't want cholesterol *and* cancer.) 'And damn her eldest sister.'

'That's 4p in the swear-box!' Sarah held out an exacting hand. 'Come on Daddy, pay up. It's 2p a damn.'

'Oh hell.'

'6p!' Sarah was crowing now.

'Daddy's going to have a baby,' carolled Snookie.

Ginny retrieved the milk-splashed letter and scanned the printed instructions from the hospital. 'Gosh! You've got to fast for two whole days. You're allowed an egg the first day, but not much else. Then, once you've taken the castor oil, you mustn't eat a thing.'

Snookie mashed her last few Sugar Puffs into the puddle of grey milk at the bottom of her bowl. 'Can we watch when Daddy takes it?'

Macabre little bitch, thought Ian, shading his eyes from the heartless glare of Ginny's new red housecoat. She'd be watching him expire with the same detached amusement. 'Beloved father of Sarah Elizabeth and Snookie Anne.' Could you write Snookie on a gravestone? There were probably rules about it. There were always rules, restrictions. You couldn't even die in peace. Messing you about with castor oil, and making you cadaverous with fasting, so you looked a perfect horror in your shroud. He snatched up his briefcase, pecked Ginny on the cheek, paused a moment before rushing for his train. 'So what d'you plan to do today?'

She clamped the Vague Look on her face, that new, suspicious, no-idea-at-all look, which had arrived with the red housecoat. 'Oh, various things,' she shrugged.

199

'What sort of things?'

'Shopping?' she suggested. 'I could get your castor oil.'

'Thanks a million,' Ian said, and slammed the front door, hard.

The nurse had a large starched bust like a bolster. 'And how did you get on with the castor oil?'

Ian shuddered, and the bolster heaved a little in a sympathetic snigger. Why did everybody think it was so damned (another damned 2p – 4p in the swear-box) funny?

'Was it successful, dear?'

'It depends on what you call successful. If you mean was I shitting more or less continuously from three P.M. till midnight . . .'

'Excellent!' said Nurse, forcing her fat fingers into a pair of plastic gloves.

No, thought Ian, execrable – the very day he'd had to visit Head Office, cowering in the gents at Cannon Street station, utterly unable to make the dash to Waterloo. God alone knew how he'd ever reached Hinchley Wood, but he'd hogged the train toilet all the way, and even when he had got home, he'd missed three-quarters of 'The Sweeney', racing up and down the stairs from sitting-room to bathroom. And all the callous girls had done was giggle.

'Right, Mr Barnes, lie on your left side and bend your knees up. We're going to give you an enema.'

'WHAT?' Ian leapt from the couch and came face to face with the bolster. 'But there's nothing left in there.'

'You'd be surprised,' grinned Bolster. 'In fact, you'd better know the worst. We're going to give you *two* lovely little enemas.'

Ian opened his mouth and shut it again. Why was the medical profession so incorrigibly and inconsiderately cheerful? Bolster was still grinning – yes, even while she whisked an alarming length of obscene black rubber tubing towards his nether regions. Something cold, hard and inexorable was splitting him in half. He knew when he was beaten.

Second time round, he was blasé – like a war veteran shrugging off the horrors of el-Alamein. He glanced condescendingly at a small scared man still awaiting his first bombardment, dressed, as all the patients were, in a green and lemon stripey gown,

200

and clomping outdoor shoes, his naked hairy legs sticking out incongruously beneath.

'Now this time please sit longer on the toilet,' Sister ordered sternly, as they approached the griping climax of the campaign. 'Fourteen minutes by your watch, and no cheating.'

Ian obeyed, though it was hard to feel dignified, let alone euphoric, sitting racked with spasms on the bog, his eyes on scruffy lino, his mind on absent Ginny. Several of the patients had brought their wives along, as company and comfort. One lovey-dovey couple was even holding hands, rubbing noses almost, between the husband's frantic dashes to the toilet. Togetherness. That's how Ginny and he had been before the damned Renaissance. Ian clutched his stomach, groaning. Toilet doors were opening all around him, then slamming shut again; dazed and stripey combatants staggering in and out of them. No one seemed embarrassed. Here shitting was *de rigueur*.

The barium enema was yet to come. The radiologist had been delayed, and there was a hushed expectancy among the nurses, waiting for their General. Ian touched the pale white shroud which had once been called his body. There was nothing left inside it – no scrap of food or drink, no organs or intestines. That trespassing rubber tube had sucked out his heart, his lungs, his soul, his spleen, and he was just an empty sack. His mouth was foul and dry, his stomach heaved. Funny, really, he'd been starving for two days and now he couldn't think of food. On the journey up to London he'd almost murdered some poor girl just because she'd been eating on the train. He'd watched her like a slavering dog while she whipped out a jam doughnut from a greasy paper bag, and bit into it vigorously, tiny grains of sugar spraying in his face. He couldn't drag his eyes away, kept waiting for the jam – an agonising twitchy wait, since the jam was well off-centre. Then suddenly, unbearably, the crimson ooze burst upon her chin and he'd felt himself reaching for his machete.

It was worse still in the taxi. The driver had been munching a bar of Cadbury's Whole-Nut – he'd under-tipped him in revenge – and every gloating poster they'd passed had been shouting food food food – Kit-Kats, bacon, biscuits, Bird's Eye, Drinka Pinta, Beanz Meanz Heinz.

Ian swung round, alerted by a stirring on the battlefield; nurses shining up their smiles, patients sitting straighter. The Great Man had arrived! He looked nothing like a doctor but was kitted out in a large black rubber apron – the sort of thing you'd probably find in the seedier parts of Soho. The nurse puffed out her bolster in his honour. 'Mr Barnes,' she called.

He was first.

It was raining again when, at last, he left the hospital – a fine sullen rain which snarled up all the traffic and snapped up all the taxis. Ian waited twenty minutes for a non-existent cab, then trailed off to the tube. If only Ginny had been there to meet him, with sympathy, soft words. His thoughts had barely moved from her in the last two hours or so. He'd watched his X-rays on a screen, and seen not his own intestines, but obscene bits of his wife doing disgusting things with private parts of Michelangelo.

'The colon's very distended,' the radiologist had muttered. But all he'd seen was Botticelli's penis – yes, horribly distended.

He phoned from Waterloo, longing to be safe back home, collapse into his bed behind the drawbridge of his own front door, and have Ginny bring him junket on a tray. The phone rang for quite some time before she picked it up.

'Hello, darling, Ian here. Look, I . . .'

'It's Kate. I'm sorry, Ian, but Ginny's had to leave. She'd no idea you'd be so long. Your supper's waiting in the oven, and I've got the two girls. I'm just about to take them back to my place. She may have to stay the night, you see. There's this very special lecturer from Venice . . .'

Ian blocked the ear-piece with his hand. He didn't care if all the treasures of the Italian Renaissance and Venice itself disappeared beneath the ocean-bed. He could see the lovey-dovey couple in the waiting-room, now back at home, entwined. She'd tuck him into bed, a cool compress on his forehead, a tray of delicate invalid-food to tempt his shattered stomach.

He kicked out at the wall. He'd lost not just his entrails, but his wife. Was it really so unreasonable to expect her to be home the day he'd been degutted in a shit-house? Or at least couldn't she have waited to find out how he was, instead of putting Leonardo before his bowels?

He slammed down the receiver, erupted from the phone-box.

Waterloo Station shoved and seethed around him. Everyone looked preoccupied, even the damn pigeons, but where had *he* to go? Ginny was the jam in the doughnut, as far as home and comfort were concerned – and Ginny was probably lolling in a gondola, listening to some siren serenade. He pushed his way morosely into the crowded station bar.

'Brandy please. A double.'

It was madness on an empty stomach (if he still had any stomach), but the second double brightened up the bar. The stuffy room expanded and the beige walls lost their stains. He decided not to die until tomorrow. He got up to tell the barman what a marvellous chap he was, and tripped headlong on the carpet, his elbow catching someone's drink, which spilt like tepid blood across her skirt.

'Damn!' she said, then added three more 'damns', each louder and more vehement than the first. Ian fought the temptation to say '8p in the swear-box', and scrabbled on his knees instead, trying to retrieve her glass. Her fierce hand grabbed it first, the two more or less colliding on the floor.

'What the hell d'you think you're doing?' asked the girl, who had long hair to her waist and the sort of cute tip-tilted nose he'd seen in Snookie's picture-books, which always went with big blue saucer eyes. He checked the eyes – which were furious-brown, flashing under Spanish-style black brows.

'Sorry. Terribly sorry. Please allow me to replenish your glass.' He cursed his strangled voice. Did he have to sound like a boring public meeting just because he was fearfully embarrassed?

'Don't bother.' She was gathering up a cache of bags and parcels, shaking out a swirling orange cloak.

'Please. I insist. What was it, Bloody Mary?'

'No, only tomato juice, but a Bloody Mary would be great. I've had a bloody day.' The bags and cloak subsided, and she grinned.

'Same here,' said Ian. 'I've had three enemas in three hours.' He burst out laughing suddenly, and the girl joined in, the two of them chortling loudly over nothing. At least it broke the tension, allowed them to swap names.

'Harriet,' mused Ian, sucking on it like a sweet, as if to judge its flavour. 'That's pretty, really pretty.' Her hair was pretty, too –

hair like Ginny's before she messed it up – natural living breathing hair, hair you could get lost in. They were soon swapping not just names, but lives – moving on from enemas (and Oxford) to ballet lessons, A-levels and St Martin's School of Art. So here he was, Ian Stuart Richard Barnes, chatting up a real live female artist! If Ginny didn't value him, then discerning women did, admired his sensitivity and style. He courted her with details of the Art-in-Factories scheme, which Holsworth was pioneering at the works. Okay, he'd never shown much interest in it up till now, but he'd been waiting for a Harriet in his life. She was already on her second drink and leaning back against him in the most delightful fashion. Dare he touch her knee – that provocative left knee, distracting him beneath her rucked-up skirt? He reached his hand out tentatively, then pretended he was brushing off a fly. No point rushing things, when they had the whole enchanted evening stretching out in front of them.

He'd take her for a little dinner – somewhere with low lights and soft romantic music, give her a taste for the older man, amuse her with reminiscences of his Management Training Course at Hemel Hempstead, dance the magic night away, show Ginny she wasn't the only one to stagger in at dawn.

He drained his own (third) brandy, resisting the temptation of a fourth. Everything was blurring very pleasantly, and the bottles behind the bar had already started dancing. Better call a halt. He didn't want to lose his touch or reek of alcohol. There might be intimate encounters, lingering farewells . . .

He tried to rehearse his lines. It was so long since he'd asked a girl out, he wasn't quite sure of the form. 'Would you care for a spot of dinner?' sounded suitably nonchalant, but that bald man opposite was listening, and reminded him of Weller at the works. Perhaps he should simply link his arm through Harriet's and wander out into the starlight, with violins playing and a Heavenly Choir hosanna-ing above . . . But it was raining and he'd forgotten his umbrella. He cleared his throat. It was difficult to whisper when she wasn't even looking at him. She seemed much more interested in the far side of the room, and was craning her neck to see over all the heads. God almighty! She was leaving – gathering up her parcels, putting on her cloak. He must forestall her at all costs. He jumped up to his feet. The floor did the dirty on him and chose the same moment to move. He almost lost his footing, clutched blindly at the chair. Once it had stopped spinning and he'd managed to look up, Harriet had gone.

'Wait!' he shouted desperately. 'I . . .' He was seeing double now. She was standing by the door, attached to someone else, a second tall and beautiful person with long straight natural hair. There was just one little difference – even he could spot it – the second person was male. He was also twenty-odd years younger, twenty-odd pounds lighter and at least twenty times more handsome than Ian Stuart Richard Barnes. And this handsome hirsute rival had linked his arm through Harriet's, and they were strolling out together into the starlight for that little spot of dinner.

Ian was sick in the night. He stood shivering in the bedroom, staring through the window at his moon-silvered square of garden, listening to the hooting of an owl. How desolate it sounded, stabbing through the silence of the lonely midnight hours. He pursed his lips, tried to hoot back in reply. Once, he could imitate an owl's cry so authentically that the delighted bird kept echoing and answering, assuming it had found a mate. Now, no sound emerged. He tried again, blowing really vigorously across his bent-up thumbs. Nothing – silence, impotence – a middle-aged failure no longer able to woo an owl or win another woman.

He flopped down on the crumpled bed, which looked empty and forlorn without Ginny's sleeping form to swell it out. He closed his eyes to think of her – saw Harriet instead – Harriet's plump dimpled knee, Harriet's long hair. He reached out to push her skirt up, undo the first few buttons of her blouse. Her breasts were full, milk-white; her soft hair smelt of summer fields, though every time he touched it, or tried to kiss her breasts, she kept shifting and receding, flirting, then rejecting him, taunting him quite shamelessly. He made one last frantic lunge for her, then kicked her out of bed, threw all the sweaty covers off, ditched the swollen pillows, which he'd turned into her breasts. He could feel his heart thumping through his chest, though more from fear than lust now. Supposing he had in fact woken up with a Harriet beside him, a college kid young enough to be his daughter? He hadn't even asked her second name. Next thing he knew, he'd be in the divorce courts – broken home, branded children. And it was all so easy, just a spilt drink in a station bar. Had Ginny ever spilt a drink? No, he mustn't think of that.

He stood queasy by the window, gazing out again at the row of neat back gardens, with their murky shadowed shrubs. Everything seemed as fragile as the moonlight – the owl howling for its faithless mate, the mouse cringeing before the hungry swoop of wings. Never in his life before had he experienced that frightening sense of sliding off a dizzy spinning universe. He'd lost his usual balance, his firm foothold on the world.

Wearily, he climbed between the sheets once more – sheets still damp from Harriet. 'Ginny,' he whispered, as he rolled across to her side, tried to fill its emptiness. 'I'm sorry I even risked it.'

27

'Caldos, darling, I can't, I simply can't. I'd never forgive myself.'

'Don't be absurd, Estrella. It's purely pride on your part, in thinking you're indispensable. It's just a simple operation – absolutely nothing to it, and Ian will probably be grateful for a little peace and quiet.'

'But he's . . .'

'Nonsense! Look at all the fuss you made over the last few months, fretting over the family, terrified your husband would find out. It's obviously a guilt reaction. He hasn't found out, has he? And he won't. It's time you cut loose, in any case. You're nothing but a chatelaine. If a grown man can't face a minor operation without his wife clinging to the bedpan . . .'

'Yes, I know, but . . .'

'But what, Estrella?' He made the Estrella sound sharp and dangerous, like splinters of glass.

'Well, visiting, for example. What's he going to do for visitors? And who'll wash and iron his pyjamas, and bring him grapes and things?' Ginny rolled away from Caldos and lay dejectedly on the far side of the bed.

'You have a mother, haven't you?'

'But Mummy's looking after the girls. I've them to think of too.'

'You never cease thinking of them, Estrella. Quite frankly, it gets a little tedious.' He pulled her back towards the centre of the bed, keeping his hands tight across her wrists. 'George can do the visiting. He's a natural when it comes to grapes. Too many visitors will only hamper Ian's recovery in any case.'

'But I'm his *wife*, Caldos. I love you, I do love you, but I can't just abandon Ian in hospital, while we waltz off to some luxurious health farm.'

'We're not waltzing anywhere, and it is *not* a health farm. It's a serious therapeutic establishment, specially equipped to deal with stress and overwork. Damn it, Estrella, I'm absolutely fagged out. I've been working like a dog and I need a rest. I always go to Hatton Hall the first two weeks of August, and you're coming with me. If you're that concerned, you'd better change the date of your husband's operation.'

She shivered at his icy tone. 'But Caldos darling, you know that's quite impossible. Chris moved heaven and earth getting him in so soon. There's a waiting list of a year or more. And Ian particularly wanted August because the works shut down.'

Caldos fumed out of bed and started sorting through his clothes, voice muffled as he struggled into his sweater. 'And what about *my* work? You seem to be totally ignoring the fact I have a lot of other people to consider. Many of my patients are away themselves in the summer, so I always take my own vacation then, so as to cause as little disruption as possible to their appointments. I'm a doctor, Estrella, and a very busy one, not just your private plaything.'

She slipped out of bed herself, put her arms around his waist, laid her cheek against his silky sweater. 'Look, I do understand, honestly I do, but . . .'

He almost shook her off. 'I've given you every chance to break out of your prison and you keep cringeing back again. It was the same thing with the job. I offer you a fantastic God-sent opportunity to be the toast of London, and all you do is bleat about your child's piano lessons.'

'Oh Caldos, please don't start all that again. I've told you I . . .'

'Only slaves love their chains, Estrella. I created you a princess, not a chattel.'

'I know, Caldos darling. I *am* grateful, really I am. It's just that it's not easy being a full-time princess.' She followed him over to the window, stood a pace or two behind him. 'And your job does sound very full-time – *and* in London, which makes things still more tricky. Sarah has Guides in Claygate on a Monday, and swimming twice a week in Kingston, and I *do* have to take Snookie to piano lessons. Her teacher lives five miles away. And who'll feed the dog and . . . ?'

'For Christ's sake, Estrella, you'll be a full-scale career woman, earning enough to hire a nanny – one for the dog as well, if you insist.'

'But I don't believe in nannies.'

'Sentimental nonsense!' Caldos was buttoning his jacket, unbuttoning it again, taking out his anger on the buttonholes. 'When I was a child, I had twenty-three-and-a-half nannies in fourteen years, and it hasn't done me any harm. I can't speak for the dog. I detest dogs on principle. You'll be telling me next you can't leave the goldfish on their own.'

She tried to smile, but her mouth had forgotten how. 'I'm working on it, Caldos, please believe me. I've mentioned it to Kate, and she's already agreed to help me with the children.'

'And what about your husband? Have you told him?'

'Well, no. Not exactly.'

'Why not?'

'Well, he's a bit suspicious anyway, and what with him being ill and everything . . .'

Caldos had picked a leaf off the aspidistra and was shredding it to pieces. 'Haemorrhoids is not an illness, Estrella. It's a combination of anal character and faulty diet.'

'Yes, but it still *hurts* him, darling, doesn't it? And I do try with his diet – I'm stuffing him with bran and prunes.'

Caldos squashed the mangled leaf into a pulp. 'I've no wish to discuss Ian's alimentary canal – except in so far as it threatens to endanger my vacation plans. Well, Estrella, are you coming to Hatton Hall, or aren't you?'

She leaned out of the window. The sun was shining for the first time in a fortnight. How had they ever got to summer? Caldos belonged more naturally to winter, to raw nights and stormy skies; didn't seem to fit this tranquil garden with its old-fashioned country flowers. She breathed in the sugared scent of stocks, watched two pollen-heavy bees crawl inside the purple bells of foxgloves. A noisy blackbird was preening in a tree – a small stunted solitary tree. She turned away. 'No, Caldos, I honestly don't think I can.'

He flung his jacket on the bed, came up behind her and forced her on her knees. She was still completely naked – passive, silent, dejected by their argument. He unzipped his trousers, entered her. He was barely hard, but he thrust until he stiffened, then paused, and, still inside her, unbuckled his heavy leather belt. There was a moment's frozen silence in which neither of them moved. Then she felt him easing out of her, still stiff, but now withdrawing; heard his laboured breathing, the nervous chink of the belt-buckle as it caught against the bed. Then, brutally, abruptly, the bronze buckle struck her thighs. She could feel heat rushing into her; the angry swish of leather cutting through the blackbird's song outside. Song and pain had fused – both too fiercely raucous, yet rapturous, intense. She was singing with the bird, sobbing out 'I'm sorry, sorry, sorry', but the apology had disappeared, become only a delighted echo of the pain.

'Stop!' she shouted suddenly. It was too merciless, too much. 'No more. Please stop, please stop.' Her voice was crying out, but her body was betraying her, begging 'Yes, go on, go *on*', and he ignored her voice and obeyed her body, until they both slumped still and surfeited; he the one now whimpering, 'I'm sorry, oh, I'm sorry, my little wolf, my darling.'

She had hardly known it was pain before. It had been just a show, a ritual. But this time she was mastered by the pain, raped by it, stampeded, and she could do nothing but submit – submit and worship him.

Slowly, he stood up, replaced his jacket, buckled back the belt. The blackbird's song seemed to transport the whole lush garden, brazen and bewitching. 'So Hatton Hall is fixed then?' His voice was sun and flowers.

'Yes,' she whispered, still crouched down on her knees. She knew he liked to see the marks; see his strength, his potency.

'And you'll take the job?'

'Yes,' she said again. How could she refuse him? He had taught her the holy sacrament of pain.

She packed for both her men. Ian's case was small and shabby, and one of the cheap locks had broken. She folded chain-store striped pyjamas and schoolboy dressing gown. Caldos didn't own pyjamas – winceyette Durex was the scathing term he used for them. But even scathing Caldos would have to wear pyjamas in hospital. Except he wouldn't go to hospital, least of all with something as unglamorous as haemorrhoids. He'd die in some dramatic way, with not a bedpan or a rubber glove in sight; drowned off Viareggio like Shelley, with a nightingale sobbing out his elegy, and the moon eclipsed in grief, or buried in an avalanche on the howling north face of the Eiger. She rushed with dogs and brandy to dig his glorious body from a snowdrift. She was giving him the kiss of life, his first romantic words as he wavered into consciousness an ardent protestation of his love.

His voice was interrupted by the sound of Ian's old slippers plopping into the case – battered vinyl slippers, down at heel. She tried to plump them up, stuffed his carton of Eno's Fruit Salts in one of them and his hairbrush in the other. Why couldn't he use scent and aftershave like Caldos, in expensive cut-glass bottles, and silver-backed hairbrushes and hand-made tortoiseshell combs? Even his toothbrush looked tired. She had never seen Caldos clean his teeth. Her lover always took great care never to do anything in front of her which wasn't either stylish or exciting. And he never developed cold sores or psoriasis, or bunged up the bathroom cupboard with suppositories and Sennakot, or gargled ostentatiously every time his typist had a cold – all of which her husband did. She slammed his suitcase shut. Even that was typical – faded, unadventurous, the labels bleating 'Bridlington' and 'Bognor', instead of boasting 'Bangkok' and 'Biarritz'.

Caldos' cases were as exotic as their owner: soft black grainy leather, lined with scarlet silk, with dramatic-looking zips and straps, and his gold-plated initials swanking on the lids. He'd played Scarlatti while she packed for him, on her knees again as she folded silk and cashmere, slipped in silver hip-flasks, Italian kid-skin shoes, gold and emerald cufflinks, or calf-bound books on the Comte de Lautréamont. She had breathed in all the smells – leather and tobacco, lavender and musk; relished his initials which were embroidered on his bathrobe, engraved on gold or silver, stamped across her heart.

'Ready, Ian?' she called, still fiddling with the broken lock. Couldn't he have bought himself a new case? She was sick of his economy. All he had engraved on *his* heart was '2p off'.

'I'll miss you, sweetheart. I'll miss you terribly.'

'You'll be all right. It's a very simple operation – almost nothing to it. Everybody says so.' Well, Caldos was everybody.

He sat beside her in the passenger seat. It annoyed her really, the way he let her drive. There was nothing wrong with him that he hadn't had for years.

'You will write, won't you darling?' He was clenching and unclenching his hands, seemed as nervous as a child. 'And I'll phone you, if you leave your number. Do they allow you to have phone-calls on the course?'

'No, I'm sorry, Ian, it says specifically no calls. But I can ring the hospital and ask Sister how you're getting on.'

'I wish the girls had come.'

'Hospitals are bad for children.' Why was he making such a fuss? He'd probably have a dozen randy mistresses mincing in with hothouse flowers as soon as her back was turned.

'Well, give them lots of love and a special hug from Daddy. You'll see them, won't you, before you go?'

She didn't answer; tried to pretend she needed all her concentration to manoeuvre the car into a tricky parking space.

'Don't be in such a hurry, pigeon. I want to kiss you – here. There's no privacy in hospital. You can never say goodbye.'

She cut the kiss as short as possible, seized Ian's case and the Lucozade, and steered him up the steps into a dingy corridor. They joined a queue snailing down the hall from the reception desk. Ginny looked encouragingly around her – beige lino, corpse-grey walls. 'Aren't the pictures pretty?'

'Pigeon . . .'

'Sssh, don't call me that in public.'

'I love you, Ginny darling.'

'Ian, have you got your card? It's our turn next.'

They were directed to Men's Surgical. A skinny nurse came bustling up, her smile so shining and sincere it was like a Sunday School prize for scripture. 'Mr Barnes? Right, we'll just pop you into bed and then your wife can stay with you a while.'

Oh no she can't, thought Ginny. Mrs Estrella Barnes de Roche has to be in Chelsea by the dot of four; hasn't time to see her children, or hold her husband's hand. Ian would make her late if he didn't get a move on; was still cowering at the door, as if reluctant to commit himself to the horrors of the ward. 'Hurry up,' she urged. 'You don't want to catch a chill.'

'But it's boiling in here, Ginny. I can hardly breathe.'

The other patients all looked up when they walked between the narrow beds to the far end of the ward. She was aware of admiring glances, men goggling at her brilliant scarlet coat-dress, dazzled by her newly blonded hair.

'Cor!' said the gaffer in the next bed to Ian. 'Do a swop?'

Ian flushed with pride and pleasure, linked his arm through Ginny's, as if to emphasise their bond. The nurse smirked her approval, then drew the curtains round his bed, told him to undress. He and Ginny were cocooned in blue flowered chintz. She whisked his striped pyjamas from the case, watched him put them on. They no longer seemed absurd, but rather sad. She'd shrunk them in the wash, and his wrists emerged, looking thin and pale and vulnerable, from the forlorn and grudging sleeves. Suddenly, she kissed the wrists, clasped them in her hands. 'I brought you a book,' she whispered. 'And a coffee cake.'

She had wrapped the book in gold paper and red ribbon. He struggled with the knots. 'A hardback!' he exclaimed. 'Gosh, darling, how extravagant.' They always bought paperbacks, or got hardbacks from the library. It was one of their life-principles, like three-star petrol, or turning sheets sides to middle.

'*Early English Christian Poetry*,' Ian spelt out, perching on the bed. 'Unusual,' he said lamely, then added 'Nice', and 'Thank you'.

Ginny hugged him almost fiercely. The book fell off the bed and landed with a thud. Neither of them retrieved it. 'I'm sorry, Ian. I'm sorry,' she repeated.

He cradled her streaked hair in the hollow between his chin and the top pyjama button. 'It's all right, pigeon. I'm not really ill. Don't worry.' He was stroking the top of her head, his other arm tight around her waist. 'I'll miss you, darling. I only hope you'll manage on your own. I don't like to think of you doing all that studying.'

'Time to go, Mrs Barnes.'

The blue chintz curtains squealed back along their rails, and a larger lank-haired nurse beamed at Ian and popped a thermometer under his tongue. Ginny gathered up gold paper and empty case, then squeezed his hand and tried to mumble some adequate goodbye. Her eyes were pricking and her throat felt full of string. Ian made farewell noises through the thermometer, watched her elegant red back dwindle down the ward, turn a moment at the door, wave and disappear.

'Bowels open?' asked the nurse.

'No,' said Ian.

Ginny pulled into a lay-by just half a mile from the hospital, and switched off the ignition. She crumpled up gold paper and red ribbon, flung them through the window. If only she'd given him a gardening book, or a decent home-made cake, not that cardboard thing from Tesco's, or bought him a pair of elegant pyjamas, instead of criticising his old ones and splurging all the money on her hair. He'd have been the wolf of the ward in a pair of scarlet silk pyjamas. No, not scarlet – that was Caldos' colour. She was muddling them up again. It was bad enough with the Early Christian Poetry. Just because Caldos had spent the whole of one evening reading her 'St Andrew's Mission to Mermedonia', was that any reason for foisting it on Ian? Dear devoted Ian, who had looked up trains for her to Wellingborough, when she was going by Lamborghini to Wiltshire, and had given her ten pounds to spend – a fortune for her husband, whereas a tenner for de Roche was simply half a lobster dinner, or one substandard haircut.

Her tears dripped off the steering wheel. 'Pigeon,' she said wretchedly – her private name, her pet name, which she had rejected with Ian's kiss. She couldn't rush away like that, so casually and callously; must return and make her peace with him. She'd be late for Caldos, yes, and her lover loathed unpunctuality (in others), but she must tell Ian she loved him.

But did she love him, or was that a lie, as well? She was in love with Caldos, wasn't she, and scarlet silk bathrobes and swingeing silver brushes? If Ian were back beside her, she'd be wincing at the way he pronounced the t in often. (Caldos said 'orphan', which was infinitely smarter.) And she didn't seem to know Ian any more. Their life was such a muddle. He always said he loved her, but once you lied yourself, you stopped believing anything. If only she could talk to him, ask him outright about that treacherous black lace nightie. But he might start asking questions in his turn. And she daren't risk Caldos – it would be like cutting out her heart.

She switched the engine on. She was already on the right road for London. Her case was packed, the house locked up; she could be in Chelsea in less than forty minutes. She sat agonising, dithering, her eyes straying to the empty case she'd just brought back from the ward, and which was sitting on the passenger seat where Ian had sat himself. She read the tatty labels – Bridlington and Bognor. Bognor had been lodgings with a Mrs Ella Fish, who wore fur boots and metal curlers both at the same time, and sang 'Jerusalem' at breakfast. Ian had caught his first mackerel and Snookie had caught mumps. Ian had stayed in with the invalid all day, playing endless games of tiddly-winks and Ludo, so that she herself was free to swim with Sarah. Bridlington was a guest-house – full of geriatrics who mumbled through their bread-and-butter pudding and their 'Coronation Street'. She and Ian had escaped the white sticks and blue rinses, and giggled on the pier, splashing through the puddles, sucking sticks of rock, and Ian had bought her a funny hat with 'You're My Girl' written on the brim.

She turned round in the lay-by, sped back the way she'd come, hurtling down the bypass, cursing at red lights. She parked in a No-Parking space, dashed along the corridor, up the stairs to Grosvenor Ward. There was no nurse about – they were understaffed as always – so she slunk in through the open door and tiptoed down the ward. She heard an eager wolf-whistle, but didn't dare look round. Ian's bed was empty.

'Excuse me, do you know where my husband is?' The man in the next bed was deep in the racing page of the *Express*.

''E's on the bog. Nurse given 'im an enema. I don't reckon 'e'll be wantin' a visitor – not in '*is* position!' His raucous laugh changed key into a hacking phlegmy cough. Ginny turned away.

Ian's locker was bare – no bowl of fruit, no flowers. He'd picked her flowers at Bridlington, a bunch of mainly cow-parsley, with a few limp and fragile harebells; stuck them in a tooth-mug. The parsley had smelt strange – sickly-sweet and curdled; had dropped all over the dressing-table like wisps of scented lace. She scrabbled in her handbag for a pencil and a scrap of paper. 'Just to tell you I love you,' she wrote, folded the paper, and put it on his pillow.

Heavy footsteps were prowling up the ward. 'Mrs Barnes, however did you get in here? This is the afternoon rest period and visitors are strictly forbidden.' Sister's glasses curved upwards at the corners; her iron-grey hair was scraped right up on top. Only her mouth turned down.

'There was . . . something I forgot.'

Sister pushed past her, straightened Ian's coverlet. She plumped up both the pillows, and the scrap of paper fluttered to the floor. Ginny tried to pick it up.

'Mrs Barnes, would you kindly leave the ward. You're disturbing all the patients crawling on the floor like that. You may visit your husband at six o'clock this evening. Until eight.'

The man in the next bed guffawed. 'You'll cop it!' he said. 'Want a tip for the three-thirty? Royal Scarlet. Can't lose.'

'No thanks, I never gamble. But could you please tell my husband . . .'

'No, he could not,' thundered Sister. 'He's meant to be resting.'

She removed the *Express* and Ginny with the same fervent disapproval and marched them to the door. The scrap of paper fluttered in the draught and was swept two beds along.

'Sorry,' Ginny murmured. It was all she ever seemed to say these days.

28

Six o'clock. Visiting time. Caldos turned off the main road into a tortuous drive lined with scarlet rhododendrons. Ginny peered out of the window, seeing only Grosvenor Ward. Ian would be alone, while all the other patients relaxed with loving relatives. He couldn't even see the girls. Her mother had swept them off to the bracing air of Lowestoft, ensconced them in her sister's country cottage. She didn't approve of Ginny's education – abandoning her children and a haemorrhoidal husband, shrugging off her marriage vows, and behaving like a new-fangled career-woman.

De Roche pulled up in front of a rambling Victorian mansion, dripping wisteria and charm; squeezed his Lamborghini between a Ferrari and a Rolls. 'Isn't it absolute perfection?' he exclaimed, gesturing to the ivy-tangled folly just left of the main house, and the shimmering lake with its rare and menacing black swans.

'Perfection,' she echoed. Echoing seemed easiest when her thoughts were still on bedpans and suppositories.

'The architect was a madman, actually – shot himself and two of his builders because the tower fell down. See that tiny window on the right . . .'

'Where?' said Ginny. She hoped the man beside him wouldn't cough all night. And would her mother remember Snookie's eardrops?

' . . . related to a friend of the Earl of Pembroke. So when they built the ha-ha . . .'

She could always send some flowers by Interflora, use the money he'd given her himself. But would she find a shop? They seemed miles from anywhere.

' . . . bodged copy of the Temple at Delphi. One of the few who actually went to Greece. But he bungled the enstasis, none the less.'

She hoped they wouldn't bungle Ian's haemorrhoidectomy (what a painful word that was!) and leave him to bleed to a solitary death. But perhaps he wasn't solitary. Perhaps a mink-coated hussy was already by his side, popping grapes into his panting mouth. Why should she waste her holiday worrying about him, when he had cool erotic hands feeling him up beneath the counterpane?

A flock of stiff black lackeys descended on the car, opening doors and touching forelocks. She was swept into a chilly marble hall, with frowning alabaster busts glaring from deep niches. A disapproving grandee sneered from his gilded frame and whispered 'Whore!' She turned her back on his simpering satin knee-britches, and came face to face with a dazzling Dr Kildare. The white coat bowed in their direction.

'Estrella Caesari,' Caldos announced, introducing Ginny with a flourish. She blushed, aware that Knee-Britches didn't believe it for a moment, and that even Dr Kildare was looking rather fazed. One of the larger lackeys strutted just in front of them, carrying the car-rug, which was real ranch-mink, and huge. Knee-Britches almost fell out of his frame. Money talked at Hatton Hall. The other minions shuffled in his wake, heaving cases, hampers, cameras, cassette players, golf clubs and a riding whip. They processed into a sumptuous corridor, hung with gold-framed pictures and heady with the scent of flowers – exotic blooms in priceless porcelain bowls. Ginny glimpsed half-naked figures (real ones, not in frames) lolling in their nightclothes. Nobody seemed dressed, nor ill. Expensive radiant health oozed through the place like ozone.

'Most of the inmates are at their last gasp,' Caldos told her later, in their lemon-verbena suite with its oval satin bed. 'But they can't afford to be seen to be ill.' He stroked Ginny's pubic region with an affectionate big toe. 'Top tycoons with as many peptic ulcers as they have businesses, film producers who've broken themselves along with their box office records, actresses falling apart beneath the greasepaint . . . Kiss me.'

Ginny obliged, wondering if Ian had had his supper yet. Fishcakes and blancmange, with a cup of cold stewed tea.

'Half of them are living on a lettuce leaf. It's *de rigueur* to fast here. The sole topic of conversation is how many calories in half an inch of cucumber.'

The toe was straying to her navel, exploring it, surprising it; his other foot now joining in, doing things she'd never thought that feet were meant to do. 'But I've got a dispensation, as you Roman Catholics say. I'm not too keen on shelling out a thousand pounds or more a week for the privilege of downing a paltry glass of lemon-water for breakfast, lunch and tea. It'll be a four-course dinner for us, my love, and a decent claret to flush the system out.'

Castor oil and syrup of figs was all poor Ian would get to flush him out – and nothing in the morning. She shuddered. Supposing the surgeon left a swab inside him, like last week's TV serial? The two feet and their owner were expecting some response. She spread her thighs a little wider and tried to concentrate. 'But alcohol is absolutely forbidden, darling. It says so in the brochure.'

'A lot of things are absolutely forbidden, *mein Liebchen*. But the de Roches devote their lives to squeezing the last drop of juice from forbidden fruits.' Caldos stretched and yawned. '*You* could always fast, of course. I'd like to see you thinner. And it's said to be a first-rate aphrodisiac.'

Ginny closed her legs, accepting the rebuke. She was obviously in need of a powerful aphrodisiac, if she couldn't drag her mind away from laxatives and fishcakes when Caldos' glorious nakedness was displayed in all its splendour on verbena-yellow satin. 'All right,' she said. 'I'll fast.'

It would be a sort of penance, which she could offer up for Ian. She'd done that at her boarding school – offered up her trifling little agonies for the Holy Souls in Purgatory, reduced their pain by suffering herself. Her two luxurious weeks with Caldos wouldn't seem so wicked if she starved.

'Well, shall we look around and see who's here?' Caldos reached out for his bathrobe. 'There's obviously no point in trying to make love to you until that lemon-water sharpens up your senses.'

Ginny heard the snide behind the bantering. She had never not responded to him before.

'No, don't put your clothes back on. Nobody gets dressed at Hatton Hall. We just drift about in dressing gowns.'

'What, in *public*?'

'Estrella, you really are a tedious little prude. If you're going to make such a song and dance about every tiny thing, then perhaps you'd better sit up here in your fur boots and your overcoat. I'm off for a beetroot cocktail with my chums.'

The door slammed shut behind him. Ginny stared despondently at the yellow satin sheets. Now Caldos had lost his temper, Ian would lose his colon, and she'd lose both of them. She picked up the primrose-coloured phone. 'Could you put me through to Beechgrove Hospital . . .'

Ian was fine – playing Ludo with an appendicectomy, so the nurse reported, and finishing up all his cod and semolina. There was no mention of illicit lady visitors, but Ian had probably bribed her to keep mum. Or maybe he was canoodling with a night nurse.

Next she phoned the girls. They also sounded infuriatingly cheerful, Snookie raving on and on about Grandma's home-made nut and honey biscuits, and her mother saying, 'They'll be better for the change,' in an accusing sort of voice.

'Look, Mummy, I must go now. It's long distance, don't forget.'

Caldos would be paying for the calls, and Caldos, incidentally, hadn't bothered to return. She unpacked all his cases, polished his shoes with her face flannel, and placed the chocolate bourbons just beside his pillow. Still no sign of him. She picked up the Comte de Lautréamont and tried to read, but neither her French nor her spirits were up to it. Perhaps he was expecting her, waiting for her somewhere, annoyed that she was sulking in her room. She trailed into the bathroom, gave her face the Babette of Bond Street treatment, selected her flimsiest housecoat and crept self-consciously downstairs.

He wasn't in the billiard room – only a lone Arab with a flowing head-dress atop his gold-striped dressing gown, and hairy ankles protruding underneath. He swooped towards her with a flash of Persil teeth. 'You like play?'

Ginny backed away. She was in no mood to be initiated into an oil sheik's harem, not just at the moment. She loped along the corridor, colliding with a tall girl in a leotard, a hurry, and purple fishnet tights.

'Hi there! Coming to the abdominal class?'

'I beg your pardon?'

220

'Exercises to tone up the tum. Starts in just two minutes.'

Ginny pulled in her stomach. There were other, more important things which needed toning up, and she was getting rather frantic about losing the whole reason for keeping muscles tight. She passed a door marked 'Smoking Room', opened it a crack, and was instantly bombarded with gusts of cigarette smoke, squalls of raucous laughter.

'Come to join us in the Sin Bin?' shrilled a campy-looking man, naked except for a pair of satin running-shorts, and one gold dangly earring. 'Have a fag.'

Ginny trickled in, trying not to cough. 'No thanks. I don't smoke.'

There was a concerted shout of laughter. 'Why come in here then? This is the den of vice, my love. Smoking is absolutely *verboten* anywhere else, so all we sinners congregate in here and ruin our rotten lungs together.'

A vamp in a fuchsia négligé and toning magenta hair looked up from her nest of cushions on the floor. 'You must be a new girl. Want to stake a tenner on the next throw?'

Ginny glimpsed a roulette wheel concealed behind an exercise machine, an impressive pile of bank notes heaped beside it. 'No, sorry, I'm . . . looking for someone.' She fled, stopped pale and panting in front of a large potted palm blocking her way in the corridor, which sprouted not bananas or exotic tropical flowers, but a plethora of notices, dangling from its leaves: Sauna, Solarium, Quiet Please, No Smoking, Acupuncture, Osteopathy, Light Diet Room. Ah, that was more like it. She'd love a cup of tea.

The Diet Room was just a few doors down, and looked singularly inviting with its oasis of green plants, and its gently plashing fountain, graced by randy cherubs, who were working off their hormones on what Caldos would call distinctly phallic dolphins. Even the sleek goldfish seemed vitamin-enriched.

One lone guest was sitting on a spindly turquoise chair, tearing the innards out of a grapefruit. She had scraped the flesh completely clean and was gnawing on the pith. 'I've been known to eat the skin, dear. The only problem is they don't tell you how many calories in grapefruit rind, and I daren't exceed my two hundred a day.'

'Two hundred!' Ginny gasped. 'But that's starvation.' There were two hundred calories in half a piece of cherry cake.

'But that's exactly why we're here, dear.' The woman tipped back her four chins and squeezed a non-existent drop of grapefruit juice into her ever-hopeful mouth. 'The most expensive form of starvation known to man – or woman, come to that.' She swathed the empty skin in a paper serviette, and stuffed it in her handbag. 'I always save them for the middle of the night,' she confided. 'In case I go berserk and chew the mattress. 'Bye, dear. See you in the sauna!'

Ginny walked up to the counter, where a rosy-cheeked Nell Gwyn was flinging oranges and lemons into a voracious-looking juicing machine. 'A pot of tea, please, and two rounds of buttered toast.'

The girl staggered, dropped three lemons.

'Is it too late for tea? Well, make it coffee then – with cream.'

The girl's pink cheeks and smile had both vanished from her face. She clung whey-faced to the counter for support. 'Tea and coffee are totally forbidden.' She made them sound like bigamy or rape. 'It's the caffeine, madam, it's absolutely lethal. It damages the kidneys, overstrains the heart, plays havoc with the entire nervous system, interferes with sleep, impairs fertility . . .' She paused for breath, still looking shaky-pale; retrieved her three bruised lemons. 'Mr Fledge-Parthington simply won't allow them on the premises. We have nettle tea, or Fig and Acorn Healthy-Cup. Or I could give you cabbage-juice.'

Ginny took a tumblerful of khaki-coloured dishwater, tried to turn it into Kenco Special Blend. How could a drop of caffeine overstrain her heart when it was already completely broken by her lover? She watched a caffeine-free goldfish swim a languorous circle, then suddenly turn tail and skulk beneath a lily-leaf. An announcement on the intercom had disturbed his watery peace.

'Miss Caesari, calling Miss Caesari! Miss Caesari wanted in Consulting Room One.'

Ginny looked up from her glass. That was an unusual name – Italian, probably. Maybe she could practise her Italian here – all six words of it.

'Miss Caesari,' boomed the voice again, alarming Ginny this time, as well as just the fish. *She* was Miss Caesari! It was part of her lover's attempt to be discreet, or maybe simply window-dressing. He hated names like Barnes. She hid her untouched cabbage-juice behind an obliging cyclamen, and skedaddled to the door, pausing for a moment to ask Nell Gwyn the way.

'You're in luck,' she fluttered, having explained the (prime) location of Consulting Room One. 'Seeing the Great Man himself! Most of our guests would sacrifice an arm or leg for the honour of two minutes with him.'

'Mr Fledge-Parthington,' swanked the notice on the door. 'Therapeutic Director, Registered Osteopath, Naturopath, Herbalist, Bio-Energist, Reflexologist, Acupuncturist, Spinologist, Hypnotherapist, Iridologist . . .' The 'ists' continued in dizzying confusion, followed by a string of letters after his name which were so long and complicated they made even those on de Roche's door at Harley Street look a little puny.

'Come,' drawled a mellifluous voice, which sounded as if it had been marinated in olive oil and treacle.

Ginny came – found herself eye to chest with a tall eagle of a man, whose beaky nose and crest of hair arched in opposite directions. He was wearing a designer version of the Dr Kildare coat, buttoned at the side, and with impressive hieroglyphics emblazoned on the pocket. His office was a cross between a greenhouse and a morgue.

'Just slip your things off, Miss Caesari, and lie down on this couch.'

He himself sat imperious at the desk, rapping out staccato questions and sanctifying her answers with a gold-plated Parker pen. Height? Weight? Age? Occupation? *Occupation*. Whatever could she call herself? Certainly not a housewife any more. She hadn't made her usual strawberry jam, and the freezer was full of Bird's Eye Thaw 'n' Serve. A professional mistress, maybe? Except her man and master had just walked out on her. A full-time hostess at a Health and Happiness Centre? Well, that was Caldos' plan, and one he hoped to execute in less than two brief months. He'd dreamed up this fantastic scheme of a psychiatric health club, with every conceivable luxury, from ritzy five-star restaurants to Instant Paradise (tropical pools, unisex solarium, parakeets and palm trees), and every type of therapy, both physical and mental, from Gestalt through to ginseng. Her head had reeled as he'd described his complex plans for Surrogate Orgies, Fantasy Factories, Death Acceptance Training, with couches shaped like coffins, Dream Re-enactment in psychedelic dream palaces with surrealist backdrops, and Back-To-Childhood Rage And Fury Work-outs in specially sound-proofed nurseries. She wasn't sure how much of it was serious – you never knew with Caldos. He'd mentioned Sock-Your-Analyst Sessions, in which patients used their doctor as a sort of human coconut-shy, and Get-Even-With-God Encounters where people shrieked abuse at God, and even Sunday Bloody Sundays where repressed Al Capones could biff dummy policemen and hold up plastic banks.

It sounded quite preposterous, yet the scheme was front-page news. Caldos had been grooming it for months, working on a project which would treat patients as whole people, not just bodies slumped on couches, or mouths reciting endless monologues. And he'd no longer call them 'patients', which suggested suffering and passivity, but 'clients', which was healthier – healthier for them, as well as for his profits. He was also considering dispensing with all diagnostic labels. Terms like 'depressive' and 'obsessional', 'schizoid' and 'hysterical' often caused more misery, he claimed; endowing patients with a sense of shame and stigma, sometimes even hopelessness. One of his chief aims was to boost clients' self-esteem, remove them from the straitjacket of strict Freudian analysis – a system he was finding increasingly onerous himself. Now, at last, he was breaking out, combining a host of weird and wonderful new therapies with a thrusting business venture; the whole designed to bring in far more clients, win him fame and fortune, and provide a total shake-up for what he called his impotent profession. He'd been groping towards a reform like this for most of his professional life, and now it was almost ready to burst upon the world – a club for total health and happiness. Philip Mossman was managing the financial side, and Caldos himself canvassing support from half of London's glossier psychiatrists.

But he wouldn't rest content with just the VIPs. She and humble George had also been recruited. George would be his Front Man, and Flora and Fauna Supervisor, pruning palm trees and teaching the parrots the collected works of Freud, and, as for her

– well, that was more of a puzzle. She wasn't really sure what he intended her to do, save divest the clients of their clothes, and maybe of their hang-ups. The very thought of such a role left her cold with fear. She hadn't had a job for thirteen years, didn't know the difference between Jung and Yang, and until Caldos had corrected her, she'd thought Masters and Johnson was a superior sort of grocer's shop. Nor had she yet mentioned it to Ian. He might just allow her to do a spot of secretarial work at the local insurance office, but a playgirl at a psychiatric Bunny Club . . .

'I beg your pardon?' Ginny plopped down from her naked palm tree, back on to the couch.

'I said, Miss Caesari – twice, in actual fact – that you appear to be in a state of severe stress.'

She'd hardly even noticed that the Eagle had left his perch, and was now standing sternly over her, frowning at her naked form as if it left much to be desired. His icy hands descended, cracked a bone or two. She yelped with pain, her face and body both screwed up, every muscle stiff. Fledge-Parthington was right. She was utterly exhausted, losing weight, losing sleep, probably losing brain-cells. And was it any wonder, after months of trying to juggle two completely different roles – be a loving wife and mother, and a depraved and avid whore; answer to two different names, mug up poetry and pathology, parakeets and penis-envy, while still ironing shirts and sheets, queuing at the check-out with two tons of so-called convenience food, and trying to help with homework which got harder every week? She closed her eyes, breathed in the smells of wintergreen and camphor, listened to the rhythmic drone of a distant lulling lawn-mower. Perhaps she could relax at Hatton Hall.

The mower was submerged by the Eagle's pouncing voice, the snap-crackle of her bones beneath his fingers. 'I just don't think you realise, Miss Caesari, how you've been abusing your whole body. You've got a unilateral anterior flexion of the pelvis on the right, which is causing a scoliotic curvature of the spine and an occipital lesion of the atlas.'

Ginny hid her face. She might not understand the jargon, but the message was quite clear – mortal sins again. 'Abusing your body' was the very phrase Father Patrick Maloney had employed, though in a slightly different context. And that 'flexion of the pelvis' only increased her sense of guilt. Since she'd been making love to Caldos, her pelvis had been flexing flagrantly, continually.

'You'll be no help to the Doctor in such poor physical shape, and so clearly overwrought. What he needs is total relaxation. His blood pressure is already raised.'

'Oh my God, no!' She tried to leap up from the couch, but the nutcracker hands had moved to her neck and were unscrewing it from her trunk.

'Don't overreact, Miss Caesari. The Doctor requires a little tender loving care, not panic and hysteria. We'll do our best therapeutically, of course, but I shall have to ask you to co-operate on the all-important personal side. Dr de Roche is a brilliant man, d'you realise, and he's entitled to your hundred per cent support.' He turned Ginny on her back, started pressing on her chest with his flattened palms, like an iron on an ironing board. She grimaced as her first two ribs buckled under the pressure. But what was a broken rib compared with Caldos? He might be dead already, rigid on a slab. High blood pressure was dangerous, could result in strokes or heart attacks. And she had helped to put it up by being fraught herself, failing to respond to him, abusing her whole body.

She chafed at the door, as the Eagle explained the mysteries of her fast. Yes, she knew all about the lemon-water, but where and how was Caldos? She rushed back to their suite – vastly coldly empty – hurtled down the stairs again, to a group of starving fatties who were storming the portals of the Diet Room.

'Excuse me, I'm looking for a Dr de Roche. You haven't seen him, have you?'

'No, sorry, darling. You won't find any doctors here. They're all cranks and chiropractors. Coming for your carrot juice?'

'No, I'm in the dining-room. Special dispensation.'

Shrieks of rage and envy echoed round the corridor. Ginny tried to smile. A balding man with a resplendent Jewish nose offered her an arm. 'I'm in the dining-room myself – first solid food for a fortnight. I only hope I don't disgrace myself. May I escort you in?'

Ginny hesitated, but two seventeen-stone matrons were shoving from behind, and before she could excuse herself, she and the nose had been butted through the heavy panelled door. She glimpsed de Roche at the far end of the room, ensconced at the best table. Smirking right beside him was a deplorably attractive redhead in what looked like her little sister's nightie. Caldos' arm was planted on her chair-back with a proprietorial air, his errant fingers tangled in her hair. Her torso looked revoltingly mobile, and was undulating freely into Caldos' own Uri Geller spine. Even their two chair-legs were entwined. Caldos was sharpening up his appetite (and wit) on a giant-sized celery stalk, breaking off loving little morsels and feeding them to the mane of Titian hair. Two other couples were also at his table, lapping up his jokes, offering him their homage and applause.

Ginny absconded from the Jewish nose to join him, slipping in self-consciously beside a fox-faced female with more diamonds than dressing gown. Caldos honoured her with a vague wave of his hand, then continued with his story about Bertrand Russell and the stationmaster.

'Soya Surprise or Lentil Savoury?' intoned the waiter, frowning at their blasphemous mirth. 'Fresh salmon for *you*, sir,' he whispered conspiratorially into de Roche's left ear. 'With asparagus to start.' Caldos grinned and nodded. 'And lemon water for madam.' He set down Ginny's glass with an obsequious (sadistic) smirk.

The murky fluid looked just slightly more appealing than her glass of cabbage juice – the colour of cement, rather than of excrement, and with a little lemon debris floating on the surface. She took a cautious sip, wondering how much nourishment could be extracted from a lemon-pip.

'Christ! You're not fasting in *here*, are you?' The redhead slipped a soya bean between her Clara Bow lips. 'What a bore!'

De Roche rummaged in a capacious plastic sponge-bag which he'd secreted under the table, and unveiled three cartons of Purefoods natural yogurt. 'Fortnum's finest Normandy butter,' he confided, prising open the first one and smarming half its contents on his asparagus. 'Pâté de foie gras!' He opened the second with a flourish. 'And a little Persian caviare, in case the going gets too tough. I'm not a lentil man, I must confess.'

The redhead was enchanted. 'You naughty naughty boy! Butter's a capital crime in this establishment. A Belgian count asked for it last week, and was immediately expelled – if not decapitated.'

'Well, if you don't let Jeeves into our wicked little secret, you can help me eat it up.' He daubed pâté on one end of an asparagus spear and butter on the other, and popped it between her lips. Ginny looked away. She loathed red hair.

Caldos rooted in the bag again, produced a bottle of apple juice, like a conjuror with a rabbit. 'Bâtard Montrachet 1971,' he whispered. 'But decanted into a different bottle. You can't be too careful about your containers here. A Scottish chum of mine tried to pass off Glenmorangie as Lucozade, but then they confiscated the Lucozade on account of its high sugar content, not to mention the preservatives. I prepare my receptacles most meticulously – live yogurt pots from the health food shop, Nature's Secrets Apple Juice, guaranteed completely free from chemicals. Jeeves never suspects a thing.'

Titian Tania was making appreciative inroads into his Nature's Secrets wine. 'But how on earth do you get away with salmon? I thought they were all fanatic vegetarians.'

'So they are, darling, so they are. But even the strongest principles bend a little if you apply enough pressure of the monetary kind. The chef's a racing man. I supply inside tips, hot from the stable boys, and the wherewithal to follow them up, and – lo! – a salmon swims among his aubergines.' He daubed a little caviare on his butter-swamped asparagus. 'Last year, I primed him on the Whitbread Gold Cup, and cashew-nut rissoles changed into fillet steak. Christ did much the same sort of thing, so I understand, changing water into wine.'

Tania giggled into the Montrachet and wiped her mouth with a milk-white hand. Ginny crunched a pip, trying to remind herself that redheads' perfect (fragile) skin never lasted past their twenties. And if Tania gorged on butter, she'd only run to fat. She herself spent as long as possible chewing on a skinny inch of lemon-rind, while all the other gloating guests ate Wheat-Germ-and-Molasses-Whirl with Minty Yogurt Sauce. Caldos topped his off with three obese bananas and a generous chunk of cheese. (The Stilton had been waiting in a 'Travel-Safe' money-belt, concealed around his waist.)

The only after-dinner activity was bridge. Ginny couldn't play. Tania could. She also played fast-and-loose and footsie, and her own variation of postman's knock. Ginny was

228

left with a second-rate pop star and the Arab brigade. She tried to concentrate as an overweight oil magnate described the geography of the Persian Gulf, while eyeing her own with a lascivious leer. The crowd from the Light Diet Room were swapping recipes, a refined form of torture, slavering over the ingredients of cherry chocolate cheesecake while suffering the last stages of starvation. Ginny's growling stomach was her only contribution to the merry chat around her. She felt too weak to talk, was hugging a large cushion, to swell her belly out, though worried she might chew it up, as Snookie's rabbit did. She hoped Snookie was asleep. Would her mother remember she liked the landing light left on, and that Sarah needed . . . ?

'You can actually feel the toxins streaming out of you,' said a sallow balding woman who did, in fact, look distinctly poisonous. 'The first ten days of fasting are the worst. After that, you either adapt or go under. One man tried to hang himself in the sauna, and another ate his credit cards.'

'One diamond,' Tania called, leaning over provocatively, so that her ripe-pear breasts were on public show, almost to their stalks.

'One no trump.' The fox-faced woman yawned.

Caldos reached across, touched Tania's slender wrist, though his fascinated gaze was slightly higher up. 'Two hearts,' he breathed, hand following his eyes.

They were still playing, in the gloom. At the stroke of ten o'clock, a po-faced porter had switched the lights down low and turned off 'Panorama'. Early bed was a must at Hatton Hall. But Tania warbled to her bridge partner that she was definitely a night owl, and de Roche fluffed out his feathers and said he must te-wit-te-woo her then (ha ha), and Ginny felt like a grey and puny mouse, writhing but forgotten in his talons.

It was well past one A.M. before they finally loafed back to their yellow satin boudoir.

'Stunning little redhead, wasn't she?' laughed Caldos.

'Mm,' said Ginny, trying to clean her teeth without him seeing her. Stunning little redheads probably looked enchanting with toothpaste dribbling down their chins, but artificial blondes simply couldn't risk it.

'I'm absolutely whacked.' Caldos slumped against the pillows, using his last remaining strength to nibble on a bourbon. 'I think I'll save myself for the morning, when they start assaulting us with hose pipes and seaweed. Goodnight Estrella.'

She edged to one side as he sprawled diagonally across the bed; longed to rouse him, shake him, as she heard his breathing deepen, then slow into a growl. He was already fast asleep and he hadn't even kissed her. He'd probably made a date with Tania to share a eucalyptus bath, or do disgusting things with celery stalks. No – she mustn't think of food. Even celery seemed tempting in her present famished state. She groped beneath the pillow for a bourbon, the scent of chocolate clutching at her ravenous insides. Surely half a tiny biscuit couldn't hurt? She took a nervous bite, the sound of crunching echoing like thunder through the hallowed hush of sleeping Hatton Hall. Caldos stirred and moaned. She shoved the half-gnawed biscuit back beneath the pillow, tried to hold her breath, so she wouldn't risk disturbing him again. If he didn't get his rest, he might die that very night. He looked radiant enough, but with blood pressure you could never really tell. And how about poor Ian? He, too, was at risk; might never survive his op, especially if it was carried out by some overworked school-leaver they'd only just recruited into the creaking NHS. Perhaps she'd get a discount at the undertaker's – two funerals for the price of one. Ian would approve of that.

She longed to be like Tania, heart-free and single and mercifully asleep, with a cash register instead of a conscience. Could you get rid of a conscience, cut it out like haemorrhoids, strip it off like superfluous hair? Perhaps Hatton Hall could concentrate on her conscience, instead of on her calories; steam and massage it away, force it out with the fat.

She clasped her hands together, shut her eyes. 'Look God,' she murmured desperately. 'It's either my conscience or Caldos. I can't keep both of them. If You do exist, I'm sorry Caldos thinks You don't. But he's so committed to his atheism, it's almost a religion. He's got his own prophets – Shelley and Swinburne and that Szasz man I can never spell. And how about George Herbert? He's always reading Herbert. Surely that counts, doesn't it, shows he's drawn to penitence and prayer, if only in other people?'

She herself felt strangely drawn to Herbert, longed to meet him and confide in him, knew he'd understand her fearful state of conflict. If only he weren't dead – and dead a good three hundred and fifty years. George . . . She liked his name, a name suggesting kindliness and strength. She'd always imagined Herbert as something like her father-in-law – two kindly dependable Georges, always ready to help out. Though Herbert would be more intense and definitely more blue-blooded. He'd say 'orf' instead of 'off', as Caldos did himself, and be careful never to pronounce that confusing h in hotel. ('Otel was fearfully smart and apparently correct.) *Her* George put the h in hotel, but left it off words like 'which' and 'whether'. She was often guilty of the same, and had invented several ditties as reminders: 'WHither wHirls the wHite wHale?' 'WHile I wHeedle . . .' 'WHeels on wHeels.' Perhaps she'd try to sleep by repeating each one twenty times, and breathing out deeply on all the elongated h's. 'WHither wHirls the . . .'

It didn't work. Sleep was as elusive as God. Perhaps she'd pray to Herbert instead. Surely Caldos couldn't object to that. Herbert really had existed, as a solid historical person. You couldn't reduce him to superstition, or social conditioning, or mere indulgent wishful thinking, as Caldos did with God. And it would be no different, really, from praying to the saints – except Herbert had been C of E and her mother would go spare if she thought her only daughter had gone over to the Opposition.

She turned on her left side, did her best to show her mother firmly to the door. The Eagle had instructed her to leave all her ties and responsibilities strictly behind, and to concentrate exclusively on Caldos and herself. It sounded rather selfish, but, as Fledge-Parthington had pointed out, by helping the good Doctor, she was helping all his patients, furthering his vital work of spreading mental harmony, curing shattered psyches.

.She tried to picture Herbert in his long black cassock, with a pointed beard and solemn burning eyes. Whatever should she call him? G.H. – as Caldos did? Mr Herbert? Father? No, Father wasn't right for a pastor in the C of E, though she longed to have a father as approachable as he was, instead of her own remote and supercilious one, who'd never really helped her in her life, never been paternal in any approving or affectionate sense.

'George . . .' She cleared her throat. It seemed a cheek to use his Christian name, but formal 'Mr Herbert' sounded distancing and cold. 'Please forgive me for being so familiar, but I'm horribly confused. I feel I ought to take the job – the Happy Hostess job, I mean. Caldos says he's selling happiness, and no one ever sold it straight before, always hedged it round with other words and concepts, such as self-knowledge, adaptation, or acceptance. But if I do agree to take the job, then it's essential I find happiness myself. Caldos says we can't sell any product we don't demonstrably believe in. And to be honest, George, I'm not that wildly happy at the moment. You can't be very happy with a conscience. So perhaps I ought to stay away from Beechgrove Hospital, and stop phoning my mother and the girls. I wondered if you'd sanction that, give me your permission to be selfishly unselfish? Oh, and one last crucial thing, George – that redhead in the nightie – could you see she leaves as soon as possible? She's not good for Caldos' blood pressure. Thank you, George. Goodnight.'

She scrabbled for her biscuit, demolished it in two swift bites, started on a second. Everything seemed infinitely improved. She'd made a decision, received approval for it from a poet and a pastor, and was determined not to change her mind again. She leaned up on one elbow, smiled down at sleeping Caldos. The curtains were half-open, and a glittering spear of moonlight cut a silver gash across his chest. She almost envied that stray moonbeam – which could caress his naked body all night long. She reached across for her leather-bound George Herbert, which Caldos had given her for Easter; opened it at random, tilting the page towards the shaft of moonlight.

How fresh, O Lord, how sweet and clean
Are thy returns!
Grief melts away
Like snow in May,
As if there were no such cold thing.

'Amen,' she said. 'Amen.

'Oh Caldos,' she whispered. 'I love you. I'm yours now, yours entirely. I've cut out my conscience, so I can do whatever you want. Amen.' She leant across and brushed his eyelids gently with her lips.

'Moon-goddess,' he murmured – instantly, romantically awake.

He was a quite fantastic waker, never yawned or mumbled, or took half the morning coming to, as Ian did. (Ian could still be blathering into his elevenses, even blinking over lunch.) But Caldos came up like the sun – dramatic, dazzling, hot.

'Get up!' he urged, flinging off the covers, and erasing all the tiffs and Tanias with one impassioned kiss. She bounded out of bed, stood exultant by the window, her pale body silver-barred. He took her hand, swept her through the door, along the passage, down the curving staircase; both of them stark naked. The moon oozed through chinks and crevices, spilling like chilled pools of milk on gleaming polished floors, bleaching dark-veined marble, sweeping velvet shadows into corners. Caldos sneaked her out the back way, like a cat-burglar, stealing through a small arched door bolted only from the inside.

She stepped into the radiance of full moon, shivering in the splintery silver-cold. Although it was mid-August, the nights were still severe. The whole summer had been dismal – unsettled, wet and windy, and even now, a slyly insolent wind seemed to be touching up her body, thrusting vulgar fingers through the spaces in her vertebrae. She tried to shake it off, preferred Caldos as her lover. He was already trying to warm her up – racing her over the croquet lawn, and into the walled garden; dodging up and down the paths; spanking her with cabbage-stalks, weaving flowers and strawberries in her hair. The whole night was their plaything, the lawn their plush green eiderdown, the moon their bedside lamp. Once she was warm (and out of breath), he cooled her off again by pummelling her in the wet and sparkling grass, rolling her over and over, then kissing the startled daisies from her ears. He didn't say 'I love you', but everything else was shouting it aloud – the stars, the huddled birds, the tangled rambler roses, the huge vault of leaping sky. The tall tower clock struck three, and each solemn chime repeated it. 'I love you, Caldos,' she whispered in reply, and his eyes and hands were saying it, his body, his warm breath.

They capered over to the swimming pool, the rippling fretted water filled with broken stars. He held her in his arms and they plunged in as one body, and she felt the stars exploding in her skull, bursting in her ears. She turned over on her back and blew kisses to the moon; she floated on her front and swallowed silver baubles. Caldos swam in prowling circles round her, a hybrid creature in burnished black and silver. The whole world wore his livery tonight. She dived into black nothingness, surfaced into silver; her heart a sparking Catherine wheel, whirling round and round. Neither spoke a word. The silence of the cedars seemed to hallow and envelop them; the icy gasp of water froze their minds.

Suddenly he pushed her to her knees. They were swimming in the shallow end, and she felt a searing shaft of warmth pierce between her legs, and they rocked together in a blaze of fiery cold. He straddled her against the rail, pinioning her thighs with his own stronger more insistent ones. Her hands were twisted on the rail, her legs grazing up and down along the stone side of the pool, but she felt only the wild blade of heat knifing in and out, and the furious cold churning all around her. The Catherine wheel was almost spent. It spun in a last frantic whirl, as the water frothed and steamed. She cried out like a night bird, swooping on its prey, and somewhere underneath her cries, she was almost sure she heard him say 'I love you'.

They were still entwined and fast asleep, when a keen young trainee naturopath knocked with a breakfast tray of prunes. 'Your linden-blossom tea, sir,' he announced, jerking back the curtains with a rumble like an earthquake.

Caldos snatched the tray and swore. He lurched into the bathroom and tipped two dozen mint-sprigged prunes into the toilet bowl. The yogurt followed suit. Ginny's lemon-water was flung into the bath.

'Don't disturb us for another three hours,' he growled to the appalled white coat. 'And then I'll have four croissants and a quart of filter coffee. Make sure it's Fortnum's King's Blend – none of your dandelion root! No – don't argue, it's a special dispensation. Just tell the chef it's Catherine Wheel for the three o'clock at Kempton. And don't – repeat don't – forget the butter.'

'I have private plans for the butter,' he whispered to Ginny, removing two last daisies from her hair.

29

Ginny sat in a turquoise plastic coffin. Rivers of sweat spewed down her flushed pink breasts, across her scalded stomach and trickled off her toes. Only her head stuck out at the top and even that was dripping. The fearsome contraption was called a steam cabinet and was melting the toxins out of her, at something near the temperature of boiling oil.

'Nothing to it,' chirped the jolly little nurse, setting an oven-timer as if Ginny were a baked potato. The wretched thing still hadn't pinged, though she was overcooked and burning. The lady in the lilac coffin opposite hadn't turned a hair, despite the fact her cooking-time was longer. Her lobster face clashed with the pale mauve plastic, but she still continued blithely chatting, as if she were lolling in a deck-chair on the QE2.

'Do you have trouble with your nanny – I mean holidays and things? Ours is getting frightfully uppity, refuses to work weekends. Well, I mean it's weekends you want them, isn't it?'

'Gosh yes!' said Ginny, feelingly.

Everyone had nannies, despite the fact their children were at boarding school, and even packed off in the holidays for improving trips abroad. And a lot of them had cooks. And all these tedious staff were impossibly demanding, and wanted selfish inconvenient things like holidays, or eight hours' sleep; or were dangerous Bolsheviks who voted Labour. (She must never, never let on that Ian read the *New Statesman* or quoted Wedgwood Benn.)

The nurse prised open the coffin lid, released a red-hot Ginny, then led her to the Electronic Impulse Shower. She turned the dial to 'Fierce Cold', and pushed Ginny right beneath the jets, dodging back herself from their thundering Niagara. A second nurse in plastic combat-gear picked up several handfuls of coarse (damp) cooking salt and assaulted Ginny's bottom with it.

'Just sloughing off the dead cells, dear,' she said, hurling salt at both her shoulders. Ginny felt still more like a potato. Grains of salt were sticking between her buttocks and stinging the flushed skin on the insides of her thighs.

'Now for the Sitz,' said the first nurse, filling two old-fashioned hip baths, nestling side by side – hot water in the first one, freezing in the second. She coaxed Ginny's bottom into boiling lava, then stuck her legs and feet into liquid ice.

'Relieves pelvic congestion,' she bellowed over the noise of the taps. 'And a natural cure for frigidity.'

Ginny glanced nervously around her, but most of the other inmates were dozing on day-beds, cocooned in plush pink blankets. Her pelvis seemed to be becoming public property – every nurse and osteopath (and mere PT instructor) striving to regenerate it. She'd hardly been aware she owned a pelvis until Caldos had kindled it to life. Now it was complaining – overheating like a car engine. The nurse had set the pinger again, which was ticking slowly, cruelly.

'Three minutes that way round, dear. Then change over – bottom in the cold, feet in the hot!'

Ginny sat staring at her toes. She'd completely lost the feeling in them, while her buttocks must be blistering. The other side was worse. She lowered her smouldering bottom inch by glacial inch into the ice; her shocked and curdled stomach growling in weak protest. Neither Caldos nor the Eagle had relaxed the rigours of her fast. She longed to whistle up her cook and order breakfast, lunch and dinner all at once – plovers' eggs, a brace of grouse, a magnum of champagne; make sure the maids had cleaned the silver egg-cups, polished up the ice-bucket.

Her conscience had all but disappeared at Hatton Hall. Compared with all these pampered socialites, she was a living breathing saint. She'd spent fifteen years being cook and nanny, dishwasher and daily, while they lolled around complaining about the price of caviare, or their chauffeur's decadent habit of wanting Sundays off. She never had days off. And she hadn't had a holiday in years, not a proper one. She and Ian always took cheap rooms and the travelling iron, or camped on sites where the only running water was a rainstorm. Caldos was right – it was time she thought about herself and devoted herself to pleasure – and to him. She'd been a slave and chattel all these years, taken for granted, unappreciated, and then fool enough to feel guilty when Cinderella was taken to the ball. Well, now she'd met her Prince, midnight had struck, and both glass slippers were still firmly on her feet. She'd throw away her guilt with the pumpkin and the rags.

'Just relax and enjoy it,' cooed the masseur, edging his oily hands a little closer to her pubis. Caldos had insisted on a male masseur. 'Much more stimulating,' he informed her.

It was only now she realised what he meant. Geoffrey's hands were straying between her thighs, his fingers flicking to and fro across her private parts. She wasn't quite sure whether it was part of the standard treatment, or a de Roche-negotiated extra. It was delicious anyway. He was doing miraculous things with two thumbs and a little finger. She tried to close her legs.

'Relax,' soothed Geoffrey. 'Just lie back and let your body go.'

She spent most of the fortnight lying back and letting go, sprawled on a towel in the sauna, or wooing the sun by the swan-shaped swimming pool, or spread-eagled on her stomach in the yoga class ('Make your body like *custard*,' crooned the India-rubber teacher), or wallowing between the yellow satin sheets with Caldos and the butter.

Though apart from the nights, she didn't see much of her lover. He had met a tall tycoon from California, who wore two-tone shoes and eighteen-carat cufflinks in the shape of London buses. He did all the things which Caldos had insisted were social suicide, such as icing his wine, or sporting a matching tie and handkerchief, both in polyester. Yet there was lordly Caldos, nose to nose with a man who guffawed at Les Dawson and thought Bach was something a dog did. She couldn't understand it, except Bud Goldenberger was rich; boasted Greek islands and Bahamian banks like other people owned transistor radios. The two men became inseparable, closeted together all hours of the day; Caldos even skipping meals, which was particularly alarming. He made long-distance calls to London, and summoned Philip Mossman down for urgent consultations. He missed the posture class, and then the ping-pong tournament, and he and Philip and Big Bud were still in conference when the clock struck one A.M.

Ginny basked in a bubble bath to drown her disappointment. Caldos had promised her he wouldn't work, and yet was busier than ever. How could she devote herself to him, when he was totally immersed in a dollar-brained Yank? Even the redhead got bored and turned her attentions to a Saudi Arabian playboy with psoriasis.

Ginny devoted herself to happiness, instead. That's what Caldos wanted, after all. She invented little rules, to help her out. Every time she worried over Sarah's sinuses, she had to book a manicure in reparation. Every traitorous thought of Ian was punished by a shopping spree in Hatton Hall boutique. Her nails were shining scarlet and her wardrobe full of clothes, but it was becoming easier each day. She met the mother of four children who didn't know who Pooh was, and a lady with a baby who had never changed its nappy. She chatted to a French fashion buyer who only saw her spouse on Friday afternoons, and an American starlet who'd finished off three husbands and was fighting off a fourth. Ian and the girls grew smaller and more puny, as her conscience steamed away with all the toxins. She thumbed through *The Lady* and read the staff advertisements – perhaps she'd squeeze a nanny in their box-room, or turn the garden-shed into quarters for a cook. She browsed through *Harpers* and tried to decide between a villa in Vigo and a sixty-foot ketch in St Nazaire. She graduated from lemon-water to three diminutive strawberries, and a peach so bijou-small it looked as if it had been dieting itself.

'I loathe money,' drawled her table-mate at dinner. (Caldos was still incommunicado with the Yank.) 'Filthy germy stuff! I never touch it. If they won't take a credit card, I simply walk out. Just think where all those coins and notes have *been* – lurking in working people's squalid little pockets, handled by the riff-raff who don't wash their hands when they go to the lavatory.'

'I know,' sighed Ginny. It was enough to put her off her peach. She picked it up and went to look for Caldos. He was sitting surrounded by papers in the library. The American was pounding his fat fist on the desk.

'No problem, Cal, no problem! I'm tellin' you, Venture Capital isn't gonna give us any headaches. I've got half the Bay Street mob in my pocket. Don't worry about 'em, Cal – I know these babies. All we gotta do is guarantee they get twenty-five per cent return. Piece of cake! Now, cash-flow . . . that's a whole different ball game. It must be self-financing. Your CPA is gonna go like this . . .'

Ginny slipped away, fought a sudden pang of loneliness. They hadn't even noticed she was there. It was Sunday afternoon, a lazy stagnant time at Hatton Hall. If she were back at home with Ian, they'd be just setting out for the park with Toby and the girls, stopping for ice-creams, getting entangled in the string of Sarah's kite. Was Ian missing her, as well? Did his stitches hurt? Did Snookie wonder why she hadn't . . . ?

'Forbidden!' snapped her fairy godmother.

She sighed and trudged towards the Hatton Hall boutique. She'd have to buy a ball-gown for her penance.

On day eleven, the American went home. Ginny's spirits soared. 'Let's celebrate,' she crowed.

They sneaked out for a forbidden lobster dinner at the local Dog and Duck. The bar was full of health-farm renegades, washing down their lentils with double gins. Caldos ordered Ginny half a grapefruit and dug into his crab-topped avocado.

'Meeting Bud Goldenberger was an incredible stroke of fortune, *ma douce*. I know he's not exactly *comme il faut*, but he happens to be a multi-millionaire, which makes one so much more forgiving. And he's completely sold on my brilliant little brainchild.'

'Which one?' Caldos had a prolific family of brainchildren.

'The Happy Club, of course. He says the timing's absolutely right. Man has splurged a fortune on every material comfort, every labour-saving luxury, yet he's still weeping into his pillow every night. When he's not worrying about his dicky ticker or his cholesterol level, he's fretting over ontological insecurity, or gender confusion, or comparing egos with the man next door. He needs total reassurance, complete reprogramming. And I shall provide it! I'll treat mind and body as a whole and charge double for the privilege. *Mens sana* and all that sort of thing. I'll dig out a few Greek statues and strew them round the place. The new Hellenic era, as created by de Roche; the psychiatric Golden Age. Man will be totally remodelled – his body refurbished, his soul spring-cleaned, his psyche reconditioned, his sex-drive souped-up.' He tossed Ginny a lobster claw from his overflowing plate. 'Goldenberger wants to make it big. Not just one club, but a whole damned string of them, all the last word in luxury – very spiritual luxury, of course.'

The new Estrella didn't bat an eyelid. 'Well, George will be pleased. He can order another dozen cockatoos.'

'Oh, Goldenberger loved the sound of George, simply lapped him up. I sold him well, of course. The all-English Man Friday, handling everything from schizophrenics to stopcocks. And he was wild about our menagerie idea, even suggested a cheetah or two – patients acting out their fantasies through animals, getting close to nature, releasing the beast in themselves, talking to their plants. George could run classes in it, a sort of psychiatric Fred Streeter.' Caldos released a walletful of credit cards, arranged them in a fan-shape on the table. 'Take your pick,' he breezed, as a haughty waiter hovered with the bill.

He unfastened the top button of Ginny's emerald chiffon blouse (her latest purchase from the Hatton Hall boutique), slipped a hand inside it. '*Tesoro mio*,' he whispered. 'Let's go and walk on the Downs. I want to tell you all about Goldenberger. If I'm Jupiter, he's Midas. Between us, we're going to re-make man and turn him into gold!'

They tramped five miles across the windy Marlborough Downs, the fields spread out all around them, cows munching, gold corn high. Patchwork butterflies skimmed across the purple spikes of sorrel. They climbed to the top of the world, their heads all but touching the sky; the great grey clouds mumbling and shifting only a hand's-span away. Ginny picked a spray of harebells and wove them through his belt. He took her in his arms and kissed her, and she heard the wind blowing through their bodies, scattering his kisses like the petals of wild chicory, blazing blue around them. She had used those petals to try to search his heart, pulling each one off its flower-head, and intoning anxiously aloud: 'He loves me, he loves me not, loves me, loves me not . . .'

'You've got five different answers,' Caldos laughed, crumpling up five stalks. She waited silently, and yearningly, for him to tell her which the right one was, but he only shredded the frail petals, scattered them around him.

They walked another flagging mile, then flopped against the knotty roots of an ancient hawthorn tree. Caldos introduced her to the twigs. 'The thorns make most ingenious marks,' he told her, tracing their fierce pattern on her buttocks.

They lay chastened and still naked as the sun sank slowly down, and a soft grey light filtered through the grasses. Caldos leant up on one elbow, ran his finger gently down her face. 'There's just one thing I didn't mention, my wolf.'

'Mm . . .' She didn't like talking when it had been so wonderful.

'About the Happy Clubs.'

'What about them?' She shrugged the finger off. They'd talked of almost nothing else for the last three hours or more. She'd only just succeeded in getting Caldos to relax, to concentrate on her, instead of on his work, and now he was back to profits, clients, clubs. Bud Goldenberger made a most unwelcome threesome.

'Just a little matter of location, *cara*.'

Ginny plucked a clover leaf and stroked Adolfo with it. 'What, you want to move out of Chelsea and site them all over London?'

'No-o . . .' Caldos twisted a matching clover leaf through Ginny's pubic hair.

'Where then?'

'Well, Goldenberger thinks . . .' He paused, face taut and frowning.

She shut her eyes. They were still so high, still tangled in the clouds, but she was stumbling, falling, sliding off the earth. She knew from Caldos' voice that he was about to tell her something fateful, something dark and final which could pull her life apart. He was still playing with the clover leaf.

'Yes?' she said, as calmly as she could. She wished it were a four-leafed clover, wished she were stone-deaf.

'Not London, my nymph,' he began, tossing the small leaf away. She watched it fall, and keep on falling, over the sharp edge of the world.

'Not London at all,' he repeated. 'Los Angeles.'

30

'Dad, it's me, Ian.'

George slid back the bolts and stood glumly at the door. No hug, no flurry of welcome.

'What's wrong, Dad?'

George dragged along the passage like a wooden wind-up toy about to run down. 'I'm sorry, son, you've caught me at a bad time. I'm that upset, I don't know what I'm doing . . .'

Ian swore beneath his breath. The last thing he wanted was his father's problems, on top of all his own. He followed George down the narrow stairs to his flat. It smelt faintly like a zoo.

'Bugger it!' screeched a steel-tipped voice. Ian jumped back, alarmed. A large black bird with a bilious yellow beak and a wicked mocking eye was shaking with laughter on top of the tallest cupboard, rocking backwards and forwards on one scaly taloned foot.

'Behave yourself, Jason!' George rapped, tossing the bird a grape. 'Do you mind sitting in the kitchen, lad? I'm just finishing off my bit of washing.'

Ian glanced nervously around him. A terrapin was snoozing in the washing-up bowl, and there was something unspeakable crawling in a jar of murky water. He peered into a saucepan – nothing living there, thank God, only the greasy remnants of a corned beef hash. His father's supper, he assumed, unless it was rations for the zoo. Poor George, he thought, with a mixture of annoyance and compassion. It couldn't be much fun cooking for himself, struggling with the chores, and stuck in on his own most evenings, with only a few reptiles and a peevish mynah bird. The mynah was a new arrival, which his father must have bought for a bit of company. He could do with some himself. At least the bird could talk, which was more than Ginny managed. Half the time she was out, and the other half silent and morose. These last two weeks he'd felt trapped in his own zoo, living with a dumb and dangerous animal. His faithless mate prowled up and down her invisible cage, pouncing on the smallest thing and tearing it to shreds. He and the children stood helpless on the other side, trying to poke their fingers through the bars, only to get them bitten.

'Well, how are things?' George removed his washing from the sink and filled the battered kettle.

'So-so.' Ian slunk down to the shadier end of the table. The gate-crasher sun had barged in through the window, gilding piles of dirty socks, gold-plating specks of dust. It had no right to shine, be so bloody smug.

'Here, son, drink your tea. You're not looking all that marvellous. It's the hospital, I reckon. You're never the same once you let them cut you up. You should have had some proper convalescence.'

Of course he should. He and Ginny should have gone away together, instead of her waltzing off on that mysterious separate holiday. It was madness to have let her go. She'd returned a stranger – distant, bitter, brooding. 'Look, I'm okay, Dad – just a bit whacked out, that's all. It's Ginny I'm worried about.'

'Oh, go to hell!' squawked the bird, and settled on the window, its squat black tail ruffling the new curtains. Ian peered more closely at the curtains. Ginny hadn't finished them, hadn't even taken out the pins. They hung unevenly, with their hems still raw and fraying. What in heaven's name was wrong with her? Six months ago, she'd been the best little home-maker in Surrey.

George took his tea-cup over to the sink, followed by a sulky Jason. 'Poorly again, is she? I haven't seen her for an age. The last time she was due here, she went down with a bug. And the time before she phoned to say she'd chipped a tooth and was trying to get an appointment at the dentist.'

'Oh, I see. I thought . . .'

'I must admit I miss her. But no doubt she's got other things to do.'

Ian stared into his tea leaves. 'Are you sure she's not been up here? You see, she mentioned this weird job – something connected with Caldos – said they'd been discussing it together, so I thought perhaps . . .' He noticed George's back stiffen. He had dropped the shirts back into the water and stood now like a ramrod.

'The Doctor isn't here much now. He's winding up his practice.'

'No, Dad, surely not. You must have got it wrong. He wouldn't do a thing like that. It's his life, his whole profession.'

George's voice was tight, his body tensed and rigid. 'I'd rather not discuss it, if you don't mind.'

Ian kicked his chair back. 'What do you mean? You're hiding something, aren't you – something to do with Ginny? I'm certain she's been here, seeing Caldos, planning things . . . What's going on, for Christ's sake? You've got to tell me, Dad.'

'Silly bugger!' Jason taunted, lunging past Ian's left ear and perching on the chair beside him.

Ian clenched his fists. 'Dumb animals . . .' he muttered, glancing at the tea-cosy, an unusual quilted one, shaped like a lady in a crinoline, a gloating girl with golden hair and a contemptuous little smile, hatching the teapot hot between her legs. Ian turned her round to face the wall; dodged a soapy shirt-sleeve which George was dripping down his neck. His father had come marching from washing-tub to table, the shirt still in his hands.

'Ginny's nothing to do with it, my lad. It's me that's been messed about, if you really want to know.'

'Oh?' Ian turned the teapot round again. The golden smile still mocked him – Ginny's smile – that wanton, I've-struck-oil smile, which she brought home from her evening-classes, and wore like her diploma. He'd almost rather have her miserable, or fierce. His head was throbbing from the sun and George's voice – a hammer-hammer voice now, raving on about some club or commune, which de Roche was setting up. He couldn't really follow all the details, except that wretched Doctor's name seemed to crop up far too often.

'I mean he promised me, the Doctor did. The whole thing was cut and dried. He'd found us these posh new premises in Chelsea, five large floors, and a decent stretch of garden. I'd done a lot of work on it already, stocking the fishpond and setting up fountains and suchlike. I even had men working under me. I was the boss, you understand. It wasn't easy, with this great place to supervise as well. I was working there some nights till almost midnight, and every damned weekend, and then he orders everyone to stop – yes, just like that. No explanations – nothing – just down tools and scat. I presume he's pulling out, but everything's hush-hush. One of the builders told me he's selling back the site for redevelopment, but that's ridiculous. I mean, he's only just bought the place, hasn't he, and he was really tickled pink with it when first he signed the contract. But something's going on, Ian – he can't fool me. I hardly even see him, he's so busy. And he's got rid of half his patients and . . .'

George lurched back to the sink, ran both taps at full blast, and continued with his saga, shouting over the noise. Ian refilled his cup, though he needed more than tea to perk him up. His father sounded crazy – supervising workmen, hobnobbing with property developers, running clubs for screwballs. And Ginny was as bad – bleating on about finding her identity, and expanding her horizons, and how she had to spread her wings and see the world. Hell, she'd buggered off already, and it had only made her worse. If she went away again, he'd never get her back – he knew that in his guts. She was raring to break loose, start not just a new career, but . . . No, he mustn't think about it, must concentrate on George instead – poor defeated George, slumped now at the table, looking shrunk and faded like his shirts.

'I didn't take it quietly, I can tell you. I told Dr de Roche exactly what I . . .'

Ian closed his eyes. He had begun to hate that name. He couldn't say exactly why, except it made him feel murderous and vengeful. 'I'm sorry, Dad, I really am. It's a bloody rotten shame. Look, Caldos never mentioned Ginny, did he – I mean when he talked about his plans? Did her name come up, or . . . ?'

'Don't remember it,' said George. 'D'you realise, Ian, I've even blown my little bit of savings? Oh, I know it was damn stupid, but I wanted a few things there I could really call my own – so I'd have more of a stake in the place, feel more involved in it. That's why Jason's here, and the turtle and the terrapins. I bought them with my own money to keep at the club. But now there doesn't seem to *be* a club. The pet-shop wouldn't take them back, and I could hardly leave them to be smashed up by a bulldozer. But they can't stay here much longer. Crankshaw's going spare. I can't stop Jason swearing, and the lady from next door's issued a formal complaint in writing because she's convinced it's *me* who's wolf-whistling her each morning, and not that blessed bird. And he's getting through a pound of grapes a day. I'm at my wits' end, Ian, wondering what to do with him. I've got to know he's happy, can't just hand him over to someone unreliable. You wouldn't like him, would you?'

'No,' said Ian. 'I wouldn't.'

'Then there's Christopher, as well.'

'*Who?*' Ian looked up in alarm. Was some grotty little urchin about to burst into the kitchen – his father's latest protégé, or some hapless son or nephew abandoned by de Roche?

'He's my Hawksbill turtle. I had to stick him in the bath, once I brought him back from Chelsea – there was nowhere else suitable. But it means I'm having to wash in a tiny leaky basin. Oh, I know you'll say I was crazy to have bought them, but the Doctor seemed so certain, actually encouraged me. Now I've squandered all my savings and I can't even . . .'

'Shame!' clucked the mynah, then cackled with cruel laughter.

Ian pushed his cup away, wished he had a shotgun – one bullet for the pair of them – Jason and de Roche. 'I'm sorry, Dad. I'm not being much use, am I? It's just that I was hoping you could . . . Oh, never mind, forget it. Look, I'll phone tomorrow and you can tell me the whole story. I'm not at my best this evening.'

He eased up to his feet. The tea-cosy lady was still smiling her pale smile – that minx-like, mortifying smile which made him want to smash her. He snatched the cosy off the pot, ground her head against the table. Beneath her hollow crinoline, she was obscenely warmly moist.

'No, don't bother to see me off, Dad.' He walked upstairs alone, stood on the doorstep, trying to calm down, breathing in the stag- . nant summer air. The sun flickered against the brass plates on the door, hurting his eyes and blurring all the names. Only one name held its own – the top one: Dr C.E.S. de Roche – fancy italic script and a string of letters after it. They also seemed to smile.

Ian stood square in front of it. 'Sod you!' he muttered and punched his fist hard against the plate. It didn't even buckle. He hurtled down the steps, nursing his bleeding knuckles.

'Shame shame shame!' squalled the mynah from downstairs.

31

The September sun shone mercilessly into de Roche's Chelsea house, trailing yellow fingers over bare boards and denuded walls. The precious furniture had been bundled into a van, curtains dismantled, carpets rolled up, pictures and sculptures stripped. The house looked achingly ordinary – all its glamour departed with the fancy furnishings and the dramatic light-effects. Ginny made tea for the workmen on a primus stove.

'Lot of classy stuff you got,' Mick, the foreman, commented, puffing on a roll-your-own and dropping ash into his cup.

'I only wish I could take it with me on the plane,' breezed Caldos. 'I can just imagine my Los Angeles apartment, with tubular steel furniture, and glass and concrete walls, and the only work of art a reproduction Lichtenstein.'

Ginny turned away. How could he joke about something so distressing? She could still hardly believe that he was going. Everything had happened frighteningly fast, like some roller-coaster nightmare, or plunging avalanche. And over all the turbulence and turmoil, Bud Goldenberger had arched like a lurid neon rainbow, enticing Caldos to freedom, profit, fame. The Happy Club had burgeoned into a gigantic enterprise, which would set his name in coloured lights from Seattle to Miami. His Chelsea plans seemed puny in comparison.

Yesterday, they'd lunched with Bud before he flew back to the States, a lunch of mainly junk-foods in his vulgar Mayfair flat.

'Listen,' he'd assured them, as he ripped apart a bag of toffee popcorn, which he appeared to be serving as an appetiser, with Pepsi as aperitif. 'We're really into therapy back home. I'm telling you, the only star in Hollywood who isn't seeing a shrink is Lassie. Even Mary Poppins has her analyst. And it's not only the rich dudes. Mr and Mrs Public are right in there too, hotting up their psyches, totting up their orgasms. T-groups, Gestalt, marathons, orgies – you name it, they'll buy it. But what we do, see, is graft all that psycho stuff on to the healthy body bit – jogging and yogurt and polyunsaturates.' He'd crammed his mouth with popcorn, diluted it with Pepsi, sprayed both across the table as he talked. 'Half the guys back home are shit-scared about coronaries, or stuffing themselves with ginseng because they can't get it up, or reading up about their anxiety-neuroses. They're crazy for the Health Kick, nuts about the Body Beautiful. Right, we throw the whole goddam lot together and push it as a new gimmick.' He'd paused to stuff a Whopper in his mouth – seven different layers of pappy bun, bloody meat, salad, relish, chutney, cheese and ketchup; continued as he chewed. 'We sell 'em low-cholesterol psyches, multi-vitamin sex with sesame seeds on top, hundred-per-cent wholewheat personalities. The name of the game is the Whole Person. If you're gonna be with it, you gotta redecorate yourself inside and out.'

He'd scooped a pool of ketchup from his lap, flung his chubby arms out, as if to embrace the entire United States. 'We'll sell Whole Person Health like hamburgers – Happiness Drive-ins with a choice of relish; King-sized Contentment and Take-away Fantasies. Or how about a psychiatric laundromat? You put in your dollar and you come out clean – guilt and neuroses washed away.' He'd washed his own away with a final gulp of Pepsi, pushed the three-litre plastic bottle across to her and Caldos. Caldos had declined, heavily involved with an Haut-Gardère '61, his own small contribution to the lunch.

'But where we score, Cal, pal, is adding the British bit. You can't lose in the States with anything Olde Englishe. We sold 'em London fog, we can sell 'em London shrinks. I'll recruit a few before I leave – English accents, English education, English tailoring – with you, Cal, as our cute little English Captain of the team, our Colonel Sanders, our Big Mac, our Howard Johnson. Come to think of it, we'll have to change your name. Caldos de Roche just doesn't have that Anglo-Saxon ring about it.'

Caldos had ignored him, checked his watch, pushed his untouched plate away. He had another meeting in Fenchurch Street, in less than half an hour, to discuss liability insurance with his broker.

'It's not just a matter of money,' he explained to Ginny later. 'It's a holy crusade, *carissima*. Psychiatrists are today's new gods, providing salvation, revelation, forgiveness, love – all the things people are thirsting after.'

'But what about *British* people?' she objected, trying desperately to nail him down to Chelsea. 'Why shouldn't *we* be saved?'

'All in good time, beloved. The Yanks need us first. Besides, Estrella, imported gods carry more conviction. British gods are like British secretaries and Burberrys – they have automatic status in America.'

Ginny stared down at her hands. Caldos seemed to be halfway across the United States already. She tried to drag him back. 'Well, what about your patients then? Some of them have been coming years and years. And how about your lovely house? And George? And . . .'

'Estrella, you're so small-minded, angel. Of course there will be problems – always are with any new initiative. But problems can be solved. And it's essential we think big. Goldenberger's right – this country stifles individual enterprise, runs a mile from original ideas. I can't even get the capital in England. And if I did, the bloody bureaucrats would be breathing down my neck. Our tax laws are quite crazy. They positively discourage any modern merchant-venturers. Pioneering and profits are dirty words in England. I've outgrown England, *Liebling*, and you've outgrown Hinchley Wood. We belong together now – in California. All we've got to do is pack our bags.'

'It's not that simple, Caldos. I've got a husband and a family. I can't just leave my children six thousand miles behind. And abandon Ian and . . .'

They had been over and over it a hundred times already, back and forward, round and round. Her mind felt like Arnhem or Passchendaele – a searing battleground of mud and casualties. Whichever way she decided, there would be fatal bloody wounds. Caldos was leaving in exactly two weeks for a preliminary tour. He was to sweep through California, meeting tax experts and marketing executives, drawing up plans, buying sites for the first few Happy Clubs, setting up a pilot scheme, collecting feedback, patrons.

'I'll be away two months,' he told her. 'That'll give you time to find a nanny.'

Ginny winced. 'But I can't, I . . .'

'Once the thing's launched, I'll be flying from Los Angeles to Brussels, to open my safe deposit. Look, Estrella, surely that's proof of how serious I am. I'm putting everything I've got into this scheme, even my precious Krugerrands, which I'd only touch for a life-or-death emergency. Mossman's sold all my other assets – leases, trust funds, futures, property. It's a sacred mission, darling, and I expect you to be equally committed.'

'But Caldos, the children aren't just . . .'

'From Brussels, I'll be flying to Heathrow. It's all arranged. My plane gets in at twelve noon on Sunday 25 November. I'll have just three hours before setting off again. Our flight to LA departs at three o'clock. I've booked two tickets on it.' Caldos took her in his arms, traced the outline of her lips, allowed his sensuous finger to continue down her neck, stroke between her breasts. 'Beloved,' he whispered. 'You must be on that flight.'

'Caldos, I . . .'

He kissed her 'can't' away, kissed her mouth, her throat, her wrists, her palms, her eyes. 'Be at the airport, darling, at two o'clock. I'm meeting Mossman first for a final briefing. There'll be a mass of financial details to discuss with him, but it should only take an hour. Come and find me in the Ambassadors Club Lounge in Terminal Three.'

'But I'm . . .'

'It's on the second floor. Ask anyone. They keep it locked, of course – don't want the hoi polloi in there. But just say my name and . . .'

'Look, Caldos, I . . .'

'I'll be waiting for you there. Don't pack your winter woollies; you won't need them. I'll take care of all the arrangements – money, insurance, visas. Just bring your passport and your suntan lotion. And your precious . . . beautiful . . . beloved . . . self.' He kissed one breast with the 'precious', the other with the 'beautiful', and started to move further down for the 'beloved'.

She pushed him away. 'I can't, Caldos, I can't.' She was only a needle stuck in a groove – can't, can't, can't. Must, must.

'Ginny, you *must*.'

He had called her Ginny. He never called her Ginny. She suddenly felt real – real and ordinary, like the house. He had taken down her expensive fittings, dismantled her shining lights. The bleach was growing out, her hair showing darker at the roots. She was thin, too thin. There wasn't time for wining and dining at Arnhem, or hairdressers at Passchendaele.

They spread a dust-sheet over the bare boards and lay together, naked, but he was unable to make love, seemed on edge, distracted; even turned away, staring at the skirting instead of at her breasts. She longed to cling to him, to claim him, to chain him there in Chelsea, bind him with her love. But she was only a poor Canute; might as well command the restless ocean to confine itself to Chelsea, stop its ebb and flow, ignore the pull and dazzle of the moon. She envied him his freedom, cursed her own tight bonds. She was chained to children and to marriage vows, to cats and dogs and cabbage patches, chained to conscience and convention. She could chuck them all away for an hour or two, a day or two, if it were only a matter of a trifling job in London, or a few illicit evenings and weekends. But a whole new life across an alien ocean, where even the clocks were different . . . She'd be going to bed with Caldos, when Sarah and Snookie were crying into their cornflakes.

She was crying now herself, crying from frustration, the sheer torment and confusion at being pulled between her precious prison-home and the chance of liberation and rebirth. Caldos turned towards her, held her face cupped in both his hands, as if he were studying a picture, or weighing up some prospective purchase, which might demand financial sacrifice. She tensed against his scrutiny, aware she must look haggard; eyes inflamed and swollen, hair dishevelled, the last traces of her make-up eroded by her tears. She shut her eyes, as if to block him out, couldn't bear to see his censure, his frown of disapproval. She had let herself grow careless, almost plain.

'I love you, Ginny,' he said.

The whole of London stopped – traffic, business, telephones, transactions, railway lines – tycoons frozen in mid-bid, transatlantic telexes juddering to a halt. The earth ceased circling round the sun; the cold moon flushed, eclipsed. He had said it, he had said it. Not almost, nearly, maybe; not in hieroglyphics nor Italian;

not in passing, in parenthesis, or in jest. He had told her that he loved her, simply and directly, in English, on the floorboards. He had called her by her name. He loved her, Ginny Barnes, not a prefabricated princess. She had waited nine long months for him to say it, and now that he had done so, she'd have to kill his love the moment it was born, throttle it in the delivery room. She could suddenly feel Sarah's gigantic angry head forcing out between her legs; the midwife shouting '*Push!*', Ian squeezing her hand so violently it distracted her from the frantic pain down lower.

'Ginny, did you hear me? I said I love you, for God's sake.'

It wasn't a mistake. He had said it in duplicate, and with even greater emphasis; a carbon copy printed indelibly across her heart. The midwife cutting the cord. Ian grinning like a clown when they put the damp red baby in his arms.

'Can't,' she whispered dully.

Caldos frowned, started picking at the dust-sheet with his fingers. 'I don't think you understand. Love is something I've always refused to feel. I dismissed it years ago as an inconvenient sensation for masochists and simpletons. I've never loved anyone before. I've played with them, pretended, but always buggered off if things got too intense. It's different this time, Ginny. I can't pretend, and I certainly can't leave you.'

She shivered, though it wasn't cold. The brave September sun was still shining doggedly, bonding their two shadows in one huge distorted form. She looked beyond him through the window. The leaves were brown and gold – beautiful, but dying. There was nothing to say, but he went on saying it.

'My clubs are assured, I know that. My name's made, and my millions. But *you're* not assured. And I want you more than my millions, more than anything I've wanted in my life before.'

She shut her eyes against the sun, which was blinding and confusing her, like the harsh lights of the labour room. That insistent bullet-head inching down and down and down; Ian's sudden shout of triumph, then the sharp explosive cry of a new life.

A new life. 'Our first Christmas together, darling,' he was saying. 'Sharing our turkey, creating our own private Midnight Mass. We've got to be together, don't you understand? I love you, and that's final.'

Final. Love buried the day it was born. Ian standing beside her as they lowered his mother's coffin into the grave. 'Man's life is as grass. As soon as the wind goeth over it, it is gone . . .'

'Can't,' she said again.

They couldn't make love. Caldos stayed limp and unaroused, even when she took him in her mouth. At last, he shrugged and laughed, pulled her to her feet, started dragging on his clothes. 'It doesn't matter, darling. We've got the rest of our lives to make endless glorious love.'

He reached for her handbag, took out her diary, the small plastic-covered Imperial Biscuits diary which Ian got free from the works. He opened it at September, the pages full of chains. 'Snookie swimming lesson', 'Ian check-up, Beechgrove Hospital', 'Hoover repair man', 'Sarah, teeth (ask fluoride?)'. Ginny didn't exist.

'I love you,' he wrote on every page remaining in September, then turned to 1 October, the day he left for his preliminary tour of the States. '*Je reviens,*' he scribbled under the date.

'I love you, long-distance,' he scrawled all through October. 'I miss you,' he jotted, as the month changed to November; repeated it, repeated it, until he reached the 25th. 'Ian's boss, dinner', it said in faintest pencil. He took his bold black pen and printed right across it in large emphatic capitals: 'MEET ME 2 O'CLOCK, AMBASSADORS CLUB LOUNGE, TERMINAL 3, HEATHROW.'

He shut the diary, closed her hands across it, then placed his own hands round her own, as if sanctioning and sanctifying all that he had written.

'Don't let me down,' he ordered.

32

It was snowing. Cruel early snow, unforecast, unexpected. The airport doors snapped shut against the cold, imprisoning Ginny in an echoing fug.

'Where to, lady?' asked the porter, manoeuvring her four large cases on to a trolley.

'Ambassadors Lounge, please.'

Terminal Three looked hazy and out of focus. She'd taken too many Mogadon last night, and Valium for breakfast. If only she could sink down on the floor, collapse on to the luggage trolley . . .

'But what about your luggage, miss? You have to check in first. What's your flight number?'

'TW 761.' How on earth could he not know? It was written all over the airport, on every kiosk and departure-board, hoarding, shop and restaurant; every brazen tannoy booming and repeating it. Her heart was pulsing in time to it, her legs pounding out its rhythm. She tried to keep the porter's blurred brown back in focus. He had all the cases, yet it was she who was weighed down. Her handbag hung too heavy on her arm – sunglasses and traveller's cheques, money, make-up, passport, and a small green plastic diary . . .

'Stop!' she pleaded suddenly.

'You calling me?' the porter asked, swinging round to check.

'No . . . Yes . . . I'm sorry. I think I'll have a drink first.'

'Best to get rid of the cases, miss, then you can order a drink in the lounge. It's real fancy, the Ambassadors – waiters and ice-buckets and those cheesy things to nibble.'

He stopped at the check-in desk, unloaded all the luggage. She stood in the queue, shading her eyes from the glaring airport lights. The other passengers were a whirl of pulsing colours

254

like a non-stop fruit machine. Someone turned to speak to her. Her mouth made mumbling movements in reply. She inched her cases along the ground, and after ten years, or a hundred, it was suddenly her turn. Bright plastic smile. 'Good afternoon.' Could it be afternoon? The night had struggled on for several centuries, and the morning had been born a sallow spastic, unwilling to wake up. She was far too early anyway, had been forced to leave by tiny things at home: Ian cooking sausages which nobody could eat, dishing up fake cheerfulness in leaden greasy dollops; Snookie wearing odd socks, one blue and one blue-grey, as if to remind her what would happen once she left; Toby bringing her his bone – his smelly ancient precious bone, flopping with it on her foot, as if to chain her to the house. Then Sarah had come rushing down in tears – her fish had died, her favourite fantail goldfish, its pale and bloated corpse floating belly-uppermost on the top of the small tank. She'd cried so hysterically that Ian had snapped at her, then tried to make amends by laying on a funeral; digging a small grave. They had knelt together in the bare and freezing garden, mourning half an ounce of fish.

Her expensive leather luggage had been stowed away in Kate's house. It had seemed to cruel to flaunt it in her own. She hadn't put the labels on, feared to state her destination quite so blatantly, as if, even at this final hour, she might change her mind, return to Hinchley Wood. She watched the girl attach the labels now, weigh her cases, tag them, mark them irrevocably: 'Los Angeles'. Another snap-on smile as the luggage slid away on the conveyor belt. It was like a crematorium – the coffin gliding through the curtains with no hope of resurrection or return. She couldn't seem to get away from funerals – first burial, now burning.

Her head and hands were fiery hot as she stared down at the empty space where the cases had been standing, cases twin to Caldos' own. He had thought of everything – matching leather luggage, new updated passport, visa and insurance, guide-books on America, histories of its Constitution, map of California. He had even opened an account for her at Harrods, to buy designer dresses, beachwear and bikinis; then sent her ardent telegrams, care of the Accounts Manager. The telegrams all said one thing: 'I love you.'

And so the love-infected weeks had limped and languished

by in a fog of indecision and despair. She had watched the swallows leave, flocks of restless travellers, swinging on the telegraph wires, mustering in busy groups at the first dwindling of the light, milling round in circles, expectant and excited. They thought nothing of flying a cool five thousand miles. She herself was paralysed, pulled between her strip of bleak back garden, which sprouted nothing save a washing-line and Snookie's broken doll's pram, and the golden gates of California where everything was coming up de Roche. She'd unfolded her huge map, walked her fingers round and round Los Angeles, as if following his footsteps, getting to know the city as intimately as he did, trying out its restaurants, seeing all its sights. She could almost hear him laughing along Sunset Boulevard, or shouting out 'I love you' from the brightest bar in Beverly Hills. But once she hid the map away, there was only the rumble of her washing machine, or Toby's wheezy breathing.

And then the leaves had fallen, brittle leaves rotting to a mulch as grey November rain lashed the shivering garden. She had longed to drift down with them, lie stagnant and unfeeling in some deep and sheltered ditch.

'Right, that's all now, Mrs Barnes. Enjoy your flight.'

Enjoy. Strange word. She had forgotten what it meant. She trailed away from the check-in desk, feeling lost without her luggage, jostled by the crowds, perspiring in the claustrophobic heat. She'd better have that drink, those little cheesy nibbles the porter had described, grab a little sustenance, tune in to solid things.

'Excuse me, please, could you direct me to the Ambassadors Lounge?'

Another dazzling smile. Why was everyone so cheerful – passengers and porters, airport staff, young men? The young man put his flight-bag down, gestured to his right. 'Just turn right over there, then up the stairs, across the road-bridge, and up again, one flight.'

Up the stairs. One step, two steps, three . . . The girls had always counted them when they were unsteady dogged toddlers dragging up to bed. Ian had invented a nonsense-rhyme to help them on their way.

> One stair
> you're almost there.
> Two stairs
> big fat bears.
> Three stairs
> say your prayers.

Say your prayers. She hadn't prayed for months, and now God had disappeared. A thousand years ago, she'd entreated Him to deliver her from Caldos. Or was it the other way round? Even then, she'd muddled them both up, worshipped the wrong one. She stood rigid on the third stair and tried to bring Him back; longed to SOS to Him, fall on her knees and implore Him to reveal Himself, to shepherd her up the stairs, lead her to the promised land. Caldos kept telling her that God was an illusion. But was anything quite real? The whole airport seemed a bubble – insubstantial, fragile, something which might burst, or float away; planes made out of water-vapour, God just myth and mirage. She forced her legs to move, one step up again.

> Four stairs
> plums and pears.
> Five stairs . . .

Five stairs? What came next? Her mind was full of smog, all the rhymes forgotten. She trailed down to the bottom again. It was easier going down.

'Excuse me, lady. Could you kindly get out of the way, or use the escalator.'

Escalator. That was what she needed, something effortless and magical, to waft and coax her up, five thousand miles up. She stepped on, closed her eyes, was jolted off abruptly into a yellow plastic buffet-bar, with jabbering plastic people, polystyrene chairs. She'd better find a chair herself, and a brandy to go with it. There was still another floor to go, and she couldn't face it without a little help. She swallowed half a Valium with her drink. Her conscience was returning, and she had to block it off, blank out all the mess she'd made, the endless strings of lies. Even now, she hadn't told the truth. There wasn't any truth. She'd woven bits and pieces of it into a cowardly craven note and left it on the mantelpiece at home. They always left their notes behind the grinning china donkey on the mantelpiece. Fifteen years of notes:

'Welcome, darling! Gone to vet with Toby. Last night was wonderful.'

'Sarah haircut. Your father phoning ref. begonias. Love you, Ian. Back soon.'

'Evening-class. Supper in oven. Sorry to be late.'

'Gone to London. Evening-class extended. Don't wait up.'

'Gone to America. Don't wait up.'

She sipped her brandy. 'I love you, Ian, I love you.' Had she really written that? Love was simply a word then, a safe and sentimental state. All those schmaltzy films and love songs never tried to warn you that real love was a disease, a lingering sickness which slowly wrecked your looks and then your life, dashed your nights to pieces, flung you into hell. She didn't need to do penance any more – love was its own penance. All the months she'd been in love with Caldos, she had been tortured, torn apart.

She slumped back in her chair. If only she'd never known him . . . But that would have been another kind of death. She'd been mouldering in a backwater, stifling in a tower, before he'd resurrected her – to life-in-death. There was almost nothing left now. Her heart must still be beating, she supposed, her body ticking over, but she could feel no stir of life. Her heavy lids kept closing, her back and shoulders sagging, as if she were already jet-lagged, exhausted from some cruelly endless flight. Was it just the pills, or some last trick of love? You had to pay for love – pay with your strength and sleep, your self-respect, your children, pay with life itself.

An oily-skinned Spaniard had joined her at the table – black eyes, white flash of teeth, whiff of gin and garlic on his breath. She turned away from his heavy-handed compliments, couldn't answer anyway. Her tongue was a broken rudder, her throat clogged with wet cement. Never in her life again would she allow a man to court her. Was Caldos just a man – or demon, shaman, saviour, murderer, god?

Her murderer and saviour was actually in England; sitting in this airport, maybe only yards away. She shook her head, couldn't quite believe it. She had yearned for him and ached for him through those interminable two months, and at last he had returned; would be closeted with Mossman now, discussing the last details of his clubs. She glanced down at her watch, the tiny jewelled extravagance he had given her before he left. Forty-five more minutes and she'd see him face to face. Impossible. Incredible. She wasn't even ready, despite her weeks of preparation; didn't have the energy to greet him, the backbone to stand up. She gazed around the bar. Only she was drooping. Everyone else looked fevered and frenetic, like figures in a movie run at double speed; arms flailing, fat heads wagging, scarlet mouths clack-clacking. She held her head between her hands, trying to shut the noise out – a discordant mix of music, cackle, chinking cups, brays of raucous laughter, announcements on the tannoy.

Was it real at all, though? Maybe she was dreaming – some jagged strident nightmare which would release her in a moment to the safety of her double bed at home; Ian snuffling there beside her, still half-asleep himself, and a cat or two purring on her foot. She rubbed her eyes, tried to see things clearly – the mink collar on her suit, the fastidious Gucci shoes, with their lizard trim and haughty three-inch heels. Her hair was Bond Street blonde again, and reflected in her brandy glass – gold and amber curdled, both colours crudely bright. She closed her eyes, descended through the lift-shaft of her lids, to the duller safer shades of Hinchley Wood.

Someone touched her arm. It must be Ian shaking her out of the nightmare, or Snookie with a stomach-ache. She felt too tired to wake, to cope with husbands, children. Someone else whispering in her ear. She pretended not to hear. Too much effort to chat about the weather, or exchange banalities about holidays and flights.

'Leave me alone,' she murmured. Everything was blurring – shifting and dissolving like wisps of wind-blown smoke. Even behind the black velvet of her eyelids, there were pricklings and alarms.

How insistent people were! Two presumptuous arms around her shoulders, a clutch of cocksure fingers flirting with her hair, song of 'Eau Sauvage' cutting through the waft of a cigar. Her heart took off like Concorde, then nose-dived and crash-landed. She could only be imagining things. Whatever happened, she mustn't open her eyes. Hallucination would be even worse than nightmare. Yet her lips were opening, searching for his own lips, fumbling for a name.

'C . . . Caldos?'

'Estrella!' came the answer – confident, triumphant – and suddenly, the whole bustling jostling self-important airport was on its knees in homage to him; fifty thousand staff and passengers grovelling in obeisance; the whole grounded world his dais.

Yellow plastic had transmuted into topaz; the snow outside warmed to white spring flowers, scented showers of petals blanketing the ground. Grim men cracked in smiles, bent old crones frisked like April lambs; the sick took up their beds and walked; the bare trees put forth leaves. Yet there was only one real miracle – Caldos Miracle de Roche was against her heart again.

She couldn't speak at all, simply gazed at him and gazed at him, wondering how he'd grown so tall. His head touched the top of the control tower; his eyes burned holes through steel. All the other passengers had withered in his shadow, just flabby scrag-ends now. She kissed his hands, entwined their fingers, overlapped their feet, swapped wild and famished mouths. She must be fused in him, and joined, reborn, transfigured, leavened. She would never, ever, let him go again.

'Beloved,' he was murmuring. 'My memory deceived me. I remembered you a Cullinan, and found you a Koh-i-noor.'

She didn't understand him, but it was enough that he was there. She could desert a dozen husbands, abandon broods of children, just to hear his voice. She longed to scoop out sonnets from her handbag, match his high-flown words, instead of fumbling for a Kleenex. All that she could stutter was, 'You . . . you're early, darling.'

'Yes, that God-forsaken Mossman let me down! He was flying in from Frankfurt and his plane's delayed. A spot of engine trouble, they told me at the other terminal. Nothing serious, thank God. He'll be here in half an hour.'

She'd have gladly tossed Mossman in the waste-bin, ground him out like a fag-end on the floor. Why should she share Caldos, when his breath had set her hair on fire, his fingers freed her body from its painful long paralysis?

'I couldn't wait that long to see you,' he was saying. 'I've been

260

searching the whole airport to see if I could spot you, and at last we're . . .'

She didn't hear the rest – he was kissing her again. A teenage boy was making catcalls at them, and an outraged woman tutting about disgusting displays in public. There wasn't any public, only the private cosmos of his mouth. He had finished up her brandy and she could taste it on his lips; feel those lips seeming to scorch through flesh and bone, and, further down, Adolfo leaping to attention beneath her prowling hands.

'Feel him, *moya lubimaya*. He's ten foot tall! He's been dying of deprivation these last two months, and is absolutely determined to make up for his abstinence and pay you his respects – here and now, without any more delay.'

She laughed. Even they couldn't turn the world's busiest international airport into their private boudoir.

'I've been so damned busy, darling, Adolfo's had to stay in hibernation. But you've kissed him out of his slumbers like the Prince with Sleeping Beauty. We must go and find our hundred-years-high briar-hedge, to conceal ourselves behind.'

'Oh, Caldos . . .' He was so extravagant, so funny. Everything was funny, the whole jubilant world smiling down on them.

'No, I'm serious, Estrella. I want you, my witch, and I intend to have you – now.'

'Now? But . . . where? How? I mean, what about Philip and . . . ?'

'I told you darling, he's delayed. Extremely tactful of him in the circumstances. He's presented us with the most perfect gift any two lovers could ask for – half an hour entirely to ourselves.'

'But, but . . . Caldos, it'll take us almost that to book in at a hotel, by the time we've found a taxi and filled in those dreary forms. We'll have hardly got our clothes off, when we'll need to turn straight round and rush back here again.'

'Who said anything about an hotel, *bellissima*?'

He was marching her out of the bar, already unbuttoning his coat. She stared at him in horror. Fornication in an airport must surely be a crime. They'd land up in the cells of the Old Bailey, rather than the first-class comfort of a jumbo jet.

He paused a moment right outside the Gents. Dear God, not there, she prayed – not writhing on white tiles while a dozen men in full flood applauded from the urinals. No – he'd whisked her on, his pace increasing all the time, so that she was running to keep up with him. They were traversing the whole building, Caldos peering into doors and cupboards, one filled with plastic refuse-sacks dribbling ash and tea-leaves; one marked in bold red capitals: 'FOR EMERGENCY USE ONLY'.

'That sounds right,' grinned Caldos, wrenching at the handle. The room was full of wheelchairs.

He galloped on again, leaping down a dizzy flight of steps, and surveying the ground floor, which appeared to have fewer cubbyholes and cupboards. He stopped beside a door marked 'TERMINAL SERVICES'.

'Exactly what we want, *divina*.' He secreted a kiss in the recesses of her ear, courted the stiff handle. But the door refused to yield to him, stayed resolutely locked. He stood motionless a second, staring through the glass doors of the terminal, to the ugly concrete buildings grouped around it. Suddenly, he seized her arm and swept her through the exit, across the busy road outside. The cold air cut and circled like a scythe. Yet Caldos' hand was still burning through her own. His golden suntan made the sky look wan. He was sprinting along the pavement, past the multi-storey car park, towards the very hub of the airport, the control tower. Horrific pictures flashed before her eyes: planes crashing from the sky, smashing into each other on the runways; carnage, wreckage, and destruction, as he kidnapped the control tower, made it his seraglio.

But the tower had disappeared. They had turned into a small paved garden, sheltered by brick walls and graced with shrubs and ivies; surely too serene a spot to have been left unscathed amidst the vortex all around it. Two white roses were still courageously in flower, outsmarting both winter and pollution. Caldos broke one off and twisted it through her hair. She touched its soft face sadly, knew it would be dead before the morning.

She stared at the dark wooden cross looming in the centre of the garden. Why a cross? Why a garden? There wasn't time for questions. Caldos had urged her through a pair of double doors, into a small grey vestibule. The chill cold of the bare stone walls seeped into her limbs. God in heaven! She knew now where they were. This was the airport chapel, and Caldos was planning sacrilege.

She tried to force him back into the safety of the garden. 'Look, it's getting rather late, darling – half past one already. We don't want to rush things, do we, and supposing you miss Philip or . . .'

Caldos was reading from a framed text on the wall, one hand gesturing to the words, the other pinioning her own. 'For those who love,' he recited, 'time is Eternity.'

'Eternity' echoed round the vestibule, as if he'd called in heavenly voices to support him. He tried to lead her down the staircase to the chapel in the basement, but she grabbed the curving banister, pulled him to a stop.

'It's Sunday,' she objected. 'We can't do it in a chapel, and especially not on Sunday. It's a holy day. A service might be starting any minute.'

'At half past one? My dear Estrella, you're still quite touchingly naive. Every Reverend worth the name will be halfway through his roast beef and Château Giscours, bought with the proceeds of the collection plate.'

She clung on to the banister, mustn't think of beef. That was what she'd left for them at home – a five-pound joint of top rib, as a treat to lull her guilt. Even the chapel name, St George's, set up guilty memories. She hadn't said goodbye to George, hadn't made her usual horseradish, hadn't . . . 'Listen, Caldos, this chapel's a sacred place. It's consecrated, set apart for prayer. It says so on the notice.'

'That's all I plan, Estrella – our own private prayer and sacrament. Haven't I taught you yet that love is holy? It's only right and proper we should do it in a sacred place.'

They had reached the chapel now, a dark claustrophobic building constructed like a crypt. The lowering ceiling seemed to press her down, reminded her of air-raid shelters, confining, coldly bleak. No ornaments, no pictures, no colour except blacks and greys, the shades of sin, of guilt. She prayed that someone might come in – a priest, a nun, a prayer-group, even a casual godless tourist with a camera and a Coke. Just one single person would be enough to quash his plan. But the only sign of life was their own elongated shadows ghosting concrete walls. She watched Caldos' shadow loom towards the altar, its silhouette profaning the east end, while she herself cowered trembling at the entrance.

'Jesus is waiting for you', declaimed the poster on the chapel door, beneath a picture of a kindly man with gentle eyes and smile. She longed to take His hand, kneel with Him in prayer or meditation; blank out the sight of Caldos, now pounding back to fetch her, his own eyes smouldering in the darkness, the softest of his whispers resounding like a sonic boom.

'This is our own private paradise, my seraph. I shall bow down and pray with my head between your legs.'

'*No!*' she said, speaking with more vehemence than she ever had before. 'I don't care what you say, Caldos. It's absolutely wrong. We just can't do it here.'

She saw his whole face darken, felt the steel grip of his fingers as he pulled her into a shadowy alcove behind a small side-altar. She could see the red sanctuary-lamp burning right in front of him, crimsoning his mane of hair.

'Caldos, *no* – not there! That's where the Blessed Sacrament is kept. It's total sacrilege.'

'Take your pants down.'

His voice was so authoritative, she dared not disobey, though she tried to lose herself in the deepest furthest corner of the alcove. The cold grey concrete was reinforced with flintstones, which grazed against her face. There was no kindness here, no mercy.

'Kneel down,' he said. She knelt. She had always tried to follow his opinions – changed her mind about foods and wines and music; let him be her guide on how to dress, what to read, even how to speak. But this was something deeper, something fundamental. Even if there were no God, as he always claimed so glibly, it was still entirely wrong to insult all those who did believe, defile their sacred chapel, risk their outrage and disgust. And in some ironic way, God had never seemed so real, somehow present in this place, weeping for their sin, for her deserted home and husband, her betrayal, her deceit.

She drew her breath in sharply as something split her from behind. She was completely unaroused, felt only shock and pain, as Adolfo forced in deeper. Always before, when he'd wanted sex that back way, he'd made sure she was responsive, eased in very slowly, taken time and care. But now his slamming rhythm ignored her own passivity, mocked her fears, her scruples. He didn't even care about the risk of being found. Anyone could wander in through that casual open door. They might shock an innocent child, scandalise a worshipper or tourist. Thank God they were partly hidden by a large vase of dried flowers, but even so, it would be clear what they were doing, if anyone should enter. And she knew that God could see them – the God whom Caldos waved away like an unripe avocado in a restaurant, or an overcooked rump steak – *He* was there and watching; could see her lover's upturned feet scrabbling against the altar-step in obscenely private prayer.

Caldos used his fingers to add a second front of pleasure. Except it wasn't pleasure. She felt nothing, nothing, except terror and distaste. That, too, was a sin. It was her duty to respond to him, to welcome even pain, as she always had before. But this pain was very different – a clumsy wooden key forcing a lock it didn't fit. Everything about him seemed suddenly too big: his hot hands on her back, the violence of his breathing, his huge lion head, his hulking heaving torso. She was just a crumb which had fallen from his table; he a whole banquet in himself.

All the meals they had ever consumed together steamed and sizzled through her head; she nibbling on a prawn, while he slavered over succulent steaks, juicy chops, creamy fragrant sauces, plump puddings, drooling pies. She multiplied them by all the food he'd eaten in his life – rusks and purées as a baby, chips and bangers as a boy, beer and sandwiches at medical school, grouse at Glyndebourne, strawberries at Ascot, salmon at Lord's. She added it together: carcasses of meat, cowsful of cream, barrowloads of apples, hothouses of grapes; acres of groaning vineyards, teeming cornucopias, running over, spilling out, building him up to gigantic glossy size. She herself was a grape-pip in comparison, a piece of discarded rind. Caldos de Roche wasn't constructed out of bone or sinew, but of lobster thermidor and crêpes Suzette; his blood was Château Giscours, his lungs were banana splits; Adolfo himself a *bombe surprise*. That's why he took so long to climax. Every sexual act was double-sauced, triple-garnished, swollen out with calories, vitamin-enriched. Even now, with Mossman disembarking and God outraged, he was still tasting and thrusting, cramming and sating, as if he had scooped up treble portions of Eternity and Ecstasy with his ticket and his boarding pass.

She had gloried in it before, staggered from his bedroom shaking and exultant, mauled and worshipping. But this time, she was an empty dish scoured by a voracious spoon, all the juices sucked out of her, until she was a squeezed lemon, a dry husk. Only now did she realise how he indulged himself in everything, said 'no' to her, but never to himself. His greedy teeth were still gnawing on her shoulder, as if she were just another course – some cake or joint or carcass he had to wolf, devour. She swung round, shook him off.

He clung on by Adolfo. 'Fantastic, darling! I adore it when you move like that. You've been so strange and tense, I could hardly even feel you.'

Yes, she was responding to him now, not in passion, but in fury, lobbing her whole force and weight against him, trying to buck him off like a horse with a cruel rider.

'Wonderful!' he shouted. 'Absolutely wonderful! Oh God Almighty!' He was praying, now, praying and coming in one blasphemous gasping breath. 'It's stupendous, darling, glorious! You've never moved like that before. Oh, don't stop! Go on, go on. Yes, twist and push. Oh Christ!'

The entire chapel seemed to heave and cry, his monstrous shadow leaping right across the wall, then plunging down, collapsing.

'My Paraclete,' he murmured. 'My Redeemer.'

There was a sudden step outside, a male voice raised in singing. She recognised the hymn, spun round, pushed her lover off, fumbled for her pants. Sperm was dribbling down the backs of her thighs, seeping underneath the tops of her sheer black Dior stockings. Whoever was outside would know what they'd been doing. The whole chapel reeked of sex, accused them with its very breath. It would be stained for ever, desecrated. She smoothed her crumpled skirt as voice and footsteps both crescendoed.

'Make me feel as thou hast felt,
Make my soul to glow and melt
With the love of . . .'

It was the Stabat Mater and the sacristan. He stopped abruptly as he realised he was not alone, saw them cowering in their alcove.

Caldos pretended to be examining a floor-plaque whilst he put his clothes to rights, then swept into a pew, bowed his head above joined hands, moved his lips in prayer. Ginny dithered in the corner. Her pants were twisted round her hips, and she dared not move until the hectic flush had faded from her cheeks.

Caldos made the sign of the cross, then eased up to his feet, stopping for a moment to compliment the sacristan. 'It's an exquisite little chapel that you've got here. The perfect place for privacy and peace.' He scooped Ginny from her alcove, tossed an ostentatious ten-pound note into the collection plate, just inside the entrance.

'An offering to the Blessed Sacrament,' he drawled, as he sauntered through the doors and up the stairs, Ginny stumbling in his wake. She could still hear the sacristan's weak uncertain baritone, rising from below.

> 'Be to me, O Virgin, nigh,
> Lest in flames I burn and die,
> In his aweful Judgement Day.'

33

It was snowing again, as they burst through the chapel vestibule and back into daylight – no longer showers of spring narcissi, but cruelly stinging pellets which lashed into their faces. Ginny screwed her eyes up, tried to glance around her. Why was everything so changed, the whole vast lumbering complex of the airport now looking like a rubbish-dump, sprawled beneath a sick and flaccid sky? Caldos was late, striding on ahead of her. She panted to keep up, recalling the lines he'd declaimed to her so grandly: 'For those who love, time is Eternity.' But not, apparently, when he was meeting his solicitor. She found it hard to run. Her shoes were far too high, and one of her suspenders had come undone, the left stocking loose and puckering. He slowed for her a moment, but his feet were still tap-tapping on the pavement, nervous fingers pacing up and down his watch-case.

'Look, I'm sorry, my dove, but I'll have to go on ahead. Mossman will be frantic. You come on more slowly and amuse yourself with a coffee and the *Tatler*. I'll meet you in the departure lounge. It's quite simple. As soon as you hear our flight called, just go through Passport Control, and you'll see the lounge straight in front of you.'

Ginny tripped on a loose paving stone, grabbed his arm to save herself from falling. Both hands were already grazed from the chapel wall. 'But, I thought you said the *Ambassadors* Lounge . . .' Was she a VIP no longer? Had she been demoted from the ice-buckets, the fancy snooty waiters?

'I'm sorry, beloved, but it's a lot later than I realised. There's a hell of a backlog to discuss with Philip already, and I shan't be seeing him for at least another year.'

'But can't I come with you?' She couldn't bear to lose him again, be widowed again, cast adrift in the hectic roar and jostle of the terminal.

'Well, it *is* rather confidential, *mein Schätzchen*. Philip always gets just slightly paranoid if outsiders listen in on his financial wizardry.'

Outsiders? He'd been inside her just a minute ago, brutally inside her, but now she was a banished Eve, the fierce brand of the flaming sword still hot between her legs. She glanced down at her knees. Tiny jewels of blood were hardening round the torn black stockings like crimson holly berries. Sarah had broken off all the berries from the holly in the garden, spelt out the goldfish's name with them on his bare back-garden grave.

'Look, Estrella, it's only for half an hour. They'll be calling our flight in exactly twenty-eight minutes. That's hardly long now, is it?' His voice had changed and hardened, assumed the authority of Adam, Primal Man, who would brook no argument.

'But I don't want to leave you, Caldos. I mean, we've only just met up again, and . . .'

They were back at the terminal, had dived through the doors into fug-hot dazzle and drama – half the itinerant world laughing, greeting, jabbering and weeping; a thousand thousand aliens milling all around them. Caldos fumbled in his pocket, one impatient arm around her waist. 'Here, I bought you a little present on the plane.'

Scarlet box tied with golden ribbon. She read the label – 'Joy' by Jean Patou, remembered their advertisement: 'The most expensive perfume in the world.'

'*Gioia per la mia gioia.* Dab that behind your beautiful ears, *amore*, and by the time you've refastened the ribbons on the box, I'll be safely back with you.'

Gone. A streak of camel-hair, a wave of plump cigar. She watched his swift legs swallow up the steps, dart across the footbridge, then hurtle up again. He was just a pin-man now, a blur, a smudge, a nothing; she a magnet which had lost its charge.

She drooped over to the café, sore in every sense, but trying not to feel. Feelings were too dangerous, especially anger – a deadly virus which could poison your whole system, even threaten life. She must cure the virus, cast it out. There was no reason to be angry, if she saw things in proportion, and from her lover's point of view. Sex in church wasn't sacrilege for Caldos, but a type of holy communion. He'd been missing her so wildly, he'd simply come and claimed her on his knees, like a devotee, a pilgrim. It was a compliment, a tribute to her. She was his bell-tower and his lady chapel, his Mecca, his Jerusalem – all the romantic things he'd called her, which had made her proud, elated, in the past.

And, after all, she'd missed him just as avidly herself, rubbed herself sore through two empty fantasising months, imagining Adolfo roaring into her. It was probably just the pills which were making her so moody, some side-effect of stress and sleepless nights. It would be different in Los Angeles. She'd open like a lotus then, in the right relaxed surroundings; champagne by the water-bed, a triumphal oratorio on the hi-fi, and Caldos to herself.

But would she have her lover to herself? What about the Californian equivalents of Mossman – accountants and solicitors, psychiatrists and club staff, architects, surveyors . . .

She marched up to the counter, joined the queue. Stupid to be negative, feeble and ungrateful. This was her rebirth, her own personal renaissance. She must turn her back on the gloom and superstition of the Dark Ages, and stride forward to the New World. If she couldn't accept the chapel, then she must pretend it never happened, throw it out, like Caldos did with God; concentrate instead on that first ecstatic moment of their meeting in the café, just one brief hour ago. She'd known then that she loved him with a passion and intensity she'd never felt for anyone before, and, as Caldos said himself, that kind of love was holy. Why ruin their whole life together just because she was feeling out of sorts? Those feelings only sprang from the anguish of his absence, the misery and tension of the last eight endless weeks. She scrubbed her knees with a Kleenex, scoured them clean with spit. It was very simple, really. All she needed was a good strong cup of coffee, a tin of Elastoplast, and a dose of common sense.

The queue was moving slowly, trickling forward inch by restless inch. Standing right in front of her was a tiny girl in a pair of scarlet dungarees, and a shy and mousy man whose face looked as if it had shifted slightly, before the putty set. The child was jumping up, trying to see the food-display. 'I can't see, Daddy. I can't see . . .'

270

He picked his daughter up, slid her along the counter on his tray. She stared gravely at a pile of custard tarts. She could have been Caldos' child, with her dark untidy hair, her greedy eyes and loud imperious voice: 'I want that one and that one and that one and . . .'

'No, only one, Jo. You'll be sick on the plane.'

Ginny smiled. She was ravenous herself – tears for breakfast and a milligram of sperm for lunch. She longed suddenly to sink her teeth into a doughnut, drag a spoon through the obscene centre of a banana split. She closed her eyes. Through the whoosh of white whipped cream, she could see the Sunday lunch table, which she'd laid before she left. How cold and bare it looked, despite the new white linen napkins, the kind Caldos always used. He'd affected her in every way, from how she viewed the cosmos to what brand of tea she bought. The girls liked paper serviettes, garish coloured comic ones with grinning Donald Ducks on.

'Daddy, why has that lady got her eyes shut?'

'Don't point, Jo. It's rude.'

The scarlet dungarees shifted slowly into focus, shuffled back along the counter, and stopped in front of her.

'Why did you shut your eyes? Daddy, why did the lady shut her eyes?'

'Jo, be quiet, please. I expect the lady's tired.'

'*We* got up at five o'clock this morning. What time did you get up?'

'Don't be a pest.' Her father sounded weary. He was wearing a tweed jacket with two blunt pencils stuck in the top pocket. His shirt looked badly ironed. There were creases down the front of it, and the collar didn't set. 'Quiet, Jo,' he urged again.

Jo. She liked the name – tomboyish and casual, like Jo in *Little Women*. They had almost had a Jo themselves. Sarah had been Josephine for six months in the womb, until Ian had met a Josephine at work – a lame-duck hypochondriac.

'Are you going to America?' Jo asked, her dark Caldos eyes still fixed on Ginny's blue ones.

Ginny swallowed, couldn't speak. Her mouth felt full of the dried flowers in the church – teasels, helichrysum, prickling down her throat. Ian would be trying his hand at apple pie, trying to avoid the disaster of the last one, when he'd showered in fifty-seven

271

cloves. Sarah had counted them, fished them all out and put them in a matchbox. 'Wait till I show them at school!' she'd crowed.

'Daddy, is that lady going to America?'

'No, I don't expect so, darling.' The man looked tense and harassed, a tiny muscle twitching in his cheek.

'Yes,' she said. 'I'm going to America.' She'd spelt it out, at last. Always before, she'd hushed it up, tried to kid herself, kid them all, reduce the miles, the distance, distort the blatant fact. She should have made the pie herself. Snookie hated cloves.

'It's a long long way, America.' Jo was sucking her thumb, mumbling through it, black-coal eyes screwed up.

'Yes, I know.'

Jo jumped off the counter and started jigging up and down. 'Daddy, I want to go wee-wees.'

'Oh, Christ!'

Ginny caught his look of panic. Tough to leave a father on his own. They couldn't cope with wee-wees. 'Look, I'll take her, if you like. You can keep my place in the queue.'

He almost hugged her with relief. 'Gosh, thanks. I'll get you a coffee, shall I?'

'Please. A really strong one.'

'Fine. Anything to eat?'

She paused. She wasn't allowed to eat, must be slim and svelte for their arrival in Los Angeles. Caldos would claim her again, instantly, immediately, strip off all her clothes . . . 'Yes, a doughnut, please. One of those big ones there with cream in. In fact, could you make it two?'

'Right.'

He didn't even sound surprised. Could there still be men who didn't care if you were fat – or plain, or dull, or stupid? She glanced down at her crumpled skirt, her damp and snow-stained shoes. Her grazed knees were still stinging, a damp unpleasant residue slimy in her pants. It was a wonder that he trusted her with his defenceless precious child.

'See you back here then.'

She nodded, took Jo's hand, a small cold hand, lost in her hot sweaty one. She'd forgotten they could be that small. Sarah was a Titan, Snookie a giant.

'Have you got a little girl?' Jo asked.

'I've got two big ones.'

'Where are they, then?'

'Careful of the door.' She fixed all her attention on the fiddly buckles of Jo's dungarees, held her steady on the seat. There were so many things a mother had to know – rationing cloves, not ironing creases into collars. You'd never get a diploma in them, or a glowing testimonial. But you might receive a sticky-fingered Christmas card, constructed out of kitchen foil and toilet rolls, with 'Mummy' written on it in a puddle of glue and chocolate vermicelli. Well, not this year, you wouldn't.

They were standing by the basins now. She could see a fake deceitful face accusing in the mirror – spidery lashes stiff with black mascara, scarlet-painted lips. She was wearing Caldos' colours even on her face, completing his bold livery with her black stockings and red suit. She was alone in the mirror, no dark-haired Jo beside her. The child's head didn't even reach the bottom of the frame. But what was a mere child or two when you were a professional fornicator, a brash New-World career woman? She rinsed her hands, splashed cold water on her knees. The little holly berries were pricking through again. Cold white tiles, hot red blood.

'Do fishes have blood?' Snookie had enquired, when they were standing by the grave, reciting the Our Father over the goldfish's last remains. It was the only prayer the children really knew.

She blotted her lipstick, dabbed at her hair, almost too exhausted to lift the comb. It took effort to be glamorous, effort and real pain. Her feet were hurting in their expensive Gucci shoes – cripplingly expensive. If she were back at home, she'd be wearing her old jeans, soft flat comfy moccasins; hair swinging loose and easy round her face, not shackled in false curls. She took out Caldos' present, tore off all the wrappings. The bottle looked mean and grudging, compared with the grandeur of its box.

'What's that?' asked Jo, rescuing the ribbon.

'Perfume.' Caldos always told her to say 'scent'. 'Perfume' was lower-middle-class and only suited to the sort of people who wore clip-on bow ties, and put Blue Flush down their toilets (lavatories). Ian said 'perfume' – though he never gave it to her, only occasional bars of cut-price scented soap. He'd bought her a handbag before she went away, a useful one with lots of little pockets. She'd left it behind, hidden in the broom cupboard. It wasn't real leather, and had no real style or class.

She unscrewed the scent, dabbed some on Jo's wrist – smell of public toilets mixed with 'Joy'. The most expensive perfume in the world.

'It smells horrible,' said Jo. She couldn't say her r's. The door of the Ladies suddenly seemed too heavy. Ginny laid her cheek against the plastic wood.

'What are you crying for?'

'I'm *not*.' Grown-ups didn't cry over rubbishy vinyl handbags, bars of cheap Rose soap. She took Jo's hand again across the million miles of shifting patterned floor. Everything too bright – shrieking yellow tables, metallic orange chairs, the clatter of the café a pneumatic drill boring between her eyes. Split apart both ends. No, she mustn't think of that again; must think only of the future, which was about to start in ten or fifteen minutes, the moment that her flight was called; think only of her love, a love beyond all doubt now, worth sacrifice and pain. She checked her watch, walked faster.

'I want my Daddy,' Jo wailed suddenly. 'Where's my Daddy gone?'

'It's all right, he's over there.'

He was watching for them anxiously, worry stamped into his face like endorsements on a driving licence, as he stood rigid at the counter, coffee steaming, two cream doughnuts sweating on their plate. He was just about to pay, scrabbling in his pocket for his wallet as he cast fretful glances round him, face slackening in relief as they joined him at the till.

'Ah good! You're safely back.' He gestured to his tray. 'I got your doughnuts.'

A whiff of grease and sugar cut across the reek of 'Joy'. She could still smell disinfectant. 'I'm sorry, but I don't think I can manage them. I feel a bit . . .' She paused. Caldos would be gobbling canapés – Persian caviare glistening in the bellies of golden vol-au-vents; plump asparagus peeking from its duvet of smoked salmon. 'Maybe Jo could eat them for me.'

'But I've already got her a piece of chocolate cake.'

'Never mind, I'll pay for them.' She passed a note across. The man refused, embarrassed; paid himself.

'Three cakes! I've got three cakes,' Jo yelled. 'I've never had three cakes before. Put them all on this plate. I want them all together.'

Ginny arranged them for her carefully, the gâteau in the middle, a doughnut on each side. Jo poked an ecstatic finger in each one, licked up cream and sickly chocolate icing.

'Come on, Jo, for heaven's sake.' Her father snatched the plate. 'You're holding everybody up.'

Ginny noticed the dark circles underneath his eyes, the cheap unambitious flannels, the hint of real annoyance in his voice. Jo was tugging at his sleeve, whining now and fractious. 'Let *me* hold the cakes. I want to hold them. They're my cakes, they're mine. That lady gave them to me.'

Reluctantly, he handed Jo her plate. She strutted slowly after him, tongue poised between her teeth, total concentration, eyes so reverently absorbed, she failed to see the six-foot-tall American striding right towards her. He swerved at the last moment, to avoid her. She jolted back as well, plate tipping up and spilling all its contents – both doughnuts on the floor, the piece of chocolate gâteau squashed into a mulch of cream and jam.

Ginny crouched down on her hands and knees, as much to hide her face as to clear up all the mess. Jo was sobbing wildly, but there was less excuse for her to cry. She was aware of people staring, one girl even sniggering. Yes, it must seem quite absurd – a stylish grown-up woman weeping over three smashed cakes. She tried to concentrate on Jo's tears, found a Kleenex in her handbag, wiped the child's wet face. The father seemed frozen with embarrassment, offering to replace the cakes, yet standing semi-paralysed, shifting from foot to foot.

'*Jo!*' he bellowed suddenly, swooping down to pick her up. 'For God's sake stop that racket! You've made the lady cry.'

Jo broke off in mid-wail, stared at Ginny's face. 'What are you crying for? They were *my* cakes.'

'Ssh,' said a woman at a table just beside them. 'They're announcing a flight.'

Ginny pounced up to her feet, took a gulp of coffee from her cup.

'Trans World Airlines, flight number TW 761 to Los Angeles . . .'

She tried to force the coffee down, needed instant energy and strength.

'Passengers should proceed immediately through Flight Departures on the first floor, to the final lounge. TW 761 to Los Angeles . . .'

761, 761. The numbers hammered through her head. She spat the coffee back into her cup, lurched towards the exit. She heard Jo running after her, but she couldn't afford to wait. She must be there for Caldos, sitting radiant and assured, Elastoplasted with courage, drenched with 'Joy'. Whatever happened, he mustn't arrive before her, shouldn't have to wait for her, or worry that she'd lost her way, or nerve. This was the first sweet moment of her future.

She cannoned through the crowds, struggling to reach the front, jolted round the corner, saw Flight Departures immediately ahead of her, only a few short paces from the buffet. She stopped, disorientated. It had no right to be so near. She would rather have walked a hundred miles, climbed six thousand steps. She joined the queue marked 'British Passports', could hear Jo crying out, somewhere in the distance.

'Daddy, I don't want to go. I don't want to go!'

She turned round, almost angrily, saw the child shrieking and hysterical, clinging to her father, kicking with her heels against his shins, upsetting all the people in the queue. He picked her up, edged forwards, trying to quiet her screams. Ginny shrugged. It was nothing to do with her. She was almost at the desk now, her shiny new blue passport as heavy as a bible, Jo's violent yells hacking through her skull.

'Don't want to go. Don't want to go to America.'

The official at the desk had dark brows, powerful shoulders, coarse black hairs tangled on his thumbs, an ostentatious ruby ring swanking on his finger. The garish stone seemed to be flickering like the sanctuary-lamp, the whole chapel red and scorching from its glow. Red was not her colour – too hectic and too threatening. Red for lust and danger, even martyrdom. The man was speaking to her, asking for her boarding pass. She hesitated, dropped it, took a step backwards to try to pick it up. The teenage youth behind her bumped into her and swore. 'I'm sorry,' she said furiously. She'd been saying that for months, begging pardon, seeking absolution from God and priest and man.

'Don't just stand there, madam. You're holding everybody up. I need to see your boarding pass.'

She suddenly wheeled round, shoving and struggling through the swarm of angry passengers behind her, bolting back the way she'd come. She paused for just a second as she passed Jo's kicking body, then hurtled on, dodging people's elbows and their flight-bags, butting through the crowds like some frantic panicked animal. Someone tried to grab her arm, offer help, advice. She shook it off, plunged towards the escalator, vibrating right in front of her. She was free, at last, free to skitter down; the black moving handrail reaching out towards her. But the steps were going up, not down, up towards the departure lounge, where everyone was going, where she should be herself. She glanced around her desperately, could see no other escalator, nothing going down.

She jumped on to the treads, fighting with an escalator determined to go up. People tried to stop her, thrusting with their arms or bags, one old man threatening to report her. She almost hit them off. She needed all her attention to stop falling – did fall at the bottom, crashed off the last three steps and cut her knee. Bleeding again, red again. Holly berries, graves. She could hear Jo, much fainter now, but still screaming at the top. 'Don't want to go to America. Don't want to go to . . .'

She dashed past the check-ins, past TWA, Pan-Am, BA – the whole hectic airborne world going up, going up. Caldos would be looking for her, questioning the stewardess, searching the departure lounge. She swerved towards the exit, could almost smell the cold clean air outside. The automatic door had jammed. She struggled with it, hammering against the glass with one corner of her handbag. The door slid open suddenly, and she fell across it, out into the snow.

'Taxi,' she shouted. 'Taxi!'

34

The note was still there, sitting unopened on the mantelpiece. Fifteen years of notes. She slit it open, wincing at its tone. Written in blood and sweat and anguish, it sounded bland and scrappy like a shopping-list. Half a pound of butter, three tins of Chum. It had taken her two months to drag together those few scant lines, and still she'd got it wrong – desperately wrong. Where was he, dear scant Ian? Where were any of them? Kate had promised to be there, not to uproot the children for the first two weeks or so, to ensconce herself in residence, with Steve. Nanny Katkin, she'd called herself, tried to make a joke about it. 'You'll have to mind your p's and q's with Nanny Katkin in the hot-seat,' 'Eat your lovely tapioca up for Nanny.' But even Kate knew it wasn't funny. Not this time.

Where in God's name could they be? It was Sunday, stay-at-home day. Holy day, family day, violating-a-chapel day. She'd left them only four short everlasting hours ago. Left them with lies and roast top rib of beef. She could smell the beef, had put it in the oven just before she left, to stop Kate resorting to the tin-opener – the most expensive joint she'd ever bought in all her married life. She opened the oven door. The meat was burnt, shrivelled up to nothing.

She turned the oven off and rushed upstairs. Ian's wardrobe was open; the radio left on. Afternoon Theatre – a cosy lady chatting to her husband, while she tinkled teaspoons, iced a home-made cake. Did people still exist like that, normal happy families, who didn't lie or cheat? All the complicated plans she'd made, all the arrangements, lists and schedules which she'd hoped would keep her home afloat, seemed so much empty ballast now, too frail to prevent it capsizing in the end. Kate couldn't be a mother to her children. It had all been sheer delusion and deceit.

'Ian,' she called. 'Ian!'

He never left the radio on. It wasted the batteries. No reply. No one there. Something terrible had happened. God had taken His revenge before she'd even had a chance to tell them she'd come home.

She rushed into the children's room, a mess of books and toys; on Sarah's desk a sheet of Snoopy writing paper, headed 'Darling Mummy'. So she'd written already, was missing her already. Would she ever see her girls again? Horrific headlines were bleeding through her head – children murdered, kidnapped, killed by drunken drivers, drowned in rivers, gassed. Or perhaps they were alive and had gone out for a picnic. A picnic in November in the snow? With the table laid and dinner in the oven? Ridiculous. She picked up Sarah's letter, trailed downstairs again, faltered to the phone, hardly daring to pick up the receiver. No reply from Kate's house, and why would she be there? Her husband was in Hamburg, at a conference, and it was all arranged that she'd be staying with the Barneses. She tried Maureen, Susan, Mrs Foster, Jane, hadn't time or patience for all the explanations.

'Yes, I'm back, but I can't talk now, I'm sorry. I'm worried about the girls. You haven't seen them? Okay, let's meet, but can we make it . . . ?'

'Look, Eileen, it's the girls . . . Oh, I see, you've been away. No, I'm afraid I can't – not now. I'll try and phone you later, when I've . . .'

'Anne-Marie, it's Ginny here. I'm getting really frantic, just can't track the girls down. You've *got* them? Oh, thank God! Are they all right? What happened? George? But surely . . .'

She could hear Snookie yelling 'Mummy, Mummy, Mummy!' down the phone, had a reassuring word with her before grabbing Anne-Marie again, trying to make some sense of her dramatic garbled story.

Kate and Ian had gone rushing off to Harley Street, after a desperate call from George. There'd been a serious accident – not George himself, but someone that he knew. Anne-Marie didn't have the details; said Kate had been too frantic to explain, just dumped the children and the dog, and gone haring off with Ian.

Ginny's hands were damp on the receiver as she dialled George's London number. No reply. All she could hear was the empty mocking ringing tone, and the lady from the radio play giggling almost girlishly through the open bedroom door.

'Tilly,' teased a deeper voice. 'You'll get fat, you know, if you lick out all the icing from that bowl.'

Another fluting laugh. 'You're only saying that, dear, because you'd really like to lick it out yourself.'

She wouldn't turn them off. She wanted a plump and giggly lady in the house, a happy well-fed husband, sitting down to tea together, sharing jokes and icing; 'dear' to one another. She peered into the dining-room, as if hoping she might see them there, cutting cake, pouring tea; their two smiling pink-cheeked daughters spooning in jelly and ice-cream.

The table was quite bare, save for its showy white lace cloth, its starchy linen napkins; looked too cold and formal for a family, for children. Nobody had eaten, no one touched a knife or moved a chair. The hearth was cold and dead; the clock listless, barely ticking, as if holding its breath, recovering from bad news.

She dragged upstairs again. Afternoon Theatre was just changing to The Living World. ' . . . enchanting recordings of a garden snail munching on a lettuce leaf. Derek Jones chose the crunchiest lettuce and the largest snail he could find. If you listen carefully . . .'

She opened her wardrobe, kicked off her silly shoes. She had packed her winter coat away in polythene and mothballs. She shook it from its cover, pulled it on over her new designer suit. The mink collar was engulfed in boring grey-blue tweed. She removed her sapphire earrings, zipped on sturdy boots. She found a wicker basket in the kitchen, packed tea and Lucozade, bandages and aspirin, even a hot-water bottle; had to be prepared for anything and everything. She removed the beef from the oven, cut off all the burnt bits for the cats, swathed the rest in foil. There were chores to be done, even in a crisis. She was calm, deadly calm, as she locked the house, drove slowly to the station. It was almost dark, and snowing. She stood a moment, silent, in the car park, flakes of snow falling on her face, as she looked up to watch a plane pass, a large and powerful plane burning through the torpid ashen sky. Was it flying to Los Angeles, perhaps, with a Dr de Roche on board, still searching for her, calling, leaning out across the bare brown landscape and begging her to join him. 'Ginny, I love you, and that's final.'

She dodged down beside the car, as if frightened he could see her. He hadn't said it. In all their time together at the airport, he hadn't said 'I love you'. And nor had she.

Final. Even at the time, the word had sounded strange. Yet he'd seemed so achingly sincere, as if love were really costing him, wrenching him apart. She could hear his ardent voice again, intense and vulnerable. 'I've never loved anyone before, Ginny. I've always played with them, pretended.' So had he been pretending then, as well; playing with her, duping her, using love and vulnerability as just his final cards to change her mind?

'It's different this time, Ginny. I can't pretend and I certainly can't leave you.'

The plane was dying to a rumble, its wide wings lost in cloud, only the red tail-lights glowing through the grey; glowing like a sanctuary-lamp, glowing like a ruby.

'Ginny, did you hear me? I said I love you, for God's sake.'

There'd been anger in his voice that time, an anger which she'd welcomed. She'd assumed such strong emotion was simply part of love, proof that he was moved and stirred, shaken to his roots. But it could have been just anger at rejection, a proud man's rage at not getting what he wanted.

She stared up at the clouds. The plane was now a fading drone, a streak of golden ribbon in the sky. She stretched one gloveless hand out, as if to pluck the ribbon down, save it as a keepsake, save it for eternity; but even as she watched it, it was lost in whirling snow. No trace. No souvenir.

She locked the car, trudged towards the station, snowflakes melting on her cheeks, streaking all her make-up, removing Caldos' colours even from her face. She turned round one last time, to check the empty sky. Was there just a wisp of vapour-trail, the faintest mark or sign from him, a message in the sky?

'Caldos,' she implored. 'Say you meant it. Please.'

No sound, except the echo of her voice.

35

The snow in Harley Street had been trampled into sludge. Ginny shivered at the bottom of the narrow iron staircase which led down to George's basement flat. Three black dustbins were piled high with stinking rubbish. All had lost their lids, so that rusty cans and damp grease-splattered newspapers overflowed their severed necks. She had dithered there ten minutes, and still not found the courage to go in. It wasn't just the fear of what she'd find, but the embarrassment of being there at all; of explaining things to Ian, facing George's shock, or Kate's derision. She hadn't had time to set the usual lies in motion; was tired of lies in any case; longed to crawl away like a hibernating animal and hide herself until spring and truth broke through again. This strange, unending, black-and-scarlet day had been stretched out and out, like a piece of thin elastic, and she tugged and yanked along with it, until they were both at breaking point.

It was cold and dark outside, like the dregs of a sick night, yet still, in fact, only five o'clock. There were golden lights in all the houses; normal laughing people, whose lives were still intact, sitting down to tea and toast; children doing homework, mothers washing up. She would see her own girls in just a few short hours. At least they wouldn't ask too many questions, simply fall on her and hug her in relief. But Ian would ask the questions, and might feel no relief. She dared not ring the bell in case he answered it, met her with hostility and rage, even refused to have her back. Her fingers lingered on the bell-push for three endless minutes more.

'Holy Christ!' said Kate, reeling back dramatically, as she flung open the door. 'I've had shocks enough for one day. Next time you ask me to be Nanny to your kids, you might at least inform me that means doctor, nurse, ambulance driver and mortician all thrown in as well.'

They stared at one another, both wary and exhausted. Kate broke the tension suddenly, burst into a laugh.

'Well, that was a lightning trip, my love! What in God's name are you doing back already? I suppose you took one peep at California, and decided it couldn't really compare with *Mon Repos*. Or did you miss the plane?'

'Yes . . . no . . . Oh, Kate, don't ask – not now. What's going on this end, for heaven's sake? Anne-Marie said there'd been an accident.'

Kate nodded grimly. 'Yes.'

'What happened?'

'Suicide. Some young kid killed herself and it was George who found the body – still warm, or so he says. We don't really know who the hell she is, but he's been raving on as if she were his daughter.'

'But how . . . ? When . . . ?' Ginny's voice ran out.

'Earlier on today. George was on his own, so he went round to this flat in Holland Park . . .'

On his own. Ginny winced. She hadn't even thought of George alone at the weekends; could have invited him to lunch if she hadn't had the little problem of a flight to California. She was still completely mystified. Why Holland Park? Why George? 'But doesn't *anyone* know anything about it? The police, or someone in her street? I mean, surely they must know her name?'

'Yes, Angela Mary Alexandra Hammond. Miss. Unmarried. No parents. No anyone, as far as the inspector could make out. Except your wretched George, who calls her Angie. He just sat and repeated it over and over for the first hour. Angie, Angie, Angie . . . They gave him tranquillisers. He's calmer now.'

Ginny tried to unfasten the buttons of her coat, felt even more vulnerable without it, like a limp and puny mollusc which had crawled out of its shell into a murderous rock-pool. She and Kate were standing tense and shivering in the narrow draughty hall. The light-bulb had no shade. She'd promised George she'd make him one, half a year ago. Who the hell was Angie? She'd never heard George mention any Angie. But then she hadn't been around much, had she? Why should she bother with her wavering forty-watt bulb of a father-in-law, when she had Caldos as her light-house? Once, she'd known the smallest of his worries, but now that he had death to deal with, she couldn't even identify the body.

'But who *is* – I mean, *was* . . . ? How did George meet this girl?'

'Well – wait for it, love – it turns out that Miss A. Hammond, parentage unknown, was one of your fancy Dr de Whatnot's patients. He'd been seeing her five times a week for something like four years.'

'Oh Christ, no!' Not Caldos again, abandonment again; not suicide on top of sacrilege.

'Yeah, 'fraid so. Nasty, isn't it?'

'But didn't he realise? I mean, shouldn't she have been in hospital or something?'

'That's what Ian said. He's absolutely furious. He's been raging about, sweeping things off tables, cursing every psychiatrist in the land, railing at you, consigning the entire continent of America to the bottom of the ocean. He was almost worse than George. I felt I was the only sane one left.'

Ginny shrank towards the door again. There was fear mixed up with all the horror – fear of Ian, fear of Caldos. He too might be enraged, pacing up and down the plane, consigning her to the bottom of an ocean . . . She'd let him down, wasted his money, ruined all his plans. But what was that, compared with what he'd done to them, done even to his patients?

'Is he here? Ian, I mean.'

'No, he's just left for the hospital. There's a lot of kerfuffle going on because they can't trace any next-of-kin. George keeps bleating that he ought to go himself, but he's in no state to go anywhere. He's already been grilled by the police. I wouldn't be surprised if they actually suspected him. I mean, it looks a bit suspicious, doesn't it, some hysterical old man found alone with a young girl, and empty pill bottles strewn around the place?'

'So she took an overdose?'

'Yeah. Half a ton of barbiturates washed down with a quart of Scotch – the most expensive brand, of course.'

'Oh Kate, *don't*. You sound so callous.'

'No, love, just shagged out.'

'But couldn't anyone have stopped her? Her landlady, or a neighbour, or someone?'

'How the hell should I know? You sound as if you're holding me personally responsible. I did my best, for Christ's sake. If it's of any interest to you, I'm absolutely pooped. It's been a shitty day from first to last.' Kate swept back to the kitchen, started banging cups about.

Ginny followed wretchedly, paused a moment outside the living-room. She could hear the mynah bird cackling and cursing from its prison in the cellar, and above it a more strangled sound – the sound of George's crying. She'd been brought up to believe that men shouldn't cry, and didn't; had to fight a sense of shock before slipping through the door. George was slumped in his old chair, surrounded by a tide of screwed-up Kleenex; looked as if he'd aged ten years, gaunt, unshaven, pale. She ran to him and hugged him, held him like a scarecrow in her arms – tatty clothes, stick limbs.

'She's dead, Ginny, she's dead.' He seemed too confused to wonder what she was doing there at all. Los Angeles didn't exist for him, only the soft red hush of an ambulance blanket. 'I thought she was asleep. She's always pale, you see. But she wasn't asleep. She was . . .' Tears streamed down his face, unchecked, like an unimportant accessory of some deeper grief. He had wept like that when Bea died – a wife he'd idolised for more than forty years, but how could some two-bit mental case call forth the same wild anguish? Ginny grabbed more Kleenex, handed them to George. Why did she feel so furious with the girl? You couldn't be angry with a corpse.

'I found her, Ginny. I was the one who found her. She was all dressed up. She usually wore old jeans at home, yet there she was, dolled up in a sort of party frock. It didn't suit her. It was a purply sort of red, and she was far too pale for red. It made it worse, somehow, as if the only thing she'd ever bothered to dress up for was her own death.'

Ginny didn't answer. There weren't any words, not for death in party frocks; nothing she could say that wasn't inadequate, insulting. 'Look, let me make you some tea, George.' Foolish fatuous tea. Both their worlds had split apart, and all she could do was stick them up with Typhoo.

'I'll make it,' Kate griped, barging out from the kitchen. 'It'll be the seventh pot so far. I've just washed up the cups from the last lot. It seems to be all I'm good for – washing-up.'

Why was Kate so cross? There was anger everywhere – seeping up from the floorboards, churning through the flat; Ian's anger still to come.

George was trying to get up from his chair. 'It was my fault, Ginny. I killed her.'

Ginny almost shouted. 'Of *course* you didn't, George.' If anyone had killed her, it was Caldos. He was cruel and irresponsible, coaxing George into this damp unhealthy cellar, tricking him into giving up his garden, his whole leisured safe suburban life, in the name of what he called promotion; abandoning his patients to their lonely suppers of Scotch and sleeping pills. How many others had he left to die?

Kate brought in the tea, a fierce orange brew in chipped cups. She was wearing a baggy skirt and sweater the same faded muddy colour as the carpet. Everything looked so shabby, second-rate. Caldos had taught her that tragedy was dramatic and sublime – the tragedy of opera with its Wagnerian finales, its crashing temples, noble dying lovers. But this was basement tragedy – an old man in a darned and matted cardigan crying into a junk-shop cup which didn't match its saucer. The flat had never looked so mean before. Had there always been that undernourished sofa, those palsied plywood chairs? Or did it only seem so derelict because she herself had been swept into five-star living – first-class travel, first-class swanky service? She longed to veneer the whole drab place with stick-on luxury, cover up the cracks with easi-fix euphoria and opulence. And all she could offer him was a stale digestive biscuit with his tea.

He stared at it, as if even a biscuit was too much for him to comprehend. 'Yes, Ginny, I killed her. I loved her, you know, like my own child, but I killed her. God knows, I didn't mean to. I'd no idea she'd do a thing like that. But *he* knew all the time. He warned me months ago, told me not to interfere.'

'Who did, George? Who warned you?'

'The Doctor. Dr de Roche.'

Ginny shut her eyes. The little red tail-lights were burning a crater between them, deep into her skull; the pneumatic drill again, roaring from the airport cafeteria, curdling with Jo's screams. 'Don't want to go, don't want to go to America.' She should be on her way now, sipping her Veuve Clicquot, hand in hand with Caldos, soothed by smiling air-hostesses as they soared towards the sun. She hadn't even said goodbye.

'I saw her every week. He told me not to, but I took no notice, Ginny. I started a garden for her, planted seeds. She always used to laugh because the kitten dug them up again.' He pushed his cup away. His voice was broken glass. 'She killed the cat, as well – you know that, don't you, Ginny?'

'No, I didn't . . .'

'He was my cat really, but I gave him to her. I thought a pet might help – you know, something to love and care for. But she killed him. She called him George and then she strangled him. She put a ribbon round his neck and pulled it – before she took the pills. I saw him. It was terrible. And she was sitting there beside him. Sitting, not lying. And smiling. Smiling and dead.'

Ginny tried to narrow the world to the three small inches of her cup: thick white handle, clumsy rim, unseasonable roses blooming on the saucer. 'Look, George, try not to think about it. Drink your tea instead. It'll do you good.' Insufferable words. You couldn't not think about last memories: white roses, black chapels, fading golden ribbons in the sky . . .

George had struggled to his feet and was taking down a photo from the mantelpiece, an out-of-focus snapshot, too small for its frame, a fancy gilded frame with a velvet mount and fretwork on the corners. 'That's her. That's Angela.'

Ginny scanned the features of the undistinguished schoolgirl scowling at the camera, not much older than Sarah, and half her size. The hair was baby-fair, the prim mouth petulant; two thin hands clutched at a black cat. Both girl and cat looked frightened, ready to attack, claws out, huge eyes wary.

'I always kept her on my mantelpiece. She felt I was looking after her up there. Oh God, Ginny, what have I done? I've killed her, I've . . .'

'George, how could you have done? You loved her.'

Caldos hadn't said he loved her, not today. That was another sort of death, though she shouldn't even care, should decry him now, denounce him, in loyalty to George, in memory of Angie. But she couldn't suppress her blasphemous desperate love.

George was sitting bolt upright in his chair, the photo in his hands, one finger tracing Angie's sullen face. 'You don't understand, Ginny. I was angry with the Doctor.'

That word again. She wanted suddenly to lunge at Caldos, kick and punch and pummel him, maul him, kiss him, join him, never leave him in her life again. Christ, her head ached! The whole thing was impossible.

'He promised me promotion, and I was really counting on it. I wanted that new job. I've been wasted all my life – he told me so himself. That club was my last chance. I was helping set it up for him. I'd done a hell of a lot of work on it already, and I know he was damned pleased with me. I was really making progress. Then suddenly he throws the whole thing over. All my labours reduced to a pile of rubble!'

He was crumbling the biscuit between his fingers, like builders' sand. 'Next thing I know, he's off to America – just like that. Little change of plan, he calls it. More like a whopping thunderbolt, I'd say. Okay, I tell him, I'll go with you. Well, why not? I'd go anywhere to keep that job. But he turns me down flat, says I wouldn't get a work permit. Well, that's ridiculous. I'm fit and well, aren't I? And if I can help run a club in Chelsea, why not in California? But he wouldn't listen, and I hardly even saw him after that. It was a shock, Ginny, I can tell you. I felt damn near destroyed. He'd let me down, brought me here for nothing. There I was, back to being a nobody again.'

Ginny snapped her own biscuit, bit into it, hard. So all her own anguish over Caldos had been paralleled by George's. Another life wrecked and overturned. Yet she'd hardly spared a thought for him. She'd been primping her hair and touring Harrods' dress department, while George was flung on a rubbish-dump and Angie gulped down sleeping pills like Smarties. And even now, with his patient cold in a mortuary, Caldos would be fretting because his strawberries had been soaked in Kirsch instead of Calvados . . .

She jumped to her feet, stumbled to the window, peering up at the dark and star-thatched sky. That's where she should be, sitting high beside him amongst the gods and stars, while he dribbled strawberry-juice liqueur between her open lips, ignoring the cold barren world below. The honeymoon suite reserved for their delight, the peacock surf pounding them awake, the smell of flowers and freedom in the champagne morning-air of California. That was her rightful legacy, her future. And all she had instead was cold burnt beef at home, a cramped and dingy bedroom, a recriminating husband, and an almost empty wardrobe. She had lost her luggage with her lover – all her worldly goods, her trousseau, loaded on that plane.

She forced herself down from soft fruits and shining stars. Reality was strangled cats, stewed tea in cheapskate cups. George had put the photo down and was shredding a wet Kleenex into strips.

'That's how I got involved with Angela. I'd been seeing her already, now and then, but I began to spend a lot more time with her. Well, I had the leisure, didn't I, with all my club work gone? Anyway, I didn't trust the Doctor any more. I felt sure he was quite wrong about the girl. But he wasn't wrong, in fact. He was aware of things I couldn't even begin to understand.'

'Yes,' said Ginny silently. 'I know.'

'Angela got more and more demanding, until I couldn't really cope with her. She was coming round night after night, refusing to leave; ringing up twenty times a day, disturbing this whole house, upsetting other patients. I loved her, Ginny, but all I'd done was make her worse. And now I've . . . Oh God! I can't even bear to think about it.'

Ginny took his hand, held it tight between her own. '*Don't* think about it, George. You should never have had to cope with all those problems. What about her doctor? Didn't she have another doctor? Surely Caldos wouldn't have left her stranded.'

'Oh no, no, of course not. There's this new chap, Dr Stringer, but Angie didn't like him. And I wasn't too keen to tell him I'd got myself involved. You see, Dr de Roche particularly warned me not to. Oh Ginny, what in God's name have I done?'

Ginny shook another Valium from the bottle in her handbag, crushed half in a teaspoon, held it between his lips. 'Hush, George, you mustn't blame yourself. It was nothing to do with you. Caldos should never have lured you up here in the first place. You come home with us now. You'll be better off at Hinchley Wood, with your animals, your garden. You'll be safe at home. We've missed you. The girls have hated it without you. You'll be all right, you see. You can have another cat . . .'

Crazy hollow words. What could they offer her in place of Caldos? Another kitchen cupboard, another turret on her tower? George's hand felt bony-cold, smaller than she remembered it, and definitely much older; the blue veins raised, the fingers gnarled and stained. Caldos' hands were huge, could pick up all America, support and succour fifty states, hold them in his palm. She'd had those hands almost to herself, exploring her, exploding her, thrashing her wet and shrieking into heaven. Why couldn't she have remembered him like that, instead of brutish and unsparing in a chapel? Yet she still needed him, desired him. Her life would crumble, unless he held it in his hands.

'George,' she faltered. 'You didn't kill her. Of course you didn't. Caldos did. Don't you see, she killed herself because he went away. She needed him, she couldn't live without him. Maybe she was even very angry with him. She still loved him, but she wanted to pay him out . . .'

Kate burst in from the kitchen with a dishcloth in her hand. 'Ian's back! I thought I'd better warn you. I can hear him coming down the outside stairs.'

Ginny shot to her feet, rushed to fetch her coat, buttoned it across her tactless suit. She couldn't be a scarlet woman, not in front of Ian; needed some protection from his wrath. Even Kate seemed nervous, scrunching up the dishcloth, face creased in a frown.

'Look, I'd better go and prepare him, tell him that you're back. It'll be a shock for him to find you here, on top of all the rest.'

Ginny stood silent by the window, her body absolutely motionless, as if the slightest movement might make her more conspicuous, more deserving of reproach. Yet she knew if any surgeon sliced her open, he'd find turmoil and convulsion – blood roaring round her veins, heart pounding like a piston, lungs so short of breath they seemed to gasp. She glanced across at George. His eyes were closed, his fingers slack, the last half-pill beginning to take effect. If only she could sleep herself, slip away from consciousness, not hear her husband's footsteps as they charged into the room. She dared not look at him – or only at his feet; the scuffed toecaps of his shoes, the bottom inch of his tired grey chain-store flannels. The feet stopped, as if uncertain, still a pace or two away from her.

'Ginny,' he said softly. No anger, no reproaches. His voice was tweed, lead pencils, forgiveness, safety, refuge. She moved towards his arms. 'Don't cry,' he said. 'You're home now.'

She scrubbed fiercely at her eyes. She was crying for another man – a murderer.

36

Christmas Eve. The kitchen smelt of hot mince pies and cinnamon. Two cats and a new kitten purred against the stove. George was in his slippers, making a food-tray for Jason out of an old draining board. The bird had been banished to the box-room, after an impressive bout of swearing.

'Shut your eyes and wish!' yelled Snookie, snatching a mince pie, breaking it in half, comparing the two pieces, then reluctantly giving the larger one to Ginny. 'Our wish comes true, because it's our first mince pie this year.'

Ginny closed her eyes and didn't wish; was still sitting with her eyes shut and the piece of pie untouched, when Sarah rushed in from the garden in her wellingtons.

'We've finished our snowman, Mum. He's super! Come and look.'

Ginny dragged outside. The snowman stood six feet high, with powerful shoulders, sensuous carrot lips, dark hair made of coal. He was smoking a cigar. Round his neck was a scarlet cashmere scarf lent to her by Caldos one raw March night when she'd come home after midnight. She couldn't meet his eyes – black prune eyes, yearning and reproachful.

'Isn't he fantastic?' Sarah capered round him. 'The biggest one we've ever made. Let's throw snowballs at him!'

Snookie rushed to join her, scooped up snow from the fresh fall on the path, shaped it into a large and firm-packed ball. She hurled it at the snowman, knocked out one prune eye. Sarah screamed with laughter, flung a snowball at the other eye and blinded him. The carrot lips dropped off. George emerged with Toby and a rubbish-bin to empty.

'Come on Grandpa! Throw a snowball at him.'

George threw two. The snowman lost his hair, half his little buttons.

'Your turn, Mummy. Try and knock his head off.'

Ginny's hands were clumsy. She couldn't make them work; couldn't seem to laugh and shout, as the others were all doing; even Toby racing round in ecstatic crazy circles.

'Come on, Mum. Get him where it hurts!'

'No, I . . . I've left the oven on.' She rushed inside, grimacing at the noise; the thud of ruthless snowballs breaking up his body, splitting his huge head. They didn't know that even snowmen cry.

By nightfall it was milder; the snow melting into slush, and a drizzly rain spattering at the panes. The girls had hung their stockings up, settled down to sleep. The house was hushed and waiting, the only noise the drip-drip of the trees outside, and one gutter overflowing.

Ginny was still cooking. 'How was Harrods?' she yawned, from the middle of her marzipan.

'Crowded.' Ian was doing secret things with crêpe paper and gold ribbon. 'Who do you think I bumped into, in the Food Hall?'

'Who?'

'Gish.'

'*Who?*'

'Gish. You know, Gish. She came here once with Caldos. Black feathers and a funny tummy. She was streaking through Harrods all done up in mink.'

Ginny rolled a lump of marzipan between her fingers, making it larger and more lethal. 'How was she?'

'So bright and breezy, she almost blew me over.'

Ginny scraped the last shreds of marzipan from the sides of the bowl and rammed them round her snowball. 'Did you talk?'

'Not really. She was in such a rush, she wouldn't stop. She was galloping about trying to find a pair of sunglasses.'

'Sunglasses?' Ginny clawed the snowball with her nails.

'Yes. Apparently she's off to Los Angeles for Christmas. She was loaded down with bags; told me she'd been buying half of Harrods – party frocks, bikinis . . .'

Ginny jerked back on the kitchen stool, the snowball dropping like a stone, back into the mixing bowl.

293

'I think she was just boasting. She'd said she'd bought half a dozen evening dresses and nine different dressing gowns and bathrobes. Though why anyone should want nine dressing gowns totally defeats me.'

'You said Los Angeles.' Ginny found the last dregs of her voice, forced and wrenched them out. 'For Christmas.'

'Yes, that's right. Rather her than me! All that smog and stuff. I'd hate to spend *my* Christmas Eve cooped up in a plane. Hey, what's the matter, darling? You look awful.'

'Nothing.' Ginny tried to concentrate on picking little shreds of marzipan off her greasy shaking fingers. 'Did she . . . ? Was she . . . ?'

'Ginny, love, what's wrong? You sound really quite peculiar. Why don't you pack up now and go to bed? It's late.'

'No I'm okay. Honestly. Tell me about Gish. What . . . what did she look like?'

'Oh, glamorous as ever. Her hair was different, though – sort of short and curly. I wouldn't be surprised if she'd had it dyed or something. It didn't look natural – the colour *or* the style.' Ian yawned extravagantly, showing all his fillings. 'Come on, Ginny, let's go up to bed. We'll need some sleep to face those little monsters in the morning. Snookie warned me that if we're not awake and opening our presents by six o'clock at the latest, she'll pour cold water over us.'

'Look, Ian, did Gish . . . ? I mean, why the hell Los Angeles?'

'Haven't a clue. Maybe she's got friends out there, or just fancies California, or Christmas in the sun.'

Ginny eased up from her stool. She couldn't go to bed yet. There were chores to be done – four pounds of Brussels sprouts to pick over and prepare, two large bags of chestnuts still to peel. She cleared up all the clutter from the marzipan, washed the bowl and spoons. Her hands were cold white corpses in the water. She swept the rubbish off the table, trying to fix her attention just on tiny things – a coil of apple-peel, a broken cork, a clove. She fumbled for the waste-bin, slipped through the back door. It wasn't really full enough to empty, but she had to get some air. She glanced up at the sky – no stars, only clouds, and a mean rain falling on her hair. The moon looked pale and faded, scowling behind the prison bars of trees.

She could hear Ian fretting on the step, see him silhouetted at the door.

'Ginny!' he was calling. 'You'll catch your death out there.'

She turned her back, ignored him, shambled on to the lawn. The moon was glowering through the clouds, lighting up a soggy cashmere scarf, a shrivelled carrot, a few small lumps of coal. The snowman had melted to a grey misshapen lump, his prune-eyes mildewed, rotting in a puddle.

'Ginny, for heaven's sake! It's pissing down with rain.' Ian was in pursuit, peering through the darkness like a fussy fretful owl. Suddenly, she hurled the carrot to the far corner of the garden, where the compost-heap was sited, a mound of stinking rubbish, putrid, decomposing.

Her husband was still fussing, slipping on the slimy grass, warning her she'd break her neck as well. She let him take her arm and lead her in. Silently, she put away the chestnuts, left the sprouts unpeeled, settled all the animals, heated milk for drinks; trying to ignore the quiet but desperate anger, bubbling on a low gas deep inside her, like the water in the Christmas-pudding pan. She glared around the kitchen, paced into the hall and back. Everything looked tawdry: cosy cards bright with fatuous robins; heartless calendars mocking another year; pine trees moulting needles, turkeys weeping blood. Kill a tree for Christmas, gut a bird. How could her husband sit there, snipping green crêpe paper into frills, when half the Christian world was tearing up forests by their roots, strangling whole turkey-farms in the name of celebration, ripping the gizzards out of stunned castrated chickens, and dumping their dead bodies into holly-patterned plastic bags?

'Do you have to make all that mess, Ian? You told me you were going up to bed, so I've just cleared the table, ready for the morning.'

'Don't snap, Ginny love. Not on Christmas Eve.'

'And what's so wonderful about bloody Christmas Eve? All I've done is cook. I haven't even seen you. I can't think why you had to go to Harrods, anyway – least of all today.' She swooped on the Sellotape, the offcuts of green paper, flung them in the bin.

'Well, in actual fact, I was trying to change your Christmas present, the one I bought you last year.'

He was lying again. Why did everybody lie to her, deceive her, walk all over her?

'Stupid, I suppose, when I'd had it all that time. But being Harrods, I hoped . . . well, I mean, it cost so much, I knew you'd rather have the money for something practical, a steam iron, or a new electric mixer, or . . .'

Ginny banged two mugs down. Oh, a steam iron would be *wonderful* – iron out all her anger, and flatten her into a debased and grovelling door-mat, who wouldn't object to being duped, betrayed. How many traitor roses had Caldos ordered for Gish, how many humbug Christmas trees had he blighted with silver baubles in her honour? Had he warmed the bed, iced the champagne, refurbished the trousseau? Gish really needn't have bothered with all those dressing gowns and bathrobes, all those evening dresses, swimsuits, when she already had a brand-new Harrods wardrobe awaiting her inspection. All she'd need to do was make a few adjustments to the size, add a new mink coat or two. She probably wouldn't be wearing clothes at all, just her naked skin and a red rose in her hair . . .

'Anyway, they wouldn't take it back. Not a dog's chance. Said I should have changed it months ago. I did intend to, darling – even hoped you'd come along to give me moral support. Oh, I know you've never seen the wretched thing. I meant to show you, honestly I did. But somehow . . .'

Ian was stumbling on his words. She wasn't really listening. He had learnt to lie, as she had, as Caldos always did. Had he given Gish the refund on her fare? Or merely swapped the reservations? She turned the gas out under the milk, hunted for the Ovaltine. Stupid to be so bitter. There was no real proof of anything. Caldos de Roche wasn't the only person in Los Angeles. Gish might have another friend among its seven million people, a different invitation – and her own account at Harrods.

'Then I thought, well . . . perhaps you'd like it after all; maybe it wasn't so unsuitable. You're different now, you see. I know it cost a bomb, but . . .' Ian was looking sheepish, holding out a box. She recognised her giant detergent carton, transformed with green crêpe frills. 'Look, you'd better have it now. I don't want Sarah sniggering in the morning.'

Ian never bothered wrapping things – always bunged them in

a paper bag with perhaps a piece of sensible brown string. But this was an enchanted parcel. He'd even bought a Christmas-fairy gift-card, tied it on with a loop of golden ribbon. She read the words. They were very nearly poetry – limping leather-patches poetry, but poetry all the same.

'Let's go upstairs and open it.' He sounded both eager and embarrassed, like a schoolboy with his first packet of Durex. 'Then you can put it on.'

The stairs seemed steep, interminable. She kept tripping on them, stumbling, as if her feet were too shocked and feeble to manoeuvre stairs at all. Ian was clomping up behind her, rattling on about the price of Harrods Christmas cards.

'Give me Woolworths, any day.' He shut the bedroom door, awarded her a Woolworths kiss. Her mouth felt cold and shrunken. 'Well, go on, darling, open it.'

She peeled off the gold ribbon, pulled at the crêpe paper, too tired to open anything. There'd be enough of that in the morning – gift-wrapped trash she didn't want, potted plants too garish for a grave, lace handkerchiefs which couldn't cope with tears. She hacked roughly at the box, tore through several layers of tissue paper. The black lace nightdress grinned at her inside.

There weren't any feelings left, not even anger. If he had to palm his girlfriend's cast-offs on to her, well, she'd done worse herself. He was always short of money, and it probably helped to give his wife a nightie which didn't fit his mistress. No, that was plain ridiculous. Ian didn't have a mistress. Since Angie's death he'd hardly left her side, except for the daily Biscuit grind, and a trip to Father Christmas with the girls.

She trailed her fingers through the wanton lace, checked the scanty pants again, the shameless plunging cleavage. So if he didn't have a floozie, then why this piece of nonsense? Ian would never lash out on a nightie as expensive and debauched as that, not unless he was totally besotted. She knew it as surely as she knew anything about him. He'd bought her another nightdress, anyway, a substantial sterling garment in warm pink winceyette, with a Marks & Spencer label. So what was he doing in Harrods in the first place?

'What's wrong, love? You don't look very pleased.'

'Yes, I am. It's . . . nice.' She fiddled with the box, crumpled up a sheet of tissue paper. 'Ian . . . ?'

'What?'

'I wondered if . . . Oh, I can't explain, forget it. Look, Ian, tell me honestly, did you really buy this for me?'

''Course I did.' She watched him flush. 'What's the matter? Don't you like it?'

She nodded, dropped the wisp of pants on to the dressing table. How could anything so tiny cost them both so dear? Lies and still more lies, even at the threshold of Christmas. Ian had picked the pants up and was twisting them through his fingers.

'Well, all right, I admit I didn't actually choose it, but . . .'

So his mistress had chosen it for her, mocked Ian's own wife with her vulgar taste in lingerie. Rubbish! Total and insubstantial rubbish. If Ian had a mistress at all, she'd be a hockey captain or a social worker, not a Messalina. Anyway, he didn't have one – she knew it now, instinctively. Perhaps that was the value of a marriage – the unspoken things, the trust. Except how could there be trust, when he kept lying and confusing her, mystifying things? But who was she to criticise? She'd wronged him far more gravely. Her Christmas present to them all had been only Nanny Katkin and a note behind the donkey on the mantelpiece.

'Thanks,' she said, stuffing the nightie into the drawer where she'd first found it – Ian's own sweater-drawer. There would be other things to compensate. Sarah had been wrestling with a mysterious piece of knitting for the past few weeks, and Snookie was plastered with glue and an air of self-importance, and had scrawled a notice on her door: 'TOP SECRET, ENTER AT YOUR PERRELL'.

'Ginny, love, don't look so upset. It's only a stupid nightie, after all. Oh, I realise it's not your usual sort of thing, but I thought you'd like a change. Look, if you must know, I *did* choose something different for you – a sort of fuzzy nightdress, pale blue, with nice long sleeves. But . . .'

She turned her back. She was sick of nighties anyway, tired and sick of everything. She pulled off her old sweater, unzipped her faded jeans. Best to try to sleep, seek unconsciousness, oblivion.

'I was just about to pay for it, and then I met . . . well, I admit it was a bit pathetic letting him change my mind like that, but everyone was listening, Ginny, and it was damned embarrassing. I mean, Caldos de bloody Roche has got a voice like the Dungeness foghorn. Half of Harrods could hear us.'

Ginny had her pants half off. She paused with them round her knees. '*Who?*'

'Well you see, I met him in the lingerie department. I told you, darling, at the time. Christ! It must have been exactly a year ago. Feels more like a hundred.' Ian was sitting on the bedroom stool, struggling with a knot in his shoelace. 'What I didn't tell you was that Caldos chose your nightie for you.'

Ginny stepped out of her pants, clutching at the wardrobe for support. '*What* did you say?'

'I'm sorry, Ginny, but he just sort of overruled me. He said he knew exactly what you'd want.' Ian had made the knot worse, was tugging at his shoe, swearing sotto voce.

'But he'd never met me in his life.' Ginny was stark naked, her bowed pink body an astonished question-mark. Suddenly, she burst out laughing, fell back on the counterpane almost doubled up. 'Oh, Ian, it's so . . . so . . .' There weren't any adjectives. Was it absurd, outrageous, wonderful, or shameful? She hardly knew. All she could do was flop on the bed and guffaw like a cretin, her full bare breasts wobbling as she laughed.

Ian watched the wobble with interest, started fumbling in his sweater-drawer. 'Here, put it on!' He snatched up the nightie and slipped it over her head. 'Wow! You look stupendous, like a film star.' He goggled at the long expanse of thigh teasing through the side-slits, the nipples still on show, preening above the low-plunge lacy top.

Ginny was still hooting, tears of laughter streaming down her face. So she was wearing Caldos' nightie. Her lover had helped her husband choose his own wife's Christmas present, and before he even knew her. Did he assist all his old college chums with their intimate Christmas shopping? Perhaps he had a special account at Harrods to bulk-buy nighties for half the sex-starved world. How dare he interfere, ruin Ian's surprise with his own insensitive meddling, swap ice-blue for sin-black. Yet her husband seemed sublimely colour-blind; had snapped the knotted shoelace, and was kicking off his shoes, gazing at his black-lace wife with a mixture of ardour and astonishment. She was his only mistress. All those melon-breasted hussies and deep-thighed Jezebels were sheer invention. Perhaps she had even needed them, to justify her own duplicity. Ian was blameless and acquitted, panting for her even now, when it was only five sleepy hours to Snookie's alarm-call of Christmas stockings and cold water.

'Gosh, you look sensational!' That was a de Roche word, slipped in with the wrappings; her omnipresent lover worming himself even into the marriage-bed. Ian was quite oblivious, struggling with his buttons now, tearing off his shirt. 'Look, I know it's late, love, but let's . . . No, don't take it off.'

Wearily, she climbed between the sheets, pushed the nightie up around her stomach. Sex was as welcome as a cold shower, but she owed Ian everything – a year of non-stop service and seduction, a lifetime of passionate response. If there wasn't any passion, at least there was real anger, which would have to do instead. Caldos had taught her to be a harlot. Right – she'd play the role, but with Ian as her sole client. All the skills and secrets which her lover had imparted to her, she would lavish on her husband as his Christmas present. She was already gift-wrapped in Caldos' fancy packaging, but now she'd wear a wedding ring, in place of a gold slave-bangle. Alfonso had resurrected her body, gulped it down in Communion, baptised it with the manna of his loins, but now Ian alone would be admitted to those sacraments, as simple compensation.

For the first time ever, she had Caldos in her power. She snapped her fingers at him, and the whole of California sank slowly into the ocean. There was only Hinchley Wood, with masterful de Roche now completely at her service. She could fuel herself from him like some colossal pleasure-tank, dip into him, feast on him, drive her husband wild with him. Ian was already sprawled on top of her, plopping kisses on her cheek, sawing at her neck. His fingers smelt of mincemeat.

'I love you,' he insisted. She didn't answer. She was sucking out all Caldos had and presenting it to Ian. There was no rush, nor interruptions, no pain, no chapel floors. Gish was left with those. Gish had all the Mossmans and the Goldenbergers, the constant threat of loss and parting, the endless scarlet lies. She herself had only the great arias, the throbbing chords and rapturous violins. She had banished all her rivals. Caldos was hers – and hers alone

– for ever and eternity. She could summon him, dismiss him, tame and tenderise him, or expand and multiply him until she was tangling with a dozen rampant Adolfos in one night. Now she had eau-de-vie in place of bitters, strawberries endlessly in season, passion fruit which could not rot or pall, resurrection after crucifixion.

'You feel different, darling, wonderful.' Ian was labouring in and out, puffing like a steam-pump.

'Ssh,' she murmured. If he talked, she couldn't hear the wild Wagnerian harmonies, the swooning transport of the flutes. It didn't matter any more that she didn't know what an *acciaccatura* was, or the names of Paesiello's hundred operas. She no longer had to wrestle with leitmotivs, or mug up myths and music dramas. She could listen to Jack Jones now, as well as Wagner, Webern, Walton, without diluting Caldos' passion or risking his contempt. She didn't even have to worry about being overweight. She could gorge herself on Christmas cake, hog the nuts and raisins, and still drive her lover crazy with desire. And – double value, two for the price of one, which Ian would surely like – she could spur her husband into a wild Valkyrian gallop, merely on the memory of Alfonso's sensual powers.

'Ginny!' he was shouting. 'Ginny, you're incredible! It's never been as good as this.'

She smiled. Of course she was incredible. Both her men were telling her. Even her non-existent God couldn't be revengeful any more. She was wife and mother now; the larder crammed with home-cooked Christmas goodies, the children's stockings bulging by their beds, and she was lying in her marriage-bed, beneath her lawful wedded husband, offering him everything she had. This was her penance, her atonement; the fateful Harrods nightdress her stern black garb of penitence.

Ian was clutching a nightie tail in each of his two hands, pulling on them like a pair of reins, panting with excitement as he watched Ginny's soft white flesh ripple through the lace. 'Gosh, Ginny, I . . .'

She herself was melting and capitulating. The nightie was a holy vestment now, a sacramental robe. Caldos' hands had lingered over it, his sensuous breath had warmed it. She could feel her breasts plumping out in homage to him, her whole ripe body burgeoning to fill it. Ian was confiding 'goshes' to her ear. She didn't hear them, only Caldos' intimate oratorios whispered through the spaces in the lace; only Isolde's anguished rapture as she sang of love, of loss; transforming the drab bedroom into Tristan's sublime and sea-enchanted castle.

Ian sat up on one elbow, paused for breath a moment, mouth drooling, hair awry. 'Christ! I'm so excited I can't even come. I've no idea what's happened to us both.'

'Let's try it kneeling,' Ginny murmured, easing to her feet. 'Hold on a second, Ian.'

She drifted to the wardrobe. There, hidden at the back, in an abandoned Gucci sandal, was a small glass bottle in a gold and scarlet box. She unscrewed the cap and trickled the entire contents slowly down her cleavage. The scent was cool against her breasts, stinging as it reached her Venus mound. She stood a moment, smiling in the mirror. Caldos was rubbing 'Joy' into her breasts, teasing it between her thighs, then tonguing it off languorously from her nipples to her groin. She wafted back to Ian, arranged herself face downwards on the bed, the way her lover always liked.

'We've never done it this way.' Ian was sweating, jubilant. 'When you kneel, the nightie sort of floats apart. It's terribly exciting.'

She wasn't listening. She needed all her concentration to hear that swingeing rhythm lambasting through the room, as Caldos seized the silver hairbrush, fused ecstasy and pain. She could experience that pain each night, with no guilt, no shamed remorse now; feel her body smarting and prostrated from that euphoric martyrdom, transported to a different realm, an extreme and thrill of feeling which most would never know or understand.

Ian was crouching over her, his clammy hands snailing down her back. 'You smell fantastic, darling. That's new, too, isn't it, the perfume?'

'Scent,' she corrected, almost automatically, as she and Isolde melted, opened, spurred.

'What?' her husband grunted, grabbing on to the headboard, to provide some extra leverage.

She clutched the blankets, knuckles white with pain; could feel herself soaring and exalting through five thousand miles of empty singing sky. 'I only said I love you,' she replied.